ALSO BY CLAYTON SMITH

Anomaly Flats
Apocalypticon
Death and McCootie
IF (Books 1 - 6)
It Came From Anomaly Flats
Mabel Gray and the Wizard Who Swallowed the Sun
Na Akua
Pants on Fire: A Collection of Lies
The Depths

POST-APOCALYPTICON

Printed in the United States of America

First printing, 2018

ISBN 978-0-9965121-9-0

Dapper Press

For Steven Luna, a dear friend and brilliant collaborator who wouldn't rest until the story of Patrick and Ben had another chapter.

Thank you.

Hey, after this you
should read Na Akua.

POST-APOCALYPTICON

CLAYTON SMITH

1.

The end of the world was bullshit, everyone worth anything was dead, and Ben was completely and utterly alone.

Except for the dozen or so Red Caps lined up against the train car wall, watching him with looks ranging from fearful awe to general confusion.

"In the post-apocalyptic wasteland," Ben said dramatically, giving his best Charlton Heston, "who is your best and only friend?"

The Red Caps blinked at each other. Some of them shrugged. One raised his hand. "Mark?" he asked uncertainly.

Ben stared at him and tried to comprehend the answer, but he didn't try very hard. Red Caps were rarely worth the effort. "Mark what?"

"My best friend in the post-apocalyptic wasteland," the Red Cap said, gaining confidence as he spoke. "It's Mark."

Ben crossed his arms in annoyance. "Who the fuck is Mark?"

A Red Cap in the corner waved his hand. "I'm Mark," he piped up.

"Mark is my best friend," the first Red Cap explained.

Ben shook his head and waved his hands. "No. Not Mark. In the post-apocalyptic wasteland, Mark is dead." The first Red Cap and Mark both gasped. But Ben continued, undaunted. "In the post-apocalyptic wasteland, your best and only friend is…this." He bent down and picked up a pool noodle from the train floor. Mice had torn chunks out of the foam, and one end was covered in some sticky substance that Ben hoped to God hadn't come out of someone's body. He held that end away from himself.

A different Red Cap raised his hand. Ben sighed. "What?"

The Red Cap cleared his throat. "Our best friend is...a pool noodle?"

"No," Ben said, shaking his head again. "Have you been listening? The pool noodle is not a pool noodle; the pool noodle is a machete."

The Red Cap frowned. "It...looks like a pool noodle," he said. The other men murmured and nodded their agreement.

Ben wondered how painful it would be to just throw himself under the train. It would almost certainly be less painful than serving as a babysitter-slash-survival trainer for this newest batch of morons. Especially if he got Horace to ramp up the engine to full speed and use the hydraulic plow. The whole thing would be over pretty quickly, and as a bonus, the Red Cap recruits would have to spend hours cleaning his guts off the engine car. That thought actually made him happy.

"The pool noodle *represents* a machete. It is not an *actual* machete. Do not take a pool noodle off the train and into the world and threaten to cut someone's face in half with it. It will not work. We're just using it right now in training. And the fact that I have to explain this to you makes me want to firebomb the shit out of everything and leave us all for dead."

The Red Caps hemmed and hawed. They felt nothing but the utmost respect for Ben Fogelvee, the mysterious wasteland warrior of legend, because even though he'd never opened up to them about his past, they knew he had really seen some shit. They could see it in his eyes. They could smell it in his sweat. And they could hear it in his voice each time he turned away from them with that far-off look and said, "I've really seen some shit," in an impressively dramatic way. They revered him, and they all wanted to make a good impression.

Even so, they had some questions.

"But we literally have a whole train car full of machetes," said a Red Cap whose name Ben thought was Bob or Glen or something. "Wouldn't it be better if we trained with the real thing instead of..." His voice trailed off as he picked up a flaccid pool noodle and held it up. "Instead of this?" He gave the noodle a jiggle. It flopped around a little.

"Good question," Ben said, and Bob (Glen?) sighed with relief. A bad question would have set the wrong tone for his training. "First: we don't *literally* have a train car full of machetes. We *figuratively* have a train car full of machetes, and you are *literally* a disappointment to me and to the whole human race if you don't understand the difference." Bob's face fell, but Ben didn't care. He'd come to grips with the fact that there weren't a whole lot of English teachers left alive, and that most AP style guides had probably been incinerated in the name of warmth during one of the five chemical winters that had passed since the Flying Monkeys fell. So now it was up to him to save grammar. "Second," he continued, "we can't use the real machetes for practice anymore because that's how Ricky murdered Jim."

"It was an accident!" Ricky volunteered from his spot against the far wall. "I thought he was going to dodge it!"

"Well, he *didn't* dodge it, and he got a machete to the neck, and now he's buried under an overpass in Iowa. Now no one gets machete privileges, and it's all Ricky's fault."

The Red Caps booed. Ricky crossed his arms and turned away.

"Now shut up," Ben said. He'd been practicing this speech, and he wanted it heard. He held up the pool noodle for everyone to see and started again. "The machete is your best and only friend in the post-apocalyptic wasteland. As a survival tool, it's great for cutting through brush, chopping up kindling, opening fruits that are really hard to open—all that. You can probably even use it to start a fire if you strike it against flint, I'm guessing. That might chip the blade and ruin it, but if you're dumb enough to be on your own out there, then you're too dumb for a working machete anyway. Got it?" The Red Caps nodded. "Okay. So it's a good survival tool, but it's obviously better as a weapon. A machete is easy to carry; it's light enough to use with one hand. If it's sharp enough, you can hack a guy's arm off. You can saw through a pretty good amount of his gut. Or, as Ricky has shown us, you can chop halfway through Jim's neck in one blow."

"It was an accident!" Ricky reminded them.

"But the *real* reason to carry around a machete," Ben continued, ignoring both Ricky and the uncomfortable looks everyone was giving Ricky, "is because if you hold it just right, like when it's dark and you're in front of a fire on top of a hill, you'll be in silhouette, with your machete-shadow stretching across the highway, or the desert, or the rubble, or whatever, and believe me…you will look *totally badass*." Ben smirked and folded his arms across his chest. The pool noodle rested uncomfortably against his nose, but he was striking a pose, and he didn't want to ruin the effect. "With the right attitude, and the right stance, your machete will transform you into Patku, the great anime spirit of the Apocalypticon."

The Red Caps shifted their weight uncomfortably on their heels and gave each other nervous looks. They'd heard Ben talk about Patku before. And never in a way that made sense.

"Any questions?"

The Red Caps mostly shrugged. A few of them shook their heads. Mark raised his hand.

Ben scowled. "What?"

"So you're saying that looking like a Japanese cartoon is better than chopping someone's neck in half?"

"It was an *accident!*" Ricky shouted.

"I'm saying that if you look like a Japanese cartoon, you won't *need* to chop anyone's neck in half," Ben said. He thought for a second. "Unless you look like Sailor Moon. Then you will probably get into a fight."

The Red Caps all nodded their agreement.

"Okay. Everyone grab a pool noodle. For the next hour, I want you to practice posing. Your goal is to look intimidating. To look *badass*. To let everyone know that you are a *motherfucking Colombian drug lord* with that machete. Be like Patku," he said, eyeing one bulbous Red Cap in particular whose name he was pretty sure was Fred. "*More* like Patku," he said, "and less like Tinky Winky."

"I think the Teletubbies were Korean," Mark's friend pointed out.

Ben closed his eyes and rubbed them. "They were British," he said. "And for the love of God, just shut your stupid mouth."

Ben took a seat on an old milk crate across the car while the Red Caps shuffled around clumsily with their noodles. He pinched the bridge of his nose wearily and sighed. He thought back on his old life, the life he'd had before M-Day, when his biggest problem was a toss-up between student loans and the mysterious smell that came through his radiator pipes in the winter. It was a noxious mixture of natural gas, dead animal, burning mold, and, inexplicably, potatoes. It used to fill his apartment until his eyes watered and his throat clogged. He had begged Patrick to fix it, but Patrick refused, saying that he definitely *could* fix it, if he wanted to, but that Ben deserved the smell as punishment for that one time in college when he'd gone ghost hunting in Texarkana with their mutual friend Clark and hadn't invited Patrick along.

Patrick had a lot of feelings about ghost hunting in Texarkana. Or, at least, he *had* had them, before M-Day.

Stuck with the terrible stench, Ben resorted to opening the windows to get rid of the poisoned air, letting it out and letting the sometimes-forty-below-wind-chilled Chicago air in, thereby completely negating the point of the stupid radiator in the first place.

But he'd trade anything for that smell now. Anything for that *time* now.

Loan payments and ESL landlords and silverfish infestations and eggplant emojis and Miley Cyrus and toxic radiators that clanged like they were being beaten with wrenches. He'd give everything he had to get those things back.

Of course, these days, "everything he had" amounted to an old purple Jansport backpack, a small bundle of clothes, a few rusty weapons, a mostly-full notebook, and unfettered access to a dozen or so Red Caps whose lives rested pretty squarely in his apathetic hands. He doubted anyone would trade him his old life for all that.

"Am I doing it?" Mark's friend asked, spreading his legs wide and holding the pool noodle over his head with both hands.

"No," Ben sighed. "You look like an idiot. No one respects you, and no one fears you, so Ricky just chopped you in the neck."

"Oh, for the love of God!" Ricky cried.

Ben was about to inform Ricky that if he didn't want to be the team's *de facto* murderer, he should stop murdering so many people, when he noticed a trail of aqua-blue smoke blowing past the window. "Okay," he said, pushing himself to his feet and tossing the noodle aside. "Code Blue. Go get a real weapon and try not to die." He shuffled toward the door that led toward the front of the train.

"Hey, Ben," Bob called out. His voice trembled when he spoke, but a few of the other recruits nudged him encouragingly. *Go on,* they whispered, *ask him.* So he did: "Is it true that...that..."

Ben stopped and gritted his teeth. He was so short on patience these days. "That what?" he said without looking back.

He actually heard Bob gulp. "Well…is it true that…that you…cut the last assistant conductor's head off?"

There was a sudden stillness as all of the air was sucked out of the train car, drawn deep into the lungs of each Red Cap recruit holding his breath. Ben bit down harder. His teeth squeaked. His jaw quivered. His fingers dug into his palms so hard his knuckles turned white.

Bloom.

"Yeah," Ben whispered, staring resolutely forward. "Yeah, that's true."

Now it was Mark who piped up from the back, his voice soft with horror, or maybe awe: "What did you…*do it* with?"

Ben ground his teeth so hard his jaw cracked. "A fucking pool noodle," he said. Then he yanked open the door, pushed his way through, and headed toward the engine to see what fresh hell Horace had in store for them now.

2.

Ben poked his head into the engine room. "What happened? Is it a sasquatch? Oh my God, *please* tell me we're being attacked by a sasquatch." Ben had always wanted to see a sasquatch. It was pretty common knowledge around the train.

Horace frowned beneath his mustache. He tossed the remains of the sputtering blue smoke bomb out the open window and wiped the waxy residue off his fingers. "Not this time." He grabbed a pair of binoculars off the control panel and offered them over. "Something worse."

Ben looked at Horace suspiciously, then looked at the other man in the engine car, Assistant Conductor Rogers. Rogers had a short, wispy mustache, a smattering of complementary chin hairs, and beady owl eyes behind a pair of mostly-broken rectangular glasses. He didn't say anything; he just watched Ben with a mixture of trepidation and irritation. He didn't much care for Ben. He, too, knew what had happened to the last assistant conductor.

"Worse than a sasquatch?" Ben asked, snatching the binoculars out of Horace's hands and stalking to the front of the train car. "That could be literally anything. A sasquatch is the best-case scenario." He held the binoculars up to his eyes. "Where am I looking?"

"Up ahead. On the tracks."

Ben peered through the binoculars. The tracks disappeared into the yellowish-green mist ahead. "Am I looking for tracks, or fog? I see both."

"Further down, where the tracks head down between those cliffs. See that?"

"Barely," Ben mumbled, twisting the horizon into focus. "There's too much fog."

"It'll clear."

Horace was right. Horace was *usually* right, and Ben hated that. As he looked on, the desert wind pushed a tunnel through the mist, and he caught a glimpse of something on the tracks. "Oh," he said, lowering the binoculars from his eyes. Then he lifted them again and took another look. "Yeah. Okay. Definitely worse than a sasquatch."

He strained through the magnification to see the details of the obstruction far ahead. It was a woman, slight and knobby and built mostly with right angles. She was lying across the tracks on her back. And she appeared to be tied down. "Did we just roll into a Charlie Chaplin movie?"

"Maybe." Horace took back the binoculars and gave the woman another look. Then he pulled his pocket watch out of his vest pocket, checked the time, and sighed. "All right, Rogers," he said, his voice heavy with disappointment. "Stop the train."

The assistant conductor reached up and pulled back on the throttle, but Ben grabbed his arm. Rogers flinched at Ben's touch, and Ben thought about making a hilarious joke about calming down and keeping his head, but now just wasn't the time. Also, he couldn't quite get the wording straight, and he didn't want to waste the joke. "Wait," he said. "You're gonna *stop*?" He looked at Horace like he was crazy. "Don't *stop*; speed up!"

"Speed up?" Horace gasped. "I'm not going to run her over!"

"Why not?" Ben demanded. "This is a trap! This is *obviously* a trap! This is a trap taken right out of the *Idiot's Guide to Traps*! Don't stop the train! For fuck's sake, Horace, make him go faster!"

"I'm standing right here," Rogers said.

Ben ignored him. "Make him go faster!"

Horace adjusted his glasses on his nose and looked at his assistant conductor. "Stop the train," he said, his voice firm.

Rogers tugged his arm free of Ben's grasp and returned his hand to the throttle. He pulled back, and the train began to decelerate.

"You can't stop the train in the middle of the desert!" Ben cried. "This is where the sand zombies live!"

"Sand zombies," Horace scoffed. "Look, if we're attacked by dusters, we'll take care of them. But I'm not steamrolling over an innocent woman."

"Innocent? She's not *innocent*; she's part of a trap!"

"I don't care! Even if she is, I'm not going to murder her with my train!"

"You murder people *all the time* with your train!" Ben said. "You've murdered half a dozen already this morning!"

"Those were *dusters*—that's different!" Horace shouted. His cheeks flamed with anger. He hated when Ben questioned him in front of crew members.

"It's *barely* different," Ben insisted, crossing his arms. "*Barely.* And what about all those marauders you obliterated with the pushy plow last week? You exploded at *least* three of them."

"*That was different, too*! They were marauders...they meant to do us harm; those dusters meant to do us harm. That girl out there? She's tied to the tracks, Ben."

"She means to do us harm," he said through gritted teeth. "You think someone tied her there because they want her dead? If you want to kill somebody, you bash her with a bat, or you knife her in the throat, or you push her off a mountain. You don't tie her to train tracks and hope for the best. You brought me on this stupid fucking train to keep it safe. Remember that? 'Oh, Ben, nice to see you again, small world, finding you out here by the tracks—hey, by the way, you look like shit...wanna work on my train and keep it safe?' Remember that? I'm *trying* to keep it safe; *that woman wants to stab you in the throat!*" Jesus Christ, was he the only person who remembered how the apocalypse worked?

"We don't know that for sure," Horace insisted. The flush in his cheeks burned to crimson. "Even if it *is* a trap, she might have been kidnapped and used for bait...we don't know for sure! And I'm not taking that chance. Rogers, stop the train."

"I've *been* stopping the train," Rogers pointed out.

"Good."

"Terrible," Ben corrected him. "This is a terrible idea, and we're all gonna die."

"Well, Benny Boy," Horace said, mopping his brow with a handkerchief, "it's your job to make sure we don't."

"Don't call me Benny Boy," Ben grunted. "That is *our* name."

Horace frowned and cocked his head, eyeing Ben with a mixture of confusion and pity; he'd taken to talking about himself in third-person plural lately, and that was highly concerning. But it was a concern he'd have to save for later, for a time when he wasn't being led into a possible trap. He sighed. "Do you think your recruits can handle this or not?"

Ben snorted. "I don't think my recruits can handle their own hands." He smirked to himself. *That was a good one.*

"Well, I don't want any of the veteran Caps off the train. I need them to protect the cargo car."

"Yeah, yeah, yeah," Ben said dismissively, waving a hand through the air. "I'll put a couple dummies on it. But if they get knifed in the throat, I'm blaming you." He turned toward the assistant conductor and gave him his best menacing stare. "*And* I'm blaming *you*, Rogers. Because you stopped the stupid train."

"He told me to!" Rogers said defensively. One hand flew instinctively to his neck. He rubbed it, felt how solidly it connected his shoulders to his head. He liked that feeling.

Ben smirked again. "Doesn't matter. If my recruits get knifed, heads will roll." He chuckled softly. "Heh. Get it?"

Rogers blenched.

Ben cleared his throat. "Now, if you'll excuse me," he said, turning and pushing his way out of the engine car. "I have some pool noodles to attend to."

•

"All right, newbies. Who wants to die?"

The recruits glanced nervously at each other. A couple of them shrugged. But none of them raised their hand.

"You'll get to use a gun," Ben said, sweetening the pot. "A real gun, with real bullets."

Nine hands shot into the air.

"Good," Ben continued. "You'll also probably honestly die. There's a really good chance of it. Probably ninety-four percent." All nine of the hands went back down. "But you'll have everlasting glory," Ben added. Four of the hands went back up, though not nearly as excitedly. "But you'll be too dead to enjoy it." Three of the hands went down.

Mark's hand stayed up. Mark hissed something at his friend, trying to get *him* to raise his hand too, but Mark's friend shook his head violently and mouthed, *No way.*

Hmm. Smarter than they look, thought Ben.

All of them except Mark.

"If you *do* survive," Ben went on, pacing across the train car with his most authoritative step, "you will be automatically promoted to the position of Red Cap. You can trade your pool noodle in for a real machete—*not* you, Ricky," he added quickly. "You never get to touch another machete as long as you live." Ricky's face fell. Tears welled up in his eyes. Ben did not care. "So. Maybe certain death, but you get to use a gun, and if you live, you're a Red Cap. Who's in?" Mark's hand went even higher in the air; he was all in. He elbowed his friend, who sighed with resignation and lifted his hand, too. "All right," Ben said, clapping once. "Mark and Mark's friend. You're up."

"My name's Howard," Mark's friend volunteered.

"I only remember the names of people I'm going to speak to again," Ben said. "Survive this mission, and I'll think about remembering your name."

Howard grew pale. He wondered if it was too late to un-volunteer.

"The rest of you, head to the armory. Lucas is in there; he'll give you some knives and clubs and things. Arm up, then spread out. Make sure all the entrances are covered. You two," he said, pointing at Mark and Howard, "come with me."

The other recruits chattered nervously. "Ben," Bob said. "What the heck is going on?"

"We're about to be sieged," Ben said. "Because that's where Horace's stupid morals have brought us."

3.

Howard gripped his rifle. "You have any idea how to use one of these?" he asked out of the side of his mouth.

Mark shook his head. "No idea. I've only practiced with a tree branch."

"It's easy," Ben said, irritated that they obviously hadn't been paying attention during the lecture. "You put the bullets in here. You pull back on this. You aim the gun, and you pull the trigger. Got it?"

Howard glanced nervously at the firearm in his hands. "I don't know if I—"

BANG!

Mark screamed as his rifle leapt from his hands and clattered down the steps. It landed muzzle-first in the desert dirt outside the train, which had come to a complete stop just a few minutes earlier. "Holy shit!" he said, feeling both terrified and thrilled. "That was *easy!*"

Ben stared at him with dumbfounded horror. "Mark. Did you just shoot that fucking gun?"

"I did!" he cried. "I didn't mean to, but I did!" Mark shook his head in wonder and said, "Huh. I guess I'm really good at firing guns."

Ben closed his eyes and counted to five. A headache was wedging itself into the deeper folds of his brain. Sending these morons off to their almost-certain doom might end up being the best part of his day. "You are such an idiot," he murmured. "If I open my eyes and look down and see a whole bunch of red on my shirt because you accidentally fucking shot me in the body, I am literally going to murder you with a pool noodle." Mark gulped. Ben opened his eyes. He lowered his chin and gave himself a visual inspection. There was no red. He seemed to be whole. "I might murder you anyway," he decided aloud.

Mark breathed a sigh of relief and wiped his sleeve against his forehead. "I should...probably go get my gun. Right?"

Ben grunted. "You should probably get busy with your mission," he said, "or I'll find someone else who really, *really* wants to be a Red Cap."

"Speaking of our mission," Howard piped up, lifting a single finger in the air in a way that he hoped gave his interruption an acceptable sheen of politeness, "what...*is* our mission?"

Ben snorted. "You guys know that's the *first* thing *most* people would ask, right? Not 'Which gun is the loudest?' or 'Are you sure you have a red hat in my size?' Most people would ask, 'Hey, what is this insane mission you just drafted us for?'"

Mark looked at Howard; Howard looked at Mark.

Mark hemmed. Howard hawed.

They both looked down at their feet and mumbled, "What *is* this insane mission you drafted us for?"

Ben shook his head. "You're going to be sorry you asked." He peeked out between the cars and squinted into the dust-colored mountains in the distance. He didn't see any movement...but he wasn't sure he would be able to see any from this far off anyway. "Look," he said, pointing up the tracks. "See that woman?"

Howard leaned back, holding onto the handrails for support. He craned his neck. Then he gasped. "Is she tied to the tracks?" he asked.

"There's a woman tied to the tracks?" Mark thrust his head out between the cars, too, nearly pushing Howard off the train and into the barren desert. "Holy shit!"

"What did we roll into," Howard asked, eyeing the woman carefully, "a Charlie Chaplin movie?"

"Cool joke," Ben said, glaring. "It was hilarious when I said it." He grabbed both men by their shirts and pulled them back onto the metal platform between cars. "Look," he said seriously, "your job is to go out there and free that woman. You'll probably need this." He handed Howard a knife, an old tool with a rusty blade. Howard took it with what Ben proudly noted was an appropriate amount of wonder. "Cut her loose, and get back. That's your mission. Understand? Don't talk to her, don't lollygag, and for the love of God, don't bring her back onto the train. Every single fiber of my being tells me this is a trap, and that she's part of it. But Horace won't explode her with Patrick's pushy plow, because he's weak, probably made weaker by that stupid, heavy mustache he absolutely will not shave for reasons I'll never know. But we have to get her off our tracks. Understand? You go out there, you cut her loose, you don't get murdered in some all-too-obvious ambush, and you get back on this train. And you become Red Caps. Got it?" He looked at Howard, then at Mark. They both seemed to be on the verge of tears. "But to be clear: I do *not* like you. In case that's a concern."

Mark nodded stoically. "We'll get it done," he promised. "Cut her loose, don't get killed, get back on the train."

"Right," Ben agreed. "And be careful." He let his gaze wander once more along the mountainous horizon. "Just because I can't see her people doesn't mean they're not out there."

Howard wiped a sheen of sweat from his forehead. "Okay," he said, nudging Mark. "Let's just…let's just do this, okay?" Mark nodded.

"All right," Ben said. He clapped a hand on each man's shoulder. "Good luck. Don't die."

"We won't," they said in unison.

None of the three men really believed it might be true.

4.

Howard couldn't shake the feeling that he was doing something really, really stupid.

"Do you think we're doing something really, really stupid?" he whispered as he and Mark crouch-stepped across the desert, guns above their heads, sidling toward the tied-up woman.

Mark's eyes were wide with fear, darting across the horizon, desperate to find some sign of murderous cutthroats preparing to storm the train. "Of *course* I think we're doing something stupid!" he hissed.

Assistant Conductor Rogers had stopped the train about fifty feet from the woman, and the two Red Caps covered the gap easily. No one shot at them while they ran toward her, and no hordes of murderers had appeared on the hillsides and stormed down toward the train, and they took all of this as a *really* good sign. They skidded to their respective stops on either side of the woman. Howard waved away a particularly dark green cloud of Monkey dust, and they saw the woman clearly for the first time. She was both bound *and* gagged, which definitely ratcheted up the Charlie Chaplin-ness of the whole situation by a good ten or twenty percent. She was a fierce, bony woman, with dirty blonde hair, vicious green eyes, knobby joints, and a face that was caked in dust. She strained against her bonds as the two men approached, bucking her back and pulling at the ropes, grunting and groaning into the filthy handkerchief that had been stuffed into her mouth. Her hands were tied together at the wrist and cinched to her belly with the help of a thick but badly-frayed rope. That same rope wound down and around her body, crisscrossing a series of Xs down her legs and up her chest, binding her to the metal tracks.

"Jesus," Howard murmured, "how are you even able to feed rope under train tracks?" He dropped to his hands and knees, setting the gun down on the sandy gravel embankment and inspecting the rope. "It's like they had to actually dig *under* the tracks to make room."

"Who cares?" Mark whispered nervously. He held his rifle to his shoulder and slowly swept the horizon. The mist made it impossible to see too far in any direction, but he thought he saw shadows moving across the ridge in the distance. Sweat trickled along the back of his neck and dripped down the inside of his shirt. He hated that. "Just untie her, and let's go."

"Right, right," Howard nodded. He pulled the knife from his belt. "Don't worry," he said to the woman. "I'm not going to cut you." But as badly as his hand was shaking, it was a pretty unlikely promise.

"Hurry up," Mark whispered. "It's too quiet out here. It's giving me the heebies."

Howard stopped and thought for a second. He looked up at Mark, his face twisted with confusion. "Isn't it the heebie-jeebies?"

"What? No," Mark said with no small amount of disgust. "It's the heebies. The jeebies are something totally different." He returned his gaze to the distance. "Idiot," he muttered under his breath.

Howard shrugged. Then he went back to work. He lowered the blade to the rope, but he couldn't quite decide where to start cutting. First, he went for her waist, but her hands made that sort of difficult. Then he moved up her torso, but the closer he got to her chest, the more he blushed, until he could practically see the red coming off his own cheeks. So that wouldn't work, either. Then he moved the knife down *below* her waist, and *that* made him uncomfortable, too...because if he was being honest, he was still a virgin, and the mystery of the female reproductive system proved far too distracting. He moved his hand down even further and started cutting at the rope around her legs, but the way her thighs strained against her faded jeans aroused certain feelings in him that made him just want to cry.

"Will you hurry up?!" Mark said.

"Sorry, I don't..." Howard began. He wiped the sweat from his forehead and shook out his hands. "There's nowhere to—how do I—where do I *do* it?"

Mark turned and blinked at his friend. "You are such a wang."

"Shut up!" Howard grumbled. He hopped onto the tracks and began sawing through the ropes at the woman's ankles, deciding that it was a strategically chaste place to work. "I am *not* a wang."

Then there was the dull, wet sound of a rock falling into a swimming pool, and Mark fell over into the sand, a harsh stream of blood pulsing out from the gunshot wound in his throat.

"*Jesus fuck, they shot Mark in the neck!*" Howard screamed, even though the only person who could really hear him was the woman on the tracks, and she already knew, because she had seen it for herself. "*They shot him in the neck!*" he screamed again. He dropped the knife and scrambled backward off the tracks, down the slight embankment, tumbling over his own heels and landing hard on his back. The wind exploded from his lungs, and he struggled onto his belly, gasping hard for air, and clawed his way back toward the train. He shrugged off the cumbersome rifle that was slung across his back and flung it away so he could give himself a better hold on the dusty desert earth, and he squirmed through the sand like a broken snake, writhing closer and closer to the engine.

He was about fifteen feet from the train when a bullet exploded through his spine. The hot lead shattered his vertebrae, snapping his nerve roots and liquefying the marrow. His legs went numb, and he felt the bullet lodge against the inside of a rib, cracking it in half so a ragged edge poked roughly through his skin. Two hot streams of blood spilled from his body, one from his abdomen, the other from his back. And as he lay there dying in the sand, he thought, *Well this wasn't worth it at all.*

5.

"Goddammit, Horace, I *told* you it was a trap!"

Ben willed his legs to move, to run like hell out of the engine car and back to the armory, with the rest of his body in tow, but they refused to listen. Legs, Ben found, were often the most useless when you really, really needed them. Or maybe it was his eyes' fault...they couldn't stop staring out the window at the two bodies of his recruits, Mark and Mark's friend Howard, still and bleeding and lifeless and dead and already being covered with sand and swallowed by the mist.

"Of *course* it was a trap!" Horace cried, throwing his hands up in frustration. "And it was a really *good* trap! That's why it worked!" He shouldered past Ben, stomping out of the engine and passing angrily into the next car.

Ben's legs finally started to get the message, and he turned to follow the conductor, but Rogers grabbed Ben's arm. "Wait."

"What?"

Rogers didn't reply. He just nodded out the window, the color draining quickly from his face.

Ben followed the man's pale gaze and peered out through the swirling mists surrounding the train. Dark shapes moved beyond the fog. An entire legion of deep green shadows scrambled down the mountainside and ran for the train. Ben did a quick assessment of the number of approaching figures in his head. He lost count after forty.

There were only twenty-four Red Caps, even counting the new recruits.

Twenty-two, Ben reminded himself. *Goddammit.*

"Maybe they're dusters?" Rogers asked hopefully. It was a hope that Ben would have found funny if he'd had a second to process it. It was just three years ago when he and Patrick encountered their first batch of dusters in the woods somewhere between Memphis and Mobile; he never would've thought he'd one day *hope* to see those drooling, drug-addicted cannibals swarming down toward him on their stupid, stumbling, stiff and broken legs. But Patrick's hydraulic train plow was more than a match for the calcification of duster bones. One thrust from the metal wedge at full power, and they literally liquefied on contact, exploding in a red and yellow mist of blood and Monkey goo. With the train in their arsenal, dusters were barely a blip on the radar of their concern.

It was other survivors who were the real monsters now.

Compared to the other humans, zombies were a piece of cake.

"No such luck...their movements are too smooth," Ben murmured, watching the legion of mysterious strangers scrabbling toward the train. "This is bad."

He ran out of the engine car and barreled his way back through the armory, plucking a machete and a baseball bat from the shelves as he passed into the cargo room. Horace was standing in the center of the train car, barking orders to the Red Caps standing nervously in the aisle, between the rows of shelves, swinging their weapons awkwardly and hoping they wouldn't have to use them. "All right, listen up!" Horace hollered. "They don't take the engine, they don't take the armory, and they sure as hell don't take this cargo hold!"

A few of the Red Caps cheered bravely, thrusting their weapons into the air and accidentally striking them against the train car's ceiling. A chorus of "Whoops" filled the air.

"Goddammit, Horace—that's my speech," Ben spat, shouldering the conductor out of the way. He held his machete high, gripping the bat by the thick end of the barrel in his other hand. "Listen up, Red Caps! They don't take the engine, they don't take the guns, and they don't take the treasure!" he bellowed.

The Red Caps looked at each other. Some of them scratched their heads. One of them coughed.

"Goddammit," Ben muttered again. He couldn't help but feel that his words were lacking a certain motivational power now. He glowered at Horace.

"You heard him," Horace said, nodding around the room. "Take your places, men. Do this train proud."

"Do this train proud!" Ben said, louder than Horace.

The Red Caps grunted their support, then filed out of the car, headed toward their various stations.

Ben turned to Horace. "Come on...you know riling everyone up is *my* job," he snapped.

"Sorry," Horace said. "Seemed like we didn't have time for proper protocol."

He turned and headed toward the back of the car, but Ben grabbed him by the elbow. "Where you are going?" he asked, alarmed. "The engine's up that way."

"Yeah, but my lucky club is back in my bunk," Horace said, pulling himself free and heading back toward the sleeping quarters. "I'm gonna need it."

Ben cocked his head to the side. "Why? Aren't you taking control of the train?"

"Rogers can pull us out," Horace said over his shoulder.

"Well what are *you* gonna do?"

Horace set his chin. "I'm going to go get the girl."

"You're *what?!*"

"I'm gonna cut her loose."

"But she's with *them!*"

"Probably," Horace nodded. "But we need to get this train moving, and I'm not running her over."

Ben opened his mouth to respond, but a series of sharp *pops* from outside stopped him short.

The bandits had just started firing on the train.

6.

Horace gripped his lucky club and peered out into the mist.

The weight of the club felt good in his hand. It lent him a strange sense of calm. He gave the weapon a couple of good swings. *Don't let me down.*

There were a lot of weaponized clubs in post-apocalyptic America. Horace had seen probably over a thousand in the six years since M-Day. Most of them had been put to decent use and carried the dark red stains of blood that had soaked into the wood. But not Horace's. His club was unblemished; it hadn't soaked in so much as a string of snot from a sneeze. Because Horace's lucky club was lucky in the best and truest sense.

He'd never had to use it.

Things being what they were, that was lucky as hell.

He squinted into the swirling green clouds and felt reasonably sure he didn't see any shadows storming this side of the train. The short crack of bullets pinging off of the metal exterior were relegated to the other side for now. He pulled at his mustache with his free hand and took a deep breath. Then he jumped down the steps, crouched down in the sand, closed his eyes, and waited to get shot.

But he didn't.

He nodded at the club. *So far, so good.*

He shuffled forward, keeping low to the ground, using the train as a shield from the gunfire. When he came to the gap between cars, he threw himself forward with a quiet cry of determination. He hit the ground on his belly, knocking the wind from his lungs. He coughed on the sand that puffed up around him, but as far as he could tell, he was alive, and not full of holes.

He picked himself up and huffed his way toward the front of the train, cursing and cringing with each new bullet that plinked off the metal siding. He reached the front of the engine car, already out of breath. *That doesn't bode well,* he thought miserably. He looked ahead and saw the girl, still writhing against her ropes on the tracks. She hadn't been shot, at least not as far as Horace could tell, and that was good. She'd be easier to move off the tracks if she was alive. If she died, he'd have to lift her, and that would be murder on his back.

He looked back around at the bandits making their way toward the train. His heart stopped; there were dozens of them, maybe as many as fifty.

His Red Caps were handily outnumbered.

They were starting to come into focus now, pushing through the mist. There were men and women both, all wearing filthy jeans and ragged shirts. Most of them had cowboy hats, their noses and mouths covered by handkerchiefs, Old West bandit-style. They were advancing toward the train in a staggered line. There was little for them to take cover behind—just a smattering of scrub brush and a few cacti—but they were laying down enough fire to keep the Red Caps inside the train, afraid to peek their heads out.

Whoever these people were, they weren't being cautious with their ammo. And that in itself was pretty terrifying.

Horace pulled back and leaned against the train. He took a deep breath and made the sign of the cross with the club. "Jesus, help me save this girl, save the train, and make up the time we've lost." He patted his pocket watch for extra luck. Then he turned and ran out into the open air and up the tracks.

•

"What is he...doing?" Ben asked, disgusted.

Rogers shook his head slowly. "I...do not know," he admitted.

They watched through the engine windows as Horace tripped over his own feet and went flopping onto the dirt like a monk seal. Rather than pull himself up to his feet and keep running like a real human being, he decided to roll clumsily toward the bound woman, wincing in pain each time his ribs rolled over the big wooden club. After a half dozen or so rotations, the struggle was apparently too much; he changed tactics and army-crawled toward the woman instead, but unlike a regular army crawl, where a man might use his elbows to pull himself forward, Horace used his feet to *push* himself along, so essentially he ended up skidding along the desert on his belly, his arms held flat out to the sides and completely, utterly, confusingly useless.

"This is fucking tragic," Ben murmured. "I should go lead the Caps." Horace's weird, twisting lurches were mesmerizing. "But I...I can't look away."

"It's like a physical manifestation of bad poetry," Rogers threw in, his voice quiet with awe. "I almost *want* them to take the train so they'll kill me and I won't have to watch this anymore."

"You can close your eyes. Or look away. Like a decent person would do. A person who really should be helping to fight off a siege," Ben said as he remained staring out the window and not moving to help fight off the siege.

"You were right," Rogers admitted. "We should have just run her over."

"I am *always* right," Ben reminded him. "Don't you ever forget that."

Rogers nodded solemnly. "Should we do something to help him?" he asked, nodding out at the struggling conductor.

"The best thing we can do for him is to pretend like we never saw this travesty," Ben decided. "And probably also not let the train fall to bandits."

He finally pulled himself away from the window and grabbed the emergency shotgun that was mounted to the side of the control panel. He checked for shells, pumped the handle, and headed out, gun-first, into the space between the cars.

7.

Horace was in a lot of pain. But he didn't want to show weakness in front of a stranger.

"I'm fine!" he hollered out, even though the woman was gagged and obviously had not asked how he was. Nor did she look like she was particularly concerned, if he was being honest with himself. If anything, she looked pissed off that he was taking so long. Her eyes blazed with impatience. "Sorry," he said between labored breaths. "This isn't normally my job."

He got to Mark's dead body, the blood around his neck wound already congealing. The sand had soaked up a good amount of the gore, and Horace had a sudden flash of memory: an art project he had made when he was in grade school, an old Coke bottle that he had drained, cleaned, and re-filled with a dozen alternating layers of brightly-colored sand. Green, blue, yellow, orange, purple, pink, and red. Blood red.

The sand saturated with Mark's blood was deep red and beautifully crystalized. It would have made a very handsome sand project layer. He wondered if it would hurt Red Cap morale if he gathered a bit of Mark-blood sand and made something beautiful out of it. He would mean it to be a symbol of hope, of something extraordinary growing from something tragic. But he doubted the others would see it like that.

Then he wondered why the hell he was thinking about blood-sand artwork, and if he was finally starting to crack up.

He crawled over Mark's corpse, which was maybe a disrespectful thing to do, but his body was on autopilot now, with the bullets whizzing and the clock ticking and the blood thundering in his ears, and he just needed to reach the girl in whatever way his physiology deemed best.

Besides, it wasn't like anyone was watching him.

He hurdled the corpse and threw himself the last five feet, propelling his bulk with a sharp kick of his feet. But he kicked a little too hard and propelled himself right into the girl's ribs. She yelled out in pain, and probably more than a little frustration. He mumbled an apology. "Sorry...sorry. This isn't the sort of thing I do."

He set the club down on the tracks and picked up Howard's knife. Without any of the guilt of impropriety that his former underling had felt, Horace went straight to work, sawing away at the ropes just above the woman's waist. He allowed himself a few nervous glances at the onslaught of attackers, and he didn't like what he saw. They were getting close to the train now. Very close.

Too close.

They were laying down so much fire that his Red Caps were pinned inside the train; aside from the occasional shotgun blast from near the engine car, it didn't sound like many of his men were firing back. *Shoot out the windows, you idiots,* he thought.

Not for the first time, he wondered what he had done to deserve a crew like his.

Given how quickly the raiders were advancing, he figured he had less than two minutes before they started to board the train. And he couldn't let that happen.

He cut at the thick rope with a flurry of energy, sawing like a man possessed, and after a few more seconds, the rope snapped in two. He dropped the knife and unwound the rope from around the woman's body, working downward and freeing her hands first so she could help. The woman shrugged out of her bonds and kicked her legs free. Then she pulled the gag down out of her mouth. She spat the taste out into the sand, then looked at Horace and said, "You dumb fucking Muppet...how are you still alive?"

Then she picked up the knife and jabbed it at his ribs.

Horace cried out and fell backward, and the blade sailed past his belly, slicing a button off of his vest. He sat down hard on the cold metal tracks, and the woman lunged forward with a vicious battle cry. He rolled down onto his back as the woman's momentum took her right on top of him. She straddled him and tried to pin his arms down with her knees, but Horace was pretty practiced in arm-flailing, and he managed to wriggle his shoulders free. The woman lifted the knife over her head, then plunged it down at his heart. Horace felt blindly to his left, his hand seizing the thick end of his lucky club. He brought it smashing against the side of her face, just as she was swinging the knife down, and with a dull, quiet groan, she collapsed off of him and rolled out onto the sand.

Horace scrambled to his feet as gunshots peppered the ground around him. He crouched instinctively, which he realized wasn't likely to be all that helpful; he wasn't much shorter hunched down than he was while standing at full height. He turned and ran back toward the train, but after only a few stuttering steps, he felt something tangle itself on his ankle, and he went crashing down, smashing his chin on a cross bar of the tracks. His teeth clacked hard, and something inside his mouth began to bleed.

He looked back at his foot. The woman's hand was clasped around it, and she was clawing her way up his leg, the side of her head dribbling blood. She snarled up at him, flashing a wicked, toothy grin…then she sank the knife into the back of his thigh.

Horace screamed. The knife slid in almost all the way to the hilt, stopping only when it hit bone, chipping away a few flakes of that just for good measure. He kicked back with his other foot and caught the woman in the jaw. She fell away, and he pulled himself up onto his good leg. He hobbled toward the engine, throwing his arms in the air and screaming, "Rogers! *Rogers!*" Fire tore through his leg as he dragged it behind him. He looked over his shoulder, and the woman was struggling back to her feet. Blood had smeared across her mouth, spreading up her cheeks. She smiled through the gore and didn't bother to wipe it off as she staggered after him.

Horace turned and hobbled straight toward the front of the train. He saw Rogers' pale face pressed against the glass. The assistant conductor gave him a thumbs-up. Horace struggled along, gripping his leg, wincing at the pain and at the sheer amount of warm, wet blood that coated his hand when he grabbed the wound.

The woman launched herself at him from behind with an angry cry, her shoulder connecting with his right kidney. Horace crumpled to the ground with a whimper. She stood over him, gripping the knife so hard, her knuckles turned white. With every ounce of his strength he had, Horace kicked upward with his good leg. It caught the woman hard in the crotch, and she went down, crying out in pain. "You miserable motherfucker!" she screamed.

Horace flopped over on his side and scuffled himself off the tracks, away from the front of the train. "Rogers!" he yelled. "Now!"

The engine gave a gentle hiss as Rogers pushed the red button on the console. Then the hydraulic plow rocketed forward, sledgehammered through the air, and hit the woman so hard, she exploded on impact. Bits of bone and gristle plopped to the ground like some sort of grotesque Marilyn Manson rainstorm.

An ear landed on Horace's chest. "I am *not* a miserable mothereffer," he said into it.

Then he brushed it off his shirt, pulled himself up, and limped back up into his train.

8.

On a scale of one to ten, Ben put his chance of survival at minus eight.

"We've got a problem," he hollered over his shoulder as Horace pulled himself up the stairs and into the train car.

"Add it to the list," Horace grumbled. He tested his leg by putting some weight on it, and it immediately gave out beneath him. He collapsed to the train floor in a heap.

"I'm almost out of shells." Ben popped four new cartridges into the shotgun. He took aim through the window and fired. Someone outside the train yelled, "Ow! Son of a *bitch*!"

"Send someone to the armory for more," Horace said, out of breath. He wiped the sweat from his cheeks, then scanned the car with tired eyes. "Where the heck is everybody?" he asked.

Ben fired another round out the window. The body of a raider hit the sand with a dull thud. "I sent them to the armory to get more shells. They didn't come back. Which means they're not only dead, but also majorly disappointing." Ben cocked the shotgun and aimed it at a raider who was approaching the train. "One more step, and I'll shoot your crotch right off your—" But before he could finish the threat, a bullet struck the outside of the car just two inches from his window, and he fell back into the train. "Goddamn!" he declared. "I think they mean business."

"Ben—" Horace began.

Ben interrupted. "Can you get me more shells? Without dying? I'm down to two. I don't think I'll—no! *No!*" he screamed out the window. "You stay in the desert, or I swear to God, I will send you to hell in eighty-seven different pieces." The marauder outside fired at the car, which only made Ben mad. "Oh yes I *will* shoot you in the face," he said, more to himself than to the bandit. He pulled the trigger and made more or less good on his promise to blast the man into multiple pieces. Possibly even more than eighty-seven. "Scratch that. Just one more shell." Ben took his eyes off the chaos outside and noticed for the first time that Horace was lying on the floor of the train. "Horace! Are you serious? This isn't *naptime*—this is shoot some people in the face before they take our train time!"

"Sorry," Horace sighed. He wondered how much blood he'd already lost. "Just…catching my breath." He reached up and grabbed the armrest of the nearest seat, then he pulled himself up to a half-crouch position. Blood spurted across the aisle.

"Ew," Ben said, watching with a sour face. "Did you let someone shoot you?"

"She stabbed me," Horace admitted. He stiffened his good leg beneath him and slid forward along the aisle. "Sit tight. I'll go get you the shells."

"Oh, for God's sake." Ben pushed his way out of his row and thrust the shotgun into Horace's hands. "Here. Take this. I'll go after the shells. Just make sure if anyone boards this train, you shoot him hard enough that his friends want to slit their own wrists when they see how gross his exploded head is, because you only have one shot left, and if they don't kill themselves, they will kill the *shit* out of you."

"Got it," Horace said, taking the gun with a grimace.

"And do *not* use it on yourself," Ben warned, narrowing his eyes. "If you die, you do it by bleeding out or getting eaten by the cannibals."

"They're cannibals?" Horace asked, alarmed, but it was too late. Ben was already sliding open the door and passing into the next car.

"Shells," Ben murmured, scanning the shelves of the armory. "Where…are the shotgun shells…?" It was probably not the right time for him to admit to himself that even though he'd gotten considerably better at guns since M-Day, he still wasn't what one might call "good"

29

at them, and he had no idea which shells fit which guns. The fact that he knew shotguns took shells at all was something of a victory. As he slid his eyes over the stacks of boxes piled high on the metal shelves, he might as well have been trying to decipher a wall of hieroglyphics. "Shit," he whispered. "I suck at this."

He leaned in to inspect the boxes of ammo more closely, but then he heard the bang of the shotgun blast from the next car. Horace had fired the gun. "Son of a bitch," Ben muttered. "He'd better not have offed himself." He grabbed one of each of a half-dozen different boxes, loaded them into his arms, and hurried back toward Horace's car. He kicked the rectangular switch plate near the base of the door. It slid open, and Ben cursed under his breath.

The bandits had boarded the train.

"I told you to shoot them *harder*," Ben seethed through clenched teeth.

There were seven bandits in the car, with more mounting the stairs in the back. They were lean, but they didn't seem hungry, like so many did in this post-apocalyptic world. They were ropy, but strong, and not a single one of them had the ashen pallor to their skin that usually signified malnourishment and desperation, as if they were well-fed. They wore bandanas over their mouths, and their hats were crammed down on their heads, but judging by the hair that tumbled out from under some of the brims and by the general shapes of their bodies, Ben estimated that between one and four of them were women. The others might have been men.

The one Horace had shot was lying on the ground, clutching his leg and whimpering in pain. He was roundly ignored by the others.

"Drop them boxes," said a tall man who stepped forward and pulled the bandana away from his nose. With his other hand, he leveled a six-shooter at Ben's chest. Ben figured this was probably for some sort of effect; six-shooters were stupid, and also impractical for hijacking a train. The man had probably tossed his *real* gun just before boarding the car and pulled this one out of his waistband so everyone would think he was a real rootin' tootin' asshole. Ben was not impressed.

"Drop 'em," the man said again, and by the way he set his jaw when he said it, everyone in the car knew he meant business.

"But they'll go all over the place," Ben said, not taking his eyes off the man in charge. "It'll take, like, an hour to pick them all up."

The man's eyes blazed. He took a step forward and lowered the gun so it pointed at Horace's good leg. He cocked the hammer. "Drop. Them."

Ben shrugged. "You're the boss." He threw the entire armload at the bandits, then dove out of the way, ducking into a row of chairs and covering his head with his arms.

The boxes of bullets scattered in the air and collided with the front line of surprised bandits. A few of the boxes burst open, spilling rifle slugs and shotgun shells across the carpet. The rest just fell harmlessly to the floor, fully intact. The bandits looked around at each other, raising their eyebrows and shrugging their shoulders.

The leader let his arm fall slack at his side. He tilted his head and gave Ben a curious look as Ben cautiously lifted his head above the seat-backs. "What...did you think was gonna happen?" he asked, genuinely interested.

Ben glanced down at the bullets that lay scattered across the train floor. He stood up straight and put his hands on his hips. "Honestly? I thought they might all explode on impact," he admitted.

The bandits murmured their disapproval. "Do you have *any idea* how bullets work?" the leader asked.

Ben shrugged. "No. I guess I really don't."

The bandit frowned. His henchmen and henchwomen chattered to each other, confused, and he silenced them with a hiss. They fell silent and straightened up. "Listen, idiot," he said, "why don't you tell us where you keep the cargo, and we'll—"

But he didn't bother to finish his sentence, because Ben was suddenly no longer listening. He juked left, toward the train window, then right, toward the aisle, then left again, then he dove right, throwing himself into the space between the seats and hurling his body through the door and into the next car.

The lead bandit sighed. He looked down at Horace. "Is he always like that?" he asked.

Horace shrugged. "Yeah."

The bandit motioned toward the door with his revolver. "Come on," he said to his crew, stepping over the fallen conductor. "Let's go."

•

Ben was a panther—a lithe, graceful predator who moved with the power and fluidity of water.

"Ow," he said, cursing as he collided with a metal shelf.

Halfway through the armory car, he gripped the edges of the shelf and pulled. The whole steel structure came tipping over, lodging at an angle against the shelf on the other side, creating a barricade through the car and sending dull sabers and sharpened mop handles scattering across the floor. Satisfied with the obstacle, he turned and leapt back into panther mode, pouncing through the next door and through the Red Caps' quarters, on into the cargo car beyond, only running into three seats and colliding with just two Red Caps, and given how crazy everything was and how much everyone was running around covered in blood and reeking of confusion, Ben thought that was pretty good.

He dashed into the cargo car and tapped his foot impatiently as he waited for the door to slide shut. Finally, it did, and he threw the locking mechanism that one of the Red Caps had rigged up. It wasn't a very *good* locking mechanism, but it was a small wedge that could be jammed into the back of the door, and though it wouldn't keep anyone out for long, it would keep them out for a minute or two.

And a minute or two was all Ben needed.

He dashed into the shelves and gave himself only a brief second to wonder why the cargo shelves were bolted to the ground, but the armory shelves were just shoved loosely into a stack. It just seemed inequitable. The cargo hold wasn't nearly as well-stocked as it had once been, back when Ben and Patrick had boarded Horace's train for the first time. Those had been the heydays of the apocalypse—the caviar days, the days of good and plenty...when post-apocalyptic capitalism was at its best, and there were men- and women-of-plenty in every corner of the country selling off their excess to the rest of America and paying people like Horace for safe, timely, and reliable transport.

But so much had changed in just three years. The M-Day survivors were being pulled to their wits' end by the stresses of post-apocalyptic life, and this led to harsher words, which led to bigger fights, which led to meaner battles...which ended in general slaughter. People were picking and losing fights in record numbers, and seeing as how ninety-nine percent of the population had already been melted into goo by the Flying Monkeys, that didn't leave a whole lot of folks standing...add to them all the people who were getting sick, and that meant there weren't many folks still paying to ship goods across the country.

But even though the shelves were sparse, that didn't make them any less important.

Oh, no. Not by a long shot.

There were plenty of high-value items in the cargo hold these days. There was a full Confederate Civil War soldier uniform, complete with gloves and sidearm. There was a fairly worn but wholly-intact copy of Uncanny X-Men #266—the first appearance of the mutant called Gambit. There was a tin of Spam that the owner claimed was the last remaining can of spiced ham on Earth, and for all Ben knew, he was right.

But more valuable than all of these things was the polycarbonate briefcase.

And it was more valuable by far.

It wasn't the briefcase *itself* that was particularly valuable, though it probably hadn't come cheap back when such things could be purchased in stores and swiped through on credit cards. It was a heavy duty piece of work, a custom Zero Halliburton with six different locks, a biometric scanner, and an indestructible hinge system. It was said to be untamperable, unbreakable, and unopenable by anyone who didn't have the keys, the code, and a properly programmed thumbprint. So it wasn't exactly a slouch in the "has some value" department.

It was what was inside, however, that made the briefcase the most valuable cargo Horace had ever carried.

In the years after M-Day, a dull shock had spread through the world, an unwillingness to accept the new reality. A lot of survivors couldn't handle the fact that they'd survived; suicides were common, depression was rampant. One of the few things that held what was left of society together—that gave people hope—was that when everything else collapsed, one rule remained: if you survived the Flying Monkeys, it meant you were immune to the dust. You were healthy; there was something within you that could combat the effects of the poison, and even though you could still die in a knife fight, or be shot in the face, or be ripped apart slowly and eaten by dusters, the dust itself couldn't hurt you. That was the rule.

But in the more recent days of the apocalypse, that rule was being challenged.

In the fourth year after the apocalypse, people started getting sick. Not a lot of people…not the majority of people…but a few of them. They would come down with a fever, or their skin would take on a sickly, jaundiced yellow hue, or they would break out in hives; the early indicators were different in everybody, but eventually, the coughing fits would set in, and the sneezes…and they would start choking up globs of an emerald green mucous, and they would sneeze strings of green snot flecked with blood. The sickness would get worse quickly from there, and soon a yellow ooze would leak from their noses, from their ears, from the ducts of their eyes. Dark stains would spread across the fabric of their pants, both in front and behind, and that was when they knew it was almost over…because the next stage was the excreting of the yellow-green Monkey fluid from their pores, little drips and drops squeezing out from the skin, coating their limbs in slick, sulfurous goo, dripping down their cheeks, dribbling down their legs, pooling in their shoes. Most died of dehydration; they were considered the lucky ones. Those who pressed on passed the leaking stage moved on to the next and final phase of the sickness: their bodies would swell and expand from the inside at an incredible and horrifying rate; their skin would bubble out into thick blister boils, and they would rupture—their flesh would burst open, squirting greenish slime and blood, until their bodies spilled out most of what had been inside. What remained was often nothing more than a soggy sack of skin and bones saddled with strings of yellow-green muscle and tendon splaying out in the wind.

They called it the Green Fever, and it was spreading.

It was just a rumor at first, a story whispered in the shanty towns along the tracks—a warning, a nightmare, a bedtime story that was whispered to misbehaving children. But the stories became more and more frequent, an accepted mythology, and before long, everyone claimed to have had an encounter with the fever…this person's brother, that person's friend. Soon, Ben was seeing it for himself every time the train rolled into another town. He saw a woman coughing green in Elko…a little boy leaking green from his skin in Newton…an elderly man sneezing bloody goo in Gallup…an advanced-stage teenage girl, stumbling into the street in a fit of fever, bursting right in front of his eyes in Altoona.

He'd had to wipe the bits of her skin from his cheek.

It was in all the towns now, and all the spaces in between all the towns. People were dying everywhere. The apocalypse was having its own apocalypse.

Once you came down with Green Fever, your chance of survival was zero percent.

Everyone who got sick died.

Everyone.

But the silver case was going to change that.

Because according to the man who entrusted it to Horace's care, inside the case was the cure.

And if it was true—if the serum or powder or pill or whatever it was inside the silver case could *actually* cure the Green Fever—that made it the single most valuable item on the face of the planet. Which also made it the likeliest reason for the ambush.

Ben rushed forward and snatched the silver case from its shelf. He pulled at the latches, but of course, they didn't budge. "Goddammit," he cursed under his breath. He needed to open that case.

He reached up and grabbed another piece of cargo from the shelves, a bowling ball that had been signed in gold marker by some nerd who bowled for a living and who probably had zero chance of having any real respect from any real person when he'd been alive. "Your life was wasted," Ben told the signature as he pulled the ball down. He lifted it over his head, then brought it crashing down on the silver case.

The latches popped open.

Ben stared at the case, incredulous. "Wow. Let me guess: made in America?"

He shook his head as he heaved the ball away and pulled open the case. Five Dasani water bottles were lined up along the inside. At some point in their mostly-inconsequential lives, the bottles had been emptied of their water, and they had been filled with a syrupy, almost viscous bright-orange liquid. Then they had been sealed, with the caps screwed on tight and dipped in thick yellow wax. A ring of white medical tape had been wrapped around the seal, and the letters JRB had been scrawled on the tape by a hasty hand. Ben picked up one of the bottles from the case. "This isn't an antidote," he said, screwing up his face in confusion at the thick orange liquid inside. "This is LiveWire Mt. Dew."

A gunshot pinged against the train car, and Ben snapped back to attention. He pulled the other four bottles from inside the case and loaded them into his arms. He nudged the case closed with his elbow and pushed it back into place on the shelf with his knee. Then he hurried across the car, dropped to one knee, and unloaded the bottles on the floor. He pulled out the purple Jansport—old, ragged, and perfectly unassuming—and shoved the bottles inside. Then he zipped the bag shut and stuffed it back onto its shelf. "Perfect," he said, proud of himself. "Just like Patrick would do it."

That is not at all how I would do it, the voice of Patrick insisted inside Ben's head. *I haven't been gone nearly long enough for you to forget how well I would do things.*

Ben sighed. That voice had been haunting him more and more lately.

"Shut up," he grumbled. "It's *exactly* how you would do it."

Switching the bottles isn't a terrible idea, Patrick admitted. *It's not the best idea...but it's not a terrible idea. We'll call it 'Ben-smart.' But if you're going to do something 'Ben-smart'—which, to be clear, is 'Patrick-stupid'—then you're going to need to go all the way.*

"What the hell does that mean?" Ben demanded.

Go all the way, Benny Boy. Go Ben-smart all the way.

"What do you mean?!" he said, getting irritated.

I mean, Patrick-stupid harder! Patrick cried.

Ben closed his eyes and shook his head. "If you weren't dead already, I'd kill you all over again."

A fist slammed against the window set into the train car door. Ben jumped. "Shit," he said. "Out of time."

Okay, okay, said Patrick. *In the interest of the current timeline, I'll just tell you. Okay? Not because you deserve a quick answer, but because if I don't help you, you'll probably get all butchered up, and then I won't be able to lord my genius over you later. For that reason, I'll just tell you: the suitcase is empty.*

"Yeah. I know." Ben rolled his eyes. "I emptied it, stupid."

He imagined Patrick burying his face in his hands and shaking his head sadly. *No, no, no*, he said. *I know you emptied it. You didn't refill it. That's the problem.*

Ben gasped. "Shit," he said. He allowed himself a frustrated sigh. "I hate it when you're right."

I know you do, Benny Boy. I know you do.

Ben dashed back across the car and threw open the briefcase again. If it *was* the case the bandits were after, they'd pick it up and know instantly that it was empty.

He glanced up at the door window. The King of the Bandits was standing on the other side, but he wasn't looking in; he was shouting directions over his shoulder, directing the others off the train and around to the back of the car. Ben snatched the nearest thing on the shelf, the Civil War uniform, and stuffed it into the briefcase. He tested its weight. *Still light*. He threw in the can of Spam, too, and two stuffed rabbits they were supposed to drop off in Albuquerque. He hefted the briefcase. "Perfect," he decided with a smirk. "I am Indiana Jones and the motherfucking bag of sand."

The bag of sand in Indiana Jones was too light, Patrick pointed out. *It made that big rock ball crash down, Alfred Molina died, everything went to hell.*

"Shut up," Ben said. "Alfred Molina was already dead by then."

Oh yeah, Patrick said thoughtfully. *You got me there.*

The door behind Ben slammed open, and he dropped the briefcase. Three of the bandits stormed into the car...he had just enough time to flick the clasps closed before they came around the shelving, guns held at their hips, barrels pointed in the general direction of Ben's crotch.

"Hands," one of the bandits growled from behind her handkerchief.

Ben raised his hands into the air and twisted his hips a bit, cocking in one knee to protect his precious nethers. "What do you want?" he asked. He intended to sound stoic and pissed off, but his voice didn't quite get the memo, and it squeaked like a balloon being rubbed by a sugared-up toddler.

The bandits didn't reply. One of them lowered his gun and jogged up the length of the train car, kicking away the shim and sliding open the door. The leader strolled in, walking casually down the aisle, glancing around at the windows and the shelves, taking stock and nodding thoughtfully, as if he were some bigshot tycoon who might like to buy this particular train car someday soon.

Ben gritted his teeth. If there was one thing he hated, it was casually murderous dickholes.

"Put down your guns," the leader said, his voice suddenly smooth as cream. He motioned downward with his hands, and the other two bandits lowered their revolvers. They stepped back and took up sentinel duty by the door. The leader stepped down the aisle and strode up to the shelves where Ben stood, crooked and self-guarding. The bandit holstered his gun and spread his hands wide in a show of innocence, or maybe peace—which Ben didn't exactly buy, since he and his friends had just rained bullets down on the outside of the train until the metal resembled the surface of the moon, and they'd likely killed a whole mess of Red Caps and recruits in their attempt to enter this car, too. If Ben survived the hour, he'd probably be responsible for tallying up the bodies, and then burying them, and then finding new recruits in the next town, and then starting all over with the training, and goddamn it all if that didn't make him want to stab himself in the heart.

"Rumor has it there's something special on this train," the leader said, throwing an arm up on the shelving unit and leaning slowly forward. "A real treasure. You know what I mean?"

"Yeah," Ben said, nodding. "I know what you mean." He nodded toward one of the racks, at a small plastic CD case. "The last Yanni album on Earth. Goddamn, I hate to part with that."

The leader's eyes burned. "You get one more chance here, friend. Think real careful about what you say next," he warned. "You know why we're here. Pass it on over, and you get to live."

Ben sighed. His shoulders slumped, and he bowed his head in defeat. "Okay," he said quietly. "It's not worth all this death. Just...okay."

The leader smiled as Ben turned toward the shelves. He reached toward the briefcase, but moved past it and picked up a different treasure from the next shelf, a tribal statuette of some archaic fertility god. Carved from wood and hardened with age, the figure was about two feet tall with a humanoid form that culminated rather severely in a massive, fully engorged wooden penis that was about eight inches long and anatomically dubious, to say the least. Ben swung the idol with a grunt. The business end of the penis struck the bandit just below the eye with a loud *thock*.

The man stumbled backward, surprised. He lifted a hand to his cheek. His fellow bandits stared, open-mouthed. Ben looked down at the idol and its substantial erection.

For several moments, no one spoke.

"I'm sorry," Ben finally said. "That was...that was weird for all of us."

The bandit's face began to darken. He drew his pistol and held it at his waist, keeping it trained on Ben's chest. "Enough," he said with a sigh. "Drop the dick. Give me the case."

Ben gritted his teeth. He tightened his grip on the idol. "Look," he said, setting his feet and bracing himself for an attack. "I don't want to die. And I don't want to get shot. But I've got *one fucking job* to do on this train, and it's to not let you have that case. So if you want it, you're going to have to go through me."

The bandit shrugged. "Fine," he said. Then he pistol-whipped Ben in the temple, and the entire world went dark.

9.

Horace slapped Ben in the face. And if he were being honest, it felt pretty good, so he slapped him again.

"Christ, stop it—I'm alive," Ben soured. He opened his eyes and struggled to sit up. A dozen small explosions set themselves off behind his eyes, and he tumbled over against a shelving unit with a groan. "But I can be convinced not to be," he added.

"You're lucky," Horace said seriously. "Most of the Red Caps weren't." He eased himself down to a seat in the aisle, using the shelves for support. He'd tied a strip of cloth around his leg wound, and it was soaked through and dripping with blood.

"You don't look great," Ben pointed out. "You're pale—er...paler. Than usual." He blinked hard, trying to clear the bursts of light from his vision. "And that's pretty pale."

"I'm losing blood fast," Horace agreed.

Ben glanced slowly up at the shelf above his head. When the bursts of pain-light cleared, he could clearly see the edge of the silver briefcase peeking over the ledge of the shelf.

"What happened?" he asked, rubbing his eyes. "How long was I out?"

"About half an hour." Horace tugged on his bloody bandage, sucking in breath as a bolt of pain shot through his leg. "They're gone now."

Ben reached up and grabbed at the briefcase. His hand was shaking, and the handle kept swimming in and out of focus. But on the third try, he snagged it, and he pulled it down onto his lap. "But they didn't get the briefcase," he said proudly, running his hand tenderly over its ribbed silver exterior. Then, more to himself than to Horace, he said, "I did a great job."

"You did an *awful* job," Horace said. "They didn't take the case, but they *did* take the bottles of antidote. Found 'em in that purple backpack you slid under the shelves."

Ben's heart stopped. "Fuck," he said. "Fuck-fuck-*fuck*!" He leapt up over Horace, misjudging the distance and accidentally dragging his toes across the conductor's bad leg. Horace whined in pain, and Ben hit the ground and rushed forward, sliding to his knees on the other side of the aisle and scrambling among the shelves. "No, no, no, no, *no!*" he cried. He dug through the scant cargo, flinging canned beans and grease-smeared Troll dolls in every direction. "Goddammit, *no!*"

"What?" Horace asked, squeezing his eyes against the pain and gingerly patting his bandage.

"'What'? Are you serious? Are you fucking blood-blind?! They took the bag with the antidote!"

"I know," Horace said, wincing as he shifted his weight. "The damage to our reputation is..." But instead of finishing the sentence, he swooned and fell over onto the floor of the train instead.

"Great," Ben grumbled, eyeing the conductor with disgust. "Just fucking great." He ran his hands over his scalp, still unused to the unruly puff of hair he felt there.

He took a deep breath. He struggled to calm his mind.

He narrowed his eyes.

He knew what he had to do.

He had to go after the bag.

"Horace," he said, not looking down at the unconscious conductor, "give me forty-eight hours. I'll get the antidote back."

Horace snored softly in response.

It was all the confirmation Ben needed. He ducked between the shelves and pressed his hands against the window. The glass was smeared with a yellowish grit of post-apocalyptic grime, and he made a mental note to make the recruits wash the fucking train, if there were any recruits left alive to order around. Through the cloudy glass, he made out a hard-beaten path of horse hooves in the dry, cracking dirt. The trail ran up the stunted mountainside and disappeared over the edge, out into the desert beyond. "Idiots," Ben grunted with a smirk. With such an obvious trail, he'd be on them by sundown. He'd be back on the train with the bag before midnight.

You've gone sand-crazy, Patrick's voice said.

"Shut up," Ben grumbled. "I can do stuff."

He pushed himself away from the window and ran to the door that led to the back of the train, crushing Horace's hand under his shoes as he did. Horace snored louder.

Ben hurled himself between the cars and smashed face-first into the adjoining car's door, which did not respond when he pushed the button to open it. He gave his head a shake, blinked the swirling world back into focus, then kicked the stupid metal door until it grudgingly gave and shuddered its way open. He pushed through and walked purposefully toward a nebulous shape in the corner that had been draped with a greasy olive-green military tarp. He gripped a corner of the tarp and dramatically whipped it away. It got caught on the thing beneath, and Ben pulled at the snag. It didn't come loose. He cursed aloud and shook the stupid tarp until it slipped its hold. Ben stumbled backward from the sudden release and nearly fell over, but caught himself at the last moment, even though he did take a lump of tarp to the face. It smelled like mold and rotting meat, inexplicably, and Ben retched. He gathered up the tarp in his arms and threw it down onto the floor, then kicked it for good measure.

You're really Benning this up, Patrick pointed out.

"Shut up," Ben said. He rubbed his hands together and gazed lovingly on the thing he had just uncovered: a 2001 Triumph Bonneville 790cc motorcycle, shiny and stunning in a deep black body and chrome plating, with a 360-degree crank, parallel-twin engine that had been retrofitted to run on cooking oil instead of gasoline. This made the Triumph more than a little unreliable, but it was really the only option. Ben didn't have a horse, and walking was bullshit. He'd had enough walking to last him a second apocalypse.

Horace wouldn't love the idea of him taking the motorcycle—it was for "train emergencies only," the conductor continually reminded him, and even though this particular situation did fit that bill, he was no dummy. He knew "train emergencies only" meant "not for use by Ben under any circumstances."

In Horace's defense, Ben was not great at the operating of even simple machinery.

Do you have anything resembling the slightest idea of how to drive that thing? Patrick asked, his voice heavy with doubt.

"I've seen *Easy Rider*," Ben replied smugly. "I'm going to be *amazing* at this."

He blew on his hands, because he liked the mental image of it, then he sidled up to the motorcycle and gripped the handlebars. With a sort of awed reverence, he pulled the bike up off of its kickstand. The weight of the thing carried itself over, and Ben screamed as the five-hundred-pound bike smashed to the floor, narrowly avoiding his toes.

"Shut your mouth," Ben grumbled to the empty air around him.

Patrick remained quiet, but it was an unmistakably smug sort of silence.

10.

"I don't like this," Horace said, grimacing from Ben's stupidity as much as from the pain in his leg. "I don't like this one bit."

"Are we seriously out of backpacks?" Ben moaned, searching the shelves.

"Yeah...we were just down to the Jansport."

"How can we not have any other backpacks?!"

"I don't know, Ben, this isn't a J. C. Penney."

"J. C. Penney?" Ben said, his face screwed up in disgust. "How *old* are you?"

He ran down the shelves, picking out supplies: a can of sliced potatoes, a handful of granola bars, a few tins of beans, an extra t-shirt. "How am I supposed to carry all this stuff?"

"Well," Horace sighed, "we've got that." He pointed to a low shelf, way in the back.

"Oh, no," Ben said, shaking his head violently. "I am *not* wearing a fanny pack."

"It'll hold everything," Horace sighed. "It's really big."

"I *know* it's really big," Ben glowered. "That's half the reason I'm not wearing it. Jesus, Horace, I'm not going for a powerwalk around the mall." He pushed his supplies together into a haphazard pile on the floor.

Then he added another can of beans. "Hey, do we have a can opener?"

"No."

Ben blinked. "No?"

"No. The last one broke."

"What the hell have we been using to open cans?"

Horace shrugged. "The boys just sort of smash them against sharp rocks until they give."

Ben shook his head in amazement. "How have I let things go so far to shit?" he wondered aloud.

"By not pitching in on scavenger days," Horace suggested pointedly.

Ben glowered. "That was rhetorical." He moved down the row, digging through their cargo. "Do we *seriously* not have any other backpacks?!"

"No," Horace said, sounding fatigued. "It's the fanny pack or it's nothing."

Ben ground his teeth until they squeaked. "Fine. I'll wear the stupid fucking fanny pack."

"I don't think you should. I don't think you should be going at all."

"Well, we don't have a whole lot of choice, do we? We need to get that bag back. If we don't, then the best case scenario is we lose all credibility and never work in deliveries again, then starve to death and get eaten by zombies. Worst case scenario is the client sends a professional hitman after us, and he stabs us through the neck with punji sticks, then we get eaten by zombies." Ben grabbed gently at his throat. "Blood was made to stay on the inside," he pointed out.

Horace sighed again. He tugged on his mustache and checked his watch. "Might not matter if we get the cargo back or not," he said, shaking his head ruefully. "Not delivering it on time is just as bad as not delivering it at all." He tucked his watch back into his vest pocket and winced. "I can't stand being behind schedule."

"All the more reason for me to take the motorcycle!" Ben insisted, stuffing his supplies into the oversized fanny pack. It was stitched together from patches of supple brown leather, and the fact that it felt so goddamn soft in his hand absolutely infuriated him. "I bet that bike is faster than ten horses put together."

"Ben, the fact that you have no concept of how much horsepower the motorcycle has is just one of the many reasons why I don't like the idea of you taking it out," Horace said, shaking his head. "But I don't know that we have much else in the way of choices. I'm too hobbled to go after them myself, and I need Rogers here to help me repair the damage to the train. Those bandits shot it up pretty bad...it's going to take some work to patch it. And of the few Red Caps who survived the attack, there's not a single one I'd want to send out into the desert after them."

"It's true," Ben agreed. He clipped the fanny pack around his waist. "I'm our best hope for mission success."

"And I'll feel less guilty if you're the one who dies."

Ben frowned. "Thanks."

Horace shook his head. He gripped his leg and tightened the tourniquet he'd cinched around his thigh. Finally, he said, "If you think you can handle the Triumph, you've got my blessing. And my thanks. But keep in mind: we're sitting ducks out here until the engine's fixed. We're down to eight Red Caps and a couple of recruits, and that's not nearly enough to hold off another attack like that one. Every hour we're stuck here is an hour we can't afford. Once we get the old girl up and running, we need to go. You hear what I'm saying?" He looked gravely at Ben. "Once we're able to go, we're going. No exceptions."

"Oh, gee, whatever will I do if I come back and you're not here?" Ben asked, rolling his eyes. "Maybe I'll, I don't know, follow the tracks that head in one direction that the train can't possibly deviate from?" He turned and headed toward the armory car. "I'm going to need some weapons," he said.

"We can't spare much," Horace warned, hobbling down the aisle after him.

"I won't *need* much," Ben replied. "A machete. A tactical baton. A hammer. Oh—and a baseball bat. With a big-ass nail to drive through it."

Ooo, ask him for a pipe wrench! Patrick suggested.

"And a pipe wrench. I'll also need a pipe wrench."

Attaboy.

"We've got your machete and a few cases of guns," Horace said. "You can take the machete. But leave us the guns."

Ben paused. "That's it? Just the machete?"

"That's it."

"What happened to the bat?!"

"Those assholes took it."

"Why would they take a bat and leave a machete?"

"For crying out loud, Ben, I don't know, maybe they have an intra-mural team."

Ben glowered. "Fine. I'll take my machete. But if I die because I don't have a sweet-ass baseball bat with a nail driven through it, I'm going to haunt the hell out of you."

"I don't doubt it," Horace replied with a sigh. "For some reason, I just don't doubt that one bit."

11.

A pair of Red Caps eased the Triumph out of the train car and wheeled it out onto the rocky sand. Ben nodded approvingly, crossing his arms, setting his jaw, and hoping the sunlight was catching him just right. This was an important moment. He wanted to strike a certain pose.

"That's good," he said, and the Red Caps stopped the bike.

"Good luck, Ben," said a Red Cap named Ralph. He was a brutish-looking man with what could only be described as "piggy eyes," but he was smarter than he looked, and a good man to have on the team. He was so good, in fact, that Ben had bothered to learn his name. Ben wasn't great with names in general, and with most of the Red Caps getting themselves killed so often these days, memorizing them often wasn't worth the effort. As soon as you had it down, *bam!*— the idiot got himself shot by a shrapnel slinger or impaled on a piece of rebar after falling into a death pit. Then you had to recruit a new one and learn *his* name. It was ridiculous. But Ralph had been with the train for over a year now, and he was a pretty decent lackey.

The man to Ralph's right nodded his agreement. "Good luck," he echoed. He wasn't a Red Cap—not officially. He was still a new recruit and hadn't earned his hat. But Ben knew his named was Morgan… not because he was worth remembering on his own, but because Ben liked to yell "Morgaaaaaan!" at him the way Kurt Russell did it in that scene in *Tombstone* where Morgan Earp died on the pool table. No one screamed the name Morgan like Kurt Russell screamed the name Morgan. But Ben liked to think he was a close second.

Ben gave them each a nod of recognition, then scanned the rest of the group assembled there. Horace hadn't exaggerated...they'd taken some hard losses in the raider attack. Bodies of Red Caps and recruits lay strewn about the desert, fanning out from the train like a trail of fallen dominoes. There were fewer than twelve left standing, all told, down from the two-dozen-strong they'd been earlier that morning. Seeing the survivors gathered together like that, meek and broken and nervous about the chances of their survival out there alone in the desert, it set a hot ember burning in the pit of Ben's stomach.

The train's crew might be a bunch of lunkheads. But they were *his* lunkheads, goddammit.

He tightened the fanny pack and slung a leg over the seat of the Triumph. He wrapped one hand around the throttle, and he closed his other hand into a fist and thrust it into the air. "This is for us," he shouted to the assembled men. One of the new recruits clapped. No one else followed suit. The recruit dropped his hands and cleared his throat, embarrassed. Ben closed his eyes and shook his head. Then he started again: "This is for us. All of us. It's for me, and it's for you. I will track down the sons of bitches who murdered our brothers, and I will reclaim that property they stole from us. And I. Will. Return."

The Red Caps raised their eyebrows. One of them coughed. Horace sighed from his perch up at the top of the engine's stairs. "Daylight's wasting," he pointed out.

Ben frowned.

You should have done Bill Pullman's speech from Independence Day, Patrick said. *They'd have cheered to that one.*

"Shut up," Ben muttered. "That speech doesn't even apply."

Yeah, but people just love it so much.

Ben lowered his fist awkwardly and brought it down on the handlebar. He cleared his throat. "Okay, then," he said to the men. "Fine. I'll just go to almost certain death for nothing. No problem." He turned the key in the ignition, then jammed his heel down on the peg. It didn't budge; his shoe hit hard and sent a painful jolt up through his kneecap.

"It's...not a kick-start anymore," Horace pointed out from the train. "We changed it when we changed the engine. Just push the start button."

"I know it's not a kick-start," Ben hollered, annoyed. "I fucking *know* that." He scanned the bike for the start button and found it near the grip of the handlebar. He jammed it with his thumb, and the motorcycle roared to life. Satisfied, Ben nodded and pulled a pair of sunglasses from his pocket. He'd been saving them for this moment. It was going to be dramatic as hell.

He flipped the shades open and slid them up his nose. The Triumph trembled and roared beneath him, wobbling his voice as he said, "I"ll s-s-see you-u g-g-guys on the oth-er-r-r sid-d-de." Then he drew up his feet, twisted the throttle, and ground the tires across the desert hardpan, sending dirt and rocks flying back at the train. The Red Caps cried out and dove for cover, most of them taking a handful of gravel to the side of the face. The bike ripped forward, and Ben fell backward, screaming with terror as he held onto the motorcycle like a paraplegic cowboy riding a psychotic bronco. His shrieks echoed across the desert, splitting the air over the roar of the Triumph's engine, until the bike tore headfirst into a huge boulder jutting up from the sand. It smashed into the rock with a sickening *crunch*. The back wheel flipped up over the handlebars, and Ben was thrown airborne, screaming and sailing across the desert for fifteen feet before landing chest-first on the hardpan and skidding to a grinding halt on his face at the base of the ridge.

"Should we go help him?" Ralph asked the conductor.

"Nah," Horace said. "If we keep helping him, then he won't learn." He turned and hobbled back into the train. The other men trickled in after him, a few of them chancing glances over their shoulders at Ben, and sort-of hoping that he was, at the very least, alive.

Ben, on the other hand, was sort of hoping he was dead.

"No such luck," he grumbled into the earth. Puffs of sand plumed up under his lips. He took a breath and choked on the dust. "I hate my life," he said aloud between wheezes.

You're the same old Ben, Patrick said happily, his voice welling up with emotion. *Just...more so.*

Ben dragged himself to his knees. He touched a hand to the side of his face. He drew in a sharp breath against the sting, and his hand came away smeared with blood and sandy grit. He moaned and sat back on his heels, taking deep breaths to try to chase away the pain. The Triumph lay over to his left, the front tire blown and mangled, the handlebars twisted, with dribbles of cooking oil leaking from a jagged hole in the gas line. He hauled himself to his feet and, in a fit of embarrassment and frustration, but mostly embarrassment (he could hear the snickering of the Red Caps from the train), he hauled off and kicked the ruined bike. Then he immediately leapt away, thinking it might explode, because he had seen so many movies in his life. But the motorcycle did not explode. It just lay there, mocking him silently.

"I hate everything," he grumbled.

And everything hates you, Patrick agreed.

Ben set his jaw and turned to the train, giving them a quick wave so they knew he was more or less unharmed. The Red Caps hung out the doors of the Amtrak cars, laughing their stupid heads off and giving him grand, sweeping arcs of goodbye with their hands. Ben made a mental note to fire them all after he'd saved their livelihoods. Then he turned his back on the train, the tracks, the Red Caps, and the motorcycle, and he strode out into the desert alone.

12.

The blonde woman stared straight ahead, sipping her beer, actively tolerating the stale, sour flavor of the long-expired bottle and sloshing the flat, malty liquid around in her mouth from cheek to cheek to give it a little froth.

She swallowed. She winced. She took another sip.

A tumbleweed rolled by outside.

"Seven cans! Seven good cans!" The wiry man at the far end of the bar was screeching to the bartender, a bored-looking older man with engine grease on his elbows and a bushy, dusty handlebar mustache sprouting from his upper lip. "Seven cans, not far gone, not too far gone, not as bad as you'll get from any other one in this whole district—I promise you that...seven good cans, not far gone, and I get three measly fucking ounces?!" The wiry man gestured wildly at the three shot glasses in front of him. Each was full nearly to the lip with some clear-ish sort of home-made demon or other. "And not even a bond—not even a *drop* of bond! Seven good cans, for three ounces that ain't even got a drop of bond?!"

The bartender sighed. The droop in his eyes and the pallor of his cheeks spoke volumes. They said that this conversation was well-worn territory; they'd had it before, many times, and they'd have it again, many, many more.

"These cans are expired, William," the bartender said, nodding to the seven grimy, dented cans of food the wiry man had brought as payment for his morning libations.

"Of *course* they're expired—*every* can of *everything* is expired!" William cried. "But they're not *so* expired."

"They expired four years back."

"Four years back! Exactly right! That is *exactly* my point!" William hollered, throwing up his hands and punctuating every other word by pushing a palm through the air. "They expired four years back, and you know they only stamp them cans good for two or three years, even though they're good for ten, maybe twenty years, probably twenty years for *sure*—you *know* they do that, so these cans were sealed fresh right before M-Day, maybe just *days* before M-Day, could have been even *minutes* before those Jamaican fuckers took us down—that might make these, hell, the freshest cans left in the whole wasted world of existence!"

The bartender picked up one of the cans, turned it around, and pointed to another, smaller stamp on the other side of the label, nearly faded away. "This one says it was canned four *years* before M-Day."

William lowered his hands. He tilted his head and frowned. He hadn't seen those dates.

"Furthermore," the bartender continued, "it's high and mighty generous to call these seven full cans. These are the smallest cans I've ever seen...ain't nothing to them."

"It's tuna!" William exploded. "Of course the cans are small, it's tuna—those are *tuna cans*! That's some high quality shit right there; that is *tuna*, that is the *dolphin* of the *sea*!"

"The *chicken* of the sea," piped up another man from the other end of the bar. This one was shorter, and plumper, and had the burst-red nose of a lifetime drinker. "Dolphins *do* live in the sea, you idiot."

"Chicken, dolphin, who gives a shit—it's all just zoology!" William yelled. "Now, those are seven good cans, not too far gone, and I want *six* ounces—of something *bonded*!"

"And what do you care about bond?" the slouchy alcoholic threw in. "J.W., don't you give him an ounce more of any single thing, I brought in those three motorcycle tires, and all I got was this quarter-bottle from some bullshit distillery in Alaska, so don't you go giving him anything more for seven cans of bad fish."

William opened his mouth to protest, but the bartender held up his hands. "Everyone's got exactly what they're gonna get, and if you don't like it, you can be banned like old Jim Hersch."

"Old Jim Hersch," William and the alcoholic both muttered in unison. They turned their heads and spat on the floor.

"No need to get all sensitive," William said sourly, wrapping his forearm around his three shot glasses and protecting them from some imaginary threat. "You know I'm grateful for whatever scraps you can provide."

"Thank the Lord Jesus," J.W. said, rolling his eyes.

The blonde woman continued to sip on her beer as she listened carefully to the sniping and whining from the other patrons around the bar. Unlike most people, she didn't mind other people's incessant blathering. Chatter was good. Chatter was camouflage. She could hide under it like some ancient sea creature beneath the ocean waves, a leviathan hidden just inches away behind a murky curtain. So she drank her flat beer, and she listened carefully to their words, because words were information, and information was power, and power was currency. Her time with the Source had taught her that.

As the bickering of the locals droned on, she finished her beer and tilted her head at the bartender, signaling for another. The droopy man obliged, grabbing for the next bottle in line below the counter, not bothering to look at the label, because it didn't matter anymore.

All the beers were expired. They all tasted like the same awful shit.

The woman shifted on her chair. It was an old, rusty thing, with a thin sliver for a back and a wobbly disc for a seat. It had once been padded, but most of that foam had torn and fallen away, and the whole thing felt like it might collapse with the slightest breath. She had more than enough heft to bring the stool down to its final demise, bigger than all three men in the bar, save perhaps the bartender, who might've been a lineman for some overly-adored high school football team a few decades back. Her dusty canvas pants strained across her thighs and stretched against her calves, and the long sleeves of the Henley shirt she wore hugged her thick arms tightly, like huge rubber bands. She pulled at the cuffs of those sleeves, pulling them down to her palms each time they tried to creep up her wrists.

Her cheeks burned as the bartender popped open her next beer. "Can't promise it's good," he said, eyeing her suspiciously. "Can pretty much guarantee it ain't."

She didn't respond. She took the beer and put the bottle to her lips, drinking down a third of it in one go. The bartender raised an eyebrow, then grabbed another full bottle from behind the counter and set that one in front of her, too. "Back-up," he explained. The woman nodded.

"Now, hold on, here...what's she paying that gets her an open tab on beer—*real* beer, *bonded* beer?" William demanded.

"Beer isn't bonded, idiot," the slouchy alcoholic snapped.

"You answer the question!"

"Hold your horses, William," the bartender said. But he turned his drooping eyes to the blonde woman just the same, and she felt the color burn even darker in her cheeks as she avoided returning his stare. "We treat strangers good here. I'm sure the lady can pay her way."

William snorted. "Lady. She's a lady like a bull's a heifer."

J.W. shot his hand out and backhanded William from behind the counter. The wiry man went tumbling backward with a shout, knocking over a set of wire shelves. J.W. had set up the bar next to the train tracks in an old Phillips 66 gas station in the middle of the desert, a station that had enough trouble getting business back before the apocalypse, and whose tanks had been tapped dry in the years since. The place was mostly cleaned out now, but the triangular cashier's counter made for a decent bar, and though the coolers hadn't cooled anything in over half a decade, they made for good enough storage of what scavenged liquor J.W. was able to scrounge up through his network of desert pirates. Thick chains threaded the handles to the coolers and were locked up tight with huge padlocks, the keys for which hung from J.W.'s belt.

The Slushee machine still sat on its counter, the sticky-sweet syrup long hardened against its dull metal sides, and the hot dog warmer still held half a dozen mummified hot dogs from an age long past; J.W.'s greatest happiness these days manifested when he managed to get a patron so drunk that the poor bastard would brazenly—and, eventually, regretfully—accept the bartender's dare to eat one of those petrified pork poles. It was second to none for entertainment these days.

Projectile vomiting was the new Netflix.

William struggled to his feet with the help of that decrepit hot dog warmer now, shooting J.W. an ornery glare. But the bartender didn't notice. His eyes were still fixed on the woman sitting across the bar.

"We treat strangers good here," he repeated. "And I trust the lady has come prepared to pay for what she's drinking."

The woman clenched her jaw. Still not matching the bartender's gaze, she reached down to her belt and slowly drew out a shiny Bowie knife, clean and sharp, looking pre-apocalyptic in its spotlessness and shine. The handle was scrimshaw elk antler, carved to resemble a prairie dog standing at attention. It was a beautiful piece of cutlery, a finely-honed blade that was meant for a cleaner time, a better time, but had wound up in the miserable shithole of post-M-Day existence anyway, along with the other unlucky survivors.

J.W. hadn't seen a knife like that in ages. No one had, at least not out here in the desert. He touched the handle with a quiet reverence. "For this?" he mumbled, his eyes suddenly bright in the glow of the blade. "For this, you *do* get an open tab."

The length of the shadows inside the gas station caught the woman's eye. "Train go past?" she asked the bartender, her voice thick with gravel.

"Not yet," J.W. replied. He knocked the counter twice. "Reckon it's a little late."

"Shit, that conductor ain't never late," the slouchy drunkard piped up.

Just then, the doors of the Phillips 66 burst open, and a thin, scraggly man tumbled in, heaving and out of breath.

"Fellas! Look at this!" the man said, getting his feet firmly beneath him and beaming around at them as he showed them his shoulder. A dark red trail of blood streaked the sleeve of his shirt, near the bicep. "I've been shot!" he said proudly.

"I always knew it would happen someday," William said. "I just always thought it'd be me to do it."

J.W. crossed out from behind the counter and inspected the smaller man's shoulder. "Just a graze," he decided, after giving the man's arm a close once-over. "Shit, George...what the hell happened?"

"Trouble down in the valley!" the man said excitedly, hopping onto an empty stool. "Down at the tracks. That old Harold and his train come through—"

"Horace," the red-nosed drunk corrected him.

"Harold, Horace—who cares? The train come through, but get this: there was a *woman* tied to the *tracks*!"

"What? No shit?" J.W. asked.

"Who was it?" William said.

"Don't know. Some woman I ain't never seen."

"Did they hit her?"

"Nope; stopped the train short. And then they get off to go cut her loose, and a whole goddamned *army* come swarmin' over the mountain, ridin' on horses, raisin' hell, and firin' every gun this side of the Rockies. Killed maybe fifty men. Maybe a hundred!"

"Bullshit," J.W. said.

"I seen it!" the man insisted. "I was out checkin' my traps, up on the ridge, I seen it sure as I see your ugly mug right now. It was some big set-up. The bandits come over the mountains, and the girl on the tracks, she was with 'em! I seen her get up and jump on one of them horses when they was done, but she cut down Harold first."

J.W. started. "Horace is dead?"

"Likely! They killed them train boys, then they got on board, were on for a long time...then they come back off, holdin' some backpack like it's the fanny diaper of Christ. They put it in a metal box, lock it up tight, and zoom, away they go, back on their horses and up the mountains." The man slapped both his palms on the counter and leaned forward hungrily. "Now if that bit of news ain't worth a shot of real, I ask you, what is?"

"Don't you give him bonded!" William cried.

The woman stood up, and the stool scraped back, lost its balance, and fell over. The men in the bar jumped. "Where?" she demanded. All told, this was more than she'd spoken in over a week. The words came out harsh, scratched like a record.

The man squinted, leaning close and sizing her up. "West," he said finally, pulling in his glass and throwing back the shot. He wiped his lips with the back of his sleeve. "About two miles, and a little bit north."

The woman downed the rest of her beer, then grabbed her canvas knapsack from the floor and held it by the cinched top.

William scoffed. "Most expensive two shitty beers I've ever seen," he complained.

But he needn't have called it out. The blonde woman was already reaching out for the knife, and she closed her hand over the elk-antler handle. J.W.'s size and general droopiness belied his own speed; he clapped his hand down on the woman's wrist, pinning it to the bar.

"I don't think so," he growled.

That was a mistake.

The woman dropped the knapsack, clenched her hand, and brought her meaty fist down on the bartender's wrist, hard. Something cracked, and J.W. fell away, howling in pain. The scraggly man moved for the gun tucked away in his boot. With one smooth motion, the woman grabbed the empty beer bottle on the counter and smashed it across the man's face. Glass exploded across his temple, shards lodging into the milky whiteness of his right eye. He screamed and clutched his face as a cloudy mixture of aqueous humour and blood seeped through his fingers. The woman sensed movement from her left. She spun again, slicing the knife horizontally through the air, and a thick, deep line of red opened up across William's shirt.

He gaped down at his wound. "You stupid cow!" he cried. Then he fell over, dead and quietly leaking on the floor.

The blonde woman shifted her gaze to the slouchy alcoholic. She raised an eyebrow in a silent challenge.

"I think *all* beer should be free," he said, raising his hands into the air. "No problems here."

She slipped the knife back into the scabbard at her hip. She grabbed the unopened bottle of beer and stuck it into her bag. Then she tossed it over her shoulder and pushed her way out of the old gas station, letting the moans and cries fall away as she stepped back into the desert and headed toward the train.

13.

Ben was hot, and he hurt, and he *really* had to pee.

"I think I punctured my bladder," he whined, holding the place at his side where he was pretty sure his bladder lived, just below his ribcage. "It's leaking blood all over...I can just fucking *feel* it."

If you punctured your bladder, you probably wouldn't have to pee, Patrick pointed out. *You would probably have to lie down, because your body would be riddled with frothy waste, and you would be just absolutely full to the brim with poison.*

"I could have to pee that poison out," Ben reasoned.

And you wouldn't leak blood, Patrick continued, barreling right on past Ben's weird rationale. *Your bladder's not full of blood. It has blood in the tissue that makes up the bladder, sure, but it's not* full *of blood. Do you have any idea what human bodies are? Or how urine works? I am very worried about you.*

"Look, I just have to pee," he said.

It's not called "leaking" when you urinate. It's called urinating. You know when people say "taking a leak," they don't mean it's literally leaking, right? Unless your penis does *leak. Does your penis leak? Wait! Ben! This is important. Focus, now. This is important: Does your penis leak?*

"Sometimes I like it better when you're dead," Ben sighed. But something tugged at his stomach as he said it, like the sensation of falling, and a hot flush rose in his cheeks. "I'm sorry," he said quietly. "I... don't."

You're adorable, Patrick said. *But I don't like you like that. Now go find a place to pee before you wet your stupid pants.*

Ben stopped his slow trudge across the hardpan and took a look around. The mist was thin here, pushed out by the wind slipping down the mountains that loomed back behind him, by the train, and while Ben was generally glad for any break in the monotonous, roiling green mist, he sort of wished the wind would stop blowing. The landscape was bleak and bare as far as he could see, and damn it all if it wasn't just the most depressing view in the world.

Well, it wasn't as depressing as Reverend Maccabee's forest of corpses. Or the gymnasium full of empty cribs Ben had stumbled into outside of Shreveport. And it was definitely better than the field of half-buried limbs he'd had to side-step through when he was running from the dusters down in Texas. So okay...maybe this wasn't the most depressing view in the world. But it wasn't about to win any Best in Show awards, either, and Ben would have given his left arm for a nice water feature to break up the desertscape.

"It's terrible out here," he observed. "There's nothing but dirt and sand and more dirt and more sand, and a whole hell of a lot of sadness. It's like a Road Runner cartoon, where the pictures just repeat themselves, over and over and over."

I loved the Road Runner.

"Of course you did. You were a human Wile. E. Coyote. Now where am I supposed to pee?"

Anywhere, Patrick said. *Literally anywhere. This place is a fifty-thousand-square-mile litter box.*

Ben toed at the rough sand and pushed it into a little pile. Then he kicked the pile into the air. The wind blew it back into his mouth, and he choked until he cried. "I can't pee out here," he gasped, struggling for breath. "I can't just do it out in the open."

There's no one around. This is the apocalypse. Everyone is dead.

"Not everyone."

Almost everyone.

"That's not everyone."

No one's going to care if they see you peeing in the desert. That'll be one of the least offensive things you've done in public.

"That's not true," Ben protested.

What about that time you pulled down your pants and ran across the quad, then tripped and fell junk-first onto that ant hill?

"Well I'm not talking about college!" Ben cried.

It was 3:00 in the afternoon. On a Tuesday.

"I said I'm not talking about college!"

The dean was very *surprised.*

"I don't like peeing in public," Ben said, bringing Patrick's cruelty back to center. "I need a bush."

I have a hilarious joke about your genitalia and a bush, Patrick said, *but I'm not going to share it with you, because you're crabby.*

"Good." Ben squinted into the bright fog and scanned the desert. There were a few rocks, but none of them were big enough to offer good cover. A tumbleweed bumbled past, and he briefly considered catching up to it, but the wind wasn't slowing down anytime soon, and the tumbleweed was going to keep on tumbling, and peeing while moving was never an ideal solution. Especially when Ben hadn't thought to pack a towel. He fidgeted with the buckle of his fanny pack, and he sighed. There was only one other option: a small grove of cacti out on the far reaches of his visibility, about halfway to the horizon. There were about a dozen cacti all told, huddled pretty close together, almost as if they'd been planted there with purpose.

It was his only hope.

Sure, Patrick said, reading his mind. *Go put your dick next to a cactus. What could go wrong?*

"I can't go if I don't have cover," Ben replied, indignant. He looked down at the horse tracks that he'd been following from the train. The tracks pointed straight ahead, and the cacti were clustered directly to his left. He didn't want to lose the trail, but he *really* had to go. "I can't go without cover," he repeated. He took a deep breath and stepped away from the trail.

The cactus grove was farther away than it looked. Ben's bladder crushed against his insides with every step, and before long he was stutter-hopping across the desert, trying desperately to make it to the cacti before he wet himself. By the time he reached the nearest cactus, he was sweating from the effort, and he leapt behind it and unzipped his fly in one awkward, graceless motion. He gasped with relief as he let the stream go.

"That was close," he said aloud.

I see you, Patrick's voice whispered, sounding close to his ear.

Ben shrugged off the voice with a frown. "Stop it, go away." He stepped back from the voice, and his heel jammed against a rock rising out of the sand. He cried out as he pinwheeled backward, a stream of urine zinging through the air, and he fell straight back into a second cactus, a mean and prickly bastard that jammed its needles straight into Ben's ass. He screamed and jerked himself away from it, overcorrecting in his haste and nearly plunging crotch-first into the first urine-soaked cactus in front of him. He stepped to the side just in time, and he barely avoided serious genital injury.

And there was urine just *everywhere*.

"Goddammit!" he screamed, shaking himself dry and struggling with his zipper. "Goddammit!"

I'm going to be honest with you, Patrick said, sounding entirely too amused, *I absolutely saw that coming.*

"Son of a bitch!" Ben cried, bouncing in pain. He twisted his neck and tried to see the damage to his own rear. "How bad is it?! Are there needles in me?!"

How am I supposed to know? Patrick asked. *I'm just a voice in your head. I don't even have eyes.*

Ben felt gingerly around his jeans and found only two needles, inhaling sharply as he carefully gripped each one and whimpering in pain as he yanked them out. "I hate the desert," he whined. "I should have thrown myself into the ocean when we were at the Gulf."

Great seafood there, Patrick noted, sounding his approval. *Death by drowning, with a delicious buffet.*

Ben hiked back across the desert, fuming with anger and annoyance. He stomped through the sand, leaving shallow prints in the hardpan. He grumbled to himself as he stalked back toward the marauders' trail. When he finally reached the wide swath of horseshoe prints in the earth, he stopped. He looked left. He looked right. He looked left again. "Shit."

What?

Ben put his hands on his hips. "Which way were we going?" he asked.

Patrick's voice sighed. *You can't be serious.*

"Ah, hell," Ben mumbled.

You are so, so directionally stupid, Patrick sighed.

"Which way is it?" Ben was starting to panic.

Go the way the hoof prints go.

"The hoof prints go both ways!"

Heh heh. "Go both ways."

"Look!" Ben shouted, pointing down at the ground. "They're half-mooned that way, and they're half-mooned *that* way! Which the hell way is the right way?!"

How should I know? Patrick demanded. *I'm in your head...I only know as much as you know. Which, I'm learning, is terrifyingly little.*

"Shut up, shut up!" Ben cried. He gripped the top of his head with both hands and dug his fingers into his hair. "Fuck!" He threw his head to the left, then he snapped it to the right. Both ways looked exactly the same. "*Fuck!*"

See, this is exactly why, on our trip, I was in charge, Patrick said, a little too smugly for Ben's taste.

Beads of sweat popped out along his forehead, and his palms began to itch. If he went the wrong way now, he'd lose half a day, at least. And who knew how long the trail would last. The wind was already filling in the hoof prints with little sprinklings of sand. If he went all the way back to the train, he'd almost certainly have no trail to come back to.

And also, the Red Caps would see you and laugh at you so hard.

"Shut up!" Ben snarled, slapping his palms against his temples and squeezing his eyes shut, willing Patrick's voice to be silent. "You're not talking to me. *You're dead.*"

That, Patrick said, *is true. But I live on. In your heart. Where it is weird, and squishy, with a surprising amount of blood flow. Especially right now.* Patrick sounded concerned. *Are you nervous about something?*

"Arrgh!" Ben screamed. He struggled out of his fanny pack and hurled it angrily at the ground. It hit the sand with a *crash*, the cans of food smashing hard against each other inside. "Dammit!"

Now, Benny-Boy, that's no way to not be pathetic, Patrick warned. *There's an easy way to set things straight here. Which way did you turn when you went off the tracks and toward the cactuses?*

"It's cacti," Ben corrected through gritted teeth.

Both are acceptable, and you know it. Don't be pedantic. Now, which way did you turn? Left or right?

Ben closed his eyes and dug his fingers into his eyelids. He tried to think back, but so much had happened since then. He'd gotten so many cactus needles jammed through his skin. It was hard to remember.

"Left," he decided. "Wait. Right. No, right. Yes. Right. Left. Maybe left. Or right? Gah!" He threw his hands up in frustration. "I don't know!"

Ben, I want to ask you a serious question, Patrick said, his tone grave, *and I need you to answer me honestly: do you know your left hand from your right hand?*

"Yes, dammit! Look!" Ben held up the forefinger and thumb on each hand so that together they formed a sort of goal post. "The L on the left stands for 'left.'"

Okay, just to be absolutely clear *on this, is that how you still tell your right from your left? Because you are a grown-ass man.*

Ben pulled his hands through his hair and fell down into a crouch. Something deep inside of him was screaming, some voice lodged in the root of his chest, and he wanted to let it out, to shriek into the wind, to curse life, to curse the Jamaicans, to curse whatever god would allow him to survive in a ruined world, a god who had decided to haunt him sometimes about driving a railroad spike through his brain, just to make it stop. "I don't know where we're going," he whispered, his voice thick and clouded with tears.

He waited for an answer. But no answer came.

THOOMP! The arrow plunged into the ground just two feet to Ben's right. He jumped to his left, open-mouthed and awkward from the shock, and landed hard on his seat, banging down on the desert scrub. Two-thirds of the arrow stuck out of the ground, bending slowly, back and forth, quivering as it swayed. "They're *shooting* at us!" Ben cried in disbelief, even though he had no idea who "they" might be, and also even though he was numbly aware that there was no "us" there to speak of. "With *arrows!*"

Cripes! Patrick cried. *Run away!*

Ben snatched his fanny pack off the ground and scrambled away from the arrow, but after a few frantic steps, he stopped again. With wide eyes, keeping his body low to the sand, he held his breath and scanned the horizon. He didn't know who had fired the arrow, or where the ambush was coming from. A step in any direction could be a step closer to his assailant. He cursed under his breath. "Now what?" he muttered.

I think it's time to stand and deliver, Patrick said.

Ben grumped. "Great," he said sarcastically. "I'm excellent at fighting."

He gripped the handle of the machete and pulled it from his belt. It was the same one he and Patrick had carried from Chicago to Florida, and the same weapon that had seen Ben through the last couple years of wandering the ruined earth alone...not because he was good at wielding it, because he most definitely was not, but because it was a hell of an intimidating blade, the sharp edge pitted with use, the rubber handle cracked and split and held together with duct tape. The metal was splotched with blossoms of rust and rivulets of dried blood that seemed to have seeped into the substance and soaked it through, staining it forever, no matter how Ben wiped the blade, or washed it, or set it to disinfect in the fire.

The machete hadn't been used well. But it had been used often.

He held the weapon at his chest and shoved the pouch of the fanny pack to the side to get it out of the way. The yellowish mist was roiling through the desert in waves, first thick, then hazy and clear, then thick again, a living thing that gathered itself in a breath, then dispersed in an exhale. It set the whole desert shimmering and shifting, wavering in and out of focus. Ben spun slowly on his toes, eyeing the horizon warily, searching the shifting fog for any sign of life.

And the arrow wavered lazily in the air, creaking in the stillness.

Ben's eyes latched onto the swaying shaft of the arrow. It jutted out of the ground at a slight angle, with the feathers of the fletching pointing in the general direction of Ben's right. The arrow had come from there, then.

It took you a really long time to figure out how physics work, Patrick whispered.

Shut your stupid mouth, Ben silently urged back.

The path away from the arrow's angle, and therefore away from the person who had fired it, would lead Ben away from the hoof prints, out into the desolate and unknown wild of the American desert. The thought of losing light out there, where the scorpions and the sand spiders crept across the desert, where the temperature would sink to near-freezing when the sun slipped down past the horizon…the thought of being alone in the desert with no trail, no markers, and absolutely no sense of direction scared him more than an overzealous archer with blessedly bad aim. He sliced the aging machete through the air a few times, relishing the hum of the tarnished blade slicing through space. He *would* stand. He *would* deliver. He would send a whole army of archers to their collective deaths, he decided, giving the machete a few figure-eight swings. He would do it anime-style.

Oh no…you have *gone sand-crazy*, Patrick said, sounding worried.

"I've gone sand-pissed-off," Ben corrected him. "It's a whole different thing."

Someone's shooting arrows at you, and your only shield is a pleather fanny pack, Patrick pointed out.

Ben tilted his head. His friend's disembodied voice had a point. "Well," he said slowly, deciding his fate as he spoke, "I'd rather die here with an arrow through my heart than out there in the desert with spiders in my mouth."

In this scenario, how do the spiders in your mouth lead to your actual death? Patrick asked.

But Ben didn't have time to explain. "Shut up," he hissed, crouching low again. "Someone's coming."

Out in the distance, across the dusty scrub, a silhouette appeared in the swirling mists. The figure moving toward him was tall, impossibly tall, and Ben wiped his sleeve against the sweat of his brow. The striking height made the silhouette imposing enough on its own, but what really sent a chill down Ben's spine was the fact that the man wasn't just heading his way. He was running. No, not running…*sprinting*, with long, lumbering steps, his arms cocked out at the elbows, flailing at the wrist as they pumped like pistons, propelling his body across the sands. "Dammit," Ben said, spitting a glob of mucous between his feet. His shirt was sticking to his back, and a hot, clammy flush crawled across his skin.

He had one machete, a few cans of food, a ragged old fanny pack, and precisely zero battle buffaloes. There was no way he was ready to fight a duster.

They're called "politicians," Patrick reminded him.

Ben ignored that statement. He hardly even heard it. The blood was shooting through his veins like water from a fire hydrant, roaring and crashing in his own ears and drowning out the world. He hadn't gone toe-to-toe with a duster in over a year. Not since the days after he left Fort Doom.

After everything went to shit.

Ben shook the memories from his head. He needed to focus. The duster was gaining ground fast. Ben dug his heels into the dirt. He flipped the machete into his left hand and ran his right palm across the sand, coating it with grit for better grip on the rubber handle. He closed his hand around the machete once more, grinding his teeth against the sting of sand digging into his skin. He had one shot at bringing the monster down. The Monkey dust made the addict's arteries harder than stone; the rusty blade would just glance right off any sort of chop to the body. He would have to drive the point of the blade straight through the duster's eye and hope he could jam it in with enough force that the metal could grind past the hardened eye socket and lodge in its brain.

You don't really have the coordination for that, Patrick pointed out.

"I know."

This isn't a very good plan.

"I *know!*"

But…maybe it'll work out.

"Great. Thanks."

And by that I mean, maybe he'll eat you so fast and so viciously, you'll hardly feel it.

"Stop helping."

Sorry.

The breeze kicked up the mists, and for a few moments, the duster was hidden behind the greenish cloud. Then he exploded through the fog, pulling a yellow-green vapor trail in his wake. He was maybe a few thousand feet away, still silhouetted against the air like some shadow demon…and still running like a demon, too.

"Maybe it's not a duster," Ben whispered. "A duster couldn't fire an arrow. Right? They don't have any motor skills...they can't fire arrows."

I've seen them motor very well, and very *quickly.*

"You know what I mean," Ben hissed, sweat dripping down his back. He wriggled his shoulders in a vain attempt to blot it away. "A duster couldn't fire an arrow. It can't be a duster. Right?"

A duster couldn't fire an arrow, Patrick agreed. *But someone firing an arrow at a duster and overshooting by a few thousand yards could fire an arrow.*

"A duster *and* an archer. Great." He took a step back, thinking that maybe he should take his chances with the scorpions after all, and his heel struck a small stone buried in the ground. Thinking quickly, he switched the machete back to his left hand and picked up the stone. Maybe if he could distract the monster, he could buy himself time until the person hunting it caught up. *If* the person hunting it caught up. Then they would tackle the duster together. That was the rule of survival: attack the biggest threat first.

Once the duster was dead, Ben could worry about convincing the other person that he wasn't the next biggest threat.

Or else they'd fight until one of them was a bled-out corpse.

One thing at a time, he told himself. *Step one: distract the duster.*

He hurled the stone as hard as he could. The duster was closing the gap, emerging from the glare of the diffused yellow light; his features were just starting to come into focus as the rock struck him hard in the ribs.

"Ow!" the duster said. He skidded to a stop, panting, and clutched at his side. "Ow!" he repeated.

Ben was stunned. "Patrick," he whispered out of the side of his mouth. "Was that just you who said 'ow'? Are you throwing your voice?"

Don't be absurd, Patrick said. *You know I think all ventriloquists are pedophiles.*

Ben frowned and straightened up out of his fighting stance. His knees popped, and his back ached as he ironed out his spine. "Hey!" he called out to the duster. "Did you say 'ow'?"

The duster twisted uncomfortably, thrusting his hips to the left, then to the right, then back to the left, as if he could wriggle his ribs right around the pain of being clobbered by a desert stone. "Yes—I said ow!"

he cried indignantly. "That's what you say when something hurts you! Ow! *Owww!*"

Ben's brow furrowed beneath the weight of his confusion. "How did you learn how to speak?"

"My mom was a teacher," the duster hollered back. "Oh, and also, *speaking is something people do!*"

Ben raised his eyebrows and stared incredulously at the duster. "Are you…?" he began, his voice tilting upward, the confusion almost palpable in his throat. "Are you…*not* a zombie?"

The other man gasped. "Do I look like a zombie?" he asked, and he sounded like it might actually be an at-least-partially real question.

"You run like one," Ben said with a shrug.

"I do not!" the man cried. He rubbed at his ribs, trying to buff away the pain. By the look on his face, he was not succeeding.

Ben took a few cautious steps closer, until he could finally register the man who stood before him. He had an oversized bow slung over his shoulder, and he wasn't nearly as tall as he'd seemed from far away. What Ben had mistaken for extraordinary height was mostly being projected by an obscenely tall Native American headdress, massive and ludicrous in its extravagance of feathers and beads. It added almost three feet to the man's otherwise-average height. Two thick leather thongs hung down from either side, threaded with turquoise beads that thudded against his ears with the slightest movement.

And the offensiveness didn't stop with the headgear. The man was close enough now that Ben could see he was dressed in thick leather breeches with a beaded loincloth wrapped around his waist and draped over his crotch. He wore no shirt, but had a bear's paw tattooed above each nipple. The tattoos were fake, and poorly drawn; the lines wavered like snakes, and whatever he had used as ink was running down his chest in little drips, leaving thin grayish trails on his skin. He'd painted two streaks of scarlet red across each cheek, and he'd smeared wet ashes across his brow, his temples, and over the bridge of his nose, giving himself a dark, threatening look—or at least a look that might have been dark and threatening if some of the ash paste hadn't worked its way into his eyes, stinging them red and causing him to wipe away an almost-constant stream of tears.

This person is racist, Patrick decided.

"No shit," Ben replied.

"No shit what?" the man demanded. He unslung the bow from his shoulder and stabbed it twice into the sand, like Moses striking the rock and waiting for water to flow.

He's doing that for effect, Patrick advised. *Don't be lulled into a false sense of awe by his commanding bow usage, no matter how impressive it is.*

Ben mentally shushed him. He focused his attention on the pale Indian. "Nothing," he said. Then he remembered the machete in his hand, and he clutched it tightly and raised it a few inches, to make sure the other man got a good look. "Why are you firing arrows at me?"

"I'm not firing arrows at you!" the man cried, sounding hurt.

"Then what the hell is that?" Ben swung around and pointed at the half-buried arrow with the machete. *I can do things for effect too,* he thought, feeling a little smug.

Your fly's open, Patrick said.

Shut up, it is not, Ben shot back. He looked down at his jeans. His zipper was down. *Goddammit!* He raised his eyes back to the arrow, trying to look nonchalant. But he squeezed his thighs together, hoping he was keeping the gap closed.

"That's an arrow," the man replied matter-of-factly. His knees twitched, as if he wanted to run to the arrow, to snatch it back, but was exercising some measure of restraint.

Slight as it was, Ben did not miss the tell.

"Yeah. It's an arrow," he said, narrowing his eyes. "An arrow you shot at me."

"Ridiculous!" the other man insisted. He stamped the earth with his bow twice more. Then he did it a third time, just to show that he could. "I do not miss. If I wanted to strike-em you with the arrow, I would have strike-em'ed you with the arrow."

Ben screwed up his face in disgust. "Strike-em?" he asked.

The not-Indian drew himself up to his full height. "I am a Painted Member of the Injun Express," he said proudly. "My arrow strike-ems where I mean for it to strike-em."

"Please stop saying 'strike-em,'" Ben said, pinching the bridge of his nose with his free hand.

This is the most racist thing I've ever seen, Patrick said, his voice tinged with a begrudging sort of awe. *And I met Strom Thurmond once.*

"This is the way our people speak your white English," the man insisted.

"My white English?" Ben replied, disgusted.

"The white man has —"

"*You're white!*" Ben exploded.

The man drew back for a second, looking hurt. Then he leaned in, knitting his eyebrows together, and said, "Come on, man, cut me some slack. This is a good job. It pays in *real food*! I *need* this job. Just…come on. Be cool? Okay?"

Ben closed his eyes and shook his head. "What is happening," he said, mostly to himself.

The world has gone insane, Patrick explained. *And frankly, I'm sad to have missed it.*

The other man relaxed a bit. He slung the bow back over his shoulder, and he approached slowly, but he balled his hands into fists, just to show that he could still mean business if he wanted to. "I didn't fire the arrow at you," he said again, this time a little more gently. "I fired it at the next station. I just missed a little, is all."

"I thought you didn't miss," Ben said, rolling his eyes.

"I don't miss," the man replied.

"But you just said you missed!" Ben yelled, throwing his hands up in frustration and nearly taking his own head off with the machete.

"I said I missed a *little*," the man corrected him. He looked down sheepishly at his feet, which were clad in poorly-stitched leather moccasins. "Sometimes I miss a *little*," he admitted. "But I don't *miss*."

"Missing a little is missing," Ben replied. "And also, what the fuck is 'the next station'?"

The other man gave Ben a disheartened look and shook his head sadly. "You white devils and your coarse language," he said.

Ben clenched his free hand into a fist. *Don't murder him…you'll just get yourself covered in blood,* Patrick advised. *And you don't have any club soda. How would you ever get it out of your shirt?*

Ben worked to make his voice as even as he could. It was a superhuman effort. "Tell me what the next station is, or I will brain you with the blunt end of this machete," he said.

The other man gasped. "You would threaten me with-em violence?" he cried.

"I would threaten you with-em violence," Ben confirmed through gritted teeth. "What is the next station? What are you talking about?"

The man frowned at Ben. He continued moving slowly toward his arrow, skirting around in an arc and giving Ben a wide berth. "You've never heard of the Injun Express?" he asked. Ben shook his head. The man looked surprised. "It is a message delivery service. Like the Pony Express. But with no ponies."

"Just with 'Injuns,'" Ben said, shaking his head.

"Injuns of the Shootanote tribe," the man said proudly. "I am a proud member of Shootanote Nation. My name is Two Paws." He gestured meaningfully at the sloppy tattoos on his chest. "Like so many of my people, I am an arrowman. The stations of the Shootanote arrowmen stretch across the west. From Denver all the way to San Francisco. We are a plentiful tribe, as numerous as the stars." He gestured up toward the sky with a grand, sweeping motion.

Ben was not impressed. "You are so offensive," he informed the man.

"Not true!" Two Paws insisted. "There are, like, zero Indians left on Earth to take any offense. We've looked."

Ben narrowed his eyes. He hated the fact that this made a sort of sense. "How *hard* did you look?"

"*Very* hard," Two Paws said. His expression was very earnest, and very convincing.

"Well it's still weird," Ben insisted. "How does it work? And why did I almost get shot through the heart?"

'Cause you give loooooove a baaad name! Patrick chimed in.

I need to find your off switch before I just fall on this machete and end it all, Ben thought miserably.

There is no off switch, Patrick said cheerfully. *There is only vibrant and charming color commentary.*

"We send messages," the man explained. "Someone gives us a message that must be delivered to another place, and we write down the message and secure it to an arrow. You see?" He shuffled over to the arrow and pulled it out of the ground. He gripped it by the business end and held the feathered shaft out toward Ben. Upon closer inspection, Ben could see that there was indeed a small scrap of parchment tied to the arrow with a thin leather thong. "If you want-em to send a message from Grand Junction to Carson City, you leave it with the Injun Express. The Grand Junction Injun fixes-em message to the arrow and fires it toward-em the moon." He made another grand gesture, arcing his hand through the air. "The arrow lands near the next Injun near the horizon. That Injun pulls the arrow, nocks it, and fires it toward-em the moon." The hand sailed through the air again. "It lands near the next Injun, and the Great Journey continues. Each Injun is his own station. And in this way, we send-em messages across the many sands and mountains of the great American west."

"You daisy-chain pieces of paper? With bows and arrows?" Ben asked.

Two Paws nodded once. "Yes-em," he said.

Ben considered this. "That's…actually kind of badass," he admitted.

We definitely should have mucked around with bows and arrows more, Patrick agreed, sounding envious.

"It is badass, as the white man says," Two Paws nodded. "I do not miss. And I only miss a little." He looked down sadly at the arrow in his hand. "This was a great misfire. As I drew back my bowstring, I was distracted by a green lizard. I have not seen a green lizard in many moons." He sighed. "Green lizards are my favorite type of lizard," he explained.

Ben waved this away. "Yeah, great, look. It's fine. You almost murdered me in cold blood, but it's fine. You can make it up to me."

Two Paws straightened up again, puffing out his chest in a show of pride. "Say how, and Two Paws will atone-em."

Ben crossed his arms and tried not to cut himself with the machete. "Tell me which way is west."

Two Paws raised an eyebrow. "You do not know which way the sun sets?" he asked uncertainly.

"There *is* no sun! The whole sky is Monkey fog!" Ben cried, gesturing wildly toward the sky.

"The Great Spirit of the Sun warms us with his breath," Two Paws said sagely. Then he leaned forward a bit and whispered, "You really don't know which way is west?"

"Directions aren't my strong suit," Ben glowered.

Two Paws nodded thoughtfully. After a few moments of thought, he said, "All right. Yes. I will help you on your way." He paused to wipe more tears out of his eyes. The ashes were really running over his lids. "You have shown much goodness in the face of fear, even though you were never in real danger, because I did not hit you with my arrow, because I did not *want* to hit you with my arrow. If I wanted to hit you with my arrow, you would be dead."

Ben exhaled roughly. "Look, can we move this along? I've got a trail to follow."

"You are a hunter?" Two Paws asked, sounding genuinely interested. Then his voice turned wistful. "I have always wanted to be a hunter…"

"No. I'm not a hunter. I'm a person who's annoyed, and I have a mission. Now which way is west?"

Two Paws pointed off to the horizon at his left. "This is the path of the Great Spirit of the Sun," he said. "Follow Father Sun, and the western lands you will find."

"Great," Ben mumbled. "Thanks." He snatched up his pack, snapped it around his waist, and stuck the machete back through his belt. "Good luck out here," he said. "Don't take any blankets." Then he resumed his path along the horse tracks, heading west, leaving the pale, white Injun behind.

"How, Great Tracker!" Two Paws saluted him, waving goodbye.

"And don't fire any arrows my way," Ben replied sourly without stopping.

Then a shot rang out, and suddenly, the desert was alive with gunfire.

14.

"Shit hell!" Ben cried. The sand exploded around his feet—a burst of dust to his left, a burst of dust to his right, and every time he took a step, another bullet struck the ground just past his feet, and amid the flood of terror coursing through his body, Ben had a ludicrous flash of memory: an old cartoon clip of Yosemite Sam firing his pistols at Bugs Bunny's feet until the rabbit grabbed an old straw boat hat and an old-timey cane and danced a fast soft-shoe across the sand.

Dance, rabbit! Patrick shrieked.

"Not helping!" Ben cried above the pepper of the gunfire. He whipped his head around, searching desperately for cover, but there was nothing but desert and wispy scrub. The nearest boulder was a good two hundred feet away.

"*What is happening?*" Two Paws screamed. Every few seconds, a bullet popped near his feet, too, and he ran around in circles, jumping up and down and throwing his hands into the air like a human comic strip in motion.

Something flickered in the corner of Ben's vision. It was the flash of a muzzle, pale in the daylight but unmistakable nonetheless. The gunman was stationed behind a shallow outcropping of stone a few hundred feet to his left. "There!" he cried, pointing in the direction of the rock.

But this wasn't very helpful, because what did he think he was doing, shouting for backup from the rattlesnakes?

Ben sprinted across the sand, running perpendicular to the gunfire, heading toward the only cover in reach: the yelping, leaping Injun. The gunshots followed at a fast clip, closing in on his heels. He felt a quick and sudden pull to his right when a bullet caught the edge of the fanny pack and rocketed it off to the side. Ben lost his balance and tripped over his own shoe, and he went splaying across the sand. A bullet exploded in the dirt just past his nose. He yelled and scrambled back to his feet, ignoring the pain in his knees and elbows where he'd skidded across the hard-packed sand, and threw himself forward, struggling on his hands and feet toward the fake Indian messenger.

"Make him stop, make him stop!" Two Paws screeched, hopping in place with the bow in one hand and an arrow in the other. Then he stopped screeching, and stopped moving, and stopped breathing, too, because he'd just caught a bullet in the head, and he crumpled over dead onto the desert floor.

"Shit!" Ben screeched. He lunged forward and took cover behind Two Paws' corpse, feeling the man's body jostle against him every time it took a bullet. Ben curled himself into a ball, struggling against the awkward weight of the fanny pack and covering his head with his arms as the bullets kept flying. "*What do I do?*" he screeched.

Give him a four-count! Patrick cried.

"What?!"

Clap your hands! One, two, three four! Make it his turn to dance!

"What the fuck are you talking about?!"

That's how Bugs Bunny stopped Yosemite Sam!

"Jesus Christ, you are so unhelpful!"

Well, I'm sorry...I left the air-to-ground support in my other pants!

A bullet grazed Ben's shoulder, ripping through his jacket and drawing a trickle of blood across his collarbone. "Ow!" screamed. He sucked in air through his teeth, hissing away the pain. He ducked down lower, pressing his cheek against the hardpan. Something beneath the fallen Injun caught his eye. He shot out a hand and grabbed hold of the end of the messenger's bow. The string was pinned beneath the body, and Ben couldn't get enough leverage with his arms to pull the thing out. He scooted back and spun around on his belly, then he planted the soles of his shoes on the messenger's shoulder. He heaved and kicked...maybe a little too hard; the messenger's body skidded forward three feet and rolled over in a limp flop, so he ended up face-first in the dust. Ben snatched up the freed bow and scrambled back closer to the body, gripping the far shoulder and hauling it back, propping up the corpse on its side to give himself more cover. The bullets stopped flying, and in the distance, Ben heard the familiar click of an empty magazine dropping out of a gun. He seized the window and dove out of his cover, just far enough to grab up the arrow the Injun had dropped when his head was split open by a bullet. Then he slid back to the cover of the body and nocked the arrow in the bow. "I'm going to bow-and-arrow the shit out of him," Ben swore, breathing heavily from exertion, but also from the thrill of it all.

He'd never fired a bow and arrow.

You've never fired a bow and arrow, Patrick pointed out.

"I bet I'm a natural," Ben said seriously. The bow felt right in his hands. The size was perfect; the heft was ideal. The string was taut, and the bow was even painted a really nice shade of deep blue, one of his favorite colors. "This weapon and I were made for each other," he said, more to the bow than to his imaginary friend.

This is going to go badly, Patrick said.

"Shut up and give me moral support."

No, I won't be a party to that.

Ben hissed, and Patrick fell silent. Ben listened carefully, picking up the sounds of quiet cursing from the far side of the assailant's boulder. "Goddamn piece of shit magazine fuckers shit," the man with the gun snapped...and there was another sound, too: the scraping of metal against metal...the sound of a gunman struggling to fit a warped magazine back into place.

He was distracted. His gun was empty.

Ben had his chance.

He lurched up to his knees, held the bow in front of his chest, drew the arrow to his shoulder, and aimed at the distracted gunman's head, which had risen up behind the boulder in his frustrated struggle. Ben took a deep breath. He said a quick prayer to the gods of the desert wasteland, and he visualized the arrow flying straight, burrowing into the attacker's skull, splattering the boulder with gray matter and blood.

He pulled back the bow and fired.

The arrow shot almost straight down, and the arrowhead skipped off a rock, ricocheted across the desert, and came to a pitiful, rolling stop about six feet to the gunman's left. The gunman stopped fiddling with his weapon and stared over at the fallen arrow, confused. He looked at Ben. He looked back at the arrow. He looked back at Ben. "Seriously?" he shouted.

"Shut up, I'm having a bad day!" Ben yelled. Blood pumped hot and sharp like razor wire through his veins. He picked up a stone from the ground, stood to his full height, and hurled the rock at the man behind the boulder. For his part, the gunman was so surprised by this show of either courage or stupidity that he straightened up to get a better look at the poor imbecile with terrible aim. He stuck his head up above the boulder a little further, and when he did, Ben's rock smashed into his skull, directly between the eyes. The man groaned in stunned surprise, and he toppled backward into the dirt.

Holy shit...you did it, Patrick said.

"I *know* I did it. I'm amazing," Ben snapped back, annoyed. He slid the machete out of his belt and leapt heroically over the Injun's body, only tripping a little bit and catching himself before falling face-first into the scrub. He jogged cautiously to the rock and peeked over the top of the boulder. The gunman lay on his back, moaning quietly and clutching his forehead. The gun had fallen away and lay just out of reach.

Ben scrambled over the boulder, scraping his knee and cursing internally at the pain. *Why don't you just go around obstacles?* Patrick wondered. Ben ignored him. Going *over* things was a much better look.

He landed hard on the other side of the stone, his foot accidentally crashing down on the gunman's ankle. The gunman whimpered in further pain.

"Yeah," Ben said, taking credit where it was most certainly not due, "and there's more where that came from."

Nice, Patrick said.

Thanks, Ben replied.

The gunman rolled around on his back, writhing in the dirt and cradling his head. "Why did you *do* that?" he whined.

"Why did I do what? Hit you with a rock?"

"Yes!"

"*Because you were shooting at me with a machine gun!*" Ben cried, throwing up his hands in disbelief.

"It's a semi-automatic," the gunman corrected him.

"*Boy* does that not matter," Ben said. "You were *shooting at me*."

"So what? If I'd hit you, it'd be over...you'd be dead, no pain, you wouldn't have to worry about it. But I got hit with a rock, and now I'm gonna have a migraine all day!" He struggled up to a seat, still holding his head. "This is awful," he moaned sadly.

Ben stuck the rusty point of the machete against the man's chest. "I can make it stop, if you want."

The man looked down at the blade. His face softened. He held his hands up in a show of surrender. "Okay, fine. I'll take the migraine. But I am not happy about it, and I want to be heard on that."

"Yeah, yeah, I hear you," Ben said, rolling his eyes. He was wondering if he should just hack the guy to death anyway when he noticed the man's clothes. He wore old leather chaps over his jeans, with a broken-down pair of boots and a ratty flannel shirt with a dusty blue bandana tired around his neck. "Holy shit," Ben said, his eyes growing wide. "You were at the train."

The gunman glanced nervously around, as if looking desperately for help. "Umm...no?" he said, trying to sound convincing and failing completely.

"Yes you were, you side-saddle motherfucker," Ben said, his face growing hot with anger. "You stormed my train. You killed my Red Caps. You killed my *interns*. You took the antidotes." He shook his head slowly, fighting back against the rage that was filling his soul like helium in a balloon. "And goddammit," he seethed, "you stole my fucking *Jansport*." He raised the machete over his head, gave it a quarter-turn, and brought it down hard, slapping the man in the face with the broad side of the blade.

"Ow!" the man cried. "Stop hitting me with things!"

"No!" Ben said, machete-slapping him again.

"Ow!"

"Damn right, 'ow,'" Ben glowered. He pressed the point against the man's neck once more. "Now. I'm going to give you one chance to answer my questions. You hear me? Give me a single answer I don't like, and I open up your throat." The man nodded slightly, straining against the sharp metal on his neck. "Good. Now. Where's the rest of your gang?"

The man squeezed his eyes shut. "I don't know," he said. Then he opened one of his eyes, just slightly, checking for Ben's reaction. Then he closed the eye again and continued to look pained.

"Goddammit," Ben said. "Look, I'm serious. Did you not hear me? You get *one chance* to answer. Now, goddammit—answer!"

Not to be a pain, here, but you're technically giving him a second chance right now, Patrick pointed out.

"Shut up," Ben hissed.

"You just told me to answer!" the gunman said.

"You shut up, too," Ben snapped, "and answer the question!"

"Which do you want me to do," the man wailed, "shut up, or answer the question?"

"Shut up and answer the question!" Ben screamed. He pinched his temples with the ring finger and thumb of his free hand. He felt like something inside of him was splitting, like his skull was being broken right in half, and his mind was being torn into halves along with it. "Where is the rest of your gang?"

"They headed back!" the man cried. "Okay? They headed back!"

"All of them?"

"Yes. All of them. Everyone but me."

"Why did they leave you behind?" Ben asked suspiciously.

"I'm supposed to make sure no one's following us. If they are, I'm supposed to take them out."

"You didn't do a very good job," Ben pointed out.

"I know," the man nodded shamefully.

"And there are no more of you out here? It's just you?"

The man nodded. "It's just me. That's how it works. One stays behind; they leave him a horse a few miles away, and he waits twelve hours. Then he comes home. Everyone else is gone. Everyone else went back."

"Back where?"

The gunman sighed. He shrugged his shoulders resignedly. "Back to the Lab."

Ben took his hand away from his temples and looked down at the gunman quizzically. "The Lab?"

"Yeah," the man nodded. "The Lab."

What the hell is the Lab? Patrick asked.

"What the hell is the Lab?" Ben repeated. The man paused, biting his lip in hesitation. Ben pressed down with the machete, and the point of the blade punctured the man's skin, drawing a small bead of red at the base of his throat. "Spill it, or I spill your blood, all over this desert."

Meh, Patrick said, sounding unimpressed. *I give that threat a six out of ten.*

"It's a...compound," the man finally said. "Two days' ride northwest. Near the Green River. It's...where we live." The man frowned. He pointed over his head, toward the horizon. "My horse is back that way, tethered to a Joshua tree. There's a map in the saddlebag. It'll show you the way. Let me bring you there." He lay back in the dust, resting his head on the hardpan and rubbing the bridge of his nose. "I need some Excedrin," he whined.

"Yeah, well, too bad. You missed the last drug store by about half a decade."

Six-point-five out of ten, Patrick said. *You're getting better.*

Ben ignored his dead friend and pressed on. "How many people are there? At this Lab? Total?"

"I don't know," the man sighed. "Maybe...maybe forty? It's been as many as sixty, but...but we're always being sent out on runs. Probably thirty or forty there right now."

"Sent out?" Ben asked, raising an eyebrow. "Sent out by whom?"

The man grimaced. *You're pressing him too far,* Patrick warned. *He's giving up too much, and he knows it. Careful.*

"Just tell me who's in charge," Ben said, softening his edge a bit. "Who's the son of a bitch that told you to steal my backpack?"

Nice, Patrick groaned. *Real soft.*

"The Doctor," was all the gunman said.

Ben waited for more details, but none were forthcoming. "What doctor? Doctor who?"

Heh, Patrick chuckled. *Doctor Who.*

Can you just please be quiet for three minutes and let me lead this interrogation?! Ben demanded.

Sorry. Proceed.

Thank you.

"Just…the Doctor," the gunman said, squirming uncomfortably. "He's a real doctor, honest-to-God. He's smart. He knows things. He makes things. When he needs supplies, or errands run—things like that—he sends us out. I don't know anything about his work, I swear to God. He doesn't tell us. We don't ask. That's the deal. We don't ask questions, and he lets us stay, keeps us safe, keeps us fed. Okay? He gets to work, we get shelter and strength in numbers. It's copa—copa—copa—shit, I can't think of the word," he moaned.

Copacabana, Patrick suggested.

"Copacetic," Ben said.

The man nodded. "Yeah. It's that. Everything's good. It's a good life."

"Yeah. It's full of goodness. You just slaughter innocent men, women, and interns every day, but it's such a good life."

"Not *every* day," the gunman insisted. "And *never* women." He paused for a few seconds, then added, "Unless they're uppity. Then it's fair game."

Oh, I do not like these people, Patrick glowered.

"Same," Ben said aloud. He slapped the gunman with the machete for a third time.

The man whimpered. "Please stop hitting me."

"No. Get up. You're taking us to the Lab."

The man shook his head. "I can't," he whispered, and tears leaked from the corners of his eyes. "They'll kill me for bringing you in."

"I'll kill you for refusing," Ben said through gritted teeth.

The man flailed his hands and kicked his feet in frustration. "I don't know what to do!" he wailed. He beat the sands with his fists. The pounding of the earth caused something in the shadow of the boulder to stir. A dusty rattlesnake uncoiled from the shade and hissed as it slithered toward the two men, the pale gray diamonds on its skin contracting and expanding with the torsion of the snake's deadly approach.

"Holy shit!" Ben cried, leaping away and stumbling back across the scrub.

The snake sidled up to the petrified gunman lying on the ground. "Oh God," he whispered, his eyes as wide as hubcaps. "Help me!"

The snake rattled its tail, a deathly maraca sizzle that sent chills vibrating through Ben's bones. It lifted its head and slithered up onto the gunman's knee, flicking its tongue irritably. Then, fast as a shot, it opened its mouth, lunged forward, and sank its fangs into the man's upper thigh.

"*Holy shit!*" the gunman screamed. He swatted at the rattlesnake with his palm, but the snake was in deep, clamping down hard. The gunman rolled around in panic and agony, shrieking and beating at the snake and yelling hysterics. Finally, the snake retracted its fangs and dropped from the man's pant leg, slithering slowly back off to its space in the shade. The gunman looked up at Ben in disbelief, his face already chalky white, his entire body trembling from adrenaline and poison.

"Quick," he whispered, struggling to his feet and stumbling forward, "you gotta suck out the venom." He grabbed his groin and framed the wound on his upper thigh. "You've gotta suck out the venom!"

Ben backed away slowly. He, too, had gone white as a sheet. He raised his hands defensively, stepping backward. "I...I'm not..." He swallowed, hard, eyeing the man's wound. "Dude, look: I am *not* sucking poison out of your crotch."

The bandit's eyes welled up with tears. Then his knees gave out, he collapsed onto the sand, and he laid his head down on a rock, sighing weakly and resigning himself to a slow and agonizing death.

Horrified, Ben continued to back away, not taking his eyes from the fallen man, or from the snake a few yards further away. "I'm...I'm sorry," he muttered. He hurried backward, nearly tripping over the Injun's corpse. "I'm...I'm seriously sorry," he repeated. "But you tried to murder me, and I am *not* putting my lips near your junk."

Then he turned and ran off toward the direction of the Lab, leaving the gunman and the rattlesnake to their intertwined fates.

Look, if it's any consolation, I'm with you on this one, Patrick said as he ran. *That dude did* not *look hygienic.*

15.

About thirty minutes later, Ben found the horse. It was a skittish, mistrustful creature, tied to a dry, bedraggled Joshua tree, just like the bandit had said. Ben held up his hands and moved toward the horse cautiously from the front, so it could watch his slow and careful approach. "Easy, boy," he whispered, inching closer. The horse pulled back, shaking its head, but the reins held strong, and it couldn't move far. It stepped to the side, watching Ben warily. "That's it. Come on. I'm a friend."

A friend who just let your master die, Patrick said.

"Shhhh," Ben whispered soothingly, both to Patrick and the horse. He moved past the horse's shoulders and gently reached out for the saddlebag. He flipped it open, wincing and quietly willing the horse not to flinch. He had to stand on his tiptoes to reach blindly into the bag, and his hand pushed past a canteen and something hard wrapped in an oilcloth, probably a piece of salt-meat. Below that, he felt a thickly-folded piece of paper. He seized it and pulled it out, backing away from the horse.

The map had been old when the apocalypse was new—soft and frayed at the edges, crisscrossed with yellowed strips of Scotch tape, the ink fading and worn. But someone had taken a fresh marker and circled a spot near a bend in the Green River, out to the northwest. The Lab. Ben folded the map and stuffed it into his fanny pack.

"All right, horse," he said, rubbing his hands and speaking softly, "I'm gonna ride you now, and you're gonna take me to your home. You know how to get to your home, don't you?" He unhitched the horse. The animal whinnied, its eyes white and wide with fear. It shook its head, its black mane waving wildly. "Whoa, whoa—easy!" Ben said, his heart pounding. But the horse jerked again, rearing back on its hind legs, and Ben dropped the reins, screaming, "Shit-shit-shit!" He dove away, avoiding the horse's front hooves as they kicked and pinwheeled through the air. Then the horse came down hard on all fours, shook its head at Ben, skittered around to the right, and bolted off into the west, kicking up little plumes of dust as it galloped away into the green mist.

Wow. You're a real-life Horse Whisperer, Patrick said as they watched the horse disappear.

"Shut up."

By the time the sun went down, Ben had covered several more miles on foot, and he was hot, dusty, tired, and all-around ready for a nap. But he also had the pesky desire to not get eaten by coyotes, spiders, scorpions, or snakes in the night, and the only thing for it was to try to build a fire before he ate his can of dinner beans and curled himself up to sleep. He started collecting little bits of scrub as he walked, malnourished and bedraggled branches and roots that he picked up off the sand or hacked loose with the machete. Each time he grabbed a bit of brush, he stuck it under his arm, and Ben imagined that from a distance, he looked like something out of *Mad Max*. And that, he thought, was pretty cool.

About twenty minutes after sundown, he came to a suitable spot to set up camp. The desert wind had blown the sands loose from a wide platform of stone, which meant if anything venomous wanted to inject poison into *his* crotch, it would have to come up and around, and wouldn't be able sink its teeth into him from the sands directly below. He tossed his fanny pack down in the middle of the platform, along with his machete, and set to work separating the pieces of dry brush. The bigger pieces he set off to the side, while he made a low pile with the smaller bits, stacking them up around a tuft of dried desert sandwort. He pulled out an ancient Zippo from the fanny pack, and on the fifth try, a flame sparked and flickered to life. Cupping his hand close against the wind, he bent down and lit the sandwort until the smoke gave way to pale flames. He pushed the sticks closer together, setting more across the top of the pile so the brush formed a little wooden cabin, and within a minute, the brush had caught fire too, popping and hissing as the pale gray of the wood gave way to dark carbon ash. Ben reached for the first few larger pieces of brush, leaning them up above the fire like a teepee, and soon, just as the pink of the sky began to fade away to deep blue, and as the yellowish-green fog deepened into a purple-reddish haze, the fire was high and crackling, throwing long shadows across the sands.

"I," Ben said, looking down on the flames smugly, "have made fire."

"Well, to be fair, the lighter made fire," said a voice from the darkness. "You just built it a little house."

Ben jumped out of his skin. He tripped over his own feet and nearly fell ass-first into the flames, saving himself at the last second by planting a clumsy hand on the ground and pivoting around awkwardly, coming to a skidding stop on his belly on the far side of the fire, well out of reach of the machete. He lifted his eyes to the figure that melted forth from the desert, emerging from the dark mists. It was a man, tall and thin, with a baton in one hand, a spoon in the other, and a head that was two sizes too big for his frame.

The man stepped into the light of the fire, and Ben exhaled with relief. "You have *got* to stop doing that," he breathed. "Jesus, Pat."

Patrick Deen smiled happily as he folded himself down, plopping onto the stone platform, his knees and elbows akimbo. "I will never stop not stopping it, Benny Boy," he said, tossing the baton onto the ground and sticking the spoon in his back pocket. "One of these days, you'll pee your pants. And that will be when I know that my work has still only just begun."

Ben pushed himself up off of his belly and dusted off his clothes. "Look at this," he complained, grabbing the hem of his shirt and pulling it down so Patrick could get a good look at the fabric. Ben frowned. "The rock just tore a new hole."

"If you don't want to rip your clothes, stop falling down so much," Patrick said, shrugging. "Look at me. I hardly ever fall down, and just look! No holes!" He sat up straight and held himself out for inspection. Then he took note of his left hand, and he grimaced at the gaping hole in his palm. "Well. This one doesn't count."

Ben shook his head and drew himself into a seat across the fire from his friend. He grinned down at the flames and indicated them with a nod of his head. "Pretty good, though, huh?"

"It is a passable flame-house," Patrick agreed, placing his palms on his knees. He wore only a pair of jeans and a thin t-shirt, and he closed his eyes and smiled, letting the heat of the fire warm his bare arms. "It's not even close to the *best* flame-house I've ever seen, mind you. The *best* flame-house I've ever seen was right before Game Five of the 2006 World Series, when my weird uncle made a twenty-foot bonfire in his backyard and caught his own oak tree on fire. The firemen came, and Uncle Frank paid them a hundred bucks to wait ten minutes to put out the fire so he could throw a teddy bear in a Chicago Cubs jersey onto the flames and watch it melt and burn." Patrick's eyes glistened over with tears. "We weren't even playing the Cubs," he whispered in quiet reverence. "It was *glorious.*" He waved a hand through the air, wiping the memory away, and looked back down at Ben's fire. "But this one's pretty good, too. For a Ben-fire."

"I'm good at things now," Ben said proudly. "I build fires, I order people around, I swing machetes...sometimes I hit things with machetes. I'm basically Survivorman."

"Does Survivorman wear a super-sexy fanny pack?"

"It's the only thing we had!" Ben cried.

"No, I like it!" Patrick insisted. "It's *huge!* I've never seen a fanny pack so big. Is that a fifty-gallon?"

"I hate you," Ben grumbled.

"You and my middle-school gym teacher have a lot in common. The hatred is one thing," Patrick said. He coughed. "The fanny pack is another."

"It's the price I'm paying for survival," Ben said miserably.

"You haven't died yet. That's very, very impressive," Patrick conceded. "If I'm being honest, I did *not* think I'd be the first of us to go."

Ben's face fell. He looked down at his knees, and he wiped his hands on the legs of his jeans. "I never thought about that," he said quietly. "I still don't. I don't think about that."

"Benny Boy! You wound me!" Patrick cried, pressing a hand against his chest. "You would lie to me. *Me!* Your old pal, Patrick! Your bosom buddy! Your *amigo* best-o! Your platonic post-life partner! The scandal of it all!"

Ben shook his head. "I'm not lying," he said. His fingers suddenly became busy scratching at a splotch of old mud that had dried on his jeans. "I *didn't* ever think about it."

"Ah," Patrick said, thrusting his pointer finger into the air, "but you *do* think about it now. You *do* think about it. Otherwise…" He spread his arms wide and gestured down at his body. "What am I doing here?"

Ben sighed. He mopped his hands down his face, pulling the bottoms of his eyelids down and drying his eyes against the heat of the fire. "I don't know," he admitted, losing himself in the flicker of the flames and avoiding the sight of the friend who sat behind them. "I don't know what you're doing here. I don't know why I hear you talk to me. I don't know why you *show up* sometimes. Like you're real. Like you're alive. Like I didn't leave you bleeding out on the Magic Kingdom parking lot." Ben closed his eyes, and hot tears spilled out between his lids. "Jesus Christ, Pat," he choked. "I don't know anything, and I don't want to see you or hear you anymore."

"Ah, Benny Boy," Patrick said, frowning across the fire. "It can't be easy. I know." They sat quietly for a few long minutes, looking at the flames, Ben sniffling into his palms, Patrick picking distractedly at the crusted scabs along the edge of the hole in his hand. Finally, he broke the silence. "It's nice now. If that helps." He shrugged his shoulders, staring down intently at his palm. "I don't know if it does. But it's good. Now. Things are less…fucked up." Now tears were glazing across his eyes, too, and his voice turned soft, and grated with emotion. "Annie is here. And Izzy. God, Ben…I'm with Izzy, every single second, every single *moment* of every day. They're with me, and they're *real*, and we're a family again." He wiped his eyes with his forearm. "I have my family back," he whispered.

Ben shook his head. "I know," he said quietly, his words barely audible over the crackling of the fire. "It's good that they have you." His voice broke, and he shook his head, clearing his throat and wiping the snot from his nose with the collar of his shirt. "Shit, Pat. It's good that they have you. It's good you have them. I just…" His words left him, evaporating in a cloud of dust and hot wind, and he tried again. "I just wish…"

But the words wouldn't come.

"I know," Patrick said, nodding sadly, not looking his friend in the eye. "I know you do. So do I. Sometimes. You know?" he sighed. "I love being with Annie. I love being with Izzy. They are my world. But… it's not…I don't…I don't know." He shook his head. "It's not the *whole* world."

Ben cleared his throat, a small, contained cough that shot out into the desert and died amid the fog. "I miss you, I guess. I'm alone, and the world is a fucking nightmare now, worse than before, and I just fucking miss you."

A heavy stillness saturated the air between them. Patrick picked up a branch of scrub from the pile and poked at the fire. The flames popped, and a thousand tiny sparks shot up into the sky, fading into darkness as they descended back to the earth. Patrick took a heavy breath, and he dug deeper into the fire. "Do you ever get worried that you...you know...*see* me?"

Ben laughed again. He pressed the heels of his hands against his eyes and pushed against the tears. "I do," he said, nodding. "I do worry about that. It can't be healthy, right?"

"Oh, *definitely* not healthy," Patrick agreed.

Ben shrugged. "Maybe I'm just that lonely," he sighed. "I don't really have any friends here, you know?" Patrick didn't respond, just looked sadly down at his knees, and Ben reached over and threw a few more branches on the fire. "Or maybe I have a brain tumor. I mean, if I really think about it, I probably *actually* have a brain tumor, right?"

"Oh, on a scale of one to ten, I'd say there's a nine-point-five-chance that you have a tumor," Patrick agreed. "You probably don't want to hear this, but there is almost no other option."

"Fuck," Ben sighed. "I knew it was a tumor." He shook his head sadly. Life wasn't exactly of the highest quality these days, but he'd take it gladly over the slow, painful, rotting death at the hands of cancer. "Fuck," he said again. He looked up, meeting Patrick's eyes across the fire. "I don't want to die like that," he said.

"Seems reasonable," Patrick agreed, nodding sadly. "I don't want that for you either, Benny Boy. I want you to grow old and miserable and crabby as hell. I want you to have that chance."

Ben frowned. "I should go see a specialist," he decided.

"That's so stupid," Patrick said, shaking his head. "For two reasons. One, have you *seen* what doctors are like these days? It's the Wild West! Do you really want someone sawing into your brain with just a few shots of homemade alcohol to basically not-numb the pain? Cripes, even if you survived the surgery, you'd go blind from the hooch."

"I used to have medical insurance," Ben said miserably, remembering the old days.

"Besides, number two, don't you remember Rule Thirty-Three?"

"Vodka is doctors now," they both said in unison.

"Right. Vodka is doctors now," Patrick nodded. "You'll have to drink away your tumor. The Rules of the Apocalypse have deemed it so." He made a grand gesture with his arms, sweeping them up toward the heavens. "And if you're lucky, the Great Spirit of the Illinois will be with you in your endeavor."

Ben snorted. "I think the Great Spirit of the Illinois is a couple thousand miles away."

"The Great Spirit of the Illinois is with us always," Patrick corrected him sagely. He touched his chest lightly. "She dwells within our hearts. And she will help the vodka to shrink your brain tumor, or else she will become indifferent in the attempt."

Ben shook his head. "I hope I'm not dying of cancer," he said, burying his face in his hands. "I'd rather throw myself in front of Horace's train."

"Well, if this little mission goes well, you'll get the chance!"

"Thanks," Ben said miserably.

Patrick nodded proudly. "I am helpful," he decided. Then he stood up, stretching his legs and clapping his hands encouragingly. "Well, it's just about time for me to go," he said.

"My tumor and I have had enough," Ben muttered.

"So it would seem," Patrick agreed. He smiled across the fire. "What you're doing right now…it's a good thing, Benny Boy."

Ben bit his top lip in thought. "It's the thing I need to do," he said, almost to himself.

"And I hope you survive it. It, and the cancer. Because I am seriously going to need you to write my biography."

"For the last time, I am not writing your biography!" Ben cried, throwing up his hands in frustration.

But he couldn't help but smile.

"Be good, little one," Patrick said, returning the grin. "And for the love of God, stay safe, will you?"

"Don't tell me what to do," Ben said.

"I wouldn't dream of it. But be safe anyway." He backed away, giving Ben a little wave. "Take care of yourself. And I'll be with you. In case that helps."

"I know you will," Ben said. He gave Patrick a stiff, uncomfortable nod, and Pat melted away into the desert night.

"And it does," Ben whispered to the darkness. He stoked the fire distractedly, pushing around the ashes. "It does help."

16.

Horace fought back his tears and wondered if his mustache was big enough to hide the fact that he was biting the hell out of his bottom lip in a desperate struggle against the pain.

"What did you bring them up here for?" he hollered, channeling his agony anger.

Ralph pulled the red cap off of his head and used the crown to wipe the sweat from his brow. He'd been working all evening on hauling the bodies of his fallen brethren onto the train, and it hadn't really occurred to him until just now to wonder why. "Well...the train is their home. Right?"

Horace closed his eyes and took a deep breath. Without opening his eyes, he said, "Son, how many people in your family died since M-Day?"

Ralph scratched his head. "Since M-Day, or *including* M-Day?"

Horace counted to five. Eyes still closed, he replied, "Including M-Day. How many of your people died on M-Day, or since?"

"Oh, geez," Ralph said, shaking his head nervously. "I don't know. All of 'em, I think."

"All of 'em," Horace repeated. "And how many of them did you bury inside your house?"

Ralph tilted his head and screwed up his face in confusion. "In my house?" he said. "Well…none of 'em."

Horace pinched the bridge of his nose. "Yep. None of 'em. You know why?"

"Umm…"

"Because you don't bury people where they live, son. You understand that, don't you?"

Ralph's cheeks flamed red, and he looked down at his feet. "Oh. Yeah…I guess I do."

"So I'm gonna ask you again. What the hell did you bring them up here for?"

Ralph frowned. He glanced over at the stack of corpses piled up between the shelves of the train car. "I…don't know," he admitted. "I'm sorry. I ain't never been responsible for something like this before."

"No one made you responsible for it this time, either," Horace reminded him.

"I know, sir," Ralph fretted. "It's just there ain't many of us left, and the bodies were just lying out there, and it just seemed like maybe I shouldn't leave 'em there. It seemed…disrespectful."

Horace sighed. "Well…you're not wrong there," he said. "These were good men. Good Red Caps. Far better than many I've known. They deserve better than to be dead and bloated on the desert floor."

"Yeah," Ralph agreed sadly. He wiped the snot from his nose and sniffled the rest of the mucous back up into his sinuses. "They…" he began. He wrinkled up his nose, looked at Horace, and said, "They're startin' to smell pretty bad," he observed.

"Yeah," Horace said. "They are. So how about you respectfully get them off my train?" Ralph was silent and didn't make a move. Horace opened his eyes. "Son, you're gonna have a hard time getting those bodies out the door if you wait 'til rigor mortis sets in…" he began.

But Ralph wasn't listening. He was gaping. His eyes were as big as fists, ogling something over Horace's shoulder. He slowly raised his hand and pointed in disbelief. "It's a lady-giant," he whispered.

Horace struggled to turn. When he managed to wriggle himself around, he looked up at the big figure in the doorway: a tall woman, and broad, with arms like ham hocks, and curly blonde hair. She filled the frame of the doorway, her hands slowly clenching and unclenching, forming into a pair of fists like sledgehammers. At her belt was a hunting knife with a long, shiny blade.

"Aw, shit," Horace moaned.

The woman stepped into the car, and the whole train shifted. A glass vial rattled off of its shelf and smashed onto the floor. No one noticed.

"Can I help you, ma'am?" Horace asked, and he wondered if maybe it was "ma'ams," because he was seeing two of them. He blinked back the pain from his eyes, and the two giants swam together and formed one huge person.

The woman raised one finger and pointed out the windows, toward the west. "Where?" she rasped. Her voice was the rattle of a rockslide in a dry gully.

Horace grimaced uncertainly. He tugged at his mustache. "Where what?" he asked wearily.

The woman exhaled hotly. She shot out a hand and grabbed the edge of a shelving unit. She jerked it forward, knocking everything on its shelves to the floor. Then she jerked it backward, then forward again, then backward, rocking it violently until the whole unit snapped off the braces where it was bolted to the ground. She grunted as she grasped the metal shelving with both hands, lifted it over her head, and slammed it down on the row of Red Cap corpses. Bones cracked and flesh squelched, and she raised the shelves again, brought them back down hard—again, and again, and again, beating the dead bodies until they broke open, and then she pulverized them some more. Clumps of gore and tissue burst across the car, coating the western windows and splattering against seats. Horace's hand flew to his mouth, where it did little to stem the flow of bile trickling up from his throat. Ralph just stood in place, jaw open, the crotch of his pants soaking through with urine.

At last, the woman threw down the shelves and slammed her fist against the bloody windows. "*Went where?!*" she screamed.

"Th-the bandits, they went toward the sun," Ralph gasped, his hands trembling at his sides. He slowly lowered himself to his knees, bowed his head, and stretched his hands forward in supplication, a poor Neanderthal bowing to a vicious and vengeful god. "They went straight out, straight west. Oh, God, please don't kill me...they went out west, straight west. A little north." Ralph sat like that, in a puddle of his own urine and fear, for several long seconds that stretched on like hours. The train car was silent but for his own sobs and the sound of Horace retching. His arms still forward, raised and shaking, Ralph slowly lifted his head and opened his eyes.

They were once again alone in the car. The woman was gone.

17.

Things were quiet at Fort Doom. Night had fallen, and everyone was asleep...everyone except Ben, who was on watch. Not because it was his turn, but because he'd swapped nights with Dylan that week. "It's all just rainbows and knife points, man," Dylan had told Ben somberly over dinner, inhaling deeply from his cigarette of ash. "And just the world, it's so *crimson*. Nothing is off-brand again."

Ben had been living at Fort Doom for a little over a year. He spoke Dylan's disjointed, esoteric language as well as any of them could. He raised an eyebrow at James. James nodded his agreement. When Dylan talked about crimson things, it almost always meant he was in a firebug mood. That's what they all called it: his "firebug mood." Because "propensity for brutal self-flagellation by fire" just sounded so harsh. On the nights when Dylan spoke of crimson things, he would, if left to his own devices, scorch some piece of his own flesh with a homemade iron brand, a long, thin rod of metal with the end twisted into a crude lightning bolt, a tool that somehow kept reappearing, even though the rest of the Doomers disposed of it every time Dylan came down from a firebug mood. Two months earlier, out of exasperation with Dylan's knack for sniffing out the brand in the alleys and rooftops—and, in one case, even beneath the graveyard soil of Mobile, Alabama—Ben had taken the boat out and flung the iron thing into the gulf.

Two weeks later, they found Dylan shivering in the smoking ashes of the previous evening's fire, naked but for a pair of moldy socks, with three fresh lightning bolts seared into the skin of his thigh. The branding iron rested loosely in his quivering grip.

So Dylan wasn't allowed to take the watch any time he talked about crimson things...or when he said "mulberry," "suffragation," or "kaleidoscope." They were all used to taking Dylan's shift; it was a matter of rote when you lived in Fort Doom. And it was Ben's turn in the rotation that night, so he'd nodded his head and finished his dinner and climbed up the ladder to the crow's nest while the rest of the crew cleaned up the dishes, smothered the fire, and tied Dylan to the post they'd installed in the center of his cabin so he couldn't add to the cruel hieroglyphs that patterned his skin like a pox.

On her way into their cabin, Sarah had stopped beneath the crow's nest, her large, sad eyes practically glowing in the moonlight. Sometimes, Ben imagined that she could cry tears of mercury, streaming silver down her sharp cheeks and dripping off the slope of her chin.

She was so beautiful, in her sadness, and in her love, and in her passion, which she hid beneath an ember that smoldered in her soul, burning low, but burning always, growing and glowing white-hot and radiant in their quiet trysts, in her nighttime gasps, in the furtive daytime glances she reserved for Ben when she wasn't sure she could make it through the daylight chores without feeling his breath on her skin. And some days, she couldn't, and she wouldn't, and they'd steal seconds behind the shed; they'd borrow against their time beneath the pattering drips of Patrick's irrigation tent, or they'd run to their cabin, hide from the world, and lose everything in themselves, until James came calling, clearing his throat outside their door, a gentle reminder of the work yet to be done before the sun went down.

She looked up at Ben that night, from beneath the nest, and Ben saw her mercury tears in his mind, and he smiled, and she smiled, and his was crooked, and hers was perfect, and he gave her a wave, and she placed a hand on her belly, and his heart broke to see the swell, and to think of the life inside, the new survivor who was his, his own, and her own, and it filled him with a well of confusing emotions so perfect and alien to the rest of the post-apocalyptic nightmare that he wondered if his chest might burst.

If it was a boy, they'd name him Patrick. If it was a girl, they'd name her Isabel.

"It's a girl," Sarah always assured him.

"How can you tell?" Ben wondered.

"I can tell," she would always respond. And Ben didn't doubt that she could.

Ben blew her a kiss, and she tilted her head. She touched her fingers to her lips, and he smiled and shook his head. Sarah ducked into their cabin, to give herself over to sleep, and Ben settled in, his back against the wall, to watch, to see, to protect, to survive.

But he had woken early that day. It wasn't his night to watch. He'd woken early, and he'd gone for a run, a long one—eleven miles this time—with a knife at his hips and a blade in his shoe, and then he'd plowed and planted most of the southern garden by hand, and he was tired. He was so tired now, in the darkness, in the quiet, thick night, with the air heavy as cotton, and warm from the heat of the gulf. And with everyone else asleep, Ben's eyes grew dry as autumn leaves, and his eyelids began to droop, and he gripped the rifle harder, squeezing it and twisting so his palms burned with the friction, but it wasn't enough to keep him awake, it wasn't enough to stave off the night, and there, in the crow's nest, high above the ground, the protector of Fort Doom fell asleep with a sigh.

•

Ben jerked himself awake. His heart pounded; his breath came in gasps, and a thick sheen of sweat coated his head, his cheeks, his shoulders, his back. He threw his eyes wildly to either side, and his present came creeping back, filling in his vision with the truth of the desert, and the stone platform beneath him, and the fire that had gone out against the spot where Patrick had spoken from across the grave. He closed his eyes. He took deep breaths. He planted his hands on the stone.

He cried for an hour.

18.

By the time the sun struggled to break the horizon, Ben had already covered three more miles of desert.

The day was already warm, warmer than usual. The desert had always been a hot place, of course, but most days now, the Monkey Fog provided cover from the sun, diffusing the light and the heat and keeping the ground cooler than what would have been considered normal before the end of the world. Even so, Ben was now trudging deep into heart of the desert, a dangerous place in any age, and the sun burned through the fog here, roasting and cracking the hardpan with its heat, which became trapped and thick and suffocating in the soupy net of ever-present mist. Ben wiped sweat from his forehead and wriggled uncomfortably against the sticky cling of his soaked shirt. He wished he'd brought a few changes of clothes. And he wished he'd brought a hat.

"And an air conditioner," he mumbled aloud. He waited for Patrick's retort, maybe something about how heavy it would be, or how he'd need an eighty-mile-long extension cord. But his dead friend was silent. He hadn't said a word all morning, nothing since his appearance at the fireside the night before.

Maybe he didn't have anything else to say. Maybe Ben's subconscious couldn't handle hearing his voice anymore.

Either way, Ben was lonely.

"I hate this fucking apocalypse," he said quietly.

He stopped and dropped to one knee, opening his pack and pulling out a bottle of water and the old, ratty map. Ben had no markers with which to judge how far he'd gone. He wished not for the first time in his life (or the twentieth) that the country actually had physical, tangible dividing lines between its states. Not walls or anything...nothing to hinder travel. But maybe a heavy rope anchored into the ground, or a series of super-permanent lines of paint— *something,* so a guy on foot could tell if he had made it across the Colorado state line.

"The founding fathers were lazy," Ben complained.

Where do I even begin, Patrick sighed.

Ben screamed.

"Jesus, Pat, will you start *warning* me when you're gonna open your dumb, stupid mouth?!"

And how exactly would you like me to do that? Patrick asked. *By saying that I'm going to say things before I say them?*

Ben clapped his hand over his chest, feeling his heart hammer beneath his palm. "Jesus," he repeated, closing his eyes. "Just either be here, or don't be here."

You're in the driver's seat. I'm just an imaginary passenger on the brain tumor train.

"Don't remind me." Ben opened his eyes, shook his head, and returned his focus to the map. But Patrick wasn't about to let him off that easily.

Even if there were actual, physical lines between the states—which is such a stupid, stupid idea—do you seriously think the founding fathers would have been the ones to put them there?

"Why not?" Ben asked. "They're the ones who wanted a country. They should have marked it properly."

First of all, there were, like, six states when those old, white racists wrote that glorious Constitution.

"Well, it would have been a start," Ben insisted.

Second of all, I don't even know what else to say to any of this, because it's one of the dumbest things you've ever said, and that list has a lot of greatest hits.

"I stand by it," Ben said. He studied the map. He frowned. He turned it 180 degrees. He cocked his head. "This is upside-down," he decided. He turned it back around. He considered the lines. He frowned again. "Is this even what the United States looks like?"

Again, I ask: how am I the one who died early? Patrick sighed. *Yes. This is what the United States looks like. This is right-side-up. I feel like you're being willfully stupid. It's the only explanation for you and how you work.*

"I'm not good at directions," Ben sighed.

No kidding.

Ben stabbed his finger at where he thought the train probably was, given the towns they'd passed on this leg of the trip that had been large enough before M-Day to be marked on the map, and he drew an imaginary line more or less west. He was probably still in Colorado. And he was heading away from the Rocky Mountain range, and generally following the arc of the sun, so he knew he was going at least vaguely in the right direction. The circled Lab was still pretty far away.

"This is where we're headed," he said. "The good news is, there's a river behind it that runs north and south...this guy here. And if we hit that river, then we just need to follow it north, until we find the Lab."

Your ability for stating the obvious things that I already know is extraordinary, Patrick said.

Ben considered the distance between his position and the black circle. There was a lot of empty desert between the two points. A lot of space for dusters to roam. A lot of space for survivors to stand their ground. "Think we can make it?" he asked.

Patrick was silent for a moment, as if mulling over the question. Finally, he said, *Probably best not to ask.*

"Yeah," Ben grumbled, folding up the map and stuffing it back into his fanny pack. "I don't think so either."

The desert terrain was uneven and jagged, the foothills of the Rockies giving way to a blunt and brutal landscape of crags and cliffs. Progress was slow, and by the time the sun was high in the noontime sky, Ben had only covered another couple of miles. He was hot and thirsty, and his muscles were weary and strained, and his eyes were in a constant fight for focus...which was why it wasn't all that surprising when he clamored over a ridge, peered down at the valley below, and saw a thriving, lively town, blanketed with lush green grass, dotted with pools of crystal-clear water, with an apple orchard in the center, and a mercantile, and a restaurant, and a courthouse, and a bank, and a few other well-kept buildings lining the town square. There was a smattering of low, simple, carefully tended cabins sprawling away from the downtown and trailing off into the desert.

It was a nice place...a clean place. A thriving place. A green place, out here in the desert, and that made sense to Ben, because as thirsty as he was, and as tired, his brain was ripe for a good hallucination.

He pinched his eyes between his finger and thumb and gave his head a good shake. When he opened his eyes again, the town was still there, scratched out into the dust, but now he saw it for what it was: a dilapidated ghost town, dry and lonely and abandoned to the apocalypse. There was no grass; there was no water, no apple orchard in a town square...just sand and rocks, and the scraggly scrub of desert brush that had never borne fruit, sparsely dotting a lonely outpost that had fallen into ruin. The clapboard buildings had rotted and begun their collapse, and the cabins that may have once housed a lively population were now rickety shanties, their wood planks bleached and splintered by the sun, and they served as homes to only memories and ghosts, and probably a fair share of desert vipers.

"That's more like it," Ben said, nodding happily, finding comfort in reality.

It's weird to be so pleased by ruin, Patrick pointed out.

"It's a weird time to be alive," Ben shrugged.

I'll take your word for it.

Ben ambled his way down the slope, toward the little ghost town. It was funny to think that there was a time when an abandoned town like this one would have given him the creeps. That was in the Old Life, back when the status quo wasn't chock full of madmen and murderers and machetes and rapists. Back when ghost towns were the exception. But now they were the rule; it was usually more unsettling to see a town full of people. The places that survived—*those* were the ones that gave Ben the creeps. There was no telling what people had done in order to stay alive, to stay together. The new history of survivor towns was almost always horrific, unimaginable. Society was unsettling in this new era.

Ben actually felt at peace in the abandoned towns, amid the ruin and the quiet. There were ghosts in those places, shadows and shades, and they kept his own ghosts busy, so he could find the time and the quiet to just be.

This particular town seemed to be one of the faux-Old West variety. They were pretty common in this part of the country: charming little pop-ups cobbled together in the style of the Wyatt Earp west, cheap tourist-trap towns that existed for the sole purpose of drawing in East Coasters and road-trippers with a vintage sensibility—or at least a basic interest in Clint Eastwood movies. The idea was to replicate a film-screen Old West town, give passersby a place to park their cars, a saloon where they could spend their cash, a corral where they could lose their minds over the sight of a few sick horses, and then, after a sepia-toned instant-print photo op with women in bustles and men in waistcoats, they would be on their way, a few hundred dollars lighter than when they'd entered, but satisfied that they'd just had a real-life, honest-to-God Western experience.

Ben shook his head. Most of the time, he didn't really miss people.

There had once been a road that led into the town, and though it had been reclaimed by the desert, Ben could still see the faded outline of where it had run. Beyond the buildings lining the main strip, cheap shanty houses dotted the desert landscape, maybe three dozen of them in all, and on the outskirts, far away from the cheap illusion of the Tombstone era, was a smattering of buildings more modern in their purpose, if not their construction: a post office, a food market, and what appeared to be a combination schoolhouse and church.

"I bet they did this," Ben said.

Bet who did what?

"The people who lived here. I bet they're responsible for all of this," he said, gesturing out at the wider world. "If I lived in this discount Mickey Mouse rinky-dink bullshit town, I'd go into that church every single day and pray for the Jamaicans to send all their bombs and please just end it all."

Patrick paused while he thought about this. *I'd pray for a Whole Foods*, he decided.

The ghostly footprint of the faded road crept up from the south and wound straight into the heart of the town, passing beneath a sign, still half-suspended between two gnarled posts, labeling the town as Scudder's Point.

"Point of what?" Ben murmured.

Point of order: this place is lame, Patrick agreed.

Still in his delirium, Ben held up his hand for an imaginary high-five. He swung through the air. He pictured Patrick doing the same. They missed completely, and whiffed.

Nailed it.

Ben trudged into Scudder's Point. The air was still and quiet, and even the yellow-green fog seemed tense here, freezing in the air and holding its breath and waiting to see what direction things might take.

The street was lined with rickety buildings, some of them with faded-paint signs that Ben could still just barely make out, revealing a veritable who's who and what's what of Old West hovels. There was Scudder's Jail on the left, an adobe building with walls that looked like they could have been scraped through with a spoon, even in their heyday. Across the street was The Wyatt Earp Shooting Gallery and Gaming Hall. Further down the road hung a sign for Miss Kitty's Saloon, a two-story complex complete with swinging batwing doors that still hung, but didn't seem very keen on swinging. Down the block stood the O-K Corral, with its broken split-rail fences and sun-dried trough, and next to that was Chief Sitting Bull's Firewater Tavern.

"Jesus. Old man Scudder was a real racist," Ben observed.

He trudged into the town, wiping the sweat from his face. The sun felt hotter in this shallow ravine, with the worn shacks blocking whatever light breeze might try to filter through. He shuffled into the weak shadow of Scudder's Jail and unloaded the fanny pack from his waist. It fell to the ground like a lead weight. "Why is everything so heavy?" Ben wheezed.

It's not heavy; you're just half-dead. You should drink something.

"I don't think the saloon is open," Ben said dryly.

I mean water, dummy.

"You're a lot less fun now that you're a ghost."

I got separated from my funny bone.

Ben rolled his eyes. Then he grunted. "Okay. That was pretty funny."

Still got it, Patrick said, pleased.

Ben reached down and unzipped his fanny pack. "I'm starting to wonder if I brought enough water," he said with a sigh, poking around. He was down to two and a half bottles, with still a long way to go.

That's because you only packed Ben-smart.

"It's the brain tumor," Ben mumbled. "It blocks all the good-smart stuff."

Apparently.

Ben sighed. He pulled out the half-full bottle and peered into it sadly. "Dehydration probably isn't the worst way to go."

Dehydration is an awful way to go. It absolutely is one of the worst.

"Maybe you could pretend like it isn't," Ben muttered. He took a few sips from the bottle and stuffed it back into his bag, battling against his thirst. He'd need as much water as he could manage if he wanted any sort of chance of making it to the Lab.

You could just go back, Patrick pointed out. *You don't have to keep going.*

"Yes I do," Ben mumbled. He leaned back against the wall of the jail and shuttered his eyes against the glare of the desert sand. "Yes I do."

You're not responsible for the welfare of the world, Patrick said. *In fact, if I had to pick one person who I think should be the* least *responsible for the welfare of the world, it would almost certainly be you.*

Ben shook his head. "That's not why I'm going."

Then why are *you going?*

Ben didn't respond. He just sat quietly against the wall, staring down at the dust. His head was throbbing—maybe from dehydration, maybe from the tumor, maybe from the weight of his own world pushing down on his neck. Maybe from the weight of the ghosts he dragged behind him.

"You ask too many questions," he said finally.

There was a soft shuffling in the dirt, and Patrick appeared from within the jail. "The curse of the engineer," he said. "There's always another question to ask." He sighed and took a seat on the ground next to Ben, close enough that their shoulders touched. "You're really not gonna tell me?" he asked.

Ben shook his head. "You wouldn't get it."

"I probably wouldn't," Patrick agreed. "Stealing back an antidote to a horrible plague that has the potential to decimate the remainder of humanity so you can deliver it to its intended recipient and save count-less lives seems like probably the best reason to do just about anything," Patrick said. "If that's not what's driving you, it is very possible that I will not get it. But I could try to pretend like I do."

"No you couldn't. You're a terrible actor."

"The second curse of the engineer," Patrick agreed sadly.

"It's just…important," Ben said, squirming against the heat. "Some-thing I have to finish."

Patrick raised an eyebrow and looked at him suspiciously. He opened his mouth to speak, but thought better of it and settled back into his own thoughts instead. After a few moments of staring down into the dirt, he said, "If it's important enough to you to be out here staring down death, then it's important to me, too."

"Thanks."

"I mean, I would never ask *you* to go on a death-mission suicide journey across post-apocalyptic badlands for secret reasons—"

"That was literally our entire Disney World trip," Ben interrupted.

"—but if it's important to you, it's important to me, too, and we'll see it through. You and me, together," Patrick finished.

Ben nodded. "Thanks," he said again.

Patrick nudged his shoulder. "You're welcome, Benny Boy."

"I mean, it's not like you have a choice, because you're me, and I'm going, so you're going, like it or not. But I appreciate the sentiment."

"I thought you might."

They sat there in the dirt for a few long minutes, neither of them speaking, each of them thinking Ben's thoughts. Ben leaned his head back and peered out into the abandoned strip of town laid out before them. Between the heat and the glare of the sun, his eyes had a hard time focusing. "I really need more water," he decided, giving his head a tired shake.

"Then might I suggest checking that well?" Patrick asked.

"What?" Ben sat up straight and squinted down the road, at the cir-cular pile of rocks tucked away next to the corral, just barely in view. "You see that, too?"

"I see what you see."

"I thought it was a mirage."

"It probably is. But hey, it's worth a look."

Ben struggled to his feet. He steadied himself against the jail wall for balance and tottered uneasily for a few seconds, willing the dizziness in his brain to pass. "How long does it take for cancer to kill you?" he asked.

Patrick shrugged. "Depends on the cancer...what kind it is, how bad it is, how aggressive it is. How aggressive does it feel?"

"Well, since you've moved from voice-only Patrick to sometimes-fully-physically-present-Patrick, I'd guess it's moving right along."

"It also depends on how equipped you are to fight it."

"My doctors are all dead."

"Yeah. Hmm. Probably not long then. Maybe weeks? Maybe days? Months, maybe? Seven years, tops. Look, I'm not a doctor."

"I don't feel well. And I don't think it's just the dehydration."

Patrick hopped up from his seat on the ground. "Then we'd better get moving."

Ben reached down and grabbed the half-empty water bottle from his bag. He shuffled out into the sunlight, shielding his eyes and peering cautiously into the buildings as he passed. Each structure was more dilapidated than the last. Untreated, sun-bleached wood had splintered and cracked, and many of the planks had fallen away, leaving behind jagged, gaping portholes into the guts of the buildings, where rot and ruin held sway. Inside the Shooting Gallery, he could see the skeletal remains of the shooting counter; the bones that were left behind after the rest had been scrapped for firewood, or maybe harvested for weapons. Air rifles had once been secured to the countertop, but they'd all been ripped out; now only their thin chains dangled over the edge, swaying and creaking with rust. The paper targets at the far end of the shooting rows were tattered, and had mostly given away to dust.

Thick cobwebs suffocated the arms of the cheap chandelier in Miss Kitty's, the cottony strands tinged green with Monkey dust. The bar had been cleared of its liquor by scavengers, and the remains of many of the empty bottles lay broken and scattered across the wood floor, which was thick with dust. A cheap piano squatted near the front corner of the room, just inside the door, and through a hole, Ben could see the calcified lumps that were the melted and hardened remains of the pianist. Globs of him were stuck to the keys and to the bench; the rest of him had collected in a hard, dense puddle on the floor.

"Guess he's not taking requests," Ben murmured.

"Have you ever wondered why people call it 'tickling the ivories'?" Patrick wondered aloud. "It makes it sound like some serious sexual assault."

"There's some sort of joke there about music assaulting the ears. I can't quite get it. But pretend I made it," Ben said, panting against the heat.

"Hmm," Patrick said, rubbing his chin. "I'm gonna give you that one, but only because you're probably Stage Four."

"Thanks."

The well next to the corral was in reasonably better shape than the rest of the town, having been solidly constructed by a mason who knew how to dry-set a stone. Since the structure didn't rely on mortar, there was nothing to crumble and fall away, and though the stones along the top row wobbled a bit to the touch, the foundation was impressively solid. Ben placed his palms on the rock and peered down into the depths of the well.

"Well? What do you see?" Patrick asked.

"I don't—" Ben began.

"Well!" Patrick interrupted. "Get it?! *Well*, what do you see?!"

"Jesus, I didn't think it was possible for your jokes to get worse," Ben sighed. "I don't see anything…it's deep." He tested the stones in the top layer until he found one that was loose. With a grunt, he pushed it over the edge. It tumbled down into the darkness, and hit the bottom with a splash.

"I don't mind telling you, Benny Boy, a splash is a good sign. 'Cause you know what goes splash? Water goes splash." Patrick tapped his temple proudly. "I learned that in science."

"You're a goddamn genius," Ben agreed. "But how do we get to it?"

Ben circled the well, inspecting it carefully, and on the far side, he found an old wooden bucket, but the rope that had been tied to its handle had been severed, cut clean through just above the knot, leaving the bucket alone against the stones without a mooring. But even with a rope, the bucket would have been useless. Time and neglect had shrunk the wood so that the seams had pulled apart, rendering the thing incapable of holding water. Patrick began to hum the refrain to "There's a Hole in My Bucket," which Ben found immensely unhelpful.

"How else can we draw it?" Ben mumbled to himself, pacing around the well. "Think. Think."

"Oh! I have an idea!" Patrick beamed proudly. "Instead of bringing the water to you, you could go to it! You know. Just jump on down there."

"I wonder if I pushed *you* down there, would you *stay* down there," Ben mused.

"You're starting to make me feel like my ideas aren't properly appreciated."

They contemplated the well in silence.

"I could just give up," Ben decided.

"That seems pretty on-brand for you," Patrick agreed. "Or! You could try displacement."

"I definitely know what that means, because you are definitely me, and your ideas are definitely my ideas," Ben said.

"Definitely," Patrick nodded.

"But let's pretend, because of the tumor, it's all a little fuzzy right now."

"Sure, we can pretend that."

"Walk me through it."

"Put something big in the well. Something with real mass. It goes down, it pushes the water to the side, the water goes out and up. Like if you dip your hand into a full bucket, and it spills all over the place."

"Oh. *That* displacement."

"Yes, that displacement."

"Shut up, I know how that works. I just forgot what it was called."

"I know, pumpkin. I know."

"Shut up." Ben surveyed the town for the right tools. "Not a lot of options," he said doubtfully.

"No, not really," Patrick agreed.

"We could use the trough." Ben nodded at the rusty metal chute inside the corral.

"It would definitely up your iron intake," Patrick said. "Not much density, though. Not nearly."

"The piano might fit."

"It might. That could be a good start. If you like your water steeped in melted human remains."

"Hmm. Right. Pass."

"Yes. Pass," Pat agreed. "We could push in all the stones. It probably wouldn't get the water all the way up, but it'd be a start. If we could find more rocks to throw in on top of them."

"That sounds hard," Ben complained.

"Rocks are heavy," Patrick agreed. "Thank God you're the one doing the heavy lifting."

"And it'll take forever."

"It won't *not* take forever."

Ben sighed. "Well," he said, exhaling with exhaustion, "better get to work."

He pushed in the looser stones easily, giving each a good shove. But after the first layer, the stones grew heavier, and more stubborn. Ben placed his hands on one rock and pushed until his sneakers skidded backward in the dirt. "Christ," he panted. "I'm too terminally ill for this shit."

"Yes, it is definitely that you're terminally ill, and it is definitely not that you are weak like pudding."

Ben gritted his teeth. "Don't you talk to me about pudding," he grumbled. "Pudding got me into this whole stupid fucking mess in the first place." He lowered his head and burst forward, slamming into the stone with his shoulder. It grated across the surface of the one beneath it, then teetered precariously on the lip of the well before tumbling in and cracking on the wet stones below.

"Only fifty more to go," Ben winced, rubbing his shoulder.

"I'd say more like a hundred."

"Great."

"You know, here's a problem: you're gonna sweat out all the water you *do* have," Patrick observed.

"So I'm taking a gamble," Ben sighed. "Shut up and be supportive."

"I'm supportive of you. I'm also supportive in the mathematical odds against you."

"Don't ever tell me the odds."

"Okay, Han. Knock yourself out."

"Do you have any other options? This was your idea, engineer." Ben planted his feet, then threw himself forward again, tackling another stone. "I need to get that water," he grunted as he struggled against the well.

"Water's brackish," said a real voice behind him. Ben jerked in surprise, and his foot slipped. He fell down, cracking his chin on the edge of the well. His jaws jammed together, and a chip broke off one of his molars. He scrambled to his feet and reached instinctively for his machete, but his hand grabbed nothing but air. The machete was back by his fanny pack, by the jail.

He balled his hands into fists and turned to face the voice.

Before him stood a girl—a woman, really, made to look small by the long, white nightgown that swallowed her up in its thin cotton shift. It was unbuttoned at the throat, and it hung loosely off one shoulder. She was thin, her bones pressing against every inch of sallow skin. Her long, dirty blonde hair was tangled and oily, framing a fierce, thin-lipped face set with curious, intelligent eyes that were the color of sea water. Her thin arms were bare, her fingers clutching the nightgown at the waist and pulling it up so she wouldn't trip, so the hem wouldn't drag. She wore nothing beneath the nightgown. The light through the thin cotton provided ample proof of that.

And she was pale. Ghostly pale, as if she'd never been out in the sun.

"Who are you?" Ben asked warily, his eyes darting to either side, scanning for an ambush. But all he saw was the rot and decay of the old, abandoned town. "What're you doing here?"

"That water's brackish," the girl repeated. She held up one hand to shield her eyes from the sun; with the other, she reached out and beckoned Ben to come to her. "Come with me for the sweet water."

Every nerve in Ben's body stood straight up, sparking against his skin. "I don't need your water," he said.

"Everyone needs sweet water," the girl replied slowly. She had the slightest hint of a drawl. Her voice was rough and sweet, like honeycomb. "Come with me, I'll show you where we keep it."

"Who's 'we'?"

"We are." The woman bent her neck and indicated the town with the crown of her head, her oily hair dangling in the heat. "The forgotten women."

Ben balled his hands into fists. "If this is a trap..." he began.

"The only trap is the state of existence," the woman interrupted, her clear eyes radiating through Ben's bones.

He hesitated. Then he cleared his throat and continued. "I was gonna say, if this is a trap, I'll punch my fist right through your head. I know how to do it; I studied it for a long time, from a master, someone who's a master of doing that, and I swear to God, I'll punch right through it, and then I'll set fire to the entire town." He tried very hard to give his most meaningful and threatening glare.

But the threat glanced right off the woman, who didn't so much as blink. "Come," she said, beckoning once more as she turned toward the blacksmith's shop, "come, and drink the sweet water of Scudder's Point."

She drifted across the hardpan and disappeared into the darkness of the rundown blacksmith's shop across the way. Ben gritted his teeth and shook his head as he watched her go. "This is not a good idea," he muttered.

Neither is dying of thirst, Patrick said, once again just a voice in Ben's head.

"You're telling me you would go?" Ben asked scornfully.

Oh, absolutely I would go, Patrick replied. *Patrick would* always *go.*

"That's the truth," Ben spat with annoyance. "Patrick always did go."

And everything worked out great!

"Except for the part where I had to cut the head off of a psychopath who stabbed you in the stomach before leaving you to bleed out on the steps of Disney World before an army of idiots came to slaughter us both. That part didn't work out so well."

Well, that part was different. That didn't count.

"It is literally the only time that it did count," Ben replied.

Patrick was silent as he thought about this. Then he said, *Well, either way, I think you should go for the water. I would definitely go for the water.*

"No kidding." Ben glanced uncertainly after the woman, who had disappeared into the shadows of the decrepit shack. "Well, shit," he decided. "Better stabbed to death by the forgotten women than shriveling into a dehydrated corpse." He kept his fists clenched as he stalked toward the blacksmith's, and he tried to pretend that his decision was a good one.

Maybe get the machete first, though, Patrick suggested.

"Yes, I know, I was obviously going to get the machete first," Ben lied. He trotted back up the street and picked up the weapon. Then he turned back and headed toward the blacksmith shop.

He couldn't shake the feeling of a thousand eyes on him as he crossed the street.

Sunlight slashed in through broken beams in the old workshop, cutting hard strips of glare onto the dusty, dried-blood floor. Ben stood tensely in the doorway as his eyes adjusted to the gloom. The darkness faded into dappled gray shapes and melted into the form of a true black-smith's workshop. A cold forge stood silently in the center of the room, with a massive anvil squatting before it. Three pairs of bellows hung from the wall, and a small collection of hammers lay on the floor, lined up by size. The smallest one was a little ball peen; the largest was a huge sledge, with a four-foot handle and a steel head the size of Ben's two fists stacked together. An old, split barrel sat in the corner, beneath a row of hanging metal tongs. Half a dozen long, steel rods with sharp hooks twisted into their ends hung down from the ceiling, swaying gently in the air like something from a slaughterhouse.

SLAM!

Ben leapt in surprise and fell backward at the sound, stumbling out of the shop and back into the street. But it was just the sound of a wood-en door hitting other wood. The woman, silent and unseen in the gloom, had pulled open a trapdoor in the floor on the far side of the shop and let it fall. Ben peered back inside in time to catch her stooped shoulders disappearing beneath the floorboards as she descended the hidden steps.

"Nope. Nope, nope, nope. I am *not* going down into a hidden cel-lar beneath a dark room with hooks hanging from the ceiling in a ghost town after some creepy-ass desert-woman—no *way*," he insisted.

Patrick would go.

"No shit," Ben hissed. "And Ben would rather shrivel up and die in the sun like a man-slug."

Ben could hear the woman moving about through the hole in the floor. Judging by the soft scratch of her footsteps, the floor down there was paved with coarse stone. She shuffled toward the center of the room, more or less right beneath the forge, and the steps stopped. She strug-gled with something, grunting softly down in the darkness, and then there was a loud, dull scrape, like something heavy being dragged across wood. Then the steps shuffled back toward the stairs, and Ben gripped his machete. He stepped fully into the blacksmith's shop so he wouldn't be blinded by the half-dark, half-bright boundary of the doorway, and he pressed himself flat against the wall, just inside the door. With him shouldered up against the glaring shaft of sunlight streaming in through the lintel, the woman would be the one who'd have to fight the light to define his shape, making him that much harder a target.

But when the woman emerged from the cellar, her pale skin practically glowing in the darkness, she held no weapon in her hands...just an oversized mason jar full of clear, cool water.

It was filled to the brim, so that with each light step, a few droplets sloshed over the rim of the jar and spilled down the girl's fingers. Beads of condensation dotted the outside of the jar, and Ben's throat turned to dust at the sight of it. The girl approached him silently, seeming to have no trouble finding his outline in the contrasted darkness, and she held the cool water up to his lips.

But Ben fought every molecule of desire. He pressed his lips shut, held up his hands in defense, and slid away from the girl, along the wall. "I don't drink anything I don't see the source of," he rasped.

You drank moonshine out of a stranger's shoe last week, Patrick reminded him.

Not now, Ben thought back.

But the girl was not put off. She followed Ben as he slid away along the wall, her bare feet moving soundlessly on the knotted wood, and she said, "We tapped into a spring line through a cavern below the ground. You may go down and see it for yourself."

Ben snorted. He turned and glanced down into the trapdoor, into the deep well of blackness that was so thick, it practically oozed up through the wood. "No thanks."

His body burned for that water. But drinking from a stranger's cup...that's how life got cut short.

You sipped coffee from a puddle on the ground last month, Patrick said.

Ben ignored him.

"You don't have to drink," the girl said hollowly. "But the sweet water is clear. Our gift to all good men who pass through Scudder's Point." Then the girl lifted the jar to her own lips, and she drank deeply.

Thin rivulets of cold water spilled out from the corners of her lips, racing down her chin and pattering down onto her thin nightgown. The skin of her arms prickled up in gooseflesh as the cold water ran through her, and over her.

Ben's mouth turned to paste. "Okay," he managed to whisper, once the girl had drunk down a few ounces. "Okay."

She broke her draught with a crisp, clear exhale, the satisfied sigh of a thirst quenched, and she held the jar up to Ben once more. He set the machete against the wall and took the jar carefully; the skin of his palms cracked against the coldness of the glass. He sniffed the water and smelled nothing untoward. He took a sip. The cold, clear water coated his tongue like honey, and the girl was right: water had never tasted so sweet.

He tilted his head back and drank deeply from the jar, and the water quenched the fire in his chest. Most of it, he swallowed; the rest soaked into his throat, replacing the moisture the desert had stolen away, and he tried not to drink too much, or too quickly, but he'd never had such a thirst, and he gulped down the entire contents of the jar.

You're gonna throw right up in front of this kid, Patrick said, clucking his tongue in disapproval.

Ben didn't care. He'd done worse.

"Sweet water for good men," the girl said. She reached out and took the empty jar from Ben's hands. She held it to her chest, clutching it like a doll, and backed away, into the further shadows of the shed. She disappeared into the darkness, moving backwards in shuffling steps, until Ben heard her back hit the far wall, and then he heard the sound of her thin cotton gown sliding down the wood. The girl hit the floor of the shed, and the jar hit soon after, knocking against the floorboards with a *thunk.*

Well, Ben thought. *That's not good.*

Purple goodness come sun glow, Patrick replied.

"What did you say?" Ben whispered, confused. His left knee began to tingle, and his shoulders sagged, like the bones had been pulled out and replaced with gummy worms. The tingling knee turned inward, all on its own, his whole leg spinning on his toes, and his body twisted in a slow pirouette. His torso ratcheted downward as he spun, until his leg gave, and he went down on his knee, hard. He knew it was hard because he could hear the loud *thud* of bone on wood...but he didn't feel the impact. The floor felt soft, like butterscotch pudding, and then Ben's neck curled back like a ribbon, and his head rolled back with it. The room tilted on its axis, and the wood slats of the floor came up to greet him, pressing up against his back. Then they lowered him down to ground level, where he lay splayed out like string.

"What did you do?" he asked. But the words didn't come out right.

Then a new shadow grew in the rectangle of light that was the door. It had the shape of a woman, taller than the girl, and it stepped noiselessly into the shed.

"Your service is commended, Amy Jo," the shadow said. Its voice rang like rain on a tin roof. "Rest now, in the stillness of the sweet water."

Burn the soda for worry and white paint! Patrick cried. He sounded alarmed, but Ben couldn't quite make out what he meant.

"What did you do?" he said again.

The shadow moved closer, resolving itself into an actual woman as it crept. Even in the darkness, Ben could see that her features were sharp: wide, knobby shoulders, a long, angular nose, and a small, pointed chin. She, too, was wearing a thin cotton nightgown, and her dark hair was piled on top of her head in a loose bun. She considered Ben with lemur-like eyes. "Good fortune, stranger. Your presence is good fortune for us all."

The woman stepped up to Ben's waist, and her eyes traced the length of his body, as if making mental calculations. If she approved of the math, her face didn't show it, but it didn't sour over the calculus, either. She stepped carefully along Ben's legs, reaching down and easing his calves with a gentle touch so that he was no longer lying akimbo, but straight as a corpse. Then she stood at Ben's feet and looked down the length of him, as if studying a new stud horse. "Our water is yours to share, and we will saddle you with as much as you can carry upon your departure. But as all good things come for a fee, the sweet water of Scudder's Point has a simple price."

Ben's mind was thick with cotton gauze. The woman's words disappeared in the heaviness of it, where they were slowly absorbed. And the only thing he could think to say in response was, "Why do you guys talk like that?"

The woman paid him no mind, and continued with her simple so-liloquy. "The next jars of water to meet your lips will be pure. But the first cup aids the payment." She grasped the fabric of her gown near her thighs and lifted it gently, so her ankles were clear, and she stepped for-ward, placing one foot on either side of Ben's shins. "The price of sweet water is man's seed," she said.

This magazine walks for bad radish, Patrick warned. Ben couldn't have agreed more.

"I need my seed," he said absently, his tongue rolling back in his mouth.

"So do we," the woman replied, dropping her skirt over his shins. "So do we all." Then she reached down and set her fingers to work at his belt buckle.

"No," Ben murmured, working desperately to move his body out from beneath her grasp. But all he could do was wag his head sadly from side to side. His upper arms fluttered, but it felt as if everything from the elbow down was putty, and even when he raised his shoulders and strained to pull his elbows up, his wrists stayed on the ground, stringy, and dripping from his forearms, and barely holding on.

"Whaaaaat is happening…" Ben muttered as a string of drool pooled out of his lips. "Whaaaaat did…you…dooooo."

The woman lowered herself to her knees, so she was straddling Ben at his thighs, and her fingers pulled nimbly at his belt. "Seed for water," she said, pulling at the leather strap. "Nothing you'll miss for nothing we'll miss. Seed for water."

Ben tried to shake his head, and he couldn't honestly tell if it tilted or not. "No," he mumbled, coaxing his lips to action. "No."

But the woman pressed on, heedless of his words, and of his not-words. She managed to pull the tongue of his belt free from its buckle, and from there, it was just a quick flick of the wrist to undo the clasp. She yanked up at the leather, setting the long end of the belt free. Then she set her fingers to work at the button of Ben's jeans.

"No," he said again, with more confidence mustered. He tried to push her hands away, but his arms wouldn't respond.

She unbuttoned his jeans and pulled down the zipper. "The daugh-ters of Scudder's Point will be your legacy," she continued, her voice lyrical now, as if she were bestowing upon him a great gift. "The male offspring are thrown into the well, but the female children will be nurtured, and will bear their own fruit. Your seed plants the tree of their bloom." She tugged down at his jeans, pulling them off of his hips and exposing him to the world.

Tears slid from the corners of Ben's eyes and dripped onto the floor.

"Please," he whispered, closing his eyes. "Stop. Please."

He had no feeling other than a numb tingle, and he couldn't tell the state of his own body when she took him in her hand. But he saw her shift her hips in the dim light, and he felt the pressure of her lowering herself down.

19.

"Please," he whimpered again, rocking his head so slightly along the floor. "Please, just stop."

"Seed for water," the woman murmured, planting her hands on Ben's chest. "The price of thirst."

Outside, the wind shifted. The fog cleared, and the sun shone brighter through the slats of the shed. The room brightened, just a little...just enough for Ben to see a massive, hulking silhouette moving in on them from the corner of the shed. The monster glided silently, with a grace that belied its size, and as it emerged from the darkness, hardening into the shape of a woman, tall and broad, with tightly curled blonde hair and a light, ruddy complexion. Ben watched in bewilderment as she stepped up to his feet, towering over his assailant from behind. The woman was holding something, and as he blinked back his tears, he could just make out the shape of the four-foot sledgehammer. She lifted it onto her shoulder as easily as a baseball bat, and while the pale woman sitting astride him lost herself in the rhythm of her rocking, moving her lips and whispering some silent prayer, the bigger woman swung the sledgehammer down like a pendulum. It blasted through the woman's ribcage, shattering her bones and knocking her clear across the room. She slammed into the wall of the shed with a loud, pained moan, then collapsed, unconscious, onto the floor in a knobby pile of skin and cotton.

"Thank you," Ben whispered, unable to feel the hot tears that rolled down his cheeks. "Thank you."

But his gratitude melted into dread as the big woman stepped forward and planted one large boot on either side of his ribcage. She stared down at him with a hollowness that sent a chill through his whole body. She held the sledgehammer before her, like a sword ready to plunge down through Ben's chest. He sent frenzied instructions to his arms and legs, imploring them to move, and while his fingers did twitch in a furtive sign of life, he was still helpless, unable to wriggle away. His heart fluttered in his chest like a caged bird, desperate for escape. The woman tightened her grip on the handle of the sledge and whispered, "Where?" Her voice was marbles in a bag, and it took a few seconds for Ben's muddled brain to process the word...too long, apparently, because she squeezed her heels together, pressing in on Ben's ribs and slowly forcing the air out of his lungs. "Where?" she demanded again.

Ben coughed and wheezed, fighting for air. "What do you mean?" he gasped. "I don't understand."

"Thieves," she said, carefully, slowly. Her brow tightened in concentration as she spoke, like each word was a metaphysical struggle. "Where?"

"I don't know," Ben said, rocking his head to the side. "I don't know."

The woman's face darkened. She let the sledge drop onto Ben's chest, pushing out what little air was left inside of him. His cheeks began to burn as he coughed and gasped for breath.

"I—I don't—know!" he insisted between gulps of air. "I...lost the...trail."

The woman gripped the handle of the hammer so tightly, her huge knuckles glowed white. She pressed down, and the sledge bore into Ben's chest with the steady force of a hydraulic press. Something in his sternum cracked, and jets of fire flared through his ribs. He pulled for air, but air wouldn't come. He gaped and gasped like a fish on land, and his face began to swell, purple and warm. He could feel the capillaries bursting in his cheeks as he was slowly crushed toward death.

Then the woman released the pressure, pulling the sledge back off his chest, and Ben burst into short, desperate breaths. He coughed and groaned, and he managed to turn his head to the side, just enough to spit up the built-up phlegm before he could choke to death on it. Feeling and movement were slowly returning, but too slowly to be his salvation.

The woman changed her grip on the sledgehammer. She took a step forward so that she straddled his shoulders, pinning his arms to his sides with her boots. She placed the heavy end of the sledge against Ben's temple, gripping the hammer with both hands, like a golfer ready to tee off.

"No, please...God," Ben said, closing his eyes. He shook his head, and his temple brushed the steel of the sledge. It was cool against his burning skin. "Don't," he begged through quiet tears. "Please."

"Where?" the woman demanded.

"Where what, where *what?!* Where did they go? Lady, I don't know where they went, I swear to God, I don't! I'm trying to follow them. I lost their tracks, I don't know. I'm fucking lost, I don't know where I'm going," he cried, his voice pleading through tears as the adrenaline in him diluted the drug in his system. "I don't know where they are, Jesus, lady, I don't fucking know. They went west, I'm looking, but I lost their tracks, I don't fucking know. I don't fucking *know*!"

He cried quietly, there on the floor of the shed, and the woman was silent, working something out in the hidden recesses of her mind. Then she cocked the hammer back, tense and ready to swing. "Where?" she said again.

"Oh, fuck, lady, come on!" Ben cried. "I don't know! *I don't fucking know!*"

Just then, a light gray blur streaked across Ben's vision. It was the girl in the thin cotton gown, recovered from her sip of the drug. She snatched a rusty punch stock from the pile of tools as she charged across the room, then she leapt at the blonde woman, screaming like a banshee and jamming the sharp metal punch into her shoulder blade. The big woman grunted in pain, and the hammer fell from her hands. Ben shrieked as it fell toward his head. The sledge slammed into the floor just two inches from his skull.

The two women went spinning across the room. The blonde giant swatted at the younger girl, but she dug in her claws and held on like a wildcat. They bounced off the wall, and the iron punch worked itself loose from the blonde woman's shoulder. The wound oozed blood, and it rendered her right arm weak. She swung up at the girl with her left hand, her fist the size of a lunchbox, but the angle was awkward, and even though she made contact, it was just a glancing blow. The girl rallied quickly, then threw open her mouth and bit down on the blonde woman's neck. The woman snarled in pain through her gritted teeth. She jerked and spun her body to catch some momentum, and then she dove shoulder-first out the door, pulling the girl out into the street, crunching her thin bones beneath a stone-hard shoulder, heaving with anger and grinding her into the hot dust, leaving Ben alone in the shed.

The feeling in his body was slowly returning. He begged his shoulders to move, and when he tried to lift them off the floor, they responded with a flutter. He bit down and threw as much force as he had into his neck, and his head jerked hard enough to pull his left shoulder up off the ground, flopping over in a clumsy arc and turning his torso through the air so that his chest came down against the floor. His legs hadn't kept time with the rest of his body, though, and they splayed out to the side, his knees knotted together like twine.

I know this isn't the best time, but man, if you could see yourself right now... Patrick said, trying not to laugh.

"I liked it better when you didn't make sense," Ben replied.

He wriggled his hands, and they gradually responded, prickling all over with the dull-needle sensation of his nerves coming back to life. He pressed his palms into the floor beneath his shoulders and slowly ratcheted himself up off the ground. He kicked his left leg, and it careened over his hip, coming to a hard landing on the floor on the appropriate side so he could push himself up onto his knees. His legs trembled like they were filled with water, and he steadied himself against the floor with his tingling hands. He allowed himself a moment to catch his breath. The struggle outside was growing...it sounded like more people had joined in the fight.

"I've got to get the hell out of here," he murmured.

He clumsily hauled himself up to his feet and took a few uneasy steps toward the window that looked out over the main road. It took him five steps before he realized his pants were crumpled down around his ankles. "Goddammit," he said, pulling them up with numb, stilted fingers and fumbling with the button. He glared over at the broken heap of a woman in the corner of the room. "I don't normally get very excited about the idea of people getting smashed in the ribs by a sledgehammer," he said. "But boy, lady, you had it coming."

The woman coughed once, a thick, rasping sound made solid with the blood in her throat. "Help me," she hissed.

Ben snorted. "Not a chance in hell."

He crept up to the window and peered out through the corner. He couldn't believe what he saw. The blonde woman stood, huge and bleeding, in the center of a ring of maybe thirty women, all wearing thin cotton dresses, all holding makeshift weapons; shovels, sticks, knives, chains. "Where did they all come from?" Ben murmured, amazed.

He looked up the road. His fanny pack was still on the ground across the street, over by the jail. And just a little ways beyond that stood a lean, powerful horse, tied to an old fence rail by its leather reins.

"Well that's new."

Must be the she-monster's.

"Obviously it's the she-monster's...I didn't think it just wandered into town and tied itself to a post," Ben said irritably.

You never know. Horses are great with their hands. Also, you shouldn't call her a she-monster. It's very mean.

"I didn't call her a she-monster, *you* called her a she-monster, I was just using your words!"

No, I don't think so. I would never call anyone a she-monster. It's rude.

"Shut up. Listen. That horse is our ticket out of here."

Yes, because you've proven yourself particularly adept at horsing.

"Well, the alternative is running," Ben said, squinting in determination and setting his jaw. "And I fucking *hate* running."

The front door to the blacksmith's shop led straight out into the brawl in the street, where the women were taking turns lurching forward and stabbing at the blonde woman with their picks and spears, so Ben picked up his machete and shuffled around the shed, keeping close to the wall, looking for an alternate exit. Over by the trapdoor, he saw thin slits of dusty light filtering into the room from the wall. He coaxed his feet across the floor, leaning heavily against the wall for support, and stumbled over to the light. He reached up and ran his fingers over the slats. It was a shutter, and it wasn't fastened down. He pulled it open, and bright light streamed into the room. He winced against the harsh glare and waited for his eyes to adjust. Then he picked up a small hammer from a nearby table and smashed through the panes of glass.

That was literally the last unbroken window in the world, Patrick observed. *I hope you're happy.*

"Better the window than us," Ben replied.

You could have just opened it.

Ben thought about that for a second. Then he said, "Shut up."

He used the machete to knock out the sharp edges of glass that stuck to the sill, and when he was satisfied, he tossed the blade and the hammer out into the alley, sat up on the sill, swung one leg out through the opening, tried to grip the outside wall with his right hand, missed, flailed his free leg, lost his balance, and toppled over, falling out of the window and landing on his face in the dirt.

Nailed it.

Ben tucked the hammer into his belt, picked up the machete, and then crawled along the edge of the building and peeked around the corner. The blonde woman had grabbed one of the Scudder's Point women. She hoisted her above her head like a wrestler in the ring and threw her against the enclosing circle of attackers. Four of the women went down, but another one rushed up behind the blonde woman and slammed a shovel across the backs of her knees, and she collapsed into the dirt.

"Today is not going how I expected," he muttered.

He turned and crept down the street, keeping low and close to the buildings. He reached the horse and hesitated. His losing battle with the Injun Express horse the day before had reminded him just how much he hated horses. He didn't trust them. They had wild eyes, and they snorted like demons, and they were very hard to ride. "Be nice to me," he warned the horse. "I write a mean Yelp review, and you don't want that on your background." He patted the horse's flank. The horse stamped and snarled, jerking its head and scaring the hell out of Ben. "This is going well," he said. "Don't move. I'll be right back."

He peeked around the horse and saw the battle still in full swing down the street. He dashed across the road, lumbering on numb feet that were slowly coming back to life, and he skidded to a stop in front of the jail. He was snapping the fanny pack into place around his waist when a ballpeen hammer whizzed by his head and struck the wall of the jail, knocking loose a shower of paint flakes and dust. Ben jumped backward, nearly tripping over his own feet. He turned and looked down toward the brawl and saw the blonde woman staring at him. It was a hard look of resolution, a look that said, "I'm not done with you yet. Not by a long shot." Then the pack of angry nightgowns closed in again, screaming and swinging and swallowing her from view.

A chill rippled across Ben's shoulders. "Time to go," he said. He rushed back across the street and unwrapped the horse's reins from the fence rail. "Look," he said, staring the horse down, "I'm not gonna like this anymore than you are. So let's just agree to disagree, and ride like the fucking wind." He lifted one foot into the stirrup and used the fence to push himself up over the saddle. But his hip wouldn't swing, and instead of sitting astride the horse, he ended up draped over it like a sack of flour. The horse took this as its cue, and it shuffled away from the fence on skittish legs. "Hold on, hold on, hold on!" Ben cried as he fought to push himself up into the seat. But his limbs were still sluggish, and the awkwardness of the fanny pack threw him off balance, and he floundered on his belly as the horse shook its head, whinnied, and took off like a bolt across the town, weaving through buildings, jumping over divots, and racing out into the desert, with Ben screaming in terror and clinging to the straps of the saddle for dear life.

20.

By late afternoon, Ben and the horse had reached an understanding. The understanding was that the horse got to make all the decisions.

"We are going the wrong way!" Ben yelled at the stupid animal for maybe the hundredth time. But if the horse gave a single fuck, it kept it to itself.

The Lab was to the northwest, but the horse seemed hell-bent on wandering southwest instead, and no amount of cajoling, coaxing, yelling, or rein-pulling could convince it otherwise. After a couple of hours, Ben just gave up, deciding that it was better to ride in the wrong direction than to trudge through the desert in the right direction. At least they were heading vaguely west; he'd figure out the north part later.

The steady trot across the sands had given Ben time to explore his new carriage, and it turned out there was a lot to see. The horse was fully loaded. There were four separate canteens, three of them filled to the brim with water that, Ben was pleased to learn, contained no paralyzing agents. A saddle bag hung down each side of the saddle; one contained food—jerky, banana chips, dehydrated kale—and the other held medical supplies, like Band-Aids, gauze, tweezers, athletic tape, and a small jar of creamy white stuff labeled "ointment" in handwritten letters. And resting comfortably in a long holster strapped to the front of the saddle was a Remington 1100 shotgun, well-oiled and well-kept, with a pouch full of unspent shells.

"It's good to be a cowboy," Ben decided, tightening the fanny pack against his hips, then slipping the Remington from its holster and turning it over admiringly in his hands. He twirled it on his finger like a performer in a Wild West show. The gun went off, firing directly into the ground, and it kicked back, the butt punching back into his head and breaking open the skin above his eyebrow. The horse bucked and leapt, and Ben nearly dropped the gun, diving forward and clinging to the horse's neck for dear life. "I'm sorry!" he cried. "It's not good to be a cowboy! I'm sorry!"

He pretty much kept his hands to himself after that.

They rode through the afternoon, into the mists and the burning sun. Ben's ass started to tingle after two hours, and by hour four, it had completely fallen asleep. But he knew on a deep and irrefutable level that if he stopped the horse to hop off and stretch and walk around, the animal would nab the opportunity to skitter off without him, because they hadn't exactly bonded. So he sat tight on a numb ass and wondered if, given enough time and not enough blood flow, anyone had ever had to amputate a butt.

That's the new dumbest thing you've ever thought, Patrick decided.

"It could happen," Ben insisted.

Oh, and then you'd be an ass-less chap! Patrick said. He sounded very pleased with himself.

The horse pushed on through the desert mist, and the fog gave way to a stunning view ahead. The ground fell away and opened up into a deep, wide canyon, with huge channels cut into the earth, the layers of the rock forming stunning striations that seemed to shift color by depth and light. The horse ambled up to the rim of the canyon and bowed its head low, sniffing at the dirt. Ben gazed down into the open maw of earth in wonder. He'd never seen anything like it.

"The Grand Canyon," he whispered.

You're a Grand Idiot, Patick whispered back. *Unless this horse travels a hundred miles an hour, you're in the wrong state, friend. Also, you can see every single edge of the canyon. It's like the Cute Small Canyon. How are you possibly this bad at geography?*

"Well, how do I know where the Grand Canyon is?" Ben said irritably.

Because you're a person who's spent his whole life in the country where it exists? Patrick guessed.

"I haven't spent my *whole life* in this country," Ben reminded him. "I went to Tijuana that once."

We *went to Tijuana that once,* Patrick replied. *And that did not turn out great.*

"It did not," Ben confirmed. "You made a lot of *really* bad decisions."

I was using all my brainpower to know where the Grand Canyon is...I didn't have any spare brain for good decisions.

"You almost got knived by a hooker."

What a day!

"God, I loved telling that story at your wedding," Ben beamed.

I can't believe Annie went through with it anyway.

"It was her most surprising decision."

I was as shocked as anybody.

Ben grinned at the memory. "Tijuana was a fun trip," he said. He shook his head and laughed out loud. "Man. I miss that."

Me too, Benny Boy. Me too.

The horse suddenly jerked its head up and flicked its ears, listening for some secret sound. It whinnied nervously, and began to step back from the canyon with quick, skittish steps. The hairs on the back of Ben's neck stood up.

"What's wrong, boy? Or girl?" he asked. It was hard to tell the gender from above. "What's wrong, horse?"

But then he heard it too...a sound that turned his heart to ice. A quiet symphony of wet, raspy snarls that cut through the fog like shark fins through water.

"Fuck me," he whispered. "Dusters."

He yanked on the horse's reins and jabbed his heels into the animal's ribs. This time, the horse responded; it wheeled away from the edge of the canyon and took off at a gallop along the rim. Ben scanned the horizon as he held on for dear life, but the fog over the desert was thick, and every bit of brush, every outcropping of stone was a duster lunging across the desert. "Come on, come on," Ben whispered, squeezing his eyes shut and shaking his head. The wet, raspy snarls were growing louder, but he couldn't see them. Then he heard footsteps, pounding across the hardpan, uneven, unsteady, but *fast*...but he still couldn't see them. He squinted hard into the mist as the horse galloped along the edge of the canyon, straining his eyes until he finally spied the first shadows of a sprinting lunatic through the green mist, heading straight for the horse, and gaining ground.

"Fuck." Ben leaned down close to the horse's ears and yelled, "Faster!"

The horse was running at a full gallop now, but the dusters were somehow faster. They began to emerge through the cloud, furious silhouettes streaking through the sand. They melted into view—one, then another, then another, then another, moving fast, moving as a horde. Ben lost count at fourteen, and more still appeared. They swarmed in from the east; they closed the gaps to the south ahead and to the north behind. And on the west, nothing but a five-thousand-foot straight drop-off into the canyon.

The first dusters were close now, close enough that Ben could make out their features. The idea of dusters had changed since Ben and Patrick had first come across them on their way to Disney World. Many of them had evolved, or maybe devolved. The concentrated Monkey dust had continued to do its grotesque work in the blood of the junkies who ingested it, and with enough time, a new, terrible transformation began to take place. The calcified build-up on the veins and arteries became thicker and harder, until the stone-like channels pressed against the skin, showing through as dark green lines that spread like roots across the entire body. The symptoms of the Green Fever had taken hold, advanced by the intentional ingestion of the powder, and most of the dusters now had eyes that began to leak thick, viscous globs of yellow-green mucous, leaving streaks down the cheeks and along the ridges of the nose. This same thick substance would ooze from the nostrils and from the corners of the mouth, and sometimes, in severe cases, it would bead up through the pores of the skin, too, coating the duster in a thick, slippery sheen. But the dusters wouldn't explode; their hardened exoskeletons saw to that. They would just swell, and their skin would pop, but they would continue to shamble around, with raw flesh and exposed wounds, searching mindlessly for an end to their hunger.

Another consequence of the Jamaican attack borne out over time was that the yellow goo that resulted from the inhalation of the Monkey dust didn't exactly agree with the skin; it burned it raw, slowly…and with enough time, it would even dissolve away, so most dusters now had tracks of scar tissue down their cheeks and above their mouths, from the leaking of their eyes and noses, and the ones who had been dusters longest, who were oozing the stuff from their pores, had skin that fell away in patches and clumps, and the pinkish-green dust-and-blood mixture coated their muscles and sinews splotched the landscape of their bodies like moss.

The result of it all: the longer someone had been a duster, the more grotesque he looked; the more his skin had been burned away, and the more pain he was in…and the more furious he was.

The dusters that closed in on Ben now were in severely advanced stages of hardened rot.

"Not good, not good, not good, not good," Ben said, his heart racing, fear clutching at his chest. "Faster, horse!" he cried, kicking his heels into the horse's side. "Faster!"

But the horse was tired, hadn't been properly rested in days, and instead of going faster, it slowed. The dusters closed in. "Fuck!" Ben exploded. He yanked the shotgun out of its holster and leveled it at the nearest duster, only about ten feet away now. He pulled the trigger, and the buckshot exploded through the fog. It caught the duster square in the chest. The monster jerked and stumbled backward from the force, but the shot didn't even break skin. The duster righted itself and lunged at the horse. Ben lifted his left foot, moving it out of the way, and the duster slammed into the horse's haunch, right where his ankle had been, hitting it with full force. The horse stumbled sideways, whinnying and whining, its hooves scrambling sideways across the hardpan and sliding up to the edge of the canyon.

Kill it! Patrick screeched.

"*I'm trying!*" Ben screamed. He lurched forward to stabilize himself on the skittering horse, and he swung the shotgun back over his arm and pulled the trigger. The second barrel exploded, catching the duster's face at point-blank range. Buckshot broke through the skin where the duster's yellow ooze was already seeping through, and a good enough portion of the shot caught the snarling monster in its eyes, bursting through the milky green vitreous and blasting through the skull and into the brain tissue. The duster fell over, dead.

"Come on, horse!" Ben screamed at the stupid animal's head as he reached into the saddle bag for two more shells. "*Move!*"

But the horse was tired and spooked. Its eyes wide and searching, it skittered along the edge of the cliff, lifting its front legs into the air, snorting and huffing and spinning. The rest of the dusters were closing in.

Time to run, Patrick said.

"No shit." Ben shoved the shotgun back into its holster and set to work fumbling with the straps of the saddle bags, working the buckles loose. He pulled the bags away from the horse and wrapped them around his own waist, cinching them tight. Then he yanked the shotgun back out of the holster just as a second duster leapt at the horse. This time, he wasn't fast enough with his reaction, and the rock-solid duster smashed into his shin with its shoulder, pinning Ben's leg against the horse's flank. Something in Ben's shin popped, and he cried out in pain. The horse was knocked off balance, and it fell down on its side, hard. Ben was thrown from the saddle, his leg wrenched free of the duster's weight, and he slid across the sand, tumbling end over end. He skidded to a stop on his belly, and his feet slid out over the edge of the canyon. He gripped for purchase on the desert floor, and his fingers pulled deep trails of dirt behind them as his momentum pulled him over the edge of the cliff up to his waist. His hips slammed down against the wall of the canyon, and he hung there, clutching the earth, his legs dangling over the drop. The swam of dusters hit the fallen horse, ripping into it like a cloud of angry locusts. They sank their teeth in the horse's hide, and Ben watched in horror as the animal screamed and threw its head while the dusters went to work, tearing it apart with frenzied hands and teeth.

One of the dusters looked up from its meal, its mouth dripping scarlet red. It saw Ben dangling over the edge, and it scrambled to its feet, stepping over the other dusters and tumbling over the dead horse. It fell down and hit the sand hard, but pulled itself up to its knees and scrabbled toward Ben, dripping blood and saliva, hissing and snorting and reaching for him with its green, mottled fingers. The duster lunged, teeth first, and Ben did the only thing he could think to do.

He let go of the earth, and he plunged down into the open air of the canyon.

21.

The blonde woman dragged herself to her feet and rose unsteadily on wounded, shaking legs. She wiped the blood from her eyes and took stock of the other women around her. She kept losing count when she tried to tally the bodies that lay strewn across the street.

The women in their strange nightgowns had come at her with fury, fighting and clawing like demons with hot pokers up their asses. They were small, flimsy-looking things, but their bodies were like steel—hard, inflexible, unyielding. They'd given her more of a fight than she'd reckoned, and the cuts and the gashes and the gaps in her flesh and the blood that seeped through her clothes and matted her hair—all those things were testimony to it.

Most of the women were dead. Some of the others were on their way. A few were just bruised or broken, but enough to have settled them down. The blonde woman was the only one standing.

She bent down and picked up a pitchfork, stabbing the blood-tinged tines into the ground and leaning on the handle for support. She lifted her free hand to her brow, blocking out the sun, and surveyed the ghost town. Her horse was gone.

If she'd had enough blood left in her, that would have made it boil.

The man she was tracking had ridden away on her horse, and he'd taken everything with him, including the small pack he'd slung down by the jail house doors. That didn't leave her with much of anything. She spat in the dust, but she couldn't begrudge him too much. He'd managed a lot for such a small man. Besides, he'd left a trail as obvious as if he'd been riding a herd of elephants. She'd catch up to him soon.

He'd pay for stealing her horse then.

She believed him when he said he didn't know where the bandits were headed. He was too scared to be lying. But for a man who didn't know where he was headed, he was heading there too deliberately. He had something that was pointing him in the right direction, she was sure of that. A map, a compass, some marker held in his mind—something. He may not have known where he was going, but he knew how to get there.

Which didn't explain why he'd taken the horse in a different direction, southwest instead of northwest. Trying to throw her, probably. Make her think he was zig-zagging blindly across the desert. Maybe he was smarter than he seemed.

Or maybe he just didn't know how to ride a horse.

The woman looked down at her left arm. The sleeve of her Henley had soaked through with blood. One of the waifs had slashed at her with a garden hoe, and the metal plate had lodged itself in her forearm. The blonde woman had returned the favor by breaking the waif's jaw in two places and leaving her alive. But the wound was worse than she'd thought. She pushed the sleeve up her arm, over her elbow, revealing not just the hole in her flesh, but also a series of raised white lines, a close pattern of scars that blanketed her skin from wrist to elbow. They stood out in great contrast to the blood, channeling an oozing scarlet river down her arm. She pulled a dirty rag from her back pocket and mopped up the blood. She spat into the wound, rubbed a mixture of dirt and saliva into it to stop the bleeding. Then she tied the rag around the gash, cinching it with a grunt.

One of the women lying on the ground watched her with wide, scared eyes. She lifted a trembling finger at the white marks on the blonde woman's arm and whispered, "The Thirteen Mercies! The Thirteen Mercies!"

The woman gave her a boot to the face. She didn't speak after that.

She flexed her fingers, to make sure there was no serious nerve damage from the forearm wound, and satisfied, she lumbered through the mess of bodies until she found someone who was alive and conscious. It was an older woman, in her late fifties, maybe. She'd broken a shovel across the blonde woman's back, and it had hurt like hell, but she had let her live because something in the older woman reminded her of her own mother. The blonde giant crouched down next to the woman now, grabbed the front of her nightgown with one meaty hand, and hefted her up into a sitting position. "Horse?" she grumbled. "Truck?"

"No...no horses," the woman said, shaking her head, holding up her hands to try to protect her face. "We ate 'em, for food. No horses."

The bigger woman jostled her impatiently. "Truck!" she said again, her voice like nails dragged across sandstone.

The older woman pointed with a shaking finger toward a clapboard barn tucked away behind the jail. "We got a car..." she said, her voice trembling.

The blonde woman let go, and the older woman fell back against the ground. She rose and shuffled down the alley, ignoring the pain in her ankle where one of the ghostly women had caught her with the flat end of a shovel. She walked with one hand against the wall of the jail house for support, leaving a trail of blood smeared into the grain of the wood.

She reached the barn and pulled open the doors. Inside, parked beneath the hayloft, sat the woman's car. In truth, it was a Meyers Manx dune buggy, a two-seater off-road go cart with wide tires, a silver roll cage, and a cherry-red fiberglass frame. Two round headlights peeked up from the corners of the hood like a bashful pair of sweetheart eyes.

The keys were in the ignition, and the needle on the tank pointed to full. The blonde woman lowered herself into the driver's seat, rocking the dune buggy on its shocks and sinking the frame so low that it ground against the chassis. She turned the key; the buggy started up on the first try, roaring to life. The woman smiled. She hadn't even *seen* a running car in years, much less driven one. But she knew the fuel was probably spoiled, and she didn't know how far she'd get before it rocked the tank, so she didn't give herself time to enjoy the purr of the engine or the feel of the steering wheel rumbling in her hands. She threw the buggy into gear and rolled out of the barn.

She opened up the engine on the main road, spinning the tires and kicking up a cloud of dust that swallowed the litter of bodies scattered on the ground. Then she rumbled out into the desert, over the harsh terrain, following her horse's trail and heading southwest.

22.

Ben opened his eyes. He was surprised to find himself alive.

"We fell, right?" he asked, dazed. His head thumped from the back, and the sky above him seemed to tilt and pivot when he opened his eyes.

We fell, like, a lot, Patrick confirmed.

"Is this hell?"

No. I don't hear any ABBA.

That, Ben decided, was infallible logic.

He blinked a few times, hard, and with feeling. The sky spun itself back into something bordering on focus. He *had* fallen; he remembered that very clearly. There are very few eventualities, he decided, that imprint themselves on the human memory like the feeling of dropping into a lethal freefall down the side of a deep canyon. Yet here he was, settled on firm ground, looking up at the sky through a cloud of green haze, and he was alive, and the world was calm.

Then a duster leapt out into the open air above, jumping off the edge of the cliff, spinning its arms wildly in the air, and diving down toward him head-first.

Ben screamed. He rolled over, curling into a ball and covering his head with his hands. He peeked through his fingers, and his situation suddenly made perfect sense; he had fallen, yes, but he had fallen onto a flat ledge that jutted out from the wall of rock like a platter, about thirty feet below the lip of the canyon. Over the edge of this flat outcropping of stone, the air opened up for another thousand feet until it collided with the hard stone floor of the canyon.

The zombie plunged toward him and slammed into the edge of the platform. Ben heard the bones and the hardened veins in its jaw crack, and the zombie snarled in anger as it bounced off the stone ledge and out into the open air, plummeting down into the depths of the canyon.

Ben crawled carefully over to the far end of the ledge and peered down after the falling runner. He watched in awe as it hit the ground and burst apart, its hardened limbs scattering across the canyon floor in a disgusting spray of red blood and yellow-green ooze.

"Wow. I haven't seen a runner explode like that since Ponch," Ben marveled.

Ponch made them explode way *better,* Patrick insisted.

"Ponch was pretty good."

Ponch was the best.

"No, I mean she tasted pretty good. Remember?"

Patrick declined to respond to that. But Ben thought he could hear his imaginary friend crying, just a little.

Another duster zoomed past Ben's head, close enough that Ben ducked backward in surprise. He could feel the breeze as the creature dropped past him and into the canyon. Ben caught his breath and scrambled away from the edge of the cliff, backing up against the wall. Another duster streaked past, then another, and another, and soon it was raining zombies. Some of them smacked into Ben's ledge as they fell, glancing off the stone and breaking or cracking before plunging toward the canyon floor. One of them actually landed in the center of the platform and clamored to its feet, snarling and drooling its yellow-green slime. Ben scrambled to the side, away from the duster, and his hands knocked against the shotgun, which had fallen with him. He dove for it, but his hand was clumsy, and he knocked it away. The barrel slid out over the edge of the cliff and teetered, deciding whether to stay or fall. Ben lurched forward and snatched the gun just as it tipped over the lip of the stone. He swung it up by the stock, whirled around, and fired as the duster leapt. The blast caught it in its snarling open mouth and exploded out the back of its head in a spray of sickly green gore. The dead duster collided with Ben, soaking his shirt in its filth. He blenched, tried not to gag, and pushed the rigid body off of him, down into the depths of the canyon.

"Hey, watch it!" a male voice from below screamed.

"Who's up there?" a woman added.

"Wait...yeah, *who's up there?!*" the man replied.

Ben tilted his head in the direction of the voices, confused. All he saw were two little rocks, two loose pieces of debris from the hailstorm of dusters. He crouched down, inspecting them carefully. "Oh my God," he breathed, reaching out slowly and brushing his fingertips against the stone. "I *do* have a brain tumor, and it's making me hear talking rocks."

"Talking rocks!" the male rock sputtered. "Talking rocks! Did you hear that?!"

"Who does he think he is, calling us dumb rocks?!" the female rock demanded. "Who do you think you are, calling us dumb rocks?!"

"I ought to knock his block off! I won't do it, because I'm a Christian man, but I'm telling you, I should knock his block right off!"

"You *should* knock his block off!" the female agreed. "You should march right up there and *do* it!"

"I *will!*" the male decided. "I *will* knock his block off—just give me the chance! *Just give me the chance!*"

"I am going to be dead by morning," Ben realized, feeling his cranium for signs of protruding tumors. "I'm not stage four...I'm full-blown stage five."

"There *is* no stage five!" the female howled.

"It's true! It's true! If she says it, it's true!" the male agreed, agitated and extremely excited. "She would know if there was a stage five—she was a nurse!"

"*I was a physician's assistant!*" the woman screamed. Then Ben heard the sound of a sharp smack of skin on skin, and the male voice yelped in pain.

He stared down at the rocks, incredulous. "How do rocks even know what a physician's assistant *is?*" he wondered aloud.

"Oh my God! Oh my God!" the female screamed. She sounded *very* put-upon. "He thinks we're rocks! He *actually* thinks we're rocks!"

"He's an absolute abomination!" the male shrieked. Then, more quietly, he said, "You hit me right in the eye...why did you do that?"

"Shut *up!*" the female cried, and again, Ben heard the distinct sound of skin on skin.

"Ow!"

"You *are* rocks," Ben said, trying to make his voice resolute. Something inside of his maligned and broken brain thought that if he could convince the rocks that they were just rocks, they would realize they didn't have vocal cords, and they would leave him to die in silence.

"Fuck you!" the female cried.

"Honey—language!" the male gasped. Then he added, "But yeah, fuck you!"

Ben dug the heels of his hands into his eyes and pressed in, somehow irrationally hoping to clear his ears by threatening his vision. It didn't make a whole lot of sensory sense, but if there was one thing he remembered about the human brain from his high school biology class, it was that the entire organ was extremely complex and could hardly be understood by any single neurologist, and therefore was far beyond his own mental reach.

"You're just rocks," Ben insisted, closing his eyes and massaging his temples and praying for the voices to stop. "Shut your stupid not-mouth mouths...you're just *rocks*."

"Oh my *God*, does he think we're *actually* rocks? He's insane!" the male cried.

"He is utterly, totally, completely, and irrefutably retarded," the female agreed. "We're not rocks, stupid!" she shouted. "We are human people, down here!"

"You shouldn't use that word," the male said quietly. "It's horrible."

"Shut up!"

Ben twisted up his face in confusion. He stared down at the rocks. They just sat there, dull and unimpressive in the fading daylight. He pushed a finger against one of them. It rocked backward against his touch, like a normal rock, and it didn't seem to complain.

"Man. I am in serious trouble," Ben decided.

"*Yeah* you are!" the male voice shouted. And now that Ben was right up against the edge of the cliff, it sounded like the voice was maybe coming from somewhere else, somewhere that might not be the little pebble under his finger. He scooted forward and peered uncertainly over the edge of his platform.

"Oh, *wow*," the female voice said, dripping with sarcasm, "the lord above doth deign to behold us little folks below!"

Ben realized then that he wasn't lying safely on the only plane of rock stretching out from the wall of the canyon cliff. He stared down at two people, a man and a woman, both standing on a similar but smaller platform, only about twenty feet below him. And beyond them, further north along the wall and maybe another fifteen feet down, was another platform, with another person perched near the edge…and further away, another, and then another, and another, and Ben pushed himself to his knees and drew back with a startled breath as he realized that the entire side of the cliff was pocked with little breaks of stone jutting out over the canyon floor.

Most of them served as platforms for people.

Not all of those people were as vocal as the ones closest to Ben.

"Hey! You see us! You see us! Yeah, you see us!" the man said, jumping around his little plateau and pumping his arms in annoyance. "Get down here and let me punch you in the face!"

"I don't want to get punched in the face," Ben said, drawing back a bit from the edge of his cliff.

"Too bad!" the woman shrieked, standing proudly and shaking her fist up toward Ben. "You got yourself up there, and now you have to get punched right in the fucking face!"

"Why do you want to punch me in the face?" Ben cried. "I haven't done anything to you!"

"You took the best spot!" the woman screamed. She had short, stringy hair, and she bounced like a Gummy Bear. "That rock is *ours*, and I will *absolutely kill you!*"

"We will *murder* you!" the man agreed, his brown hair flopping with each angry bounce. "Do you want to get *fucking murdered?*"

Ben pulled himself back from the edge. He shook his head incredulously. "This can't be real," he mumbled, pinching the bridge of his nose.

"Oh, it's real!" the man hollered. "Oh, yeah! You don't think I can hear you when you mumble? I can hear you when you mumble! I can hear *everything!* I have the ears of a *fucking badger!*"

"He has *badger ears!*" the woman agreed. "Bring your face over to my fist!"

At that moment—and maybe it was the morning's dehydration, or the assault in the blacksmith's shack, or the attack by mutant dusters, or the cramp in his leg from the horseback ride, or the pain in his back from his fall down the mountain—whatever it was, at that moment, Ben had suddenly had enough. He hopped up to his feet, tightened his hands into hard fists, and screamed at the couple below, "What the *fuck* are you *talking* about?! Who are you?! Why are you here?! What are you *doing* here?! Why do you want this fucking rock?! *I* don't want this fucking rock—I *fell* onto this fucking rock...you can goddamn *have it*, but I'll tell you this, you string-bean, bounce-around assholes, in the last twenty-four hours, I have been shot at, beaten, roofied, raped, attacked by zombies, and I fell off a cliff—*and* I have brain cancer. So I will leave you your stupid fucking rock, but I am staying here tonight. I am resting on this rock, I am *sleeping* on this rock, I am *making it my rock*, and if I hear one more shriek from either of you about whatever bullshit you're blabbing on about, I swear to God, I will gladly, *glaaaaadly* spend two shotgun shells in the name of eight hours of peace and quiet." He picked up the shotgun, held it above his head, and pumped it for emphasis.

He stared down at the couple, daring them with his eyes.

The man looked at the woman. The woman looked at the man. She grabbed his elbow and led him to the far side of their rock. They huddled and whispered, shooting glances over their shoulders at Ben every few seconds. Ben tapped his foot expectantly, hefting the gun in his hands. Finally, the couple returned.

"We're sorry," the woman declared. "We didn't know about the cancer thing."

"Or the rape," the man pointed out.

"Or the rape," said the woman. "We wouldn't have been so mean if we'd known about those things. We're not usually very mean people."

"We've gotten meaner since the apocalypse," the man added helpfully. "We used to be much nicer."

"We used to be *very* nice."

"I used to be a schoolteacher."

"It's hard not to be mean now," the woman said.

Ben found himself nodding thoughtfully. "It *is* hard not to be mean now," he sighed.

The woman nodded too, more vigorously, gaining steam. "Yes, and it's just that we've been waiting so long for that ledge to come open. The real estate market on this cliff is cutthroat as shit."

"It's worse than San Francisco," the man added. "*Pre-M-Day* San Francisco."

Ben stopped nodding. He had lost the thread. "Real estate market?" He looked down over the edge of his platform, at the dozens and dozens of survivors camped out on the stone ledges. "You've turned a canyon wall into a real estate market?"

"Yep. And this is the toniest cliff in West Desert," the man said smugly.

"*We are not calling it West Desert!*" the woman shrieked, slapping him on the shoulder. "*We are calling it Sunrise Pointe!*"

"We haven't had the vote yet," the man explained to Ben. "That happens next week."

"You listen to me," the woman said, grabbing the man by the shirt collar and yanking him down to her eye level, "that is a *terrible* name—it is a *stupid* name, Carl...West Desert is a *stupid* name, and if you ever want to be mayor of this town, you will make a case for Sunrise Pointe, do you hear me? Because Sunrise Pointe is *beautiful, goddammit!*"

"But I'm not even sure I *want* to be mayor, Linda," Carl whined.

"Yes, you do! Yes, you *do!* You have *ambition!* You have *drive! Or was my mother right about you?*"

"Don't you dare bring your mother into this!" he cried.

"Look!" Ben shouted, holding up his hands to quiet them down. "I just need one night's sleep. Then this...ledge, or plot, or whatever, it's all yours. Okay?"

"Okay," the woman agreed, "Okay. We've been waiting for that spot for almost four years. See that dumb little ledge down there?" She pointed far to the north, at a tiny ledge that jutted out just about four feet off the floor of the canyon. "That's where we started. And we've been climbing ever since, and *that*," she said, jabbing a finger toward Ben's rock, "*that* is the *best* ledge, and we *deserve* it! That old Mary bastard who had it for the last year just *would not die*. She had the Green Fever; we thought she'd go quick, but *noooo*...she was one of the drawn-out ones! She started coughing up green a full eighteen months before she finally threw up her guts once and for all! She was so *old*, but she wouldn't *die*, and we just kept waiting, but she just wouldn't *die,* and she coughed up the green, and she swore she saw Jesus four times a day, and her eyes started leaking, but she just wouldn't *die*. But then! Then you know what happened? She *did* die!"

"She splattered herself inside-out, right there on your rock," Carl pointed out. Ben lifted his feet and shifted his weight. His face soured, and he checked the ledge for green stains. Now that he was looking for them, he did see a few dried puddles.

"She finally died, threw up her own heart right out of her throat, and the birds ate it, and she popped open, and she was *dead,* and we weren't *glad* or anything, we are *good people*, but she was dead, so we gave her a funeral—"

"We pushed her body over the edge," Carl clarified.

"That is what a funeral is here!" Linda screamed, hitting Carl across the back.

"I did it with a stick. I didn't like it," Carl said sadly.

Linda pressed on: "We are *good people,* so after the funeral, we decided to leave her ledge untouched for one week, out of respect for the dead, because we are *good people*, otherwise we'd be up there right now, but we're not, because we're *good*, but that ledge is ours by right; we are next in line, we have *earned* that ledge, and if you don't leave tomorrow, then we will punch you in the face."

"Right in the face," Carl warned.

"Okay, okay," Ben said, rolling his eyes, "I get it. One night's sleep, and I'm gone."

"Where are you going?" the man asked.

"Carl!" the woman hissed. "Don't be rude!"

"We've been threatening to punch him in the fucking face, Linda!" Carl replied. "I'm just asking a polite question."

"I'm looking for a place called the Lab," Ben said.

Linda and Carl both gasped.

"The *Lab?*" Linda whispered, and she ducked, instinctively, as if she were afraid of being overheard. "You're looking for the *Doctor?*"

"You know him?" Ben asked. He scooted quickly back over to the edge of the ledge, squatting down and listening with interest.

"We know *of* him," Linda said, her voice still low. "People tell stories."

"Like what?"

Linda looked at Carl. Carl looked at Linda. He shook his head no. Linda hesitated. "Well…" she said.

"Linda!" Carl hissed.

"Well, he should know!" she reasoned.

Carl shook his head sadly, but he didn't protest.

Linda continued. "People come through all the time with stories of what goes on at the Lab. What the Doctor does there." She shivered, and she crossed her arms, grabbing her elbows and hugging herself tightly. "Terrible, awful things."

Ben raised an eyebrow. "Like what?"

"He makes the Dead Things," Linda said quietly, her eyes wide with fear. "You know? The Dead Things?"

"Those green monsters," Carl clarified. "The ones that attacked you."

"Dusters," Ben replied, and he said it with such authority that both of the people below him nodded their agreement. "He actually *makes* them?"

"They say he's building an army," Carl whispered.

Ben furrowed his brow. "Why would he do that?"

"No one knows," Linda replied. "The way we hear it, he is absolutely insane."

"I heard he removes people's limbs while keeping them alive," said Carl.

"And that he experiments by injecting babies with dead blood," added Linda.

"He surrounds the Lab with Dead Things to keep people away."

"He shoots them up with some secret serum, to make them more powerful."

"He surgically implants radio receivers in their brains so he can control them through airwaves."

"He enslaves innocent people and makes them do his bidding, or else he'll send his Dead Thing army to march on their villages and families."

"In his old life, he was kicked out of his hospital for performing strange experiments on the patients," Carl said.

"Like Dr. Moreau, they say, but *worse!*" Linda said.

"Dr. Moreau, *but worse,*" Carl reiterated.

"Why would you want to go find someone like that?"

A cold ball formed in the pit of Ben's stomach. Its icy tendrils spread into his lungs and his chest. "His people took something of mine," he said. "I need to get it back."

Linda threw up her hands in a show of mock frustration. "Puh!" she cried. "Kiss whatever it was goodbye! You'll never get *close* to getting close to the Lab!"

"You'll be ripped apart by Dead Things like *that!*" Carl said. He tried to snap his fingers, but they just sort of fumbled.

"You still can't snap? Christ, *we have worked on this!*" Linda shrieked.

"I know!" Carl wailed.

"Anyway," Linda said, clearly annoyed, "you don't want to go to the Lab. I mean, you can't stay here, that is our ledge, and you need to go *somewhere* in the morning. But look, here's some hard truth, okay? I don't mean to be mean, but it's a hard truth: you'd be better off with the slow, painful death of brain cancer than you would be going after the Doctor at the Lab."

"Definitely," Carl agreed, nodding his head. "I'd take brain cancer any day."

"Thanks for the pep talk," Ben said miserably. He gave them a little wave and retreated back toward the center of his ledge.

"We're just trying to help!" Linda hollered up. "Do what you want. But the Doctor is a madman. No one comes out of the Lab alive."

"No one comes out of the Lab alive," Carl agreed.

"I just said that, Carl!"

"Thanks," Ben said again. "I appreciate the help." He gathered his things together, and he made a small pile of saddlebag and fanny pack. Then he lay back against it, nudging his head into a comfortable spot. He pulled out the map and studied it until he found the canyon, or at least *a* canyon, and he thought it was probably the one where he was now. He traced his finger up toward the Lab. He actually wasn't all that far off-base. The Green River was close; he just had to head north from here, and he'd find it, probably within the next day.

He tucked the map beneath the saddlebag, then he settled back onto his makeshift pillow. He stared up at the skies above, at the dark clouds that gathered above the mist, threatening a desert storm, and he sighed.

144

Thoughts of bloodthirsty super-dusters and madmen scientists jostled for purchase in his brain.

"It doesn't matter," he said to himself. "One way or the other, I guess it really doesn't matter."

He waited for Patrick to agree. But Patrick didn't say a word.

23.

Ben could see for almost a mile in every direction from the crow's nest in Fort Doom. Mobile lay stretched out to the northwest, or what was left of Mobile did. A string of controlled fires burned in the streets, and lanterns dotted a few of the windows in the taller buildings, but all was quiet. The town sprawled and trailed off to the east, where the mid-rise buildings stepped down to low huts and ruined houses, into the darkness of the outskirts, where the coyotes and the wild boars kept mostly to themselves. The bay stretched out behind the fort to the south, opening up into the great Gulf of Mexico, and sometimes the tides brought in boats and makeshift sea craft, but there had been no manned vessels for weeks, and when there were, they didn't come at night. There were no lighthouses, and the bluffs were treacherous.

It was a quiet night outside the walls of Fort Doom. And that had made it even easier to fall asleep.

He didn't know how long he was out. Too long, there was no doubt about that; the moon had climbed high above the dogwoods and was now hovering near its zenith. How long had he slept? An hour. Maybe two.

It was a sharp *crack* that woke him. The sound of a gunshot, or maybe wood breaking. The sound broke through into his dream, snapping him out of his sleep. He opened his eyes. Had there actually been a gunshot? Had he dreamed it? He thought he heard the reverberation against the walls of the fort, but maybe that was just dream residue.

He climbed to his feet and lifted the rifle to his shoulder. James had fitted a scope to the barrel of the firearm, but it was something he'd scavenged, and there was a thick crack down the center of the lens. The break made it impossible to accurately sight a target, but it was still sort of useful as a magnifier. Ben angled the rifle around to the east of the wall, where he thought the sound had come from. If it had come from anywhere at all.

Through the broken scope, he saw silhouettes of burned-out cars and abandoned houses outlined against the darkness by the moonlight, and the swaying shadows of the wild grass and weeds that had reclaimed the suburban sprawl. He scanned the horizon to the southeast, to the far edge of the bay, and then back up toward downtown Mobile, tilting the rifle upward, then downward, searching for movement.

"Nothing," he said out loud, trying to convince himself. "There's nothing there." But when he lowered the rifle, something *did* move, out beyond the wall. A dark shape flashed in the edge of his vision, over near the bay cliff. He threw the rifle back to his shoulder and searched through the scope. The shape was gone, swallowed up by the darkness… but the grass along the bay wall dropped and sprang back up, disturbed by whatever had muscled its way through.

Something *was* out there.

Or some*one*.

He grabbed the strap of the rifle and slung it over his shoulder. He climbed out onto the ladder and stepped down carefully. For a split second, he wondered if he should wake James, or maybe Annie. But that was stupid. "Let them sleep," he thought aloud. "It's just an animal."

Animals don't have guns, his brain pointed out.

"I don't know that it was a gunshot," he countered. "I don't know that I actually heard anything at all."

But he was pretty sure he had.

He climbed down the ladder, hand over hand. He jumped the last three rungs and plunged down into the ocean beneath the watch tower, sinking, drowning, breathing the cold water into his lungs…

•

"*Hey! Wake up!*"

Ben awoke with a gasp. He rolled over onto his side and coughed the water out of his lungs. Torrential rain pounded the ledge. Disoriented, panicked, he grabbed his fanny pack and held it over his head for protection. Drops of water trickled through the mesh belt and pattered against the top of his head. He shook the water from his eyes and gazed around, his vision slow with sleep. It must have been raining already for some time; not only were his clothes completely soaked through, but in the canyon down below, a thin stream of runoff had formed. It was raining so hard through the canyon that the rivulet seemed to grow wider as he watched. Lightning cracked in the distance, splitting off into an electric snake tongue in the sky, and thunder cracked almost immediately behind it.

He mopped his face with one hand and leaned over the edge of the platform. Carl and Linda were huddled together under a tarp that was doing little to keep them dry. Water pooled in the natural divots in the stone beneath them. It was soaking their clothes from the bottom up.

Linda was looking up at him, shouting something, but he couldn't make it out.

"What?" he hollered, his voice nearly swallowed by the storm.

She pointed a finger to a spot above Ben's head. "Look!"

Ben turned his face up and used the pack to shield his eyes from the pouring rain. The night was made especially dark by the thick storm clouds, and at first, he couldn't tell what she was pointing at. But then another streak of lightning flashed, this one jolting between the clouds and illuminating the entire sky, and in the wash of blue-white light, he saw the hulking blonde woman from the old ghost town crouching directly above him on the lip of the canyon.

"Aw, come on," Ben moaned.

Their eyes locked. There was cold fire behind hers, and something more like tired, dead leaves behind his. Ben sighed.

Things were about to go badly.

Perfectly on cue, the woman put a hand down on the desert floor and swung her legs over the edge. She dropped through the air, and Ben tucked the fanny pack under his arm and rolled to the edge of the ledge just as she came down hard on her feet, her thick work boots pounding the stone and shaking pebbles loose from the canyon wall. Ben pushed his way backward, his eyes wide in horror, as the woman gained her balance and charged. He scrambled to his feet, hugged the fanny pack, took a deep breath, and launched himself over the edge.

He landed on his feet on Carl and Linda's ledge, but the rock was slippery from the rain, and his left leg went out from under him. Something in his hip popped as his legs split, and he cried out in pain.

"Hey, don't bring us into this!" Linda shrieked.

"The top spot is all yours," Ben said with a wince as he picked himself up and hobbled across their ledge.

The blonde woman leapt down onto the rock and hit the ground running. She shouldered past Carl, sending him spinning backward into the canyon wall. Ben yelped at the sight of the sprinting woman, exploding through the falling water like a leviathan about to ram a ship. He took two big steps and threw himself over the side of the ledge. His stomach dropped into his ankles, and he prayed there would be something to stop his fall.

He arced through the air, his legs kicking, his lungs burning. He free-fell for twelve feet, screaming the whole way down, and slammed into the next ledge with his shoulder. The air blasted out of his lungs, and he heaved for breath, his face pressed against the cold, wet stone. There was an elderly man camped out on the ledge, huddled partway beneath a small outcropping in the canyon wall. Ben shot him a desperate look. "Don't move," he rasped. The old man nodded, his face drawn with fear.

Ben crawled forward and was scrambling for the edge when he felt the vibration of the woman landing behind him. He flipped over onto his back, still clutching the pack, and used his heels to push himself back across the rock. The woman took a bad step when she landed, and Ben heard her ankle pop. She grunted, but didn't slow. She stomped across the ledge, drawing a hammer from the small of her back. She lifted the hammer high, and Ben pushed down through his feet with all of his strength. He propelled himself back over the edge of the cliff and tumbled backward off the ledge as the woman brought the hammer crashing into the stone, where his kneecap had been just a split second before.

He fell just a few more feet, onto a small, empty ledge. He forced himself up to his feet and looked down the canyon wall. In the steady flashes of lightning, he saw his path easily from here: a series of smaller ledges—some with people on them, some empty—made a crude passage to the canyon floor.

Ben took a deep breath, and he jumped.

He pushed past the couple on the next ledge, muttering an apology as he splashed across their rock and leapt to the next, and then the next. The blonde woman barreled through behind him, and above the thunder and the rain, Ben heard a woman scream. The ledges were small, and the blonde woman had knocked someone off into the depths of the canyon.

Shit, Ben thought. *Shit, shit, shit.*

As he hopped his way down the wall, he noted with growing alarm that the narrow valley below was flooding, filling quickly. The thin stream he had seen from the top of the canyon wall was now a full-blown river, the water rushing fast, churning up greenish froth. Branches and desert detritus flowed by, caught up in merciless eddies that spun them down the new river.

And the water was rising.

He chanced a look over his shoulder. He had gained some ground on his pursuer. The woman was limping a little now as she ran. He was three full ledges ahead of her, but whatever relief that might have brought was short-lived. Just as he was nearing the bottom of the cliff, there was a deafening rumble from somewhere to the north, the sound of a desert canyon washing out, breaking away, and tumbling down into the river. It was followed by a thunderous roar that made his heart sink: the colossal crash of a surge of water.

Some sort of natural dam had just broken around the northern bend. The entire canyon was about to be flooded.

Ben lowered his head and ran as fast as he could on the slick stone, stomping through puddles and streaking past confused desert inhabitants. "Get to high ground!" he shouted as he ran. They looked at him with a mixture of bewilderment and annoyance. Ben didn't notice. As he jumped to the final ledge, the roaring grew louder, and a surge of water crashed around the bend. It sped through the canyon in a fury, a muddy, white-capped wall that threatened to wash away anything in its path.

The water below was almost up to the lip of the ledge. The river had grown wider, almost five full feet of water now between the canyon wall and the swell of earth that sloped gently upward toward the far wall. Ben looked to his right. The tremendous wave was bearing down. He backed up to the wall of stone, clicked the fanny pack around his waist, took a deep breath, ran two steps forward, and jumped as the water crashed down.

He hit the bank on the other side just as the wave smashed over his legs, whipping them out from behind him and dragging him downstream. He cried out and gripped down on a rock buried deeply into the earth, and for a few seconds he dangled sideways, holding on for his life as the river tried to drag him down. But then the wave passed, and in its wake, the river rose two feet in ten seconds, and Ben floated upward. He scrambled up the bank and climbed a few feet up the hill before planting his hands on his knees and doubling over, desperate for breath. The cold rain pounded his back, and the water rushed by, spilling up the bank as it ran, lapping at his heels.

Ben turned to look over his shoulder. He saw the blonde woman standing on one of the higher ledges, a few feet above the water line. She stared at him, her face a cold block of uncarved stone. Her eyes chilled Ben deeper than the desert water did, and he couldn't break away. For a few long moments, they stood there, on opposite sides of the river, staring at each other as the storm raged on around them. Then Ben backed slowly up the hill, reached the top of the swell, and, turning his back, he ran across the canyon floor, up toward an old cattle trail that led back up to the desert floor.

The woman watched him disappear into the desert rain. Then she turned and began the long climb back up the canyon wall.

24.

Ben wrung the water from his shirt, and it dribbled right into his shoes.

"Aw, son of a bitch," he swore. He unrolled his shirt, shook it out, and laid it over a dry stone. Then he picked up his shoes and tipped them over, draining the water out of them. "Great," he muttered. "Just great."

You are very, very bad at drying clothes, Patrick observed.

"Nice to have you back," Ben grumped. He set his shoes on the cave floor, balancing them upside down.

It looked like you needed someone to point out how bad you are at things.

"I can always count on you for that."

Reliability is so important in a friendship.

Ben dug through his pack and pulled out a bag of jerky. He hadn't eaten much the last two days, even by post-apocalyptic standards, and he was beginning to feel the effects. There was a dull ache in his head, and his stomach felt prickly and sour. He ripped open the package and tore a piece of leather-tough jerky in half with his teeth.

"Boy. No shirt, no shoes, growling over dried meat." Patrick stepped forward from the back of the cavern, his hands stuffed into his pockets. "Ten minutes in a cave, and you've gone full Neanderthal."

Ben looked up at his dead friend thoughtfully as he chewed. "Even my dry clothes are wet," he said.

"Crazy weather patterns," Patrick observed, looking out at the rain. It had slowed to a drizzle in the last hour since Ben had climbed out of the canyon.

"Someone forgot to tell the clouds that this is the fucking desert," Ben said miserably.

"Pfft. El Niño." Patrick sat down and crossed his legs. "You know what dries things? Fire. Fire dries things *good*."

"Great idea." Ben jerked his thumb out into the rain. "Go out there and don't come back until you find dry wood."

Patrick considered this. Then he said, "If we had a fire, we could dry the wood so we could make a fire."

"Brilliant."

Patrick frowned. "You seem more Ben-like than usual tonight. What's wrong?"

"Nothing's wrong." Ben swallowed the jerky and then fell back against the cave floor. He stared up at the cold, wet ceiling. "I think I'm just going to lie here until I die."

"That's a pretty good plan," Patrick agreed. "It shouldn't take very long. Wet clothes, wet cave, cold desert night? I bet you're dead from hypothermia by dawn."

Ben sighed.

"Some men would put their money on pneumonia," Patrick continued. He held up his hands and swirled them in Ben's general direction. "But you've got a real pre-hypothermia aura about you."

"My hip hurts," Ben said. He dug his thumb into his right hip bone. "I think something popped when I smacked it on that rock."

"Then you shouldn't have done that," Patrick decided. "See, this is exactly why I don't let you run near the pool. It's very dangerous to go rock-hopping in the rain."

Ben sighed again. "Why is that woman chasing me?"

"I have a very good theory about that," Patrick said. He scooted a little closer, as if he was about to let Ben in on a very big secret. "Everyone knows I was an engineer of machines, but I also like to consider myself an engineer of the mind, and of the heart. And when I look at her emotional blueprint, you know what I see?"

"What?"

"She wants the cure. It became very clear to me the moment she said, 'Where are those bandits going?' and you said, 'I don't know,' and she said, 'Oh, yes, you do know, and I want to know, too, because I want to go after them and get that cure.'" Patrick tapped his temple with one finger. "I am very smart."

"She didn't say any of that," Ben countered.

"She said it with her eyes. And with her emotional heart."

Ben shook his head. "How would she know that's what was stolen? How does she know about the bandits at *all?*"

"I've been thinking about that," Patrick said, nodding thoughtfully. "I think she must have been close by when the attack started. Passing through or something. And if I'm her, and I see a whole army of cowboys rob a well-armed train, I'm probably looking at that and thinking, 'Wow, I bet whatever they took sure was worth a lot. Maybe I should go get what they took so that I can have something that's worth a lot.'"

"Seems like a hell of a lot of work, tracking someone across the desert and getting yourself battered up with clubs and shovels, just for a backpack you think might have something valuable inside," Ben said. He wasn't buying it.

"It might not make much sense," Patrick agreed. "But my emotional mind-heart blueprint reader says it must be so. I don't know what else it would be."

"I don't think I even care why she's out here," Ben frowned. "I just don't want her to kill me."

"Oh, I don't think she wants to kill you. Something tells me if she wanted you dead, you'd be dead."

"She threatened to bash my head in with a sledgehammer."

"But she didn't."

"She swung at me with a regular hammer, back in the canyon."

"Oh, puh," Patrick said, dismissing Ben with a wave of his hand. "That wasn't a kill shot. That was a body swing. She doesn't want to kill you; she just wants to kneecap you."

"Great," Ben said, growing testy. "Why would she want to kneecap me?"

"Probably so you'll stop running away so much," Patrick shrugged. "That's why I'd kneecap somebody."

"I don't want to be kneecapped!" Ben wailed.

"Well, I didn't want John Tesh to get the satisfaction of going platinum, but we don't always get what we want, now do we?"

Ben screwed up his face. "Who the fuck is John Tesh?"

Patrick tilted his head and grimaced at Ben. "Ah, sweet Benny Boy. I do so envy your ignorant bliss."

Ben frowned. The rain had all but stopped, and the clouds had thinned enough to shine a bit of moonlight into the desert. "Maybe we should keep going," he said, thinking aloud. "Try to stay as far ahead of her as we can. See if we can make it to the Lab before she catches up."

"That's not the worst idea you've ever had," Patrick admitted. "Because she is very big, and very strong, and there is a one hundred percent chance that she breaks you in half. But I think you should chance it, and stay here and get some sleep. I mean, you should see yourself. You look awful."

"Well of course I look awful...haven't you been following along?"

"That's what I'm saying! You need to rest! Your poor little brain is naturally on the fritz as it is...you get anymore sleep-deprived, and you'll wind up falling off a mountain or eating a whole cactus."

Ben hesitated. "I should keep going," he said.

Patrick shook his head and waved his hands through the air. "Look. This is already a suicide mission. Especially if what those ledge-people said is true. If you're going to run head-first into the Oasis of Dr. Moreau, you should do it with a good night's sleep under your belt."

Ben considered this. "Yeah...I guess that's true..." he said slowly.

"Of course it's true. Trust me. I'm a heartgineer." Patrick lay back against the wall of the cave and stretched out his legs. He poked at the hole in his palm where Reverend Maccabee had driven his nail through it. "Speaking of suicide missions," he said, approaching the topic gingerly, "and specifically, this being one of them..." He tapped his teeth together, as if unsure how to proceed. Finally, he pulled his feet back underneath him, learned forward, and said, "Look, why are you doing this?"

"Doing what?"

"This. All of this. That woman's not the only one who's crazy to be out here."

Ben sighed. "Same reason as her. I have to get the antidote."

"Oh, don't tell me it's because of the antidote," Patrick said, his mouth turning sour. "No offense, but you don't like humanity *nearly* enough to put your life at risk to save it."

"Screw you!" Ben cried, offended. He crossed his arms in a huff. "I can be the good guy," he muttered.

"Oh, I know you can be the good guy. You *are* the good guy. You got us all the way to nightmare Disney World. You're the Bulldog to my Mouse Hunter. You would risk your life for *certain* people. Just not *all* the people."

"You don't know," Ben said, indignant. "Maybe I'm helpful now."

"Look. I'm not saying it's not noble to risk your life to keep the salvation of all mankind out of the hands of a zombie-loving psychopath. But can I be honest?" He looked expectantly at Ben. But Ben just stared back without assenting. Patrick hesitated. He picked at the scab around his wound. "I think..." he began. Then he stopped and took a deep breath. "I think there is a very good chance you're going on this suicide mission *because* it's a suicide mission."

"Oh, please." Ben pushed himself up from the floor of the cave and stalked out into the desert. Patrick got up and followed him. The night air was cold, and Ben huddled tightly into himself. "Why would I do that? Why would I *want* that?"

Patrick shoved his hands into his pockets. He leaned back against the mouth of the cave and dug the toe of his sneaker into the soft mud. "I know you still think about what happened at Fort Doom," he said quietly.

Ben stiffened. The twilight breeze prickled his flesh with goosebumps. "You weren't there," he said, his teeth pressed together.

Patrick bowed his head. "It wasn't your fault," he said. "You didn't—"

"You weren't there!" Ben shouted, his voice echoing through the open mouth of the cave, fading into the darkness. He looked down at his fists to see that they were clenched so tightly that his knuckles were white. He pried his fingers loose and flexed them slowly, trying to calm the blood in his veins. "You weren't there," he said again, softer. "Don't talk to me about it. You don't know anything."

Patrick pulled a hand out of his pocket and scratched uncomfortably at his neck. "You don't have to do this because of what happened. That's all I'm saying."

Ben closed his eyes. He took a deep breath. "That's not why I'm doing it," he said. "I'm going after the Jansport." He looked up then, finally meeting his old friend's eyes. "If I was going to kill myself, I would have done it already."

He couldn't tell if Patrick believed him.

Ben rolled his head and shuffled back over to the cave. He leaned against the far curve of the mouth, so he and Patrick stood like mismatched pillars, holding up the darkness. "I went back to Disney World," Ben said.

Patrick glanced over from the corner of his eyes. "You did?"

Ben nodded.

"When?"

"Three days after."

Patrick turned and faced Ben, leaning into the cave wall with his shoulder. "Why?"

Ben shook his head slowly and shrugged. "I don't know. I just wanted to see."

"See what?" Patrick asked, his voice full of curiosity. "If the Red Caps had mangled up my body?"

"I just wanted to see...*you*, I guess. Make sure it really happened. Make sure you were really dead." Ben wiped a tear from his eye and sniffed back the mucous in his nose. "It didn't feel real."

"What did you find when you went back?"

Ben scraped his teeth along his bottom lip. The memory of that day was so clear in his mind, as if it had been sealed and preserved in acrylic. He had headed back west when Patrick begged him to leave, had made it as far as the coast. The heart-shaped Jacuzzi boat had vanished, its heavy trail dug into the sand veering off to the south. Ben had stopped at the water, helpless and frustrated, with his heart ripped in half, and he'd dropped down on a bluff overlooking the Gulf and wept for his lost friend. For two hours, he sat there, looking over the water, his eyes red and swollen. Guilt began to gnaw at his chest, the guilt of having left Patrick behind. He could have stayed. He could have hidden. He could have watched. He could have made himself a witness. Patrick deserved that much.

As the sun began to set over the ocean, he made up his mind, resolutely. He turned and headed back toward the Magic Kingdom.

When he finally made it back, exhausted, depleted, and dehydrated, he paused at the edge of the parking lot. He could see the plaza near the turnstiles where Patrick had been run through with Bloom's sword. The Red Caps were long gone, off to God knows where to wreak some new havoc now that their leader was dead. Ben felt a sour anger burning in the pit of his stomach. The Red Caps could have stopped it. They shouldn't have let it go that far. They were once fathers, sons, brothers, friends. In just three years, Bloom and Calico had molded them into thoughtless, spineless heralds of torture and murder. *How does that happen?* Ben demanded, standing there in the parking lot of the Magic Kingdom. *How do actual human beings become so heartless?*

In a way, he resented them more than he did Bloom. Bloom was a creature of pure greed and anger. He wore it like a coat; his cold eyes were a death mask. He had no choice but to be vile. But the Red Caps... they had a choice, and they chose.

Ben rubbed his eyes. He gulped down some air, and he walked slowly to the plaza.

"But you weren't there," he said, standing outside the cave, shaking his head and shivering. "They left Bloom's body on the bricks, his head in the grass, and you were *nowhere.*"

Patrick closed his eyes. He pinched the bridge of his nose. "I'm sorry," he whispered.

"First I thought they'd dragged your body away. I couldn't imagine why they would do it, but I figured they must have." Ben stared down into the mud as he spoke, his arms crossed, his neck muscles straining with tension. "But then I saw a blood trail leading into the park. And that was you, wasn't it?"

"Ben..."

"You died in my arms. I left you there because you *died.* You were *dead.* There was nothing else I could do, so I left your body there, just exposed on the sidewalk for the animals to pick apart...I *left you there because you died.*" He turned and stared at Patrick, his blue eyes burning. "But you weren't dead. Not yet."

Tears welled up in Patrick's eyes. He held up his hands in helplessness. "I had one more thing to do," he said, his voice choked by his tears. "I couldn't let you die for that."

Ben felt his feet burning. Hot pulses of anger radiated through his veins. He went back into the cave, just to have a place to go, just to make

158

the energy kinetic. He snatched his shirt up from the ground, shook it out, and put it on, even though it was still damp. He walked back out of the cave, and he began to pace, shielding his thoughts. Patrick watched, and he opened his mouth, but he couldn't find the words to speak.

"I followed your blood to the castle," Ben finally said, the tips of his ears glowing pink with anger. "I followed it to the door, and up the stairs. I went into the room where they pushed you. Or maybe you jumped. Fuck, Pat, I don't know. I saw your blood. I saw the indentation where you sat on Cinderella's fucking *bed*. I saw Izzy's empty pudding cup. They just tossed it into the corner. They did, or you did, that whole trip for that little cup of pudding, and I found it smeared and empty and cracked like trash in the corner of the castle where you fell to your death—a death I could have prevented, because I could have pulled you out. I could have pulled you into the woods, we could have hidden, you could still be alive, but you're *not,* because I *left you*—do you understand that? Do you understand what that *makes* me? Can you even *begin* to comprehend how that fucking *feels?*"

Patrick wiped his eyes with the back of his scarred hand. "No," he whispered.

Ben wheeled around, his fists clenched once more, the tears now streaming freely down his face. "And you know what else I saw?" he asked.

Patrick bowed his head.

"I saw the stains at the foot of the castle. The stains of you." His face drained to a deathly white. That memory, too, was as sharp as a diamond in his mind. "We'd seen so many dusters exploded by that point, it was such a shock to see a stain of red instead of green. But there it was. There you were." His knees trembled, and he suddenly felt the need to sit. He eased himself down to the ground and put his head between his hands. "I don't know what they did with your body. What was left of it. They did take it away. Christ, I can't imagine why." He sniffed, and the sound of mucous was thick in his throat. "All that was left of you was an empty pudding cup and a smear on the concrete."

Silence hung between them like heavy laundry on the line, criss-crossing through space and blocking their view. In the far reaches of the desert, a coyote howled, and Ben had never, ever felt so goddamn lonely in his life.

Patrick gently pushed himself up from his spot against the cave wall and crossed over to where Ben sat. "I'm sorry," he said.

Ben looked up at him. The anger had seeped out of him and sunk into the desert mud. "I left you to die," he said simply.

"You did not. Now shut up and bemme."

Ben rolled his eyes.

"Bemme," he said again. He reached out and opened and closed his fingers, making a grabby hand. "Bemme!"

"Bemme *what?*" Ben exploded.

Patrick grabbed his hand and pulled him to his feet. "Bemme Ben, stupid." He threw his arms around Ben's shoulders and drew him in.

"This isn't even a real hug," Ben pointed out. "You're just a tumor-dream."

But he let himself be hugged anyway.

25.

Willis had been digging all day. His arms were sore, his back ached, and his fingers were thick with blisters, even though he wore a pair of brown jersey work gloves. He'd been at it for six hours, and he was ready to be done.

But he'd only dug ten graves. He still had four more to go.

He jammed the shovel into the soft desert dirt and kicked it in deep with the heel of his boot. "Shovel goes down," he said to no one in particular. He pulled back the handle, and a load of wet sand and dirt came out. "Mud goes up," he said. He lifted the heavy load and tossed it over his shoulder.

"The thing is, Tommy—" Willis had named his shovel Tommy, and Tommy was the only other "person" for miles, "—the thing is, Tommy, ya gotta dig 'em out when it's wet. You get it when it's dry, well, hell— shovel goes down, *dirt* comes up, sand falls back in, hole collapses, and Willis starts again." He took another blade full of earth, then he stood Tommy up and spoke to him face-to-face. "It's been dry for almost two months, Tommy. I can't dig no holes when it's dry for so long. Them bodies stack up, and no one likes that, but I tell 'em, I say, 'Stack 'em up and rub 'em with sage.' Can't keep 'em fresh, but is that my fault?" Willis waited for a response. But Tommy seemed noncommittal on the subject. "Hell no, it ain't my fault." He yanked Tommy around, then stuck him back in the dirt. "Ice'll do it, but we ain't had ice for nigh on five years. 'Rub 'em with sage,' I tell 'em, 'we'll put 'em down as soon as it's wet.' And we got that bad rain last night, so now's the time. 'Course that's why I been out here since two a.m. this mornin'. Won't stay wet for long. It's dryin' up already." He lifted out another load of sand and nodded down at it. "Look at that there. Gettin' dry." He looked up at the sun through the hazy green fog and whistled. "Gettin' hot," he added.

A black scorpion scuttled out from beneath the sand a few yards to his left. Willis tensed and watched the sand-devil from the corner of his eye. The scorpion paused, twitching its tail, as if reading the air…then it skittered forward and disappeared under the tarp that covered the stack of bodies next to the graves. *"I knew it, I knew it—I knew you'd go for them dead ones!"* Willis shrieked. He sprinted toward the pile, raised the shovel above his head, and screamed, *"Get him, Tommy!"* He brought the shovel down hard on the edge of the tarp, and again, and again, whacking the side of it with the flat side of the corroded metal. Heaving, out of breath, Willis gingerly approached the tarp. He grasped the edge, counted to two, and pulled it up, holding the shovel ready to attack. The scorpion lay dead in the sand, splattered into the hardening mud. Next to the scorpion rested a greenish-colored hand that had come detached from its decomposing wrist.

"Aw, hell," Willis cursed, "that one's gone soft." He used the back end of Tommy's blade to push the hand up against its owner's hip.

He hauled up the shovel and walked back over to his digging spot, whistling a happy tune. He went back to work, pushing the shovel in, kicking the shovel up, tossing the dirt aside. Down, up, aside. Down, up, aside.

"Anyway, Tommy, it's like I was sayin', there's just folks back in town dyin' off more and more, I can't hardly keep up. They get that green-spit cough, and hoooo boy, they're good as gone. Takes some a week, takes some a year, but either way, they get the sickness, they don't come back. They might as well dig their own graves." He stopped his work and leaned against the shovel. "Now there's an idea," he mused. He thought about the details of such a program. Then he shook his head and waved the thought away. "Nah. Too much to ask someone who's dyin' to dig their own grave, I guess." He dug down a little deeper. "I'd do it. I wouldn't wanna put no one out, Tommy. That ain't my way." He nodded to himself. "I wouldn't ask it of no one else. I wouldn't want to make people feel like—*get your shit-self away from the dead, you split-shit son of a demon!*" he screamed at a second scorpion that had surfaced near the body pile. He ran over and swung his shovel, catching the scorpion straight-on and sending it flying across the sand.

He watched the little hell-spawn arc through the air, and he smiled with satisfaction when it hit the ground. Then his eyes picked up something moving on the horizon, and his smile faded. He squatted down low and crept over to the nearest grave. He tossed Tommy down into it, then lowered himself after. He peeked over the edge of the hole and trained his eyes on the moving thing on the horizon.

At first, it was just a soft red spot, waving in the heat-haze of the desert morning. It came closer, and grew bigger, and before long the spot had resolved itself into a real shape, a cherry red car, speeding across the sand.

Willis blinked. He rubbed his eyes. He blinked again.

He hadn't seen a car in almost two years.

"Hot damn," he mumbled. He reached down and grabbed Tommy, holding him up high so the shovel could see the marvel that was headed their way. "That's a car," he explained in an awed whisper. "Get a good look, Tommy. You mightn't not see one ever again."

The car broke through the shimmer as it roared across the clay, its wide tires churning and sliding on the wetter patches of earth. It barreled toward Willis with surprising speed. "Oh, Lord," he said, his voice suddenly tight with alarm, "it's gonna roll right through the graveyard!" He looked around at the flat desert earth that surrounded him. If a person didn't know any better, that person would swear there weren't upwards of fifty-seven bodies buried in that stretch of land. Willis sighed. "I knowed I should've marked the graves."

But then he noticed something else about the car that was coming closer: it seemed to be trailing a thin pillar of dark grey smoke. Willis squinted at the oncoming vehicle, and then he saw the flash of a flame. "Good Moses!" he cried. "That there car's on *fire!*"

The buggy bore down on the graveyard, and Willis watched in awe as it and the flames grew bigger and brighter. He shook his head in wonder as it came within a quarter mile of the graveyard. And his jaw fell open in disbelief when the engine exploded in a brilliant orange ball of fire.

"Jesus Josephat!" he said, leaping out of the hole. He clutched Tommy tightly and hurried toward the car. It kept speeding forward, but its progress was slowed some by the sudden lack of motor functionality. He and the car ambled toward each other, and when it rolled to a stop, he stopped too, breathing heavily and eyeing the thing from about a hundred feet away.

He could just barely make out the silhouette of the driver through the thick shroud of black smoke and lingering flames. The figure behind the wheel didn't look to be in any great hurry to leave the driver's seat behind.

"Hey!" Willis hollered. He cupped his free hand to his mouth and tried again. "Hey! Y'all oughtn't stay in there!"

The door of the buggy popped open, and Willis took a stutter-step backward. The figure that climbed out of the little car was the biggest, brawniest, curliest-haired woman he'd ever seen.

She slammed the door, her ruddy cheeks glowing crimson with anger and blood, and maybe with the heat of the flames. Willis felt his own blood drain from his face, and he took a few more steps backward. The woman turned to face him, looking almost surprised, as if she'd just now registered his presence. She held a wad of paper in one of her ham-hock hands. She stuffed it into her pocket. Then she balled her hands into fists and marched in Willis' direction.

"Tough luck 'bout them cars!" he said, stumbling backward as she approached. "Don't care for 'em myself, tendin' to trust my own two feet like I do." He hit a hard rock buried deep in the sand, and he fell backward, smacking the ground hard on his seat. The woman bore down, her teeth glinting in the sun. Willis held his shovel before him with both hands, trying desperately to ward her off. "Don't you come near me—I know kung fu!" he shrieked, squeezing his eyes shut and curling into a fetal position.

The woman stomped up to the prostrate gravedigger. She stared at him, her eyes on fire with fury. She reached down and yanked the shovel out of his grasp.

"No, Tommy, no!" Willis wailed, reaching out for his lost companion. But the woman took the shovel and stomped back to her smoking car. Willis watched in horror as she stepped up to the side of the burning engine, lifted Tommy above her head, and then proceeded to bash the shit out of the engine, shrieking a primal scream as little bits of ruined metal and shattered fiberglass flew through the air.

Willis covered his head with his arms, shrinking away from the fury of the scene and crying a wellspring of tears over the brutal trauma she was imposing on his trusted friend and graving tool. And then, just as quickly as it had begun, the violence was over. The woman lowered the shovel, gave the fender of her car one last, good *WHACK*, stomped back over to where Willis lay, and threw the shovel into his lap. Willis grasped Tommy lovingly and drew him close, nuzzling the chipped metal shovelhead with his cheek.

"Horse?" the woman demanded. She stood over Willis with her hands on her hips, and her midsection blocked out the sun.

"N-no, I feel f-fine," Willis said, tapping his throat to show her it was in good working condition.

"Horse!" the woman bellowed, and Willis felt the vibration of it tear through his bones. "To ride!"

"I ain't got one!" he cried, shrinking back even further, clinging to his shovel. "I use my own two feet!"

The woman glowered down at him. She seemed to be making some sort of calculation behind her dark, angry eyes. She pulled the wad of paper from her pocket and opened it up, smoothing it out. She held it out to Willis, and he peered at it cautiously. It was an old map, soft at the edges, crisscrossed with tape. "Where?" the woman demanded, her voice autumn leaves on a washboard.

Willis took the map with a trembling hand. He inspected it carefully, wanting to make sure he got it right. He found the Green River, and he found the Utah-Colorado line. He jabbed his finger into the space between the two markers. "Here," he said. "'Bout two inches away from your circle." He handed the map over, then he shrank back, trying to blend in with the desert floor.

The woman stared down at the map. She seemed satisfied enough. She folded it up and tucked it back into her pocket. Then she simply turned and stalked off across the desert, heading in the direction she'd been heading already.

Willis watched her go with disbelief. "Tommy," he whispered, his lips so close that they brushed the metal of the shovelhead when he spoke, "I do believe we just dodged a proverbial bullet."

Tommy didn't have anything to contribute to the conversation, but Willis expected that he agreed.

Willis watched her go, and when she was far enough away that she was just a spot near the horizon, he pulled himself back up to his feet and gave her a mocking salute. "Good riddance," he said. Then he sneezed. An electric green goo splattered into the sand. He frowned and wiped his lips. The back of his hand came away green, too.

"Aw, shit," he said sadly.

He sighed.

Now he had *five* more graves to dig.

26.

Ben opened his eyes. An armadillo sniffed the air just inches from his face.

"Shit!" Ben screamed, scrambling backward on his arms and legs. The armadillo screamed, too. Then it turned around and toddled out of the cave.

Ben's heart hammered in his chest, and he placed a hand over it to try to get it steady. "Jesus Christ," he muttered, shaking his head. He blinked the sleep out of his eyes. He'd never felt so groggy in his life.

He reached for his socks and his shoes, which had mostly dried overnight. He pulled them on clumsily, then pulled himself up to his feet and crawled out through the mouth of the cave.

Something was wrong.

He frowned and scratched his head.

Something was off.

But he couldn't quite place it.

He scanned the desert. Brown mountains to his left. Brown mountains to his right. Sun coming up on his left. Dry creek bed to his right. Cacti on his left. Armadillo on his right.

Wait, go back, Patrick's voice said.

"What? The armadillo?" Ben glared daggers at the little creature and kicked some dust in its general direction.

No. Before that. The sun. The sun is coming up on which *side?*

"The left."

Didn't it come up on the right yesterday?

Ben furrowed his brow. He put his hands on his hips. He looked to the left, to the sun. He looked to the right, where there was darkness over the mountains. He looked back to the left. "Wait, which way is west?" he asked, turning in a circle, confused.

Normally, I'd like to use this sort of question as a teachable moment, but to save myself untold frustration, I'm just going to tell you that yesterday, the sun set to your left, so it would stand to reason that that's where west is.

Ben cocked his head. He crossed his arms. "Then why is the sun rising over there?" he asked. He rubbed the sleep from his eyes. He just felt so *groggy...*

I'm gonna let you figure that one out on your own, Patrick said. *Wake me up when you get it.*

Ben huffed. He wished he had some coffee. Coffee would know why the sun was rising in the west...he was sure of it. He groaned and tapped the heels of his hands against his brain. "Urgh! Why am I so *tired?*" he asked, stifling a yawn. He ruffled up his hair in confused frustration. He decided to lay out the facts as he knew them. "Okay. The sun rises in the east. The sun sets in the west. Yesterday, the sun set over there." He pointed to his left. "Now it's rising over there." He thought about this. He thought about it some more. He rubbed his chin. He scuffed his foot. He tilted his head. He bit his lip. He worked his brain as hard as he'd ever worked it before. "Holy shit...I slept through an entire *day?!*" he cried.

There it is! Patrick exclaimed happily.

"I slept so long, the sun is *setting?!*" Ben slapped his forehead with his hand. "Why didn't you wake me up?!"

And how, exactly, would I do that?

"I don't know! You're in my brain! Pull some wires or something!"

You know brains don't have wires, right? I mean, you know that. Right?

But Ben wasn't listening. He ran into the cave and scooped up the fanny pack. He pulled it open, looking for the map.

But the map wasn't there.

"Oh, shit," Ben groaned.

What? What's wrong?

"I left the map back in the canyon."

Oh, cool, Patrick said. *If there's one person in the world who definitely doesn't need a map, it's you, for sure.*

"Goddammit," Ben muttered. He threw everything back into the pack, zipped it up, and threw it over his shoulders. "We're on our own."

He hurried out into the desert, praying that he was headed in the right direction. "I can't believe I slept until sunset. That's a whole extra day Horace has to wait with the stupid train, so *they're* all probably gonna get slaughtered by something, just sitting there like that, or else they'll just decide to give up and go," he said, annoyed as he hustled toward the mountains in the north. "Oh, and don't forget Lady Psychopath, who is *definitely* somewhere ahead of us just waiting to ambush us and pull us apart with her bare hands!"

I'm intangible, Patrick said smugly.

"Yeah, well, if I die, you die," Ben grumbled. Then he hesitated. "You know. Again."

Eh, it's not so bad, Patrick decided. *When you're dead, you don't have to worry about desert animals stalking you in the night and ripping your flesh from your bones.*

"You're not helping. Stop not helping."

Oh, and when you're dead, you don't have to walk anywhere! That's pretty nice, too.

"Yeah, well...some of us still have to climb over mountains while trying not to get mauled by sand-bears, so pipe down, will you?"

Sand-bears? Patrick asked, confused.

"Yes, Patrick—sand-bears! I don't want to get mauled by sand-bears, or sand-wolves, or sand-snakes, or sand-anythings, so be quiet and let me focus!"

Snakes don't really maul people...

"Shut! Up!" Ben shouted. "We are *way* behind schedule! We have a *lot* of ground to make up, and I am walking harder than I've ever walked before!" He took three more steps and tripped over a prairie dog hole. "Dammit, Patrick, what did I tell you?!" he cried.

I didn't say anything!

"Well *keep* not saying anything," Ben said, pushing himself back to his feet, "I am *trying* to *focus!*"

They continued on in silence for a while after that.

The terrain became harder and more dramatic, the desert floor giving way to mountains that rose and fell sharply against the sky. The hills stretched on toward both horizons, and as far as Ben could see, the nearest low crossing was a road maybe a mile away, a thin ribbon of smooth trail against the rough texture of the rocks...but it was a switchback that wound its way back up the side of the mountain, and there just wasn't time. So as the last light of the sun disappeared over the horizon and the moon began to glow, Ben hoisted himself up over boulders and lowered himself down dangerous crags, walking upright when he could, pulling himself up on his hands and knees when he couldn't. For three hours, he strained against the desert, taking breaks every twenty or thirty minutes to drink some water or have a snack from his dwindling supply of food. He hadn't planned on being out in the desert this long, and his chances of starving to death or dying of dehydration were growing every hour. The horse taking him in the wrong direction hadn't helped his progress, and sleeping through a whole day wasn't great, either. And given his lack of directional prowess, there was the constant nagging thought that he still might not be moving toward the Lab. *This was such a stupid idea,* he chided himself as he struggled his way to the top of a bluff, feeling for handholds and pulling himself along by inches. *I should just let them keep the bag.*

That wasn't an option, of course.

But it was sort of cathartic to pretend.

He reached the top of the bluff and pulled himself to his feet with a groan. He stretched his arms, flexing his worn and tired muscles, and then he put his hands to his lower back and leaned backward, bowing his spine. He twisted his neck to the left, then twisted it back to the right... and saw a great bonfire burning near the base of the hill.

He dropped to his belly and scooted back, so he could just barely peek over the edge of the cliff. The fire was far away, at least a thousand feet, but he could make out two shadowy figures sitting beside it. The bonfire threw its light in a bright halo that illuminated the campsite, and Ben could just make out two separate tents, and a pair of horses hitched to a tall cactus.

"What do I do, what do I do, what do I do," he whispered. Approaching two strangers in the dead of night was a surefire way to get yourself shot. Or worse. Ben had heard stories of wandering cannibals in the

170

desert, and while he didn't particularly believe those stories, he found himself a little more willing to be convinced right then. Sometimes, he would come across the bodies of men or women that were just strung up in trees, or staked to the ground and covered in honey, their skin eaten away by wolves, or flayed open by a knife, and often for no apparent reason at all. When he found bodies like that—people murdered outright by methods that took time, and planning—and when those bodies had been left with their pockets full...that was when he knew the killing had happened for sport. He'd seen it more and more often in the last few months. People were getting mean. People were getting bored. Creative slaughter was a thing to pass the time.

Approaching the fire would be a bad mistake.

But he needed food. He was low on water. He might be lost. If he kept pushing on alone, there was a chance he'd end up dehydrated and starving, dragging himself around the desert in pointless circles. If he didn't find help, he wasn't sure he'd make it to the Lab...and even if he did make it, he'd be too weak to do anything but lie down and die against the Doctor's army. And as much as he'd seen horrors of inhumanity out in that wasteland of a world, he'd also seen goodness, and generosity, and kindness. He didn't see them very *often*, but every once in a while, a post-apocalyptic wanderer could really luck out.

Or he could be tied to a tree with his own small intestine, with his kneecaps shattered and his toenails pulled off. He'd seen that twice.

"Any advice?" Ben asked.

Oh, how nice of you to grudgingly acknowledge my superior critical thinking skills, Patrick said. *Yes, as luck would have it, I have lots of advice.*

"Great," Ben grumbled. "Let's hear it."

Okay, ready? Patrick asked. Ben could practically hear him rubbing his hands together in sly excitement. *Here it is: Moccasins.*

Ben blinked. He blinked again. "What?"

Moccasins! They're comfortable, stylish, and totally timeless. Everyone should own a great pair of moccasins. Especially you, given the current setting. Moccasins have a great desert aesthetic.

"I meant advice about this particular situation!" Ben hissed.

Oh, Patrick said. *Then no. Not really.*

Ben rolled his eyes. "Great."

Well, hold on, Patrick considered. *I do have one thought. But I'm pretty sure you're not gonna like it...*

27.

Ben held out his arms. He looked himself up and down. "Oh hell no," he said.

Look, I told you you wouldn't like it, Patrick said. *But I'm so glad you tried it, because seeing you now, in all your awful glory, I seriously think this might be the best idea I have ever, ever had.*

Ben frowned. "No," he said. "Hard stop. I am *not* doing this."

Patrick had described his plan as genius, an adjective that Ben had found ominous from the beginning. Boiled down to its idiotic basics, the idea was this: Ben had to approach the figures around the fire; his survival almost certainly depended on their kindness. But since he couldn't count on not being slaughtered for fun, he had to convince them that he was a greater danger to them than they were to him. *Now, you are small and not very threatening,* Patrick had explained, *and that has always been true. It is more true now that you let your hair grow. You're going to have to convince them that you're dangerous. You're going to have to make them think you are absolutely bat-shit crazy.*

Ben gave himself another once-over. At Patrick's direction, he had ripped up his shirt with his machete so it had slash marks across the belly, and only one sleeve. His shorts were turned inside-out, the pocket pouches full of sand and pebbles so they stuck out like white balloons.

He'd used some of his precious remaining water to make a paste of mud and had smeared it across both legs of his jeans, from thigh to ankle. He'd made a painful and perilous makeshift crown from a handful of branches of desert scrub, and he'd pricked his finger with the point of his blade and streaked a bit of blood on his forehead and down his neck. He'd plucked a bit of lilac from a bush on the mountaintop and stuck it behind one ear. And he had removed his tennis shoes. He'd tied one of them by the laces to his left wrist, and he stuck his right hand into the other, wearing it like an imbecile's glove.

You look beautiful! Patrick squealed.

"I'm not going down there like this."

This is the best and greatest plan I've ever had. Better even than Disney World! This is it! This is my life's work! Ben could practically hear his imaginary friend choking up. *You are a glory-creature now, like a beautiful, badly handicapped macaw.*

"I am not going—"

Ben, shhh. Ben, Patrick interrupted him, *shhh. Listen to me now. Shhh. Listen. Ben. Listen.* He paused for dramatic effect. *Ben, you're ready.*

"Oh, fuck that! I am not going down *there* dressed like *this!*" he hissed. "They're not going to be scared of me; they're going to think I'm an asshole!"

You are *an asshole, but look how stupid you look!*

"I don't want to look stupid!"

That is between your parents and God!

"I am not wearing this!" he snapped. He reached for the scrub crown and hit himself in the face with the shoe that was dangling from his wrist. "Ow!"

Don't you dare take that off! Patrick cried. *You are perfect! You are my Sistine Chapel!*

"I don't want to be your Sistine Chapel!" he cried, throwing the shoe off of his hand and working angrily at the knot around the other wrist. "This was a stupid plan, like *all* of your stupid plans, and holy shit, *why* in the name of *Christ* can I not just *not* listen to you for *once?*"

You seem very upset right now. It may be worth arguing about your terrible life choices when maybe it's not so important that you be quiet.

"I *am* being quiet!"

False.

"And if I hadn't let you drag me on that stupid fucking road trip from hell," he continued, throwing both shoes to the ground and ripping the crown from his head, "we would still be in Chicago, you would still be alive, and I wouldn't be out here dressed like a fucking asshole, trying to trick some strangers around a fire into thinking I'm bat-shit crazy so I can take their food before going off to fight a mad fucking scientist with a hard-on for dusters!"

He stared out at the empty air where he imagined Patrick would have stood. His chest heaved and fell, heaved and fell, out of breath and out of words. He stood there in the darkness, staring through nothing, holding a prickly scrub brush crown in his hands.

"Who's got a hard-on for dusters?"

Ben whirled around just as someone shone a light into his eyes. He shrank back, squinting into the glare and holding a hand to his brow so he could see. There were two silhouettes behind the lantern.

The two men from the fire.

Ben realized that perhaps he wasn't being so quiet after all.

It's not the right time, but I told you so, Patrick whispered.

"Who's got a hard-on for dusters?" the first man demanded again. "And how would that even *work?*"

"We're not asking because we're interested for ourselves," the second man said quickly. "It's just...it's a curious thing to think about."

"Also, I want it to be known that I do not like your idea of taking our food," said the first man.

"Good point, brother," the second man nodded. "And for the record, I've seen crazier."

"Oh, yes, we have definitely seen crazier," the first man agreed.

Ben closed his eyes. *Stupid,* he thought. *Stupid, stupid, stupid...*

His shoulders slumped with resignation, and he raised his hands into the air. "I gave myself away by shouting at an imaginary friend," he said, and then he laughed, quickly, a short burst of frustrated laughter. "Well," he said, shaking his head and smiling bitterly, "it pretty much doesn't get any more humiliating than this."

Then one of his inside-out pockets burst at the seams, and a small stream of pebbles and sand spilled out.

Ben sighed.

"If you're going to kill me, at least let me turn my pants right-side-in first," he requested sadly.

"Who said anything about killing you?" the second man asked.

Ben opened his eyes. He shrugged. "I don't know. You just sort of assume it these days."

The first man—the one with the lantern—took another step closer. He held up the light, as if inspecting Ben's face. "Brother," he said, his voice heavy with curiosity, "am I off my wine, or have we seen this sad person somewhere before?"

The second man stepped forward as well, his face still hidden in the darkness behind the lantern's glare. He raised his hand and rubbed his chin. "Hmm," he said. "Now that you mention it, brother, he *does* possess a particularly familiar sort of pathetic look, doesn't he?"

The first one nodded slowly, considering this. "Friend," he said finally, "I do believe we've met."

Ben squinted suspiciously. "I can't see your faces," he said, sliding one foot quietly backward in the sand, angling himself away from the men and grabbing the handle of the machete in his belt. "Who are you?"

The man holding the lantern slid back the metal shutter, throwing the light into a full circle, and illuminating his face, and that of his companion. "I am Brother Mayham," the first one said. "And this is Brother Waywerd."

Brother Waywerd bowed deeply. "*Oom-la-doh-me-soh-no-fay*," he chanted.

"*Ay-fah-glo-lo-haf-ee-nay*," Brother Mayham replied. "May the Great Centralizer and the hunger of the Post-Alignment Brotherhood be with you." Brother Mayham looked quizzically at Brother Waywerd. "Hunger? Is that the right word? There are so many intricacies of the common tongue that I do not understand."

Ben groaned, his disbelief total, and all-consuming. "You have got to be kidding me," he said.

Deep inside his brain, Patrick suddenly recognized the butchers of his buffalo, and he began to wail. Ben closed his eyes and clapped his hands over his ears, but that just made the wailing worse. The monks of the Post-Alignment Brotherhood frowned at him with curiosity.

And Ben decided that maybe he should just use the machete on himself and end it all.

28.

Ben pulled his other shirt out of his pack and sniffed it. "Woof," he said aloud, rearing his head back against the stench of stale sweat and mildew. Then he shrugged.

At least it was a whole shirt.

He pulled it on, then grabbed a stick from the fire, doused it in the dirt, and rubbed the charred end over his torso to try to mask the awful smell of him with the scent of smoke. The brothers watched with wide eyes.

"Is that a cleansing ritual from your order?" Brother Waywerd asked.

"Yes! Yes!" Brother Mayham threw in. "What was it you called it? It was…ah! The Order of Patri-Benicus!" He clapped his hands delightedly at being so good at remembering things.

Ben snorted. "The Order of Patri-Benicus is dead," he grumped. "Now it's just the Disorder of Ben."

"That is very interesting," Brother Waywerd said seriously. "You must tell us about this Great Disorder. Is there a penetrative element?"

"Sorry, what?" Ben asked. Patrick hadn't stopped screaming in his brain, and it was giving him a terrible headache. *Will you shut up?* he thought.

POOOOONCH! POOOOONCH! POOOOONCH! POOOOONCH! POOOOONCH! Patrick screamed.

Ben willed the brain tumor to work faster.

"I asked if there was a penetrative element. Is that not the right word?" Brother Waywerd asked, looking to Brother Mayham for support. "It has been so long since we have spoken anything between us but Latsish, I fear my control over the common tongue is more enervated than it has ever been." Brother Mayham nodded his sad agreement.

"There are no elements," Ben said, waving the thought from the air. "Penetrative or otherwise. Jesus." He leaned back against his rock and pressed the heel of his hand against his forehead. "I don't suppose you have any aspirin that's been expired for the last four years?" he asked.

"Oh, the Great Centralizer frowns upon unnatural medicine," said Brother Mayham.

"Yes," Brother Waywerd agreed, pushing his horn-rimmed glasses up his nose. "The medicine of science is precarious, and ill-gotten. Scientists were so preoccupied with whether they *could* make cures, they didn't stop to think if they *should*."

"*Kyrie-eh-so domin-oos,*" Brother Mayham said.

"*Dom-ah doos-uh eff-ree-ay,*" Brother Waywerd replied.

"Forget I asked," Ben muttered. "Forget I ever said anything. Forget everything. Forget that I was ever here." He struggled to his feet, silently begging Patrick to stop his internal shrieking. "I should go."

"No, you mustn't!" Brother Waywerd cried, jumping up and throwing out both hands. "You are a friend here, Brother Ben! We have food, we have water, we have a Bengal tiger, we have wine—you are welcome to share our fire and energize your biology before heading off on the Centralizer's path for you."

"I'm sorry, you have *what*?" Ben asked.

"Water," said Brother Mayham. "And we would be honored to share it!"

"No, the other thing."

"Oh. Food? Yes, we have food, and what we have is yours."

"Did you say you have a *Bengal tiger*?" Ben said, loud enough to hear himself over the cacophony of Patrick. And Patrick must have heard the question, too; he immediately stopped screaming and fell into complete attention. Ben sighed with relief.

"Oh, yes!" Brother Waywerd said. "His name is Marvin. Come— sit, relax, and rejuvenate. Much has changed for us and for the Order since last we met! We have much to tell you!"

Ben rolled his head and cracked his neck. "I don't know," he said doubtfully, "I've got this voice in my head that won't stop screaming over the fact that you ate our buffalo."

"*We* ate your buffalo," Brother Mayham said, indicating all three of them. "And if memory serves, that buffalo was delicious."

Ben licked his lips at the memory. Ponch *had* been very, very good.

Don't trust them, Ben! Patrick warned. *They lure you in with their lunacy, then they rip out your heart and kill it in humiliating ways and dry strips of it over a fire and make you eat it for dessert!*

But they also have water, and non-Ponch food, Ben pointed out. *Plus, they think they have a tiger, and I one hundred percent need to figure out what the hell that's all about.*

Patrick had a hard time arguing with that.

Fine, he said, his voice haughty in Ben's ear. *But I am attending this fire under protest. Don't expect me to contribute to the conversation, because I refuse.*

"Thank Christ," Ben mumbled.

Even if you beg *me.*

Got it.

Even if you desperately need me to speak.

I got it, shut up!

Hmpf, Patrick grumped. *Fine.*

Ben sat back down, crossing his legs and holding his hands out near the fire. The monks nodded their happy approval. Ben looked first at one monk, then at the other. They watched him eagerly, their smiles wide and bright in the flickering flames of the fire. "All right, I'll bite," Ben finally said, breaking the silence. "What the hell are you two doing out here?"

"What a truly wonderful question!" Brother Mayham cried, clapping his hands together. "No one has asked us that question yet!"

"Most people we meet seem preoccupied not with why we are here, but when we are going," Brother Waywerd said sadly.

"Yes, that's true," Brother Mayham nodded. "We are not well-liked."

"You don't say," Ben said flatly.

Brother Mayham shrugged. "The world is not a place to make sense of things, I always say."

"I've never heard you say that," Brother Waywerd said suspiciously.

"I say it all the time!" Brother Mayham insisted. He turned back to Ben. "Now, to answer your question: we are here because we are spreading the Word of the Order." He said this with a breathy voice, and with large, round eyes, as if he were entrusting Ben with the secret of life itself.

Ben coughed.

"Spreading it to...whom?" he asked. He looked around. "This is a desert."

"Ah, very astute!" Brother Waywerd said cheerfully. "This is our staging ground! From here, we will coordinate our efforts, and from here, we will spread the Word of the Order to..." and here he, too, lowered his voice and took on a rather moony gaze. "...*others.*"

"Boy, am I sorry I asked," Ben sighed.

But Brother Waywerd continued, as if he had not heard him. "You see, Brother Triedit has sent Brother Mayham and myself into the western reaches so that we may spread the light of the Post-Alignment Brotherhood, and thereby grow our number."

"Wow...so all that gender transmutation must not be taking, huh?" Ben rolled his eyes.

"Not as quickly as we would like," Brother Waywerd admitted, his face pained.

"But Brother Wyldgarden has developed a very strong liking of chamomile tea!" Brother Mayham chipped in. "It is a very promising lead."

"Yes, very promising," Brother Waywerd agreed, "yet total transmutation still seems a long time in coming for the Brothers in our order. And also, there are new forces in the East that threaten our number."

"New forces," Brother Mayham agreed sadly.

"The Source is all-consuming," Brother Waywerd sighed.

"The Source is all-consuming," Brother Mayham repeated.

"So we have not increased our number through mammalian reproduction, and we are dwindling in size from the new threat. Therefore, to encourage the growth of our ranks, rather than wait for the imminent childbirth of our genderly transmutated members—"

"Which *will* happen," Brother Mayham interrupted.

"Which *will* happen," Brother Waywerd nodded, "we have been sent to spread the word of the Post-Alignment and to try to grow our numbers."

Against all rational odds, Ben actually found himself curious. "How's it going so far?" he asked.

"Oh, very well!" Brother Mayham said happily. "We have Marvin!"

"And Marvin is...the Bengal tiger?" Ben asked, to clarify to himself that he was still holding the thread of the conversation.

"Yes, Marvin the Bengal tiger!"

"Who is a tiger, and not a member of the Order." Ben looked around. "And potentially invisible, or imaginary."

"Oh, he's not invisible *or* imaginary!" Brother Mayham said. "So things are going pretty well!"

Ben shrugged. Who was he to begrudge a tumor dream or two? "Great," he said. He twirled a finger in the air. "Just the absolute fucking best, all around." He rubbed his hand against his forehead, pushing back at the dull pain. "You know, I'm actually...I'm actually really glad you guys are here," he admitted. "Better you than some of the other lunatics out here."

"Oh, how nice of you to say!" Brother Waywerd exclaimed.

Brother Mayham noticed Ben prodding his skull. He pulled his satchel close and opened the flap. "Does your head cause you such problems, Brother Ben? As I was saying earlier, we hold not to the poisonous chemicals of pre-modern science. But we *do* have our own natural remedies for dulling insidious pains." He pulled out a bladder flask and offered it to Ben. "This will help."

"Ooooh, no," Ben said, holding his hands up in refusal. "No way. I am *not* drinking frog's blood."

"Oh, no...this isn't centerwine," Brother Mayham laughed.

"It's forbidden to take centerwine beyond the boundaries of the Order's lands," Brother Waywerd said. "And besides, centerwine is not to be used for the dullification of pains. It is for stimulating mammarian development only."

"I remember, I remember," Ben groaned.

"The boobular region," Brother Mayham added helpfully. "Bazoombas."

"Yes, I know, bazoombas, I remember!" Ben squeezed his eyes shut and rubbed his temples. "My headache's going away," he lied. "I don't need it."

"Your headache doesn't *look* like it's gone away," Brother Waywerd observed. "Your headache *looks* like it's drained all the blood from your face."

"I can see your eyeballs throbbing," Brother Mayham added.

"Share our wine, Brother Ben!" Brother Waywerd encouraged him. He took the bladder flask from Brother Mayham's hands and walked it around the fire. "No frog blood whatsoever. I swear on the Great Centralizer."

Brother Mayham gasped. "Brother Waywerd! We must never make oaths against the Great Centralizer's name, She-Slash-He who will bring half of all men to glorious womanalism and who will restore a sexually vibrant and fertile seed-ground to the crotchular areas of all believers!" he cried.

"I would not cast an oath against the Great Centralizer if the oath were not of the severest truth!" Brother Waywerd retorted. "And this is among the truest truths I have ever avowed, and therefore I will not apologize, but will take my solace and comfort in the knowledge of the Great Centralizer's mercy where all things true and of moderately-good-to-extremely-good-intention are concerned." He waggled the bladder in front of Ben's nose. "Share our wine, Brother Ben. Dull your pain, and then we shall discuss your journey."

Ben raised an eyebrow up at the flask. "It's *not* centerwine?" he said, hesitant. "And there's *no* frog blood?"

"It is not centerwine. And there is no frog blood whatsoever."

"It's just regular wine?" Ben said.

"It's just regular wine," Brother Waywerd confirmed.

Ben pressed his lips into a thin line. His head *was* thumping from all the ruckus Patrick had made about his stupid fucking buffalo. And a little wine *would* help dull the pain. "All right," he conceded, reaching up and grabbing the flask. "Thank you. Thank you for this. I appreciate it." He took the bladder and saluted the monks of the Post-Alignment Brotherhood. Then he opened his mouth and squirted a stream of wine down his throat.

He smacked his lips. The wine was sweet, but earthy, with a distinct berry flavor. It was good...very good, actually. A lot better than the counterfeit schlock that passed for table wine those days. "Thank you." He squirted another mouthful of the sweet nectar and savored it on his tongue before swallowing. He handed the bladder back to Brother Waywerd. "Thank you," he said again. "I appreciate it. What's it made from?"

"Snake blood, do you like it?"

"Oh, come on!" Ben shouted, spitting and coughing into the dirt.

"Do you *not* like it?" Brother Waywerd asked, confused. "It stimulates the spermalins."

"In the testiculars," Brother Mayham added helpfully.

"No! I do not like it! No! I do not!" Ben cried. He retched. Nothing came up. He tried again. Nothing. The snake blood was part of him now. "I can feel its diseases," he gasped, feeling at his throat and his chest. "You poisoned me with wine, you sons of asses! *Again!*"

"It's flavored with cactus flowers," Brother Waywerd offered. He squirted some wine into his mouth. "Mm. Yes. You can really taste the botanicals."

Ben rolled over onto his side and curled up into a ball. "I hate everything, and also everyone," he said. "I want to be extremely clear about that."

"Is it not fermented enough?" Brother Mayham asked, furrowing his brow. "Brother Waywerd, how long did this sit in the fermenting chamber?"

Brother Waywerd shrugged. "It is hard to say with any certainty," he said, crossing his arms and tapping his chin with one finger. "But it was in there at least three days."

"Three days?!" Ben exclaimed.

"Hmm, yes, that is the proper amount of time," Brother Mayham mused. He considered this for a moment, then threw up his hands. "I cannot imagine why the extreme alcohol content has not made the wine pleasurable for Brother Ben."

"Alcohol doesn't form in three days!" Ben exploded. "The alcohol content of that snake blood is zero!"

"It also has cactus flowers!" Brother Waywerd chirped happily. "For flavor!"

"Why would you call it wine?" Ben cried. "Why would you think it would be something you could actually reasonably call 'alcohol'?!"

"Oh, strong alcohol is discouraged by the Post-Alignment Brotherhood," Brother Mayham chided. "Three days' worth is the maximum fermentation we are allowed."

"You just drank the strongest stuff we have ever made," Brother Waywerd pointed out.

Ben mopped his face with his hands. "I should have let that blonde brute smash my head in with her hammer," he moaned.

Brother Mayham looked at Brother Waywerd. Brother Waywerd looked at Brother Mayham. They shrugged.

"Let us prepare our evening meal," Brother Waywerd suggested, turning and digging through his knapsack. "Perhaps Brother Ben could use the time to tell us of his current adventure?"

"Yes, exemplary!' Brother Mayham said, stabbing a finger triumphantly into the air. "Let us forego the normal meal of beans and packaged rice, and let us warm the celebratory Spam!"

Brother Waywerd gasped. "Goodness, brother!" he cried, placing a hand against his chest. "The Spam? Truly? Is this such a night of celebration?"

"Without question!" Brother Mayham replied joyfully. "Our long-lost Brother Ben is returned to us!"

"I'm not your brother," Ben reminded him.

"And we would celebrate his journeys: the one that brought him to us, and the one that will carry him away!" Brother Mayham continued. "And we would hear of the great adventures of his friend Patrick, whose presence we miss, but whom we hope to see again soon!"

Ben's breath caught in his lungs. His head felt dizzy, prickled over with darkness. His shoulders went slack, and he slumped closer to the fire.

"Brother Ben?" Brother Mayham asked gently, standing up and looking down at Ben with alarm. "Are you okay?"

It had been years since Ben had been taken by surprise with questions about Patrick. He'd assumed he'd outgrown the shock. The hardship of it. The breathlessness of realizing that there were people who didn't understand that Patrick Deen was gone from this world, gone forever, dead and gone and never to return. At Fort Doom, they had asked him. And later, Horace had asked him. The few Red Caps who had been on the train with them the first time— the ones who hadn't been loyal to Bloom—had asked him. And it had wrenched his guts to talk about it, each and every time, but they deserved to know, and so he had faced it, faced the unbearable pain of it, but eventually he had thought, *This is it, this is the last time, there's no one else in the scattered, broken world who knows Patrick who also knows me, and who knows that we were friends, and I won't have to explain his death ever again.* And he had been foolish enough to believe that, to cling to it, for almost two years now. But here came the monks of the Post-Alignment Brotherhood, and of course they didn't know, how could they, and of course they wanted to know about Patrick, how could they not, and of course they mentioned it in passing, how could they have done otherwise, and it all made perfect sense, but even so, it broke him, because he thought he had left all that behind, but he hadn't, it was still his job, still his burden, to explain Patrick's death, to detail the horror of it, to relive the pain of it, and maybe he would never be free, and even if he would be eventually, he wasn't free now, and it cracked him inside, hearing it now from these men. These men who knew Patrick, but who didn't *know* him, and who cared about his now-life despite that.

Except there was no now-life. Not for Patrick.

Three years later, there was nothing left but a pain that would not subside.

"He's gone," Ben said quietly, his throat tight.

The proclamation grew large in the air between them, expanding so wide and so heavy that it threatened to smother the flames. And indeed, the fire seemed to flicker low for a moment. But then Brother Waywerd nodded solemnly, and he raised the bladder toward the sky. "To Patrick," he said, and he drank down a gulp in Patrick's honor. He passed the wine to Brother Mayham, who toasted their fallen friend as well. Then he offered the flask to Ben.

Ben considered it. He pushed the tears away from his cheeks. He had cried more in the last few days than he thought anyone was capable of anymore, this far down the post-apocalyptic timeline. "Ah, fuck it," he said, and he snatched the bladder, opened his mouth, and squeezed in a stream of wine. "To Patrick," he said, and he drank.

"Well!" Brother Mayham said, clapping his hands and breaking the silence that followed. "It *is* a celebration, then! A celebration of life, and a celebration of those who lived!"

"Yes!" Brother Waywerd cried. He grabbed three cans of Spam from inside his knapsack and held them triumphantly up to the moon. "Tonight, we honor the Great Funnel of Life!"

Ben snorted. "Don't you mean the great circle of life?"

"Oh, no," Brother Waywerd chuckled. "In our Order, we believe life is not a circle, because circles go around and around, continuing for all eternity. Circles are infinite, and life is certainly not. Therefore, the idea of life as a circle is…hmm," he said, tapping his finger to his lips. "What is the word in the common tongue?" he asked.

"Dumb-dumb," Brother Mayham suggested.

"Ah, yes; the idea that life is a circle is dumb-dumb. Rather, we say life is a funnel. You are thrown into the top, you spin around for a time, and at the end, you slide to the center and drop out the bottom. It is the Great Funnel of Life."

"To the Great Funnel of Life!" Brother Mayham cheered. He drank deeply of the snake wine. His face soured. "Perhaps more cactus flower next time," he mused.

Brother Waywerd peeled open the Spam cans and pushed them into the ash near the fire. "Brother Ben!" he said jovially, rubbing his hands together. "While the celebratory Spam warms, regale us with the story of your current adventure. From whence do you come? To whence do you go?"

Ben sighed. "Where do I even start?" he said, shaking his head. The last few days were so full of horror and sadness and adventure and even a little joy — joy at seeing Patrick, at having their old conversations, even if doing that meant Ben's own impending death by cancerous tumor.

But when he thought about it…when he really, actually thought about it…the whole thing came through pretty easily.

"There was a raid," he said. "Our train was attacked. It was a good plan, a strong attack…and I tried to protect what they wanted, but it didn't work. It backfired. It backfired so hard. They took what they wanted, but…they took more than that." Ben shook his head. "They took more than they know. And I've been chasing them. I need to get back what they took, so I've been chasing them. I thought getting there would be the easy part, and taking it back would be hard, and I'm sure taking it back *will* be difficult, but the getting there has been…" He stopped, and he exhaled hard while he searched for the right word. "The getting there has been fucking stupid," he finally decided. "But I need to get it back; I need to get my bag, and the guy who sent the raid, he's some guy called the Doctor, and he has a Lab, and *that* sounds ominous, and it turns out, it probably *is* ominous, because the rumors are all about his experiments with dusters—that was the hard-on I was talking about earlier…they say he has a lot of dusters, and he conducts a lot of experiments, and he's a psychopath, and you can't even get into the actual Lab because of the armies of dusters, and maybe that's true, shit, I don't know, I don't know how I'm going to get inside, but I *have* to get inside, okay, because they have my backpack, and I need to get it back. I shouldn't have even— fuck." He shook his head and held up a hand, strong against the night. "It's my fault. I need it back. I need to get it back."

Brother Mayham looked up, his head cocked in confusion. Brother Waywerd met Brother Mayham's eyes, and they both shrugged. "Brother Ben, remind me why you hoped to approach our fire?" Brother Mayham said.

"We found you in slashed shirts, with shoes for hands," Brother Waywerd reminded him.

"Yes," Brother Mayham nodded, "slashed shirts, with shoes for hands. That seems extra of the ordinary. Why would you take such measures to reach our humble fire?"

"Because I need help," Ben sighed. "I need food and water. I do *not* need your gross-ass snake-blood wine," he clarified, "but I do need enough to keep me going another day or two. I'm low on supplies, I've got a psychopath on my tail, and I have no idea how much further it is to the Lab, so anything you can spare, I would be very grateful for. I have barely enough food and water for the night, and I definitely don't have enough to make it back, if I get out of this stupid mission alive. Whoever's fire this was, they were my only hope." Then he added, "I'm weirdly glad it was you two."

Brother Mayham and Brother Waywerd exchanged a confused look.

"Brother Ben," Brother Waywerd said, pushing his glasses back up his nose, "where, exactly, do you think you *are*?"

Ben lifted his head from his hands. He stared at Brother Waywerd.

"Is this some sort of Buddhist shit?" he asked.

"Oh, we're not Buddhist," Brother Mayham explained, furrowing his brow. "We're with the Order of the Post-Alignm—"

"I know, I know—I know what order you're with," Ben groaned. "And I have no idea where I am. Weren't you just listening? Probably about a million fucking miles from the train that's probably not waiting for me anymore, and about a million fucking more from this stupid fucking Lab!"

Brother Mayham closed his eyes and looked a little pained. "Forgive me, I'm not as well-versed in the common tongue as I would like to be, as you know. But am I to assume that your words are bolstered with crude epithets of frustration?"

"Yes!" Ben shouted, throwing his hands up in the air. "Yes! Yes! Epithets of frustration! For fuck's sake, yes, I am *seething* with crude epithets of frustration!"

Brother Waywerd tilted his head to one side. "But...Brother Ben," he said quietly, his voice muddled with confusion, "there's no reason to be. You're not a million miles from the Lab." He lifted his hand and pointed toward the north. "The Lab is right over those hills."

Ben started. He pointed at the hills over their heads. "*Those* hills?!" he said.

Brother Waywerd nodded. "Yes."

Ben's jaw fell open. He kept his finger pointed at the low mountain range. "Those hills right there?"

"Yes."

"The Lab is on the other side of those hills right there?!"

"Yes!"

Ben gaped. His eyes felt like they just might fall right out of their sockets and float away like helium balloons. "Wha—? Bu—? Wh—?" he stammered. His brain clicked and spun, clicked and spun, like an engine trying to turn over. "*Well, why didn't you say that in the first place?*"

Brother Waywerd shrugged. "I assumed you knew."

"No, I didn't know!" Ben shrieked, jumping up from the ground. "The Lab is *right there?!*"

"You've come an awfully long way in the right direction for someone who's been lost the whole time," Brother Mayham observed.

"Holy shit, I *made* it!" Ben said, shaking his head in disbelief. He gave a low whistle. "I am a human compass. I am a glorious goddamn human compass!" He began to pace around the fire. "You know, I always knew I had a gift," he insisted. "People gave me a hard time, and maybe I didn't *always* know which way Lake Michigan was, and maybe I didn't *always* point north when I thought I was pointing north, but I *knew* that deep down inside, I really had something. Ha!" He clapped his hands and jumped up and down, stomping out the desert dirt. "I actually made it to the Lab! Wow." He stopped jumping and clutched his side, where a sharp pain had formed in staunch protest of his uncoordinated celebration. He plopped back down onto the ground. "I don't want to jinx it," he said, grinning despite the pain, "but that was easy."

"You were just saying it was very hard," Brother Mayham pointed out.

"I never said that," Ben replied, waving the thought away. He laughed again. "I did it. I *actually* did it!"

"You still have to get over those hills. There are rattlesnakes," Brother Waywerd said helpfully.

"And scorpions," Brother Mayham added.

"Oh, yes, there are *many* scorpions," Brother Waywerd agreed.

"Shut up, stop ruining things," Ben snapped.

"Also, Brother Ben, I don't know if you've been properly warned. But Brother Mayham and I have looked out over the place of the Lab, and it is completely surrounded by a horde of those oozing green deadman monsters."

"I said, stop ruining things!" Ben grumbled. "It doesn't matter. I'll figure it out." He rubbed his hands together excitedly. "Okay. Okay! We are back in business! How's that Spam looking? Yessir! A little food, a little water, and let's get this shit done." He turned his stare into steel, and he crossed his arms, striking his most dramatic pose. "I've got a goddamn job to finish."

"Yes, and we'll go with you!" Brother Mayham chirped happily.

Ben's face fell. His dramatic pose loosened. "Oh. Uh...no, I-I'm actually more of a...solo act," he explained gently.

Brother Mayham looked at him curiously for a moment. Then a light of understanding washed across his face. "Oh!" he said brightly. "No, I didn't mean all the way to the Lab! Ha ha! No, no. Goodness! No! Ha ha! Storming the Lab is certain and absolute death. Even if you somehow made it in, you wouldn't make it out. Not with the militia that lives inside. And even if you made it past *them,* they say the inner sanctum of the Lab is where the doctor you speak of lives and carries out his terrible experiments." Here, Brother Mayham's voice became soft and furtive, as if he were afraid of being overheard. "They say he makes the monsters out of dead men."

"They say he reanimates them," Brother Waywerd added, shivering at the thought. "He uses electricity, and he sews up their wounds with barbed wire, to make them stronger."

"So they say," Brother Mayham said.

"So they say," Brother Waywerd agreed.

"*Som-la doh-ti far-go-lah,*" Brother Mayham chanted sadly.

"*Dos-toy Ev-sko tar-na-lee,*" Brother Waywerd replied.

"No, we will not accompany you to the Lab," Brother Mayham concluded. "I, for one, am not yet at the bottom of my Great Funnel." He gasped then, and placed a hand to his chest, as if he had made an impolite offense. "Oh, but I *do* think it is *wonderful* that *you* have come to the bottom of *your* Great Funnel, Brother Ben!"

"Oh, yes!" Brother Waywerd agreed. "And to face the bottom of your Great Funnel with such *cheer*! What courage!"

"Yes, we have the utmost respect for your choice," Brother Mayham nodded. "It's just that *we* would prefer to live."

"For now," Brother Waywerd said.

"For now," Brother Mayham agreed. "But if you would accept the company, we will walk with you to the top of the hill."

"Oh! Yes!" Brother Waywerd said brightly. "We'll walk with you to the top of the hill!"

"We have to go there anyway," Brother Mayham explained.

Ben raised an eyebrow. "Why?" he asked. "What's at the top of the hill?"

Brother Mayham laughed. "Why, Marvin is, of course! Have we not mentioned Marvin?"

"Oh, I'm sure we mentioned Marvin," Brother Waywerd said. "He's a Bengal tiger. We shall walk with you as far as Marvin, and then we will send you on your way."

"To fall out of the bottom of your Great Funnel," Brother Waywerd explained.

"Yes, to your death," Brother Mayham said brightly.

Ben's mood took a sharp downward shift. He glowered down at the fire and snatched up a warm can of Spam. He prodded the meat with two fingers and began tearing off little chunks. The monks' prognostications about his Great Funnel had pretty much evaporated his hunger, but what the hell. He needed to build up his strength.

The Lab was close.

And it was going to be a long night.

29.

"You see, Marvin is an important tool in our plans of brotherhood expansion," Brother Waywerd explained as they climbed the dusty hill in the moonlight, led by Brother Mayham's lantern. "Marvin is our pit boss."

Ben stopped. "Whoa, wait," he said, closing his eyes and shaking his head. He planted his hands on his hips. "Pit boss?"

"Yes," said Brother Waywerd. "Is that not the proper word? I apologize, I'm not—"

"You're not fluent in the common tongue, I got it, I got it." Ben made an annoyed gesture with his hand, and they resumed their climb up the hill. "Why do you think a Bengal tiger is your...pit boss?"

"It's about spreading the word in a non-threatening way, you see." They were all three breathing hard as they struggled up the hill in the dark, and the irregular pattern of Brother Waywerd's speech made the whole sermon that much more idiotic. "We have modeled our outreach program after the manner in which Native American tribes used their brightly-lit and often dirty casinos to spread the glory of their culture."

"Uh...I'm pretty sure that's *not* why they ran casinos," Ben pointed out.

"Spinning dials!" Brother Waywerd continued, unabashed. "Whirling lights! Inexpensive cocktails! Waterfalls of coins! These were the things that made the Indian tribes great before the great, dramatic cassocks of European holy men took hold of their simple native imaginations and caused the great conversion from gambling-based theology into a more fashion-forward religion."

"I cannot imagine the incredibly specific upbringing you must have had to make you think that *that* is the true history of the Native Americans. I bet it was just an absolute haywire wonderland," Ben said. He wondered if he didn't actually feel a little envious of an upbringing like that. It was probably chock full of completely idiotic wonder. He wished he had some more idiotic wonder in his life sometimes. He sighed with a touch of sadness. "I just grew up middle class in Missouri."

"The Missouri tribe was well-revered in the Old World for its prowess at the keno board," Brother Mayham said sagely.

"There was no Missouri tribe," Ben pointed out.

"Eventually they became known as the Pokenos," Brother Waywerd continued, "and that is how the Pocono Mountains got their name."

"The Poconos aren't even *in* Missouri," Ben said, shaking his head. He took it back; idiotic wonder was overrated. "And how does any of this make a Bengal tiger the pit boss of your sex-change religion?"

"Ah!" Brother Waywerd cried, thrusting a finger into the air, and losing himself so completely in his triumph that he missed a step, stumbled over a rock, and fell onto a cactus. "I'm fine! I'm fine!" he screeched, peeling himself off the plant and hopping from one foot to the other, his face screwed up in pain. "Praise be the Great Centralizer! *Taw-nay brawnay oom-lat-tey!*"

"Accidental flagellation by nature is an extraordinary gift from the Great Centralizer," Brother Mayham explained.

"Cool religion," Ben replied, rolling his eyes.

Brother Waywerd fanned his punctured body with his hands and tried his best to smile. "As I was saying," he continued, "the pit boss is central to the casino's survival. Without the pit boss, there is corruption, betrayal, and loss. Am I using those words correctly?"

"You're making casinos sound a little bit like a Lifetime movie, but sure, I follow you," Ben said, nodding. "So what?"

"So the pit boss is the lynch pin to the entire casino operation. And in much the same way, Marvin is the key to the survival of *our* operation."

"And your operation is…what, exactly?" Ben asked.

Brother Waywerd rubbed his hands together with enthusiasm. He looked slyly at Brother Mayham. Brother Mayham's eyebrows jiggled up and down, and his tongue wagged out of his mouth.

They were both very, very excited.

"Brother Ben," Brother Mayham said, now hopping from one foot to the other and clapping his hands like a loon, "we are going to spread the gospel of the Post-Alignment Brotherhood through the thrills of our very own traveling circus!"

Brother Waywerd squealed with delight and joined Brother Mayham in the hopping from foot to foot. "Picture it!" he cried. "A three-ring circus! Clowns over there! Acrobats over there! And Marvin the tiger in the center! What a wonder! A fully trained, precisely perfect circus orchestration that travels the American West and, through its revelry and joy, spreads the good word of the Post-Alignment Brotherhood!"

"We haven't exactly decided *how* we'll use joy to spread the word," Brother Mayham admitted. "Our order is not historically a brotherhood of revelry."

"Yes, that's true...we haven't *quite* threaded those two disparate and dissociated ideas together. The circus on one hand, and a sexual transmutation for the purposes of the propagation of Brother Triedit's vision on the other, we can't...*quite*...seem to find a way to bridge that gap."

"Oh, but it *will* be fun, won't it, Brother Ben?" Brother Mayham gushed, clasping his hands over his heart.

Ben shrugged. "Well, it's dumb. But I'll be honest, it's not the dumbest thing you weirdos have got going on."

"Encouragement!" Brother Waywerd beamed. A single tear spilled over his eyelid and rolled down his cheek. He brushed it away with a gentle finger. "Thank you, Brother Ben," he whispered. He reached out and grabbed for Ben's hand. Ben pulled back, and the monk grabbed empty air. But he still looked very touched. He held that empty air tightly and whispered again, "Thank you."

Ben cleared his throat. Their affection made him uncomfortable. "Okay, so...we're almost to the top of the hill, where's this supposed— *JESUS CHRIST!*" Ben screamed and dove backward as an actual tiger leapt out into the moonlight just a few feet from where he'd been standing. Still screaming, Ben crawled behind a rock that was way too small to conceal his body, and he clutched it tightly, as if gravity might upend itself, and he'd float free from the earth if he didn't dig his nails into the stone. "Fuck, it's a *tiger—fuck!*" he yelled.

Brother Mayham pursed his lips and looked down at Ben, confused. "Yes, that's what we said." He looked at Brother Waywerd. "We did say Marvin was a tiger, did we not?"

"Yes, several times," Brother Waywerd agreed.

"I didn't know you meant an *actual fucking tiger!*" Ben said. "I thought we would come up here and find some stuffed animal kid's toy, and you'd be like, 'This is Marvin, our real-life tiger,' and I'd say, 'Wow, that's exactly what I expected from you lunatics.' This is a *real tiger!*"

Marvin padded around in the little clearing of earth, his tail swishing slowly, his yellow-orange eyes holding Ben in their sharp, reflective stare. He was a fully-grown adult male, with vivid black stripes slashing across caramel-orange fur. He was over ten feet long from head to tail, and he snorted as he paced the earth, sending little dust devils spinning up into the night air. There was a thick iron collar fixed around his neck, secured to a long, heavy chain with half-inch welded links. The chain trailed behind the tiger and led to an iron fencepost that had been hammered into the ground back in the shadows of a small grouping of cacti. Marvin strained against his collar as he tested the limits of his confinement, but the chain pulled him back.

Ben reached down and patted at his crotch. He was relieved to find that he had not wet himself.

"Why in the absolute fuck do you have a *tiger?*" he demanded. He slowly raised himself up from the ground, his eyes locked with the animal's. He took a few more steps back down the mountain, holding his hands up high, in case that helped.

"Isn't he wonderful?" Brother Mayham said cheerfully.

"Who gave you a *tiger?!*"

"We found him!" Brother Waywerd replied.

"You *found* him?!"

"Yes! The Great Centralizer works in mysterious ways."

"And not always through felines," Brother Mayham pointed out.

"Yes, that's true, Brother Mayham. In fact, *rarely* through felines, I'd say."

"Well, not *that* rarely, brother."

"This is—" Ben said. His mouth continued to move, but no more words came out...only the sounds that make up the beginnings of letters.

With an impressive and enduring strength that he hadn't known he had, Ben managed to tear his eyes away from the tiger. This allowed him to focus his full visual incredulity on the monks, and he focused it on them as hard as he could. "You two should not have a tiger!" he cried.

"He's for our circus," Brother Mayham said.

"I don't care if he's for the second coming of Jesus Christ, he shouldn't be here!" The tiger gnashed its teeth at this remark, and Ben screamed.

"I think you're hurting his feelings," Brother Waywerd said with a frown.

"Marvin is sensitive," Brother Mayham explained.

"He is a wild animal who is at the top of the food chain!" Ben cried.

But Brother Mayham laughed. "Brother Ben, surely you know the Great Centralizer has put *humans* at the top of the food chain! This is true in almost all important religions."

"Not in South Carolinian Root Revival," Brother Waywerd pointed out.

"No, not in South Carolinian Root Revival," Brother Mayham agreed. "They believe that the top rung of the evolutionary ladder belongs to the silky camellia shrub."

"They *do* make some interesting points," Brother Waywerd mused.

"That is *blasphemy*, brother!" Brother Mayham shrieked.

"I don't care who thinks what is at the top. I am telling you—right now, in this moment, unless you've got a fucking bazooka under your robes, that tiger is *it*," Ben said, leveling a finger at Marvin.

Brother Waywerd looked absolutely crestfallen. His cheeks drooped sadly, and his eyes wobbled with the tears that coated his irises. "I wish you wouldn't say such things in front of Marvin, where he can hear you so plainly," the monk said, stepping up to the tiger and rubbing his head. "We already told you he's sensitive."

"Don't pet the fucking tiger!" Ben shrieked. "What are you *doing?*"

But Brother Waywerd shook his head sadly. "Brother Ben, you hear, but you do not believe. Marvin is a gift from the Great Centralizer. He is central to the spreading of our message. We will build a glorious circus around him, and he will help the ranks of the order to swell." He scratched behind Marvin's ears. Marvin seemed to like that.

"Marvin is kind and gentle," Brother Mayham agreed, watching with simple pleasure as his brother-in-the-word patted the tiger. "He is practically a full member of the Post-Alignment Brotherhood, he is of such a sweet nature. He would never raise so much as a claw against myself, or Brother Waywerd. Marvin is a calm and contemplative creature, good-natured and loving and—*SWEET CENTRALIZER, BROTHER WAYWERD, WATCH OUT!*" he screamed.

Ben watched with horror as Marvin sprang into action, twisting his head as quick as a snap and sinking his teeth into Brother Waywerd's arm. Brother Waywerd screamed as Marvin tore through his flesh. "It's just a misunderstanding!" he shrieked. "Marvin is kind! He is—*OH CHRIST, HE SLICED MY STOMACH OPEN!*"

And it was true. With his huge, sharp teeth still sunk into Brother Waywerd's arm, the tiger had swiped at the monk's abdomen with one great paw. His claws had torn through the muscle and tissue like a warm knife through butter, and Brother Waywerd's insides began unspooling themselves through the seams, spilling out onto the desert earth. Ben clamped a hand over his mouth. He turned and vomited into the brush. Through the suffocating sounds of his own heaving, he heard Brother Mayham scream, "*Bad Marvin! Bad Marvin!*" And then there was another crunch, and when Ben made the mistake of looking back over his shoulder, he saw that Brother Mayham no longer had a face.

The two monks collapsed to the ground in a heap. Brother Waywerd gasped, his eyes bright with disbelief, and Brother Mayham gave one last guttural moan, his throat coughing up frothy bubbles of blood through the space where his jaw used to be. And then the only sounds were the crunching, slurping, and tearing of Marvin the tiger enjoying the fresh meat of his kill.

Ben retched again, but he had nothing more to give except bile and air. He stumbled away from the scene, half-watching the tiger's movements, half-turning away from the unspeakable gore. Marvin disinterestedly watched Ben make his retreat, blood dripping from his muzzle, strings of Brother Mayham—or maybe Brother Waywerd—caught between his teeth. Then Ben melted into the shadows, scrambling over the far side of the mountain, and the tiger resumed his meal, pulling against his chain.

30.

Can I share an unpopular opinion? Patrick asked.

Can it wait until I'm not dedicating every ounce of energy to trying to hear if a tiger is sneaking up on us? Ben shot back, annoyed.

It can. *It* can *wait. But it* won't. *I like to be heard,* Patrick explained. *Besides, there's no point in listening for a tiger. If it wants to sneak up on you, it's going to sneak up on you. You won't know you're prey until it's too late.*

Great, Ben thought miserably. He had skirted around to the far side of the hill and was going around it rather than over it. He was scared, he was exhausted, and he still felt sick to his stomach. *Fine. What? What is your unpopular opinion?*

I'm glad you asked! Patrick replied. *I think those monks deserved it. Cosmically. For Ponch.*

Oh, for crying out loud.

Hear me out! Just hear me out. Monks eat buffalo; monks show no remorse. Nature hides its awful vengeance for three years, until tiger finally eats monks. It's all a part of the Great Funnel of Life.

I don't think "man eaten by tiger" has been part of the Great Funnel of Life for a few centuries.

Well, that's how these things go, Patrick said. *You go along for a millennium or two, not having to worry about tigers, and all of a sudden, bam—eaten by tiger. I mean, you throw a tiger into that funnel, and I'll tell you this, bloody chunks are falling out the bottom.*

"Stop," Ben whispered. "I'm already sick enough." He steadied himself with one hand against the slope of the small mountain and stepped carefully over a small animal den in the dirt. He straightened up and patted the dust from his hands. "Besides," he said, nodding out at the landscape before him, "we're there."

He'd lost track of the time that had passed since he'd stumbled upon the monks, but now, as he stood on the far side of the desert hill, the east had already begun its pre-sunrise glow, and it illuminated the desert before him with an otherworldly pink and purple light.

The first thing Ben saw was the building, what he assumed must be the Lab itself. It was actually an old airplane hangar, abandoned long before M-Day, by the look of it, and repurposed as a secret stronghold now. The doors of the hangar were all closed; Ben saw several small windows above each door. He was certain there would be men and women with long-range rifles stationed behind those windows, guarding the entrances. There was the large entrance on the front end, of course, where small aircraft had once wheeled into the building, but there were smaller doors, too—three of them set right into the larger airplane door, and several more lining the broad side of the hangar.

Huge, rectangular holes had been cut into the metal structure along the side, and other, smaller structures outside the hangar were connected to the main building through a series of what looked like massive duct-work tunnels that had been fitted into the rectangular slots in the hangar, so that it looked like one massive warehouse with eight large pods sticking out of the sides. One of the pods was an RV; another was a huge, multi-room camping tent. One was a prefabricated work shed, and one was a massive metal shipping container.

It's like something out of a super low-budget sci-fi movie, Patrick decided.

Ben nodded. It was exactly like that.

There are underground sections too, Patrick said. *Look at those concrete pads. They have hatch doors that lead down.* And indeed, the entire property was ringed by large concrete platforms, about eight feet by eight feet, that extended about three feet up from the ground. Set into the top of each platform was a round door with a handle.

"Whatever they're doing in there, they've got a shit-ton of space to do it," Ben muttered.

Lots of potential escape routes, Patrick pointed out. *If things go bad inside. Or* when *things go bad inside, I guess I should say. It's definitely gonna go bad inside.*

"Thanks. Your optimism is always appreciated," Ben grunted.

Hey, here's some good news! Patrick said. *At least there's not actually an army of dusters swarming around the entire...*

His voice trailed off as the first light of the sun crested over the far horizon. The pink-purple light of the desert twilight gave way to a rosier glow, and looking now, they could see a mass of shapes writhing in the darkness, small from this distance, but unmistakable. They hadn't noticed them earlier because the desert floor around the hangar was so thick with dusters that they looked like one solid mass. But now, in the brightening light of dawn, they saw that the structure was completely surrounded by an entire horde of dusters, thousands of them, shuffling and milling around like a hive of lazy bees.

"How are they so contained?" Ben whispered, his voice an equal mixture of fear and awe. "There are no fences...why aren't they spreading out?"

"Dry moats," Patrick said, appearing in the darkness and crouching down next to Ben. He pulled Ben down to the ground too, in case there were lookouts. "See?" He pointed down at the base of their hill. A wide channel had been dug into the earth, about twelve feet wide and maybe twenty feet deep—too wide to jump, and too deep for a person to climb out on his own, without the help of a ladder or a rope. The channel curved around in a huge, wide circle that ringed the entire property, a dry moat that enclosed about ten full acres of desert land. The channel was full of dusters who had either jumped or fallen in. They were too mindless to help each other out, so they milled around, bumping into each other, snarling and hissing.

"Pretty elegant solution," Patrick admitted.

"Why are they so docile?" Ben asked. "They're not running. Have you ever seen a duster not just fucking *furious* and *running?*"

"Good question," Patrick said. He scratched his cheek. "Maybe they're too sick. You can see how many of them are leaking green, even from here."

"Maybe they're too hungry," Ben countered. "Do dusters get weak if they don't eat?"

"Everything gets weak if it doesn't eat."

"So it could be that."

"Could be both."

Ben shook his head in amazement. "How the hell do the bandits get in and out?" he wondered aloud.

Patrick chewed his bottom lip as he pondered this question. "I have no idea," he finally admitted.

"Underground tunnel?"

"Maybe," Patrick said, but his voice was heavy with doubt. "They'd have to go deep to get beneath their own moat. And we know they're bringing out horses." He shook his head slowly, thinking. "No, it doesn't seem likely."

Ben rubbed his jaw, and he sighed, incredulous. "What the fuck," he said.

"Yeah. What the fuck," Patrick agreed.

"So what do we do?" Ben asked. "Just wait until someone goes in or comes out? So we can see the entrance?"

"Maybe," Patrick said, considering. "Or..."

Ben raised an eyebrow. His eyes slid over to his imaginary friend. "Or?" he said.

Patrick looked back at him. "You're not going to like it," he warned.

"Oh, I'm sure I won't," Ben replied. "I like almost no plan you've ever come up with. I don't see any reason why I would start liking one now."

"It's worse than the bat-shit crazy, handicapped macaw plan."

"I have no doubt."

"It's worse than that time we got jumped by Spiver because I wanted to watch the puppet show."

"Just tell me."

"Well...I was just thinking...it might be useful for us to introduce a little bit of chaos into the situation. Cause a huge distraction, and take out a bunch of the dusters in the process."

"Okay," Ben said. "And where are we going to find that kind of distraction?"

"Well, that's the thing, Benny Boy. It would need to be a distraction that can jump a twelve-foot ditch…and then cause some real damage. I mean, some *real* damage."

Ben's heart sank. "Ooooh, no," he said.

"I told you you wouldn't like it."

"Absolutely not."

"Ben, I'm just saying…"

"*Absolutely not.*"

"When you have access to a tiger, you should use it."

"No. No way in hell. Absolutely not. You hear me? No. Way. In. *Hell.* There is *no fucking way* I am actually going *back there* for that tiger."

•

A little while later, they were back by the tiger.

"This is absolute fucking lunacy," Ben muttered through his tightly clenched teeth. "This is the dumbest thing we have ever, *ever* done, and that is saying a *lot.*"

"Yeah, but it's *exciting!*" Patrick squealed.

The tiger was lying down in the clearing, propped up like a sphinx. Brother Mayham's femur stuck up between the tiger's paws…or maybe it was Brother Waywerd's. Marvin wasn't interested in the bone at this particular moment. He just held it there between his paws, like an unlit requiem candle.

Aside from the femur, there wasn't much left of the monks: tattered pieces of cotton robes, a pair of feet still in their sandals, and a few small piles of bone, gristle, and other human gore. "I don't know how much a tiger normally eats," Patrick said admiringly, "but I'm going to go ahead and be the one to say it: I am *impressed.*"

"What is he doing?" Ben murmured without moving his lips, hovering at what he desperately hoped was outside the reach of the tiger's chain. "Why is he staring at us?"

"Probably the same reason I like to look at pigs and think, 'Wow, I can't believe delicious bacon comes from *that.*'"

"Helpful."

Ben slid one foot slowly up the hill. Marvin watched, but did not move. Ben followed with his other foot, and in this painfully slow manner, he inched his way up toward the high ground. Patrick followed him with his regular, easy steps, his hands stuffed casually into his pockets.

"What's our plan, here?" Ben whispered.

"Well, Tiptoe McShuffleton, in sixteen days, when you finally reach the stake in the ground, you should slip the chain off of it and ride Marvin into battle against the zombie horde."

Ben shook his head and gritted his teeth. "There is so much about that plan that is so awful," he said.

"But also so much that is just so, *so* awesome," Patrick countered.

"So we slip the chain. The tiger goes free. We turn him loose on the dusters. We run in during the chaos and get inside the hangar."

"Yes, basically, but I want to be clear that you keep saying 'we,'; this is really a 'you' thing. I'm just here for moral support. I would never do something as stupid as this."

Ben snorted. "This is exactly the level of stupid that you would do," he said.

Patrick tapped his lips as he thought about this. Then he shrugged. "Yeah, that's true."

Ben shuffled around the tiger along the perimeter of the chain's reach. Marvin watched him out of the sides of his eyes, and when Ben passed beyond his field of vision, the tiger shook his head, licked his lips, and began to gnaw quietly on the femur. Ben lifted his eyebrows in surprise. "Maybe he's not interested in us," he decided.

"He's probably full. I want to reiterate that two monks is a *lot* of monks to eat in one sitting."

"That means we're probably safe. Right? Tigers only attack when they're hungry...right?"

"It's a tiger, Benny Boy, not my Aunt Dottie. Now, Aunt Dottie, *she* would only attack when she got hangry, and boy, did she *turn*. It was like going to visit a food werewolf every Christmas. Tigers, though...tigers are not Aunt Dotties. They might attack for all sorts of reasons."

"Like what?" Ben asked quietly, skirting around behind Marvin's haunches, still far out of reach.

"Like if you threaten their young, or if you invade their territory. Wild animals like personal space. Animal Planet was always *very* clear on that point."

"How much personal space? What's the bubble?"

"If you're asking if walking up to the stake and mucking with the chain puts you squarely in Marvin's personal territory, the answer is definitely yes."

"Great," Ben moaned. "Why are we doing this again?"

"Do you have a better plan?"

Ben pressed his lips together in frustration. "I cannot fucking believe that I don't," he grumbled. He shook out his fingers and puffed out his cheeks, taking six short blasts of breath. "Okay," he said, shifting his weight like a boxer, rolling his shoulders and bouncing on the balls of his feet. "Okay. I can do this. Okay. I'm gonna run in, free the chain, and run out."

"Oh, God, no—don't *run,* are you *insane?!*" Patrick cried, throwing up his hands. "Are you *trying* to get mauled?!"

"Well, I don't know!" Ben hissed. "I never watched fucking Animal Planet!"

"Obviously! Cripes, Ben, you don't go *running* at a *tiger!*"

"Well! I want it over with fast!" Ben replied.

"Unless the 'it' you're talking about is *your life,* I *strongly* suggest moving slowly," Patrick said.

Ben grumped. "Fine. I will walk *slowly* toward the Bengal tiger, wet myself, shit myself, and hope against hope that I can set him free before he rips my fucking face off."

"And don't forget about after," Patrick added.

"After what?"

"You also don't want him to rip your face off *after* you set him free. He'll have more free rein to do that when he's loose."

"Jesus, Patrick, *why* am I doing this?!"

"Because when you have a tiger, you use it!" Patrick said happily.

"Great."

"And because, honestly, with the tiger, you have a chance. With the dusters, you're dead. And if the dusters somehow *don't* kill you, the bandits will. It's really weird if you think about it, but if you want inside that hangar, teaming up with a tiger really is your best option."

Ben looked doubtfully at the tiger. "I'm not entirely sure the other options aren't preferable."

But Patrick waved this away as nonsense. "Look, here's what you do. You take your machete—"

"Oh yeah, I have a machete," Ben said, brightening considerably.

"You take your machete, you creep in, you free the tiger, and then you dive into the cover of those cacti over there. If the tiger comes, you blow him up with the machete!"

"Not how machetes work."

"And if that fails, just curl up into a ball, and the cacti will protect you."

Ben sucked on his bottom lip and twirled the machete as he surveyed the grouping of cacti and contemplated this plan. "What if *I* get stabbed by the cacti?"

Patrick shrugged. "Wouldn't be the first time."

"True."

"And let me ask you this: which is better, being stabbed by cactus needles, or being stabbed by the stomach acid of a Bengal tiger?"

"I have a guess," Ben said miserably. He took some deep breaths and swung his arms like a swimmer preparing to dive. "I can't do this, I can't do this, I can't do this..."

"Yes you can!" Patrick grabbed Ben by the shoulders and gave him a good shake. "Listen to me! Yes! You! Can! You can tame the wild tiger! Haven't you read *Life of Pi*?"

"No."

"It's easy! Tigers are *very* easy to tame. If I learned one thing from that book, it's that tigers are *very* easy to tame."

"Is that true? Did the book really say that?"

Patrick shrugged. "Sure."

"Well, how did they do it in the book?"

"Excellent question! It's not a *they*, it's a *he*. And the 'he' is a very young boy. And if a very young boy can tame a tiger, surely a grown-albeit-rather-short-for-a-human man can do it." Patrick went into full professor mode, clasping his hands behind his back and pacing along the side of the hill. "The thing that *really* helped tame the tiger was the fact that the stupid thing was scared of water." He looked out at the desert that stretched to every horizon. "I guess we don't have that going for us," he said.

"What else?" Ben asked.

Patrick held up his hands and shrugged. "Beats me. I only read the back cover."

"Great."

"I do know this, though," Patrick said, wagging his finger knowingly at Ben's chest, "the longer you wait, the more time old Marvin's digestive system has to work. The longer you wait, the hungrier he'll be."

Ben grimaced. "Fine," he said. "Fuck it. Fine." He gripped the machete in both hands, holding it like a baseball bat. He took a deep breath. "If I die, just remember: I've always hated you."

"You're not going to die. You're going to conquer that tiger, and you're going to ride him into the Lab!"

"I'm not riding him."

"We'll see."

Ben took a cautious step inside the perimeter. He clenched his teeth and kept his eyes trained on Marvin. But the tiger was still engaged with his bone. Ben took another step, and another, treading softly across the desert dirt, his sneakers quietly scuffing the dust. His heart hammered in his chest, and he couldn't catch his breath. His palms itched, and he tried to tighten his grip on the machete, but his hands just spun on the handle, slick with sweat. *What am I doing, what am I doing, what am I doing,* he chanted to himself, but his brain was white noise, full of the static of danger. Soon he was ten feet from the stake…then five feet… then three feet…

Marvin lifted his head and flicked his ears. Ben froze. Sweat spilled uncomfortably down his back and into the waist of his jeans. Marvin turned his head, and Ben saw the creature's massive muzzle in profile. The tiger opened his mouth and yawned, and Ben's knees gave out as he stared in awful horror at the size of the creature's teeth, still flecked with the pink foam of blood. Ben fell to the ground, clutching the machete. Marvin turned, and his yellow eyes bore directly into Ben's. Ben's insides melted into water, and through the fuzzy void of his brain, a single insane thought came buzzing through: *Maybe if I pee myself, he'll think I am my own territory.*

The tiger wrinkled his nose, and his flat, pink tongue lolled out of his mouth through his teeth. He considered Ben in this manner for a few moments, a few long moments that felt like years…and then the tiger pushed itself up onto its feet, circled around, and padded slowly toward Ben, dragging the chain behind him.

"Oh, fuck-fuck-fuck," Ben gasped. He scooted forward on his shins, dropped the machete, and reached for the chain. His fingers slipped on the warm metal, and the tiger started to move more quickly. Ben gripped the chain loop and slid it up the stake, but the tiger shook his great head, and the chain rattled, pulling the loop tighter, and it would slide no further. "Come on, come on, come on," Ben hissed. He pulled at the loop, trying to loosen it, and the tiger moved forward. Ben shook the sweat from his forehead and tugged desperately on the loop. The chain gave, just a little, and he pushed it up. The tiger lowered his head and leaned down on his front paws, crouching, preparing to pounce. "Oh, fuck!" Ben cried. With one last grunt of effort, he threw the loop over the top of the stake, then turned and dove into the cacti, driving shoulder-first into the needles. He hit the ground hard, screaming in pain and fear.

The screaming went on for a good thirty seconds, with Ben covering his head and shrieking like a terrified goat. But eventually, it occurred to him that the tiger had not pounced. He gathered his courage and opened his eyes.

Drool from the tiger's jaw splattered directly into them.

"Ugh!" Ben cried, forgetting to be terrified because he was so absolutely disgusted. "I don't want your sick tiger diseases!" Then he realized that he was talking to a wild Bengal tiger that was standing close enough to drool onto his face, and perspective came rushing back. Ben shrank down, pressing his entire trembling body down flat onto the earth, ignoring the pain of the cactus needles in his shoulder. "I'm sorry," he whispered, his voice hoarse with fear. "I'm sorry. Don't eat my face. Please, God, I'm sorry, don't eat my face." His fingers reached blindly for the machete…but he had left it at the base of the stake.

The tiger took a step into the grouping of cacti, easily avoiding the needles. He leaned down and sniffed Ben. Ben squeezed his eyes shut and gritted his teeth, waiting for the pain of death.

But it never came.

The tiger nosed around, his whiskers grazing Ben's cheeks…and then he pulled back, turned, and trotted down the hill, dragging his chain behind him.

Ben opened one eye. He opened the other. He sat up. "Hey, wait!" he hollered. He pushed himself to his feet and shouldered his way out of the cacti, taking a few more needles in the palms of his hands and cursing under his breath. He leapt out into the clearing and watched the tiger trot across the desert. "Hey! You idiot! The dusters are *that way!*" he said, pointing toward the north.

Patrick ambled down into the clearing, sidling up next to Ben and watching the tiger go. He let out a low whistle. "This was *not* one of the ways I saw this going," he admitted.

"You stupid fucking tiger!" Ben hollered. "I just risked my *life* to free you! Go charge those fucking zombies!" He picked up a small rock and hurled it after the retreating Bengal.

"One minute, you're wetting yourself next to a cactus, and the next minute, you're throwing rocks at a wild tiger." Patrick slapped Ben on the shoulder. "My favorite thing about life is that it always surprises you." He turned and hiked back up the hill.

Ben just stood there, flabbergasted, staring at the tiger as the creature became smaller and smaller, until he was just a speck of dust in the desert, and then he was gone completely.

Ben broke his gaze, shaking his head, and he turned around and followed Patrick up the hill. "I didn't wet myself next to a cactus," he grumbled, feeling his crotch, just to be sure.

If he had continued looking out over the desert for just a few more seconds, he might have seen the small, almost-indiscernible silhouette of a woman trudging across the hardpan in the haze of morning heat.

31.

"Well that was pointless," Ben grumbled, plopping down onto a boulder perched on the top of the hill. He shifted the fanny pack around so it sat in his lap, and he dug out a bottle of water the monks had given him. He unscrewed the top, tilted his head back, pried open his eye with one hand, and poured water into it, grunting in discomfort. He shook his head, blinked a few times, and wiped his eye on his sleeve. "Can you get a disease from getting tiger drool in your eye?"

"I'd be shocked if it was possible to *not* get a disease from getting tiger drool in your eye," Patrick said.

Ben sighed. He took a drink. "One of these days, I'm going to stop listening to you."

"Frankly, I'm amazed you still do," Patrick admitted, taking a seat next to Ben. "If I'm being honest, half the decisions I made on the way to Disney World were just to see if you'd actually go along with them." Patrick smiled at the grand memory of the trip and shook his head in wonder. "You never disappoint, Benny Boy."

Ben grunted again.

"Hey, come on, how bad can my advice be? You haven't died yet," Patrick pointed out.

"I'm about the only one," Ben muttered. He stared out over the valley below, at the monstrous hangar and the duster horde that milled around it like dazed cattle, terrifying in their sheer number. With the sun beginning to climb in the sky, the world was bright enough for them to see exactly what they were up against.

"Remember the first time we saw one?" Ben asked, gazing out over the sea of shuffling half-humans.

"I do," Patrick nodded.

"You called them 'politicians'."

"Yeah. That wasn't really fair to the dusters," Patrick said.

Ben snorted. "The first one almost ate my foot. Remember that? Tore right into my shoe with his teeth."

"I broke a bat over the back of his head," Patrick said proudly.

"He chased us into that cabin. And then more of them came, and more, and we were surrounded. Remember that?"

"Yeah." Patrick prodded at the edges of the hole in the center of his left hand. "We climbed up to the roof and looked down, and you started crying like a girl-baby."

"I didn't cry," Ben insisted.

"Well, you probably wanted to," Patrick said.

Ben closed his eyes and saw himself back on that roof, surrounded by the snarling, angry dusters. "I'd never seen anything like it," he said, remembering the sound of their fingernails scratching against the house. "I thought we were dead for sure."

"I had my doubts, too," Patrick admitted.

"That was the most scared I'd ever been." Ben opened his eyes. "That was, what—twelve dusters? Maybe twenty?"

"Something like that."

Ben opened his eyes and stared out over the valley. Thousands of dusters jostled each other for space. When the wind blew, he could smell the stench of them, the sweet sourness of rot. "I remember *that*," he said quietly. He drew up his knees, hugged them close to his chest, and watched the duster horde.

Patrick turned his head and considered his friend. Then he, too, looked out over the dusters, and the wide channel surrounding the Lab, and the cut-outs above the doors that hid rifle barrels in their shadows. "I know what you're thinking," he said finally.

"No you don't."

"You're thinking you should just charge in. Try to jump the ditch and see what happens."

"No," Ben said, his voice quiet, and dry.

Patrick hesitated. He shifted himself on the ground, crossing his legs and placing his palms on his knees. "Ben, you know that would be it, right? That's death. There's no hope of anything other than death."

"I know."

"Even if you somehow made it across the ditch—and Jesus, Benny Boy, I've seen you jump...you would *not* make it across the ditch—but even if you did, what, do you honestly think you could fight your way through a few thousand blood-thirsty, meat-hungry politicians and reach the hangar alive? And even if you somehow did *that*...the gunmen would shoot you on sight."

Ben nodded slowly. "Yeah," he said. "I know."

Patrick stared at Ben. His eyes twitched, and his brow crinkled, and Ben could see from the corner of his eye that his imaginary friend was trying to work something out. "Ben..." he said.

"Jesus, Patrick," Ben replied quietly, looking down at his hands, folding his fingers. "I told you. If I wanted to kill myself, I would have done it a long time ago."

Patrick frowned. He leaned forward, propping his elbows on his knees. He looked down between his legs, and he picked up a pebble from the ground. He rolled it over between his finger and his thumb, thinking carefully, thinking his own thoughts. Thinking Ben's thoughts. Finally, he said, "It wasn't your fault."

Tears welled up in Ben's eyes. He scrubbed at them with the collar of his shirt, annoyed. He ran a hand over his face, and when he looked up, his eyes were red, and tired. "Yes, it was," he whispered, his voice low and broken, and dry as the desert wind.

•

Ben stood outside the walls of Fort Doom, helpless, anxious, his fingers twitching, his legs flinching, his whole body desperate to help, to *move*, but having nowhere to go...the flames rose up; they flared out, they licked the grass near his feet, they kept him barricaded in a prison cell of heat and anguish.

And the screams. He knew the voices as intimately as he knew himself. James. Annie. Amsalu. Dylan. And Sarah, and Isabel, forever...

Sarah and Isabel. Their cries reverberated against the smoldering wood, rang out across the scorched fields. Scared, confused, angry, alone. *Where is the watch?* the screams sang through Ben's very bones.

They called for him to save them. They screamed for salvation against the fire that blackened their skin.

Ben pushed forward, shielding his face with his arms, but the fire was too hot; it blistered the skin of his forearms and pushed him back, back into the cool night, back into the grass, where he sank down to his knees. An endless stream of tears spilled off his chin, and his own screams mingled with the torture and pain of his loved ones inside the walls. They cried out for him; he heard his name, *Ben, Ben, Jesus Christ, Ben*, and he collapsed with his whole body, convulsing into sobs, his skin blackened with soot, his lungs clouded with smoke, coughing and crying and spitting and screaming, as the world around him burned, as the loves of his life grew quiet in the fire.

•

"They burned because of me."

"No. They didn't."

"Yes! They did!" Ben shouted. He couldn't sit still anymore; his limbs were suddenly jittery, too full of blood, and he jumped up to his feet. "They died in that fire because I left my post."

"They would have died in the fire anyway," Patrick said quietly.

"There wouldn't have *been* a fire if I hadn't left," Ben shot back, his voice high and tight. He was walking now, stepping left, wheeling, scuffing right, stabbing his heels into the dirt, dancing a clumsy, angry *pas de deux* with the past. "I was on watch. It was my *job* to watch. And I fell asleep. I fucking fell asleep, and I heard something—it was *nothing,* it was *nothing*...it was a sound from my goddamn *dream*, and even if it wasn't, what the hell did I think I was gonna do? What was the actual fucking *point* of going out there, of looking into a...a...a *rustling* in the grass, a crack of a stick—Christ, even if it *had* been a gunshot, why would I have gone out there? What did I think I was going to do?! My job was to *watch*, and to protect the fort, to stay *inside* the fort, but I didn't...I climbed down, and I left." He jammed the heels of his hands to his temples, digging them in, as if maybe, if he pushed hard enough, he could sprain the place where the memory lived and blot it out of his brain with a deep, bleeding bruise. Tears streamed freely down his cheeks now, and his steps became more erratic, palsied, his shoes kicking up eddies of dirt and sand, his whole body spinning, like an animal caught in a too-small cage. "I *left*—fuck, I didn't just *leave*, I walked for twenty minutes, to investigate a sound that didn't even *exist*!"

"You don't know that it was a sound in your dream," Patrick said.

"It doesn't matter!" Ben screamed, throwing out his hands, clawing at the air with his palms up, begging for alms of understanding, or rationalization. "Are you even listening to me?! It doesn't matter! I shouldn't have been out there either way! I left, and they got in." He stopped walking, his feet stopped moving, and the tears began to pour. He started to sob. He raised his hands to the top of his head and pressed down, wishing he could push himself deep into the earth, cover himself up with rocks and soil, breath in the dirt, let it fill his lungs, let it weigh him down in the darkness. "I can still smell the smoke," he said, his voice cracking through his tears.

Patrick pushed himself to his feet. He approached Ben carefully. He reached out and touched his shoulder. "Ben, it wasn't your fault."

"Yes, it fucking was!" Ben yelled, slapping Patrick's hand away. "There was nothing in the grass, and I turned to walk back, and the sky was orange, and the flames...God, they were already so high," he whispered, his mouth thick with mucous. "They got in, and they set my whole world on fire."

"Ben," Patrick said lightly, reaching out, but hesitating, pulling back his hand, standing helplessly. "You couldn't have stopped it. You would have burned, too."

"I would have stopped them," Ben said, shaking his head miserably. He crossed his arms over his head, lifting his ribcage, freeing his lungs, trying to breathe, but his chest heaved, and he couldn't hold in the air, and he wondered if he might suffocate, right there in the desert, surrounded by air. "They shouldn't have even gotten in. I would have stopped them, but I wasn't there, they saw the watchtower empty, and they came, and they set their fires. I ran back. I ran so hard, but my feet kept slipping in the grass, and the faster I ran, the longer it took me to get there, and the fire spread, I could see it over the walls, and then the walls caught fire, too. By the time I made it to the gates..." He lowered his arms slowly, the memory seizing him, wrapping its ashen fingers around the valves of his heart and squeezing, pulling down the veins, dragging the heart down into the pit of black, burned remembrance. Ben crumpled to the ground, and when he spoke again, all the feeling had gone out of his voice, all the emotion, and his words were a distant train whistle on the breeze. "The fire was too hot. I couldn't go in. So I stood outside. I stood outside our cabin, and I listened to her scream."

Patrick pressed his thumbs against his eyes, pushing back on his own tears, pressing back against Ben's torment. "Ben…it wasn't your fault."

"Stop saying that," he replied hollowly. "You weren't there. You don't know, because you weren't there. You weren't there because you were dead. Because I didn't protect you. I left you to wait for the Red Caps, I left you to die—I *let* you die, and then I let Sarah die, and I let our baby die. Sarah thought it would be a girl. We were going to call her Izzy. I listened to Sarah scream as she was burned alive by a fire I didn't stop. I listened outside the wall while my daughter boiled to death inside of her, without even the simple fucking benefit of knowing why." Ben looked up at Patrick. The tears had mostly dried, but his eyes were as red as a dusky sunset, his lids swollen and raw. "No, I don't want to kill myself," he said quietly, shaking his head. "But I'm not fighting to stay alive, either. There's an in-between place, and I live there. Like a shadow."

Patrick stood in the sunlight, casting his eyes downward, nudging at one ankle of his blue jeans with the toe of the other shoe. "But is that why you're doing this? Tracking down the Doctor and his raiders? Because you want out of the in-between place?" He looked Ben directly in his red-rimmed eyes and asked, "Are you hoping they'll make the choice for you?"

Ben snorted a short laugh. "No," he said, shaking his head and smiling ruefully. "The in-between place *is* my choice." He looked out over the valley, at the inscrutable Lab. "I'm doing this because they took the one thing in the whole stupid world that has any chance of making all of this worth anything at all."

Patrick opened his mouth to reply, but just then, the sound of rusty gears churning to life screeched across the desert. Instinctively, Ben dove behind a rock, and Patrick squatted behind him. Together, they peered out at the Lab, where the large hangar door was slowly wrenching itself open, its squeaky metal rollers grinding harshly along the tracks. Some of the dusters near the entrance took notice of the commotion and came to life, snapping out of their dreary trudging and working themselves into a frenzy. They hurled themselves toward the door, snarling and spitting and gasping for breath. But they stopped a few yards from the opening door, as if they had run into an invisible force field. The dusters in front skidded to a stop, some of them falling to their knees, while the ones behind crashed into them, frantic and angry. They piled up there, before the hangar door, until the ones on top scrambled away, retreating back to the drowsy throng, and the pile dissolved as the dusters that had flooded into the space now shouldered their way backward, still angry, still snarling, but edging their way back from some invisible line.

The door creaked to a halt, leaving an opening about six feet wide, barely a sliver compared to the full monstrous size of the hangar door. As Ben watched from behind his rock, a man on an electric dirt bike nosed his way out of the hangar. He moved slowly, clad in a leather jacket, jeans, gloves, and a comically oversized helmet with a mirrored visor, walking the bike forward, rolling toward the duster horde.

"Holy shit," Ben whispered. "What the hell is he doing?"

"Ritualistic self-sacrifice?" Patrick suggested. "Maybe they've sentenced him to death by duster for the crime of dressing like an extra from *The Warriors*."

But as the rider moved forward, the dusters pushed themselves back, as if the motorcycle—or perhaps the rider himself—was extending the invisible boundary that the dusters couldn't cross. The rider wheeled around to his left, guiding the bike away from the hangar, toward the hills where Ben and his tumor-dream were crouched. As he moved, the boundary moved with him, and he steered the bike into the throng of shambling dusters. They pushed themselves out of his way, forming a channel for the bike's safe passage, and then they closed in behind the rear tire as it moved forward so that the rider seemed to be traveling in a huge bubble that the dusters couldn't penetrate. They snarled and rasped as he passed, and some of them took swipes in his direction, but they were too far to reach him, and the attacks seemed half-hearted at best.

When he was about a quarter of the way to the dry moat, the driver seemed to grow impatient, and he gave the bike a little gas. The dusters clawed each other to get out of the rider's way as he cruised safely through their ranks.

"What in the absolute hell…?" Ben breathed.

Patrick had no opinions to share.

When he reached the edge of the moat, the driver pulled the bike to a halt and set the kickstand. He pulled the glove off of his right hand and dug into the pocket of his jacket. He pulled out a small remote control and pushed one of the buttons. Something down in the dry moat rumbled to life; the dusters down in the channel scurried over each other, trying to get away from the space beneath where the biker sat. Metal creaked against metal, and a platform began to rise slowly from the bottom of the moat.

"No way," Ben said.

He watched in awe as two gigantic steel accordion-style hydraulic arms pushed the metal platform up from the base of the ditch, extending until the platform was level with the desert floor on both sides of the moat. The scissor arms jerked to a stop, and the platform swayed a bit as the whine of the hydraulics screeched and faded away.

"That is some incredibly unimpressive tech," Patrick said, crossing his arms. "I'm a mechanical engineer," he reminded Ben smugly.

"I know, you always fucking talk about it," Ben grumbled.

"Would you like to know how *I* would have built a retractable bridge in a dry moat?"

"No." Ben tightened his fanny pack and trotted along the ridge of the hill, keeping low to the ground. Down below, the rider motored across the platform, braked on the other side, and clicked another button on the remote, sending the platform groaning back down to the bottom of the moat. Then he stuffed the remote into his pocket, pulled on his glove, revved the tiny engine, and peeled out, spraying pebbles and dust back across the channel, pelting the angry dusters on the other side.

The rider pointed his bike toward a gap in the little mountain range, just to the east of the hill where Patrick and Ben were perched. Ben pushed off the ground with one hand and burst into a run, sprinting as hard as he could down the mountain.

"Where are we going?" Patrick hollered, hurrying after Ben. "You know my body doesn't run fast!"

"Keep up!" Ben shouted over his shoulder. "This time, *I* have a plan!" His feet pounded the dirt, avoiding rocks and divots in the ground where he could, plowing through them when he couldn't, stumbling and sliding, racing the dirt bike to the foot of the hill. With clumsy fingers, he fumbled with the zipper of the bouncing fanny pack, wrenching it open as he ran. He dug one hand inside the pack and rummaged around until his hand closed on an unopened can of Campbell's bean and bacon soup. He yanked it out of the pack, breathing hard and slapping the ground with his thin, worn sneakers. The whine of the dirt bike's engine shot through the air, growing louder as it neared the gap in the hills. Ben lowered his head and pumped his arms, and the bouncing fanny pack threw him off balance and sent him careening forward, but twisting sideways. He pushed through, pumping his legs, ignoring the fire burning in his blood. The dirt bike came into view, curling around the bend and speeding through the gap. Ben raised the can of beans, took aim, and hurled it as hard as he could. It caught the rider in the helmet, and he pulled the handlebars, then overcorrected, skidding his tires in the dirt and losing control of the bike. The front wheel slammed into a basketball-sized rock half-buried in the ground, and the back tire kicked up, throwing the rider forward. He flew through the air, flailing his arms and screaming into his helmet. He arced like a bottle rocket, then streaked back toward the earth. He slammed head-first into the desert hardpan, and his body crumpled in like an accordion, the force driving his helmet across the sand and dragging him along with it, and then he came to a stop, and was still.

"Wooooo!" Ben cried, jumping triumphantly and pumping his fists in the air. "Yes! Did you *see* that?! Did you *see*—" He looked behind him, but Patrick had vanished. Ben grumped. "Hmpf. Figures. Someone else has a plan that works, and you can't take it."

It's more about the fact that you made me run, Patrick's voice said. *You know I'm not built for running. You* know *that. Now are you going to tell me why you brained Swan the Warlord over there?*

"Infiltration," Ben said smugly.

You're going to put on a dead man's outfit? Patrick asked, disgusted.

"What? No. He's not *dead*," Ben said, gesturing to the rider's body, lying in a heap on the ground. Then he paused. He craned his neck and looked intently at the body lying prostrate in the dirt. "Is he?"

I definitely heard a neck crack, Patrick said. *I know a neck crack, and that crack was full neck.*

Ben frowned. He trotted the rest of the way down the hill and carefully approached the fallen rider, tiptoeing across the hardpan. "Hey. Buddy?" He waited for a response. The rider didn't move. "Hey. Heeeeeey." Ben kicked a little dirt toward the body. Nothing. He approached the body slowly and nudged the rider's ribs with his toe. "Hey, guy?"

Oh, he is definitely dead.

Ben sucked in air through his teeth. "Whoops," he said.

Well, you were gonna have to kill him anyway.

"Not necessarily," Ben replied.

Oh, your plan involved politely asking him if you could borrow his clothes and his bike so you could go break into his home and murder his friends, and he was going to say, "Oh, yes, by all means, let me shrug on out of my coat," and he was going to do that after you'd knocked him off his dirt bike with a can of soup? That was your plan?

"I'm not going to murder his friends."

We'll see.

"And he didn't have to *let* me borrow his clothes, I could have… like…I don't know…" Ben made some jerky, uncomfortable hand motions through the air. "…subdued him."

Oh, yes, with all your martial arts prowess, and perhaps with the rope that I suppose you remembered to pack before you left the train.

Ben sighed. "I…did not pack a rope."

Ben, Ben…sweet, dumb Ben, Patrick said, and Ben could picture him shaking his head in disappointment. *You always bring a rope.*

"Well, I didn't bring a rope!" Ben exploded. "And it doesn't matter, because I don't need one, because he's dead!"

The bloodlust has taken you now.

"Will you shut up?" Ben grumbled. He set his fanny pack on the ground and frowned down at the twisted, broken body. He flexed his fingers, trying to decide where to start.

Start with his heart, you cold, cruel monster…he probably had a family.

"I said shut up!" Ben cried. "What the fuck are you even talking about, his heart? I'm not ripping out his heart!"

The Great Spirit of the Illinois would take his heart, and she would eat it. The Illini never wasted any part of the kill.

Ben ignored his tumor-voice and crouched down close to the body, still holding up his hands and moving his fingers uncertainly. He grimaced as he reached down and prodded the body with two fingers. "Ugh," he moaned, "it *feels* dead."

It is dead.

"Yes, I understand that, thank you.

You have *touched dead bodies before, you know.*

"Yeah," Ben sighed, "but they weren't wearing helmets." He gingerly slipped one hand beneath the rider's shoulder, then he yanked it up, flipping the body over clumsily, so the arms and legs flailed and came down in a twist. Ben blenched as he reached down and pulled the gloves off the dead man's hands—first the left, then the right. The right-hand glove got stuck on the rider's thumb, and Ben had to really tug, but eventually it popped off.

Then he took a deep breath and went to work on the zipper of the jacket. The sound of it made him wince. He took a deep breath and pushed on, until the jacket fell open. Then he set about the uncomfortable task of pulling the dead man's arms out of the sleeves. It was like pulling a sausage from its casing.

When he'd extricated the leather jacket from the torso, he folded it in half and laid it on the ground, and he tossed the gloves on top of it. Then he looked down and considered the body once more. "I probably don't need the pants, right?" he asked, tapping his lips.

Well, that depends. Do you want it done Ben-style, or do you want it done right?

"Who's gonna notice?"

Who's gonna notice that a man rode out of the Lab wearing mostly-clean skinny jeans and came back thirty minutes later wearing mud-smeared straight-leg jeans? Uh, everyone?

"They will not," Ben insisted. "It's a bunch of killers and bandits, not the cast of *Queer Eye.*"

Are you willing to take that chance?

Ben frowned. He looked down at the man's waist. "He's too small. The pants won't even fit."

He is exactly your size.

"No way, I'm definitely bigger. I'm pretty big now. Not fat or anything, but bigger. Apocalypse muscle."

You don't have apocalypse muscle.

"Yes I do, I'm bigger. His pants won't even fit."

You just don't want to put your hands on his crotch.

"Well, no, Patrick, that thought doesn't exactly put me over the moon," Ben snipped. "Besides, leaving him here with no pants, it seems disrespectful."

More disrespectful or less disrespectful than killing him with a can of soup?

"I didn't mean to kill him with the soup!" Ben shouted. "Fine. You want me to take off his pants? Fine. You want me to disrespect his corpse? Fine." Ben yanked open the button on the dead man's jeans and pulled down the fly. "Happy?" He grasped the denim by the pockets and tugged the jeans down over the rider's hips, wriggling them free and exposing a pair of black cotton briefs that had faded to a mottled gray-ish mess, with small holes beginning to wear through the undercarriage. "Yep. There's his underpants. Feel good about yourself?" Ben asked. He pulled the jeans down over the man's pale, white knees and pushed them down his shins. "There. He's super-pale. Lives in the desert sun, never puts his legs out in it. He looks like a dried-up whitefish. Is this what you wanted?" He shoved the jeans down lower, then remembered the man's boots, so he set to work unbuckling the clasps on each boot and tugging them off of his feet, a task made more difficult by the fact that the boots were at least half a size too small, and Ben had to hold up each foot and rest it between his own knees so he could squeeze it to hold it in place while he pried off the boot. "Wow. He's wearing novelty socks with the genie from *Aladdin* flying around on them. I bet he thought to himself, 'Boy, I sure hope I get a chance to show these to a total stranger before the day's over.'" Ben flipped the boots out into the sand, then he tugged on the jeans from the ankles to pull them off of the dead man's legs. He thrust the worn pair of pants into the air and said, "There! We've completely humiliated a dead man's corpse. Is that what you wanted?!"

Hey, my thoughts are your thoughts, Patrick reminded him. *I'm starting to think you* wanted *to see him in his underpants.*

"I did not!" Ben cried. He hurled the jeans onto the ground, and he stomped around a bit, just to prove his point. Then he looked down at the dead man, lying there in his stained t-shirt, his once-black underpants, and his calf-high *Aladdin* socks, and he felt unmeasurable sadness. "This isn't how I thought the plan would go," he sighed.

Does anyone else think it's weird you've left the helmet on until now? He looks like something out of a porn dream from 1974.

"What the hell is a porn dream?" Ben demanded.

You know, Patrick assured him. *You know.*

Ben cursed under his breath. He marched over to the pile of clothes, snatched up the leather jacket, and pulled it on. It actually fit pretty well. "Guess he's more muscular than he looks," Ben reasoned.

Sure.

Then he picked up the pants and held them up to his own waist. He was dismayed beyond belief to see that they actually looked like they might be a little too big. "Fine," he said in a huff, undoing his pants and pushing them down. He tried to step out of them, but his shoes got caught in the fabric, and he fell over. He cursed—this time *not* under his breath—and pulled his sneakers off before kicking out of his pants. He pulled on the new pair of jeans, working to ignore the shiver that traveled up his spine at the thought of wearing a dead man's clothes so close to his own reproductive organs.

And the helmet? Patrick asked.

"I'm getting the helmet!" Ben snapped as he tied his shoes. He shook his head in annoyance and knelt down next to the dead man's head. "I'm getting the helmet," he grumbled again, under his breath. He made a sour face as he reached down and gripped the helmet by the bottom. He gave it a gentle tug, but the helmet didn't give. He pulled harder, but the way the neck had broken during the fall had left the head somewhat untethered, and so when Ben pulled and twisted, the head turned with the helmet.

Ben decided that he might throw up.

No, keep going, you're almost there! Patrick encouraged him. *You just need more torque!*

"I don't know what torque is!" Ben cried. He pulled and pulled, and the helmet slowly inched its way up the dead man's skull. Ben sat down and used his feet as leverage, pushing the soles of his shoes down on the man's shoulders as he pulled. The neck seemed to unravel and stretch... or was that Ben's imagination?

"If his head pops off, I'm going to be sick," Ben warned.

Heads don't pop off, Patrick assured him. *Unless you've been granted the apocalypse strength of ten men. In which case the soup can would have blown right through the helmet, and you wouldn't be having this problem.*

"Great." Ben pulled and twisted, and the head pulled and twisted, and the neck pulled and twisted, and once, it popped, and Ben did feel his stomach roiling, like it wanted to throw up, and he was grateful for having gotten so sick after the tiger attack, that there was nothing left to give. But the helmet moved slowly up the skull, and with a low, soft *thoonk*, the helmet came off in Ben's hands.

Oh, look—you murdered a toddler, Patrick said.

"Oh, shut up. He's twenty-five at least," Ben said, grimacing down at the young man's face.

I'd say six, max. Maybe seven. Maybe.

"He has a beard!"

He has patches of stubble.

"Besides, if he's old enough to pillage and plunder, he's old enough to get his neck broken by soup."

Pillage and plunder? What is he, a pirate of Penzance?

"He probably killed Howard. Or Mark."

You hated Howard. And Mark.

"Yeah, they could be a real couple of wangs," Ben admitted. "But all the recruits can always be wangs. That doesn't mean I want them dead."

Whatever helps you sleep at night.

"Oh, shut up." He turned his attention to the bike. He yanked it upright and was surprised to find it so light.

Oh look, a baby bike for a baby rider.

"Will you stop it," Ben said, rolling his eyes. "It's an adult bike. For adult people."

It runs on AA batteries.

"It runs on a thirty-six-volt battery," Ben corrected him.

How do you know that? Patrick asked suspiciously.

Ben scoffed. "Patrick. A lot has changed in the last three years. I've seen some shit you wouldn't believe. I've learned a lot. About the world. About myself. And I've learned a thing or two about dirt bikes. I'm not saying I'm an expert, but I'm something of a motorcycle savant."

You drove the last one right into a boulder, Patrick pointed out.

"Yeah, I don't know shit about these things," Ben shrugged. "I read the battery size on the side." He pointed to the big plastic box beneath the seat, where the details of the bike were molded into the casing.

Ah.

"How do you think it works?" Ben wondered, tilting the bike to the side, eyeing the handlebars with confusion.

Oh, look—it has an on-off switch! Patrick cried. On the side of the little black box, there was a black plastic toggle switch was stamped with the words ON and OFF. *I was joking before, but in all seriousness, this is a kid's bike.*

The switch was turned to the ON position, and Ben flicked it down to OFF, then back up to ON. He stared at the bike. "It's broken," he decided.

Twist the handle, Patrick suggested. *Isn't that how the big boy versions work?*

Ben gripped the handlebars and gave the right handle a turn. The battery whirred to life, and the tires spun in the dirt. Ben held the bike easily in place. "If I'm being honest, I am *incredibly* disappointed right now," he frowned

I bet it goes up to six miles per hour, at least, Patrick said.

"Sure seemed a lot faster when I was running after it with a soup can," Ben said.

That's because you are a very slow runner. I've known it forever, but I never wanted to say anything until just now. I know bad running, and you are very bad at running.

Ben flipped the switch to OFF and continued to examine the bike. "How do you think he buffered out the dusters like that?" he asked. "Do you think it's the bike?"

Very possible. If the 1980s movie Rad, *starring* Full House's *own Aunt Becky, taught me anything, it's that dirt bikes have very magical—or, at the very least, seductively romantic—powers.*

"God, I love that movie," Ben said.

That's because you're not a monster.

"But seriously. How do you think it works?" He inspected the dirt bike for anything that looked out of the ordinary—any sort of box, light, monitor, antenna, speaker, wire, spring, anything that looked like it wasn't integral to the original production design. But everything looked perfectly factory-made. There was no obvious sign of any modification or add-on.

Maybe it's not the bike, Patrick suggested.

Ben stood up straight. "No," he breathed, turning his head and looking back at the dead body on the ground behind him. "You don't think…?"

You have no choice, Patrick decided. *Check him for hidden things.*

"He's in his underwear and socks," Ben snapped. "There's nowhere else to check."

Well, Patrick said. *There is* one *other place to check.*

"Oh, no. No. Absolutely not." Ben crossed his arms and set his jaw. "I'd rather be eaten alive by dusters. And I am *not* being hyperbolic."

Fine. Suit yourself. But if he does have a rectal implant, now would be an easier time to fish it out than ever before.

"Absolutely not. A million times over, no. A very hard no." Ben had a thought then, and his eyes became bright with an idea. He fished into the jacket pocket and pulled out the little remote control. It had three buttons on it, a large central button flanked by two smaller buttons, one on either side. "Any chance it might be this?" he asked.

Honestly, I can't imagine what *would make dusters move away like that,* Patrick admitted. *Something in a remote, or something olfactory, or something laid into the ground like a track…I have no idea.*

"Great," Ben sighed. "Well. On the bright side, I guess it won't take too long to find out if it'll work for us or not."

If it'll work for you, *specifically. Again, I'm already dead. I really want to stress that you're on your own in this. For plausible deniability.*

"Yeah, thanks for the reminder," Ben grumbled. He stuffed his old clothes into the fanny pack, then dug a small pit in the dirt at the base of the mountain and shoved the pack into it. He pushed the sand back over it and marked the space with three small rocks. Wiping his hands on his jeans, he snatched up the helmet and pulled it onto his head, ignoring the fact that it was a little loose, even though it had been tight on the rider. Then he slipped his hands into the leather gloves. "Fuck it," he said, his voice muffled by the helmet. "Let's ride."

He threw his leg over the dirt bike and plopped down onto the seat. His knees nearly reached his wrists when he set his hands on the handlebars. "Damn. This thing *is* small."

You almost look like a normal-sized person on it! Patrick said, delighted.

Ben flipped the switch to ON. "Well. Here goes nothing," he said.

So just to be clear, your plan is to ride up, raise the bridge, cross over, keep the dusters at bay, roll on up to the hangar door, knock three times, get inside, go undetected, find your backpack, and slip back out, similarly undetected, hop back on the bike, navigate it back through the dusters, cross the moat, and motor on back to Horace and the train?

"I don't know about the knocking three times part," Ben said. "If they were smart, they'd have a complex, rotating knock-slap-tap system in place. But yes, that's essentially the plan."

Eh. I give it a nineteen percent chance of success.

"That's better than nothing."

Oh! No! That was meant to be encouraging! I honestly believe a nineteen percent chance is the absolute best that you could have hoped for. Nineteen percent is best case scenario.

"Great," Ben said. He tightened the belt of his fanny pack, and gave the side of his helmet a thump, just for good measure. "Then, as I already said, because you made me waste a great line: Let's ride."

He twisted the throttle, and the dirt bike slowly rolled to life. The battery churned out its high-pitched whine, and soon he was scooting across the desert, the bike pulling in fits and starts.

Rides like a dream, Patrick shouted in his ear.

They puttered around the base of the hill, through the channel, and rode out toward the Lab on the other side. They rolled up to the moat, to the spot where the biker had crossed over the platform, and Ben stuck out a foot, dragging the bike to a stop. "Well," he said, pulling out the remote and taking a deep breath. "Here goes nothing."

He pushed the button on the remote.

Nothing happened.

Ben looked around. The helmet's faceplate was cloudy and smeared with dirt, and it was hard to see. But he didn't hear the hydraulic whine of the platform. "Did I do it?" He pushed the button again. Nothing. He pushed it again, and again, and again, over and over and over again.

Nothing.

"Well, shit."

Maybe it's one of the other two buttons, Patrick suggested.

"Yes, obviously it's one of the other two buttons," Ben snapped. He had just wanted it to be the first button he tried. He wanted that dramatic effect.

He sighed and pushed the smaller button that was set above the big one. The hydraulics below cranked to life.

That would have been a lot more impressive if you'd hit that button first, Patrick pointed out.

"If you weren't already dead, I'd kill you," Ben swore.

The platform creaked to life, rising slowly in the moat. The dusters on the far side of the gap took notice, and they began to gather on the far end. "This had better work," Ben said through gritted teeth.

Well, if not, at least you have an escape vehicle that goes almost as fast as I can walk, Patrick said.

Ben turned the handlebars nervously as the platform slowly rose to the top of the moat. The wheel scraped through the dirt, digging a little channel into the ground. He could feel the palm sweat pooling in his gloves, and he was glad for the grip of the leather on the handles. Then the platform gave a loud *KA-CHUNK* as it reached its full height and stopped level with the top of the ditch. "Shit," Ben breathed. He took a deep breath.

He twisted the throttle and kicked off the ground, and he rolled across the bridge. The dusters had gathered in a thick knot on the far side, the ones in the back bumping into the ones in front, shoving them out onto the bridge. They stumbled forward and swiped angrily at the approaching bike. "It's not working!" Ben shouted into his helmet. He squeezed the brake, but just as he did, he noticed that the duster at the front of the pack was scuffing his feet on the platform of the raised bridge, peddling backward, his arms scrabbling frantically at the thick wall of decaying bodies behind him.

Uh, either he has stage fright, or you might actually be doing it, Patrick said.

Ben cut the throttle, but he pushed the bike forward with his feet, rolling slowly toward the far end of the bridge. The lead duster loosed an angry rattle of frustration from his throat, then he spun away from the throng and threw himself over the edge of the platform, plunging down into the pit below. Ben inched closer, and the next few dusters jerked their heads back, as if each of them had been shot in the neck, and they, too, turned and clawed at the wall of bodies behind them, scraping through and losing themselves backward into the throng.

"Holy shit," Ben said. "It *is* working."

He pushed forward more forcefully, scooting the dirt bike along the bridge, and more dusters turned course and scrambled backward, snarling and fighting their way back into the throng, spitting and hissing and splattering their yellow-green mucous on the ground. By the time he reached the far end of the bridge, the dusters had melted backward into a semi-circle around the path, giving Ben a good ten-foot berth on every side. The dusters closest to the border's edge were furious, screaming and stamping their feet, green spittle flying from their decayed and wasted teeth, but they wouldn't cross the invisible line, and if they were pushed past it, they fought like the devil's fury to pull themselves back into the angry crowd.

Ben's heart was beating quickly, vibrating the leather of his jacket. But he swallowed hard and gripped the handlebar, and he said, "Fuck it." He hit the throttle, and the tires slipped, kicking dirt into the air, before making purchase on the dry sand and rearing forward into the horde of meat-hungry monsters.

The dusters pushed themselves back, opening up the road for Ben and his bike. He motored across the platform and rumbled toward the hangar, and the dusters clawed all over themselves, fighting to get out of his way. Once he passed into the throng of them, they closed in behind him, filling in the bubble the same way they'd done to the original rider on his way out of the compound.

You're like Moses, parting the Red Sea, Patrick marveled.

But Moses wandered in the desert for forty days, Ben thought smugly. *I've only been out here for three. I am amazing.*

Well, hold tight, Patrick warned. *There's a ninety percent chance you get locked up in that hangar for at least thirty-seven days.*

Ben considered this. *Well, a ten percent chance of success isn't nothing,* he decided.

No, the other ten percent chance is that they kill you on sight.

"Very helpful."

Ben pushed on, and the bubble held, with the dusters making way. He cruised on through the snarling mob, and the hulking frame of the quiet hangar loomed ominously overhead.

Now what? Patrick whispered. *Any plans for infiltration?*

"No idea," Ben admitted. "This isn't really a plan-for situation." Then he pulled the throttle, and the battery whined, lurching forward and screeching toward the hangar doors.

The bike scooted into the shadow of the hangar, and Ben slowed to a stop outside the humongous door. He sat on the bike and looked up. He turned his head to the left. He turned it to the right. He looked around.

Nothing happened.

"Hey!" he shouted, reaching out and knocking on the massive door with one gloved fist. "Heeeeeey!"

The gears rumbled to life, and the door began to squeal along its tracks, pulling open slowly. Ben tapped his handlebars impatiently, listening intently to the dusters salivating over his shoulder, until the gap in the doorway was wide enough for him to motor through. Then he turned the throttle and scooted into the huge and somber building.

Someone shut the door behind him with a *BANG*.

32.

As soon as the door shut, Ben began to wish that he had a plan.

Shit, he thought, walking himself and the bike backward until the rear tire bumped against the closed hangar door. *Now what?*

Frankly, I'm surprised you made it this far, Patrick said. *Which is very exciting! But also, you're on your own.*

Thanks.

The inside of the hangar was subdivided into smaller sections by haphazard drywall sections that were nailed together to cordon off the different areas. Much to Ben's surprise, the windows above the hangar door were not manned by raiders with guns. There weren't any platforms set into the wall up there; it wasn't even possible to reach the windows at all. The area to Ben's left was also empty, for the most part. The concrete floor was littered with long, flat pieces of cardboard, makeshift drop cloths made from old boxes that were spray painted with the halo shapes of whatever had been worked on there. A few benches sat scattered about the space, some with tools on them, some clear of debris, and beyond those, three huge wooden chests mounded over with loose shop tools. Further down, a haphazard wall crossed behind the workshop, closing off the far side of the front end of the hangar from Ben's view. A wide, brawny man in overalls stood leaning against the wall by the far end of the door. *Must be the doorman,* Ben reasoned.

I think you could take him, Patrick said.

Shut up.

The section to his right appeared to be some sort of makeshift garage. Four old Jeeps were parked along the eastern wall. They looked like they hadn't run in a long time; most of their tires had been stripped away, and their chassis had been given over to rust. A couple of Harley-Davidson motorcycles were propped up against the far wall, too, in similar states of disrepair. Ruined cars were a common sight, now more than ever, since enough time had passed that pre-M-day gasoline had gone bad.

But lined up against another section of drywall were seven other electric dirt bikes like the one he was currently sitting on, clean and shining in the buzzing fluorescent lights that glowed high overhead. A small, bony woman with mousy gray hair and sharp shoulders was hunched over one of the bikes. Ben hadn't seen her at first; her blue jumpsuit blended in with the blue of the dirt bike. She straightened up, and Ben jumped in surprise.

"Bring it over," she called, beckoning him lazily with one hand. She hardly looked up from the bike she was working on. It took Ben a good five seconds to remember that he was wearing a helmet, and therefore avoiding detection.

For now.

She thinks you're that small boy you brained, Patrick pointed out.

I did not brain him! Ben thought back. *He brained himself. He should have been paying attention.*

Yeah, the first rule of motorcycles is, "Watch out for flying soup."

"Come on," the woman said, looking up again and snapping her fingers. "We got a run later—gotta charge, gotta charge, let's go!"

Ben cursed beneath his helmet. He gripped the handlebars and began to roll the bike forward.

You could kill her, Patrick suggested.

I'm not going to kill her.

You kill other people.

I do not kill other people.

You do. You have the bloodlust.

I do not have the bloodlust!

He rolled over to the line of dirt bikes and parked his at the end. He hopped off and pushed down the kickstand, then he gave the woman an awkward little wave and turned to go.

"Hey!" she shouted, and Ben froze. He turned slowly. She flicked her fingers at him impatiently. "Gloves. Jacket. Helmet. Come on."

Well this isn't good, Patrick decided.

Ben suddenly felt very hot inside his clothes. Sweat formed on his scalp and dripped down from the tips of his hair, fogging up the visor and filling the helmet with a heady cloud of hot vapor. He blinked back the heat, and he pulled off his gloves and laid them on the motorcycle's seat. His palms were covered in a sheen of sweat. With trembling fingers, he reached up and pulled at his zipper. His fingers were so wet, they slid right off the metal, and he gripped it again, harder, and tried a second time. He pulled down, slowly unzipping the jacket until it fell away, and he shrugged it off his shoulders, grabbing it by the collar and laying it across the seat, over the gloves. Then he turned quietly on his heels and scooted away, toward the nearest break in the wall.

"Hey!" the woman snapped. "Helmet!"

"Dammit," Ben whispered.

Did you honestly think that would work? Patrick asked, sounding genuinely confused. *You look like something from a David Lynch music video.*

Ben turned back toward the woman once more. His mind raced with possible actions and outcomes. His brain sparked as quickly as it could, calculating the probability of his survival for each one.

Not a single one had good odds.

He sighed, defeated. He could make a run for it, but where would he go? Even if he could make it to the door, find a way to open it with John Henry over at the far end holding it closed, and then slip back out into the duster horde, the mechanic would sound some sort of alarm, rally the troops...and even if he managed to swipe his jacket with the duster control device on his way out, the raiders would run him down in no time. His legs were no match for the bikes.

Ben's hands trembled as he reached up and palmed either side of his helmet. He had no other choice.

He pushed it up slowly over his chin. The sweat that lathered his cheeks and his hair made for an effective lubricant, and the helmet slid right off. He swallowed hard as he held the helmet between his shaking hands and faced the woman at the bikes.

She furrowed her brow and dug her knuckles into her hips. She squinted hard and sucked at her teeth as she stared at the unmasked rider. "Sheet says Timmy had this bike," she said, picking up a clipboard from the wall and shaking it in the air.

Oh my god, his name was Timmy...what a sweet little angel, Patrick lamented.

"Must be a mistake," Ben said, his voice dry as the desert wind. He cleared his throat and licked the roof of his mouth. "I took it. I'm back now."

The woman bore into him with suspicious, unblinking eyes. "What's your name?" she asked.

Severus Snape. Oh my God, please say your name is Severus Snape, Patrick begged.

"It's...Steve."

God, you are no fun.

"Steve," the woman repeated. She worked her mouth, as if she was chewing on the sound of the name and tasting it for sweetness. If she found any, her face didn't show it. "Don't recall any Steves," she said, her eyes narrowing even further.

"I'm new," Ben gulped.

The woman grunted. She walked closer to his bike, her eyes locked on Ben the entire time. She reached down and snatched up the gloves and the jacket, inspecting them for damage. Satisfied, she tucked them under her arm, and then she checked the helmet as well. When she held it up, thin streams of sweat dribbled off and splattered onto the floor. "It's filthy," she said, disgusted.

"Hot outside," Ben explained, looking at the floor.

She set the helmet down next to her feet. Then she examined Ben's dirt bike carefully. She titled the bike this way, and that way...she slid her eyes over every inch, looking for nicks and splits. She stopped dead when she got to the front fender. She glared up at Ben and beckoned him forward. He reluctantly took a step closer. "What's this?" she demanded, stabbing the fender with her forefinger. The hard plastic there was chipped and scuffed, and covered in desert dust and scratch marks from the original rider's spill.

"Took a...bad turn," Ben said. He swallowed, but his throat was as dry as sandpaper, and he choked on his own air. He coughed and tried to work a lather of spit into his mouth, but it wouldn't come.

"Take better care," the woman growled, and she said it with such venom, with such pure malice, that Ben's skin prickled with goosebumps despite the heat, and a cold flush shuddered through his body.

This is a Slytherin house, Patrick decided.

"Sorry," Ben mumbled. He took the opportunity to retreat, raising his hands in apology and walking backward toward the nearest door in the drywall. "Sorry. I'm new." The woman eyed him with suspicion as he stepped backward. She inclined her head, as if deigning to let him pass away into the hangar. "Thank you," he whispered. "Sorry."

Then he ducked through the doorway and into the heart of the hangar.

He turned a corner and plowed straight into another man's chest.

Ben bounced back from the impact and looked up. He locked eyes with a much taller man. Ben recognized him almost instantly. It was the lead raider from the train, the one who'd knocked Ben unconscious and taken the Jansport.

"Ah, shit," Ben sighed.

The raider shot out his hand and grabbed Ben by the throat. He was quick as lightning, and he gripped Ben's neck hard, crushing his windpipe. Ben's entire body crumpled, and he gasped for air, clawing at the bigger man's hand with his own impotent fingers. "What in the bright blue fuck are you doing here?" the raider asked, his voice tinged with glee. "Are you trying to rob us back?"

"It's...mine..." Ben gagged as tiny black flecks began to speckle across his vision. His scrabbling fingers lost their grip, and his arms fell away, useless and limp, as the oxygen evaporated from his lungs.

And the darkness drew around him like a curtain.

33.

The blonde woman stared across the moat. An entire army of stick-thin ghouls stumbled around the hangar, thick as fibers on a carpet. Their skin was sallow and thin, stretched and brittle like paper that had been soaked in water and left to dry in the sun. Most of them streamed green mucous from their noses and mouths, and a few of them had it leaking from of their eyes, and oozing out from under their fingernails. The droning buzz of their groans filled the basin like a hornet's nest.

The woman turned and stalked away from the hangar, back through the mountain pass. She lumbered up to the body that lay awkwardly in the sand—the young man with the broken neck who had been stripped of his decencies. She picked up a rock, a sharp-edged stone bigger than her fist, and hefted it as she approached the body. She straddled one of the young man's arms, gripped the wrist, and pulled the arm taut. With her other hand, she raised the rock above her head, and then she brought it down on the meat of his arm, right at the shoulder socket. Again and again and again, she brought the rock down with all her strength, bludgeoning the flesh until it broke, jamming the sharp edge of the stone through the dead man's meat, cracking it against his bone, cutting down into him over and over and over again, until the bone broke too, and the meat split, and the blonde woman ripped his arm free of his shoulder, strings of flesh dangling from the meaty place like ribbons.

She flipped the rock back onto the ground and dragged the arm back over to the channel that circumvented the hangar. The ambling monsters paid her little heed. Even the dusters down in the ditch just stalked along, moving in a slow and endless ring. She'd never seen dusters so pacified.

She hurled the dismembered arm across the ravine. It landed in the dirt amid the morass of shambling creatures with a soft *plop*. In less time than it took to take a breath, the dusters sprang to life, working themselves into a frenzy, throwing their wasted bodies down onto the newly-dead flesh, scrabbling for purchase in the skin and sinking their teeth into the lifeless meat. They tore new wounds into the arm, and the blonde woman watched without interest as they chewed the flesh and swallowed it down, and as more dusters dove into the fray, piling on top of the others, blocking the decimated limb from sight.

The blonde woman's eyes clouded over with a film of thought. The dusters weren't as docile as they seemed.

That was going to make things harder.

Not impossible. Just harder.

She glared across the desert at the hangar.

One way or another, this would be over soon.

She turned and headed back for the rest of the body.

34.

Ben looked down. He was standing in a lake of shimmering black ink.

He looked around, confused. He didn't remember walking into a lake of ink. But he must have, because there he stood, in the very center of it. The ink came up to his knees, and he watched with interest as thin black tendrils soaked into the denim of his jeans and wound their way up toward his waist.

He looked up. The lake was big. Not Lake Michigan big, but still...big. He could see the shore, but it was far off in the distance. The land behind the lake was mountainous, but the mountains weren't desert mountains. They were enormous, snow-capped mountains; they were the Rockies, except not gray and black, like the Rockies are, but a bright jade green, as if they had been hewn from precious stone centuries ago, during some ancient Chinese dynasty.

Ben looked around. In every direction, there was thick, black lake and tall, green mountain. He was in a valley, where all the black ink of the world had collected, and he stood there in its center, his clothes taking on the stain.

He turned in a full circle, searching the area. He was alone in the lake.

He heard a splash to his left. He turned to find Patrick standing there silently, his hands stuffed deeply into his pockets, a sheepish grin crossing his boyish face.

"Where are we?" Ben asked. His voice sounded wrong. It seemed to stop short and die just outside of his lips, as if he were speaking in a closed and soundproofed room.

Patrick shrugged.

'We shouldn't be here," Ben heard himself saying, and the deep pull of dread in the pit of his stomach told him instinctively that it was true. "We should go."

Still smiling, Patrick raised both of his hands in a futile gesture, as if to say, *Where will we go?*

"Over the mountains," Ben said. "We have to go home."

Patrick closed his hands into fists and planted them on his hips. He made a sad, sour face, like a vaudeville actor's exaggerated notion of displeasure, and he shook his head in a wide, slow arc.

"We've been gone too long," Ben insisted. "We have to go home."

Patrick spread his arms out wide, and he looked up toward the sky and closed his eyes, his lips curled up into a smile. He stood like that, taking in the air, and the world, for a few seconds...then he let himself fall backward, splashing down into the lake. Despite the shallowness of the ink, his body sank beneath the surface, and the thick black liquid sped in to cover him up, and Patrick was gone.

"No!" Ben shouted. He dove forward and splashed into the lake, thrusting his hands into the ink and feeling for Patrick, but he could not find him; the ink had become too deep, and as the realization of the depth occurred to him, his feet suddenly understood it too, for there was no more ground beneath them, and he plunged down into the cold, black ink, thrashing his arms and gasping for air. "Patrick?! *Patrick!*" he screamed, spinning his knees and desperately treading for buoyancy. His head slipped beneath the surface once, and he clawed his way back to the air, covered in ink, the tang of it filling his mouth. He spat and he wept, with his eyes shut tight against the sting.

But then he felt a lowering of his body. He wasn't sinking; he didn't go beneath the surface again...but he was being *lowered*. He wiped the ink from his eyes with his wet, blackened hands, and the stain of it burned in his corneas. He squinted out at the lake, and the ink ring around the mountains just above the surface bore witness to the fact that the lake was draining.

Down, down, down, the surface retreated, and suddenly Ben's feet could touch the bottom of the lake once more. And the ink kept draining, and the lake shriveled up, leaving just a damp, blackened basin, stark against the shining jade of the mountains. The ink washed past his knees and spun into a whirlpool just to his left. The ink was sucked down, lower and lower, and then the toes of Patrick's shoes broke through the surface, then his nose, and the rest of his head. He was lying on his back at the bottom of the lake, and the ink spiraled down into his open mouth, and even when the surface level had gone below his lips, the whirlpool defied gravity so it could continue its path, pulling up the ink from beneath Patrick's shoulders, like a fountain set to reverse, and spilling down into his throat, until he sucked the entirety of the lake away, and Ben was standing in a wasted crater, his clothes tinged black, the earth tinged black, Patrick covered in black, and full of ink. Then Patrick's eyes opened, and he gasped, a wet, throaty gurgle rising from his throat. Ben looked down, and a wound opened up in Patrick's stomach, and tears leaked out from the hole, spilling down his abdomen and dripping over his ribs, until his body wept an ocean, and the lake was full again, but full of tears, and Ben tried to swim away, but his arms were tired, his soul was tired, and he struggled against the salty sadness, but he could not struggle anymore, and the lake of tears took him, and he sank beneath the waves, and he breathed Patrick's tears into his lungs, and he sank to the bottom of the lake, and the world faded out into static.

•

Ben broke back into the world, gasping for air. He lurched forward in a fever sweat from his dream, but he was yanked backward at the wrist. He pulled forward again, but something held him fast. He looked down at his hands. Thick brown straps encircled his forearms, securing him to a metal table. Similar bands bound his ankles, too. He jerked his wrists and his feet, furious and confused. "The fuck is this?!" he demanded, pulling at the straps.

"Goodness, what sudden life!" A face slid into view above Ben's eyes. It belonged to an older man, his head ringed with a wild halo of fuzzy white hair, the skin on his cheeks and his forehead pinched into a hundred papery wrinkles. But his eyes, big and bright and crackling with energy, hinted at a youthful spirit, hidden behind a pair of glasses with Coke-bottle-thick lenses. They served to magnify his irises, giving him an extra boost of whimsy and life. "How do you feel?" he asked.

"Pissed off!" Ben cried.

"Mm, yes, good." The old man retreated and picked up a clipboard from a nearby table. He made a few markings with his pen. "That is a *very* appropriate response."

"Let me go!" Ben demanded.

The old man looked at him quizzically. "I don't believe that's a very good idea," he decided.

"Let me out of here, or I swear to Christ, I will rip myself free and jam this whole table right through your skull," Ben seethed.

"Yes, that's exactly why freeing you is not a very good idea," the old man said, nodding. He rubbed his chin and blinked at Ben through his comically thick lenses. "You're from the train, is that right?"

"I *am* the train!" Ben cried, pulling again at the straps. He heaved himself up as far as he could, looking wildly around the room. He was surrounded by the same plain white drywall he'd seen at the front of the hangar, but the light here was dimmer, the ceiling lower, and this room was definitely a laboratory of some sort, hidden away in the secret basement of the hangar. Beakers and thin glass vials were fitted snugly into wooden racks on the walls. There were stainless steel carts everywhere, covered in scalpels, microscopes, empty slides, Bunsen burners, small centrifuges, and about three dozen other scientific paraphernalia Ben couldn't even begin to identify. There was also a makeshift emergency eye wash station in the corner, a five-gallon water cooler jug full of water, suspended from the ceiling, connected to a plastic tube that was cinched off near the opening with a clamp.

Just next to it, on one of the steel carts, was Ben's purple Jansport backpack.

The old man made a confused face. "You *are* the train. Mm-hmm," he muttered. He made some notes on his clipboard.

"Who the hell are you?" Ben asked.

"Oh! Yes! Hello!" the old man replied, brightening quite a bit. He extended his hand. Ben stared at it, incredulous. The man moved his hand down to Ben's own secured hand and gave it a light shake. "I am Dr. Joseph Bergamot. M.D., D.O., D.H.S., Au.D., Ph.D."

"You fucking nerd!" Ben sneered.

"Oh...you must have just a bachelor's," Bergamot said, his voice sympathetic. "Yes, I suppose you would say that I *am* a nerd. I am *fascinated* by knowledge, and the general workings of people, and of the world we inhabit! Aren't you?" he asked, his voice buoyant with wonder.

Ben gaped at him. "I'm tied to a fucking table!" he screamed, yanking furiously at all of his straps.

"Very interesting reaction," Bergamot observed. He took a note on his clipboard.

"What are you going to do to me?" Ben demanded, his chest rising and falling with the force of his breath. "You don't tie someone down if you're going to kill them. You're going to perform weird-ass experiments on me, aren't you? Are you gonna perform weird-ass experiments on me?!"

"Hmm. Maybe!" the doctor replied brightly, as if this were actually the first time the idea had occurred to him.

"I swear to God, if you anally probe me—"

"Whoa, whoa, whoa!" Bergamot exclaimed, throwing his hands up in surprise. "Who said anything about anal probes? What is it you think we do here, exactly?"

"I don't know!" Ben cried. "I know you send out armies to attack trains and murder innocent people, why the fuck wouldn't you probe an ass or two when you had the chance?!"

"That is a gross misrepresentation," the doctor said, troubled, furrowing his brow. "It's...more complicated than that."

"It's not complicated," Ben said, resting his head back against the table. "My recruits were good men. They were idiots, okay, but they knew right from wrong. They were good men. And your people butchered them."

The old doctor clasped his hands, and he bit at his bottom lip as he paced a bit around the room. "I don't condone it," he said, more to himself than to Ben. "It's an awful thing, all this death. But there are bigger things at stake."

"Like power by theft," Ben said, his words dripping with contempt.

The doctor stopped pacing. He straightened up and cocked his head, staring at Ben with confusion. "No," he said, shaking his head. "No, no. Not *theft*. Theft *back*."

Ben scoffed. "What does that mean?"

"My people aren't *thieves*," the doctor said, placing a hand against his chest and sounding hurt. "No. No, train employee."

"My name is Ben," Ben interrupted, rolling his eyes.

"Ben, yes, good. My people aren't thieves. They didn't steal those bottles from you. They stole them *back* from you."

Ben wrinkled his eyebrows. "We didn't steal them."

"But *we* stole them *back*."

"What the hell does that mean?!

The doctor shook his head and mumbled to himself. He crossed the room and approached a miniature refrigerator plugged into the wall in the corner. He pulled it open and retrieved something from inside. It was one of the bottles the raiders had stolen from the train, still full of the thick, bright orange liquid. He shut the fridge and brought the bottle over to the examination table. "What do you know about this?"

"I love Tang," Ben sneered. "I always have."

Dr. Bergamot frowned. "These answers are not convincing me that you're not a danger."

Ben rolled his eyes and rested his head against the table. He sighed. "I know it's supposedly a cure that we were paid to transport to a buyer. I know we picked it up from the supplier. I know it supposedly cures the Monkey sickness. I know your people slaughtered my people to get it."

"Almost right," the doctor said quietly, almost sadly. "You *were* bringing it to the buyer. And it most certainly does cure the Monkey sickness. But the woman you picked it up from…she didn't formulate the cure." He turned the bottle over and held it so the cap was within reading range for Ben. "What do you see?"

Ben focused on the medical tape that was wrapped around the cap, and the letters that had been written there. "J-R-B," he read.

"JRB," the doctor agreed, nodding. "You know what that stands for?" He taped his finger against the letters. "Joseph. Rondigo. Bergamot."

Ben's eyes narrowed with disbelief. "*You* made the serum?"

The doctor nodded solemnly. "I did."

Ben looked at him suspiciously. "Your middle name is Rondigo?"

"Sins of the father," Bergamot sighed. "But yes. I formulated the cure. It was stolen from me, with the aim of putting it into dangerous hands. I directed my people to steal it back. And I regret the lives that were lost, I do...I regret them more than you can conceivably imagine. But I instructed my people to retrieve the cure at any cost, and they did."

"You have no idea the cost of it," Ben seethed, his cheeks flushing red with anger.

But the doctor nodded in agreement, and his eyes misted over with tears of regret. "I know," he said quietly. "The casualties in this war..." He shook his head sadly. "They are far too many to bear."

Ben screwed up his face in disgust. "What *war*?" he spat. "There is no *war*; the *war* is over, the Jamaicans won, and we lost *hard. That* was the war, there's no *new* war. Jesus!" Ben's anger bubbled up inside of him, searing his veins and boiling the underside of his skin. "The casualties have been for *nothing.* You've taken them without a war!"

The doctor gave him a confused look. "No, there *is* a war," he insisted, as if the need to explain it was the most idiotic thing he'd encountered in his life. "There's a *new* war. It's the war of life. It's the war of who lives and who dies." He approached Ben's table and planted his hands on the metal, bringing his face close to Ben's. "Do you not understand? The sickness, the Green Fever, it is absolute. *Scientifically* absolute. Everyone will experience it. *Everyone.* Every single survivor. On a surprisingly short timeline, the survival rate against the Jamaican virus is zero percent. I cannot overstate the insanity of that. *Zero percent.* In fifteen years, *no one* will be alive—do you understand that? Without my cure, humanity will reach zero percent survival. *Zero percent.* Literally each and every person who survived M-Day will suffer death in the next fifteen years. Mankind will be extinct. Not endangered; we're endangered right now. Mankind will be *extinct.* But for this cure." He raised up the bottle of orange fluid and gazed at it tenderly. "This is truly and completely, without hyperbole, mankind's salvation."

"Bullshit," Ben snarled, pulling once more at his restraints, though mostly for effect. "No virus hits everyone, one hundred percent."

"This isn't a virus," the doctor said, his face grave. "And its toll *will* be one hundred percent. There's no doubt. No immunity. One hundred percent."

"You can't know that."

"I *do* know that," he said with finality.

Small chills prickled through Ben's bones. "Fine. It doesn't matter. You made the cure, you can keep the cure. I don't want it. Just let me go." He sighed and leaned back against the table. "Just let me go."

The doctor looked amazed. "You expect me to believe you came all this way but now, faced with this, you would just walk away? That you chanced your way through my sea of hungry ones outside, and you would just…leave?" He snorted and shook his head. "I don't think so."

"Is that what you're going to do to me?" Ben asked, setting his jaw. "Turn me into one of them?"

The doctor tilted his head and considered Ben carefully. "No," he said, his voice a knot of confusion. "Is that…? What is it that you think we do out here?"

"I have no idea," Ben said.

"This!" The doctor held up the bottle of antidote and shook it frantically. "*This*! This is what we do! This has been my constant work since M-Day! *This*! We don't turn people into hungry ones; I don't send out armies for slaughter, I don't take hostages and—and perform *ungodly* experiments on them!" he cried, clearly agitated. "I've heard what they say, but I'm not a monster! I'm a *doctor*! It's for this! *This*! Only this!"

"Then what are you doing with so many fucking zombies in your yard?!"

"I've brought them here to cure them!" he bellowed, throwing up his arms. He set the antidote down on a counter near the wall and began to pace the laboratory, annoyed. "The formula isn't yet right. It works on early-stage cases, but I haven't cracked it yet for advanced stages. But mark my words, I will! I will! My work continues." The doctor suddenly looked very tired.

"Bullshit," Ben decided, squinting suspiciously. "If you're such a hero, why don't you keep them inside? Out of the sun? Out of the weather? Why do you let them drag around this place like a pack of mangy fucking dogs?"

"Well," the doctor said, giving a guilty shrug, "they *do* offer the side benefit of deterrence. I admit, I do…*use* them, I guess. I'm not proud of it! But without the added security they provide, we would fall under siege—I have no doubt about that. No, none whatsoever. They protect our work, and in return, our work will cure them. Our work will set them free. I have no doubt of that, either."

"And you didn't create them all out of living people in this lab?"

"No, of course not!"

"If they're not science experiments, then how is it you can mind-control them with a VCR remote?" Ben demanded. He would have crossed his arms in an extremely satisfied manner over this particular chess move of an argument point if they hadn't been restrained at his sides.

The doctor's eyes popped open wide in total bewilderment. "Mind control with a remote?" He rolled a stool out from beneath a counter and plopped down on it, shaking his head. "I don't know if you've watched too many movies or missed too many classes in school, but boy. I tell you. Probably both. Your generation…"

"Don't patronize me, I'm an adult!" Ben insisted. "Are you gonna tell me those dusters just decided totally on their own to let me roll on through out of the goodness of their hearts?"

"No, of course not," Bergamot said, waving his hand dismissively. He rolled closer to Ben's table. He seemed interested in the proposition of having a new and interested student, even if that student was a real dunce. "It's not mind control; it's frequency!"

"That movie sucked," Ben said.

"Yes it did," Bergamot agreed. "But listen: the hungry ones, they get that way by ingesting too much of the Monkey dust. It gets in their bloodstreams, and the liver can't process it. So it collects inside of them, and it solidifies like a calcium, or like a cement! You can understand cement, yes?"

"Yes, Ben can understand cement," Ben glowered.

"It builds like this, solidifying the blood vessels. All through their veins, all through their bodies. The ears have so many blood vessels; one of the side effects of the dust buildup is that the structure of the ear fundamentally changes. The calcium-like deposits don't absorb sound the same way the natural ear does. Higher frequency sounds ricochet through the ear drum. Do you understand?"

Ben gaped at the doctor. "Are you telling me that after all these years of fighting dusters with hammers and bats, all we had to do is *scream* at them?"

"Well, no, not exactly. But a noise of over thirty kilohertz ought to do the trick."

Ben shook his head in amazement. His eyes rolled up into his head, and he fell back against the table. "Well, fuck me," he said.

"Science is a wonder," Bergamot agreed. "We equipped each of our vehicles with transmitters. On the bikes, they're connected to the batteries," he said proudly. "As long as the bike is running, the rider is safe."

"I'll be damned," Ben muttered.

"Like on the bike you rode in on," the doctor frowned. "I won't even ask you how you got it."

"That's probably best," Ben agreed. He changed the subject quickly. "If this is your antidote, and you want it here with you, how the hell did it get on my train?"

Bergamot sighed. "That," he said ruefully, "is a rather long story."

"That sounds great. Why don't you loosen me up here, and tell me the whole thing?"

Bergamot actually seemed to consider this. He bobbed his head lightly from side to side, as if weighing the option against his better judgment. "No," he said slowly, drawing out the vowel to an interminable length. Then he said it again, more definitely. "No. Let's talk more. You seem like an honest man, but...let's just talk."

Ben sighed. "Fine. But this had better not be one of those awful supervillain-style monologues." He scoffed. "God, I hate those."

"There is a villain in this story, but it isn't me," Bergamot assured him. "There was a physicist working here, a remarkably brilliant doctor. Susannah Gustheed. I found her—or rather, she found us—when we were retrofitting this hangar. So you see, we worked on this together almost from the very start. But it was a condition of her staying here and working—an absolute condition—that she was a guest in *my* lab. I made the decisions. It wasn't a power trip, you understand, or some Neanderthal idea about idiotic gender roles. It's that I have given myself a job, and I must see it through to my satisfaction. Which means in this lab, I have the final say. We fostered a collaborative environment, and Susannah contributed so many exciting and phenomenally sound ideas to the work, I couldn't have discovered the cure without her. But I am the ultimate decision-maker. In all disputes, my word is final."

"I get it, I get it...you're the king of Junk Lab," Ben said.

"Junk Lab?" Bergamot said, taken aback. He looked around at his cobbled-together basement workspace. "It's the best I could do," he said with a frown. "It's the apocalypse out there." Bergamot wrinkled his lips in a sad expression of pain, but he continued. "Once we had tested the antidote to our mutual satisfaction and devised a formula that worked, you can imagine the sort of excitement that took hold here. The possibilities blossomed before us! There is so much you can do with a cure to an extinction sickness; there are so many paths you can walk, so many places to start! In the end, though..." Bergamot's voice became duller, and it trailed off as he became lost in some secret and painful memory. "In the end, Susannah and I reached an impasse of opinion. I wanted to turn this hangar into a factory. Replicate the antidote in as large of quantities as we could, and then distribute it to the remaining population, starting with our own people, and expanding systematically outward, through the region, and eventually across the country, as long as our resources held out."

"And she wanted to sell the formula to the highest bidder," Ben said.

Bergamot started. "Why, yes," he said, sounding surprised. Then he gave a quick, rueful laugh. "You hit on it easily. Was I really such a fool to not see the importance of wealth, even in a time as this?"

Ben shrugged. "I've just met a lot of people," he said. Then he added, "People are pretty much the worst."

Bergamot nodded, tapping his fingers on the examination table. "At this point, I might have to agree," he conceded.

"So she stole the antidote and sold it off."

"In a manner of speaking, yes. She did steal the antidote, every full bottle of it, along with the formula. I came to the lab one morning, and it was all gone, and so was she."

"How'd you track her down?"

"Well...we haven't, exactly. The priority was the antidote—the formula first, and the completed samples second. I know of only two people who have amassed enough post-world wealth to satisfy the price tag for something as precious as the cure. There may be others, but I know only of those two, and Susannah knows of them, too. She spoke of them often." Dr. Bergamot pulled off his glasses and pinched the bridge of his nose in frustration. "One to the west, in California, called Darcy Black. I know little of her...just whispers, mostly. But the other...the other is a rather formidable figure who lives out east, a man who calls himself the Source of Mercy."

Ben's eyes lit with understanding. "The Source is all-consuming," he whispered, repeating the words of the Post-Alignment monks.

"So you've heard of him," the doctor said, nodding. "Everything I know comes second- or third-hand. But I've seen evidence of his cruelty, too. The Source of Mercy, he is…well, I don't know what you'd call him, exactly. A cult leader, maybe? Like Charles Manson, or David Koresh, but sadistic. *Sadistic*," he said again, holding up his hands for emphasis. "A charismatic savage."

"Oh, he's like Barney the Dinosaur!" Ben said. Bergamot gave Ben a sad, confused look. "Sorry," he mumbled, flushing red. He held up his wrists. "Tied to a table. It's bringing out my inner Patrick."

"Your what?" the doctor asked.

Ben shook his head. "Nothing. Just my brain tumor."

"You have a brain tumor?" Bergamot replied, perking up. "Did you have an MRI?"

"How would I get an MRI? It's the apocalypse; I burned my insurance card for warmth, like, five years ago."

The doctor pursed his lips and considered Ben carefully. "Then how do you know you have a brain tumor?" he asked.

"Because I…hear voices. In my head. Talking."

"Like your conscience?" Bergamot asked, leaning forward. He grabbed a pen from his lab coat pocket and clicked it open, apparently unaware of the fact that he didn't have any paper.

"Don't write this down," Ben said sourly, trying to wave the pen away. "No. Not like my conscience; like a voice. My dead friend's *actual voice*. We have conversations, weird, stupid conversations that are exactly like the weird, stupid conversations we had when he was alive. With words that he would actually use, that I definitely do not use."

"Ah! Auditory hallucinations," Bergamot said, mostly to himself. He moved his pen as if to jot some notes, but realized for the first time that he wasn't holding any paper. He lifted his hands in confusion, as if a notebook had just mysteriously vanished from his grasp.

"Not just auditory," Ben clarified. "Also visual. Sometimes. Not all the time. But sometimes."

"I see," the doctor said, scratching his chin thoughtfully. "And no MRI…so who diagnosed you?"

"I did," Ben said, suddenly feeling defensive. "So what?"

"Nothing," Bergamot replied, holding up his hands. "Just asking."

"I know what a brain tumor is," Ben grumped.

"Oh, do you have medical training?" the doctor asked, genuinely interested.

Ben hesitated. He gritted his teeth until they squeaked. "I'm very good with tourniquets."

Bergamot tilted his head. He blinked. "Is that all?"

"Look, you're a doctor. Can you fix it?" Ben demanded.

Bergamot considered this. "I actually might be able to," he said.

"I don't want to be cut open," Ben warned. "I know that's probably how you have to do it, but I'm telling you. No lobotomies."

"Have you ever considered that it might *not* be a tumor?"

Ben snorted. "Some doctor you are. Of course it's a brain tumor. What else would it be?"

Bergamot leaned back on his stool and stared thoughtfully toward the ceiling. "As a matter of fact, there are several other maladies that can cause hallucinations of this sort. One of them is simple stress. Do you feel stressed?"

"I'm strapped to a table in the secret lab of a post-apocalyptic doctor. *Of course I feel stressed!*" Ben screamed. A man poked his head in from the hallway—a guard, presumably, his hand resting on a hatchet set into a holster at his hip. But Bergamot waved him off, mouthing the words, *it's fine, it's fine*. The man retreated slowly.

"It could be stress," the doctor repeated, "especially if you experience headaches."

"I do experience headaches," Ben confirmed. "That's the tumor."

"Possibly. It could also be dehydration. Or it could be Parkinson's... or the flu...or just run-of-the-mill dementia."

"Run-of-the-mill dementia. Great."

"I'm just saying, there are many potential causes. It could be gre—"

"I get it, I get it," Ben snapped, cutting him off. "I take it back; I don't want you to fix it. I want to die so I don't have to hear you recite every possible way I might die. Go back to the other thing. The mercy guy."

"The Source of Mercy."

"Yes, the Source of Mercy. Go back to that."

"Mm. Yes." Bergamot stroked his chin absently, losing himself in thought. "Susannah sold him the antidote, but not the formula...that, she must have given to Darcy Black. Or maybe she still has it herself. I don't know. The Source is formidable. I don't know his background. I first heard his name a couple of years ago. He seems to have come up out of nowhere, but he has amassed an extraordinary following in a very short amount of time, and extreme wealth along with it. He controls a compound—or, *compound* isn't quite right...a campus, I guess. To hear it told, dozens of people make the journey to the House of Mercy every month, all looking for the same thing."

"More beans?" Ben guessed.

Bergamot pushed his glasses up his nose. "Acceptance," he said. "The Source will accept them, with all their faults, with all their *histories.* He is willing to accept the monstrous among us for the awful things they've done, that they've felt *compelled* to do, since M-Day."

"Why would they need some stranger's acceptance?"

"Because they believe that with acceptance comes a new utopia of being."

"What the hell does that mean?" Ben asked sourly. "They get an official pardon, and then they can enter the Promised Land?"

"In a manner of speaking, yes," Bergamot said, giving his shoulders a shrug. "The Source gives you a home, and forgiveness. Acceptance. If you earn his favor."

"Okay. So what happens?" Ben asked. "How do they get this favor?"

"There's a process," Bergamot said. "I don't know every step. Just what I've heard. But there are thirteen of them, thirteen steps. The Thirteen Mercies. Each one is more demented than the next. If you complete all thirteen, you complete the process. You become what they call a Peaceful One."

"I'm guessing that name is probably ironic."

"Oh, most definitely," Bergamot nodded gravely. "The Peaceful Ones are brutal, relentless servants of the Source. In exchange for his blessing, for his *acceptance,* for what they are told will be a life of ease and bliss, they give themselves over to him wholly. They perform his will with something like a hive mind. And believe me when I say where there is a Peaceful One, there is a trail of death and pain."

"Sounds like someone I know," Ben snorted. He could still feel the pressure of the sledge hammer the blonde woman had pressed against his temple. "What are the thirteen steps? The ones that you know of?"

"They start with the Hundred Apologies, where a member of the Peaceful Ones takes a serrated knife and gives you fifty hard cuts on each arm, wrist to shoulder. Every time they draw the knife across your skin, you make an apology. If any single one doesn't sound heartfelt, they jam the blade into your throat."

"Jesus," Ben said. "That's the *first* step?"

Bergamot nodded grimly. "Those who survive—either the knife to the throat, or the loss of blood from the cuts themselves—they move on. Another step is the Beggar's Foot. They tie your ankles together, then smash them with bricks until they shatter."

"I'm sorry, people *ask* for this?" Ben said, incredulous. "They put themselves through it on *purpose?*"

"More people than you would believe. For one of the final steps, they heat a spoonful of pebbles over a fire, then force the hot stones down your throat."

"Jesus," Ben whispered. "All of that for an easier life?"

"The Source is convincing, apparently. Even though an easy life is hardly what the Peaceful Ones get." He shook his head sadly. "Only a handful survive the hot stones. I imagine most people choke. Sometimes the pebbles burn right through the esophagus. For those who *do* survive, the scarring must be...extensive. I imagine they're left with limited powers of speech."

"Holy shit...it really *does* sound like someone I know," Ben said, his eyes wide. "You said the Source is East Coast?"

"The compound is out east, but the Peaceful Ones are everywhere. That's the trick of it. They sign up for a peaceful life, but after they pass the trials, he spreads them around like some sort of perverse missionary program. They spend several years on various assignments all over the country, possibly all over the continent. I wouldn't be surprised if he has a whole network of them spread between here and there, daisy-chaining information about us and—" Bergamot stopped. He looked down at Ben. His pupils became pinpricks against stark white fields of fear as realization set in. "And watching the train," he breathed. He caught his breath and gripped the examination table, his knuckles going pale with the pressure of his grip. "Were they watching the train? Did you see a Peaceful One?"

"I more than saw her," Ben said. The doctor's panic was contagious. His heart started to thrum, and adrenaline shot through his veins. He pulled hard at his straps. "Untie me. *Now*."

"Where?" Bergamot demanded. He loosened his grip on the table and smacked his palms down on the metal surface, next to Ben's side. His entire body was trembling. "Where did you see her?"

"I've seen her fucking *everywhere!*" Ben replied.

Bergamot straightened up, his face a blazing red light of alarm. "Has she followed you?" he asked, his voice tight. "Have you led her *here*?"

"I don't know," Ben said. "I lost her a while back, maybe she—" But he stopped, and the heavy weariness of defeat bore down on his bones like a metal press. An image faded into his mind just then, quivering in its focus…an image of a piece of paper, creased from folding and re-folding, pinned beneath a saddlebag on a platform of stone jutting out from a cliff in the desert.

"What? What is it?" Bergamot demanded.

Ben shook his head. "Goddammit," he cursed himself under his breath. Then, louder, he said, "I think she has a map."

Bergamot's eyes bulged like they were being inflated through some secret valve in his skull. "To *our* location?"

"I found one of your guys in the desert. He gave me a map. I made him…I made him give me his map. That's how I found you." He closed his eyes. "I left it behind. I had to bug out last night, and I left it behind. She might have it now."

Bergamot threw his hands into his shock of hair and pulled furiously at the roots. The blood rushed back to his cheeks, flooding them a dark purple. "Rickson! *Rickson!*" the doctor shrieked.

The guard in the hallway poked his head back into the room, his hand resting on his hatchet. He looked sharply around the room, and his shoulders relaxed when he saw there was no immediate threat. "Yeah?"

"Sound the alarm!" Bergamot cried as he leapt across the room and yanked open a metal drawer. The instruments inside smashed against each other as Bergamot dug through them, looking for something. Without closing the drawer, he opened a second one, but he pulled it too hard, and the whole drawer came out. The doctor jumped backward, and the heavy metal drawer crashed to the ground at his feet, spilling clamps and scalpels and forceps and scissors across the floor.

"The alarm?" the guard asked, confused.

"Yes, the alarm—sound the alarm!" Bergamot screamed, moving onto the next drawer and pulling that one open, too.

The guard crossed his arms and shifted his weight to one leg. The emergency wasn't really setting in. He screwed up his face and said, "You mean the *big* alarm?"

"*Yes, yes, dammit, yes, the big alarm, sound the big alarm!*" the doctor shrieked, throwing his hands up in frustration. Then he jammed them into the drawer, wading through the odds and ends, scraping metal against metal and cursing under his breath at the nicks and cuts sustained by his hurried fingers.

Rickson looked uncertainly at Ben. "Sound it…for *him?*" Their prisoner seemed pretty well-confined.

"No!" Bergamot screamed. "No, no, no! Go! Now! Sound the damned—!" But before he could finish, a loud horn blared from a set of speakers overhead. The lights began to flash slowly, dimming and brightening, dimming and brightening. Bergamot looked at Rickson.

Rickson looked at Ben.

Ben looked very directly at the ceiling, avoiding any eye contact as his cheeks flushed red with guilt. "I…guess she made it," he said, his voice barely audible over the honking alarm.

A loud crash sounded from above, from the front of the hangar, then a peppering of gunshots, followed by screams. Even from the basement, and with the horn blaring, Ben was pretty sure he could hear the snapping of bones.

"Sorry," he added quietly.

Rickson snapped into action first, pulling his hatchet from his hip and scrambling out of the room. More raiders flashed by the doorway as they rushed toward the stairway that would take them to the intruder. More gunshots were fired, more people screamed, and a cacophony of other sounds Ben couldn't identify echoed around the hangar—brutal clangs and sharp snaps and quick breaks and loud pops.

Bergamot finally found what he was looking for, and he lifted a semi-automatic handgun from the back of the drawer. Given how long it had taken him to find it, Ben guessed he probably wasn't very used to firing it. There was a wildness in his eyes, and the gun trembled in his hands as he fumbled with a box of bullets and tried to work the clip.

Ben had seen plenty of unpracticed academics try to use firearms in a panic. Things were about to get *extremely* dangerous.

"Cut me loose," Ben said, working to keep his voice even. "You have *got* to cut me loose. Because trust me, you're not going to be able to face her alone."

"I have a gun," he said, as a bullet slipped out from between his fingers and rolled under the cart. He cursed and grabbed a new bullet, and pushed it into the clip.

"And you're really good with it," Ben said. "But I saw her take out an entire town. Literally. An entire *town*. With her bare hands. You need my help."

Bergamot took some deep breaths. He weighed his options as he pushed more bullets into the clip. "I don't know you," he said. "You could turn on me."

Ben shook his head. "I just came for my bag," he said. "And even if I *was* here to take the antidote, we would have to stop her first. And that's not going to be easy." A few more screams echoed up from the front of the hangar, and one more gunshot fired. Then there was a loud crunch, and the noises stopped. Ben's ears pricked up against the sounding horn. The doctor was listening, too.

"Maybe they stopped her," he said hopefully.

"Or maybe she just took out your entire army," Ben replied.

Bergamot pushed the clip into the gun. "She won't be expecting me to fight," he said. He puffed out his cheeks. "I can do this." But there was sweat dripping off his nose, and tears glistened in his eyes.

"Let me off of this fucking table," Ben hissed, straining at the leather straps. "Keep me between the two of you, use me for a human shield—I don't fucking care, give me a *chance!* You leave me on this table, I am *dead!*"

Bergamot switched the gun from one hand to the other, and then back again. He rubbed his arm against his forehead, and his sleeve came away soaked through. "Okay," he decided. "Fine." He set the gun down on the counter and turned back to the table. He grabbed the strap around Ben's left wrist and pulled the end out of the buckle. He was about to pull the leather free of the clasp when movement caught their eyes, and he screamed.

The blonde woman stood in the doorway, her shoulders scraping the frame. She was covered in blood—some of it hers, most of it not. It clung to her clothes and dripped from the tips of her hair. Red splatters marked her brow, and a pink streak crossed her eye where she'd wiped away gore to clear her vision. She was breathing heavily. One of her sleeves had been slashed open, and it dangled from her shoulder, exposing a seam of raised scars down the length of her arm.

"Shit," Ben cursed.

The doctor stumbled back from the table, leaving Ben still strapped down. "No!" Ben screamed. "Come on, goddammit, let me out! Let me out!" His voice was so high-pitched and strained that he didn't recognize it. It was a stranger's voice. A sacrificial scream.

He rocked and pitched himself, straining against his bonds, pulling with every muscle in his body. He felt the veins in his neck flood and pulse against his skin. He screamed with effort and frustration, but the straps wouldn't give. He began flailing in desperation, and the table started rocking, rising up on two legs, then crashing down and bucking back up on the other two, back and forth, until Ben threw himself too hard against the edge, and the table tipped over. It crashed to the concrete floor, vibrating hard and shaking his very bones. The knuckles of his right hand scraped against the rough concrete surface, leaving a small smear of blood beneath his hand. "*Fuck!*" he screamed, hanging sideways by the straps, his body open and defenseless and facing the blonde woman in the doorway.

Bergamot had fallen back against the counter, and the woman watched without expression as he fumbled for the gun. He picked it up and whirled around, his entire body jerking in spasms like a malfunctioning carnival ride. He closed his eyes and squeezed the trigger four times, firing across the room. The bullets exploded through the drywall on either side of the blonde woman, the nearest one missing her by eight full inches.

She didn't flinch.

"Oh, are you *kidding me?!*" Ben cried.

Bergamot squeezed the trigger again, but the gun clicked, empty. He had only loaded four bullets into the magazine.

"You stupid fuck," Ben whispered, closing his eyes. Tears spilled from the corners of his lids. They dripped onto the concrete, mixing with his blood. "You are so stupid for a doctor."

The blonde woman flexed her fingers into fists. They hung at her sides like bowling balls. "Antidote," she said, her voice raspy and chopped.

"P-P-Please," Bergamot stammered, holding up one hand in defense. With the other, he gripped the edge of the counter, as if he thought that if he held on tightly enough, she wouldn't be able to pry him away. "Please, l-l-leave me one. Just one." Terror coated his words, made them stick. "Okay? One, and I can—I can s-save everybody."

She stepped into the room, her boot thumping against the concrete like a sack of feed. Ben could smell the metal in the blood that dripped from her chin. "Antidote," she said again, with a cold impatience that turned Ben's heart to ice.

"Give her the bottles," Ben said quietly, his eyes still closed. But the blood in his body was draining to his head, and his vision was fuzzed with spots so that even in the darkness behind his lids, his saw stains of blood-red light. "Just give her the bottles."

"I-I can't," he said, his voice catching with the terrified gasps of his breath. "I have to k-k-keep it s-safe." But his biology betrayed him; he instinctively looked down at the refrigerator as he said it, just for a flash, just a microsecond of a tell, but the blonde woman saw it. She thudded toward the refrigerator. "No! No!" Bergamot yelled, throwing himself down onto his knees in front of the cooler. "Please, no! Everyone will die! Don't you see?! Everyone will *die!*"

Ben squeezed his eyes shut even harder as the woman reached down and grabbed the doctor by the throat. She pulled him up to his feet, sputtering and choking and begging with his eyes. "Not everyone," she said simply, without a single trace of emotion. Then she let her hand slip a few inches so that she held him by the chin, her thumb and forefinger against his jaws, the outer edge of her palm pressing against his Adam's apple. She gave his head a sharp, hard turn, and Ben flinched at the sound of the crack. The woman tossed the doctor to the side, and the dead weight of his body slammed against the upper edge of Ben's table. His waist caught on the upended table legs, and his body folded like a doll, hanging over the edge of the table, his lifeless lips brushing against Ben's shins.

"Goddammit," Ben whispered, shaking his head and gritting his teeth. "This fucking world."

The blonde woman pulled open the refrigerator, removed all five bottles of the bright-orange antidote, and set them on the counter. She looked down at the mess of instruments and medical supplies at her feet, scanning the floor until she found what she was looking for. She picked up a syringe and a fresh needle, sealed in plastic. She ripped the plastic with her teeth, slipped out the needle, and fitted it into the syringe. Then she picked up one of the bottles of antidote, screwed off the lid, stuck the needle down into the bottle, and drew a few milliliters of the serum into the syringe. She set the bottle back down and turned her attention to her arm. She ripped off the tattered sleeved and used it to mop up the blood, streaking it across her scars. She spied the eye wash in the corner of the room and crunched over the metal tools strewn across the floor. She pulled off the clamp and held her arm under the running water. The rest of the blood washed away in pink rivulets, pooling into the cracks in the concrete.

With her arm rinsed, Ben could see the damage she'd taken in her assault on the hangar. There were fresh cuts sliced into her arms, and a hole at the edge of her elbow that looked like a graze from a bullet. But what made Ben shudder was the series of bite marks winding around her upper arm. The shapes of teeth were clearly visible in the wounds. One of the dusters had even ripped out a chunk of her flesh, a small chunk, about the size of a peach pit, but the edges of the skin around the hole were ragged, and the gash had pooled with blood again as soon as she'd rinsed it off.

The woman tied the wet, bloody sleeve around her bicep, cinching it tight with her teeth. She flexed her fingers a few times, until a vein rose on her forearm. She jabbed in the needle and pumped the antidote into the vein, where it set to work spreading through her body and fighting the Monkey dust poison in her system.

"Will you just make it quick?" Ben asked, as she drew the needle out of her arm and dropped it onto the floor. His eyes were strained with the release of too many tears. They felt dry now, and rough, like pavement. "The bullets are on the counter...can you just—shoot me in the head or something?" The blonde woman looked down at him, but her face was cold and passive and inscrutable. Then she turned her attention to the bottles on the counter, and Ben couldn't help but laugh. "No one like you is supposed to exist," he said, shaking his head and laughing.

The sound of laughter was strange, coming from his throat, in this place. "You're a Cormac McCarthy character come to life." This somehow struck him as unbelievably funny, and he laughed harder.

The blonde woman ignored him. She considered the five bottles, then she glanced around the room until her eyes fell upon the backpack on the counter. Ben's backpack. The old purple Jansport from the train.

"Your name's probably something like...Maghlut, or...Shvearum. Some kind of name no one would know how to say if they saw it in print, and they'd have to wait for the movie." He howled with laughter, laughed until he couldn't breathe, until a pain crept into his side, and still, he laughed some more.

The woman grabbed the backpack, pulled open the main pocket, and upended it, dumping its contents onto the counter. Some snack bars, a few pens, gum wrappers, the tattered half of an old twenty-dollar bill that had dissolved away from the rest of itself sometime before M-Day, when value was still weighed in strips of green cotton paper. And a notebook.

Ben could barely get the words out, he was laughing so hard. "Man. Patrick loved Cormac McCarthy. Patrick would love *you!* He would go absolutely bonkers for the ridiculousness of you!"

The woman stuffed the five bottles into the Jansport, zipped it up, and struggled into it, fitting it around her shoulders so the nylon straps strained with the effort of holding themselves together. She looked like a grown-up playing school day with a child's backpack.

"God, Patrick, you would love her," Ben laughed, nodding. "You would think this was the most absolutely absurd fucking way to die in the world. Patrick, are you seeing this? Is it not the absolute goddamn *best?*"

But Patrick was silent.

Patrick was...gone.

"Can't watch this part, huh?" he whispered to his old dead friend. His eyes were suddenly wet. He hadn't run out of tears after all. He hung there sideways on the overturned metal table, and saltwater stung his eyes and dribbled down his temple. He saw the woman pick up the pistol, saw her pop out the clip with practiced ease, watched her load it up and slide it back into the grip of the gun. Saw her come around the table, the gun in her hand. Saw her step up to the table, saw her lift the gun.

Ben nodded again, crying now almost as hard as he'd been laughing moments before. "Guess I'll come to you this time," he said through the film of mucous that coated his tongue. "God, and Sarah. I'll see you so soon. And Isabel, my Isa—" His voice broke, and he sobbed. The pain in his heart was overwhelming, too much to bear, but also beautiful, and swelled with hope. He'd be with them now, with his family, in the place they'd gone before, where fires didn't burn, skin didn't crackle, where people weren't mean or petty or violent, where there was no falling, only flying, and where they would be whole, where he would find them whole. Where he would be whole. "Soon," he whispered.

And then he laughed again, laughed because the pain in his heart was a heavy memoir, typed in the black ink of guilt and regret, and the blonde woman was about to be a match set to that book, and it would burn like blazes, down to the ash, and the pages of memory would be gone, blown away on a hot desert wind, the words blackened and disintegrated, and they would not be strung together again.

"Soon," he said again.

Soon. The word returned to him, whispered not by Patrick, or not *just* by him…it was a small chorus, it was Patrick, it was Sarah, it was a third voice he hadn't known, would never get to know, but now he *did* know it: his own Isabel. *Soon,* they chanted, their voices filling his ears. *Be whole.*

Ben blinked. He shook the tears from his eyes. He looked up at the woman. "Do it," he said. It was encouraging; an invitation. He smiled, without malice, without pain, without fear. "Do it."

The blonde woman crouched low. She brought the barrel of the gun within inches of Ben's skull. She considered him calmly, with her cold, disinterested eyes. "My name is Alma," she said, her voice rasping across the unseen scars in her throat.

She set the gun on the floor, just out of Ben's reach. Then she stood up, turned, and was gone.

Ben hung there, bewildered and alive, alone in the basement of the empty hangar. He heard the squeal of the main door and the whine of a dirt bike, and then there was silence.

He hung there for several minutes, his ears prickling, and hearing nothing more.

She had left him behind in the Lab.

"What in the absolute fuck?" he wondered.

35.

Ben sat on the boulder, chilled by the cool night air, lost in the crackling flames of the fire.

For the tenth time since making camp, he ran back through the events of the last eight hours, trying to get them to process, to make sense, or something close to sense.

Back in the hangar, sideways and alone, he'd managed to shimmy himself enough that he could move forward an inch or two at a time, even with Bergamot's dead weight draped over the top, scraping the table sideways across the floor. He'd moved for the gun first, was actually able to pick it up and hold it, but a few awkward rotations had made it clear that trying to shoot through the leather straps around his wrist was going to result in a missing hand. Besides, he knew, Alma had left the hangar door open after she'd ridden away on the bike, and a gunshot would draw the dusters in. His mind raced for another solution, which presented itself in the form of a scalpel that had hit the floor along with all the other instruments from the drawer during the doctor's panic. A few dozen more precarious scoots, and Ben was in reach of the blade.

Things had progressed quickly from there.

Once he sliced through his bonds, he headed to the counter and snatched up his notebook, the pens, and the snack bars. Then he climbed upstairs and did a quick search of the building for anything else he could use.

The quantity of death in the hangar was staggering. Every raider was dead...every single one of them. She had slaughtered them all. Ben was no Gil Grissom, but best he could tell, Alma had found the corpse of the man he'd killed with the soup can and had used him as a shield to push her way through the dusters. Ben found what was left of it just inside the front door, ragged, clotted with blood, ripped to shreds by scores of chomping teeth, bones broken from the blunt force of hardened dusters smashing into it from all sides.

The rest of story was less clear. The bodies closest to the door had all been bashed in with something hard. At least one of them had a handle-bar from a dirt bike buried in his chest. There was also a wrench on the ground, covered in blood, hair, and bits of bone. At some point, she'd gotten ahold of the gun, and the carnage had come more easily. Thirty more bodies lay splayed across the floor further into the room, their chests and legs pocked with bullet holes, sprays of blood spread out behind them in sunbursts on the concrete floor.

Ben wasn't sure how she'd gotten across the moat. She must have jumped. Even loaded down with the weight of a corpse, she must have been powerful enough to clear the distance.

Ben had wheeled all three of the remaining dirt bikes over to the door and flicked on the batteries to keep the dusters at bay. Then he did a quick pass of the hangar, scavenging food, water, a knife, two guns, some ammo, a lighter, a handful of other things. He tucked one of the guns into the back of his jeans and stuffed everything else into a big camping knapsack that was hanging near one of the cots in the sleeping quarters in the back of the building. Under a mattress, he found a half-empty bottle of moonshine. He figured that meant it hadn't made anyone blind, so he stuck it into the bag, too.

In the center of the hangar was a room full of folding chairs, and there was a map of three states tacked up on the drywall. The location of the hangar was marked, as were about a dozen other places across the desert, including one red circle that Ben figured was probably the location of the ambush, and the spot where he would find the train...if Horace hadn't given up and hauled away. Ben studied the path, traced it with his finger a few times, then pulled down the map and folded it up, tucking it into the bag. There was a compass pinned to the wall, and he took that, too.

He traced his steps back down to the laboratory, slipped his notebook and his pens into the front pocket of the knapsack, then returned to the front of the hangar, turned off two of the bikes, removed their batteries, and stuffed them into the bag. It took a little searching, but eventually he found a remote control for the bridge, kicked haphazardly beneath a workbench during the scuffle. He grabbed that, too. Then he cinched the knapsack, slipped his shoulders through the straps, mounted the last working dirt bike, and kicked off into the desert, parting the sea of dusters and speeding toward the horizon, away from the setting sun.

He didn't even bother going back for the fanny pack he'd left buried in the desert.

Guided by the compass, warmed by the moonshine, he had ridden through the starlit night until the first battery died, and the headlight dimmed to darkness, and the dirt bike rolled to a bumpy and unceremonious stop somewhere west of the Colorado line.

Alma hadn't left a trail. And Ben hadn't worked to find it.

Now, with the fire burning high, with the moonshine balanced on the boulder and a half-empty can of corn at his feet, Ben sat with the notebook in his lap and wondered why he was alive.

"Nice of you to show up," he said to the shadows beyond the flames. "Now that it's all over and everything."

"I don't like violence," Patrick replied, melting forward into the light. He walked up to the fire and warmed the coldness of death from his hands.

"Strong words from a guy who once shoved a man from a speeding train."

"And look where that got me." He rubbed his hands together, and the scarred edge of the hole in his right palm glistened in the light.

"Why didn't Alma kill me?" Ben asked.

Patrick shook his head slowly. "I can't begin to imagine what motivates a person like that to do anything she does. But if I had to guess, I'd say she's probably sweet on you."

Ben snorted with laughter. "Yeah, she seems like a real romantic."

"She loves you like she loves hanging men by their own entrails."

"Not likely."

Patrick shrugged. "Who knows?" he said. He circled around the fire and eased himself down on the other end of the boulder. "Maybe it's best not to know."

"Maybe," Ben agreed.

"Maybe someday you'll get a chance to ask her."

"God, I hope not."

"I don't know, Benny Boy. I'm not sure we've seen the last of her. People like that..." Patrick said, nodding slowly, his eyes mesmerized by the flames. "...people like that, they tend to last."

Ben rubbed his thumbnails together, lost in quiet thought. He picked up the moonshine and pulled out the cork. He took a swallow, and he winced as the alcohol burned down his throat. He held the bottle to his lips and blew across the mouth. A low *wooooooooooo* carried out into the desert and was swallowed up by the stars. "Just a few square miles from normal," he said softly.

Patrick scuffed at the hardpan with the toe of his shoe, carving divots into the sand. "What did it feel like?" he asked without looking up. "To know you were about to die?"

Ben clutched the bottle in both hands. He leaned forward, propping up his elbows on his knees, watching the sparks from the crackling wood as they popped and danced high into the air. "It felt..." he paused as he searched for the right word. "I guess it felt...vulnerable."

Patrick nodded. "It's nice to feel vulnerable sometimes."

The corner of Ben's mouth turned up into a half-smile. "Who would've thought," he said.

"Who would've thought," Patrick agreed.

They sat in silence for a while, safe in the circle of the firelight while the world continued to spin in the darkness. Ben set the moonshine down on the desert floor and returned his attention to the notebook in his lap. He tapped his thumb on the cover, drumming a secret tattoo.

"You didn't get the antidote," Patrick said.

"I didn't go there for the antidote," Ben replied. "I told you that."

"And you didn't go there to die."

"No."

"Okay," Patrick said. "So what *did* you go there for?"

Ben didn't respond. But he kept tapping on the notebook.

"*That?*" Patrick said, pointing down at the book, incredulous. "The notebook that you left in the Jansport? *That's* why you chased an army of bandits across the desert? *That's* why you faced off against Alma the Hun? *That's* why you almost fought a *tiger*? *That's* what this whole thing was about—a *notebook*?"

Ben pressed his palm down on the cover, felt the warmth of the leatherette beneath his hand. He ran his fingers over the book, feeling the dappled texture ripple beneath his skin. "It's not just a notebook," he said.

"Oh, I'm sorry, a *Moleskine*," Patrick said, rolling his eyes. "You snobby nerd."

Ben snorted and shook his head. "That's not what I mean, dummy." He thought for a moment, and then he added, "But yeah, it *is* a Moleskine, so you need to show some respect."

Patrick slapped his hands on his knees and said, "All right, I'll bite. What's in your precious dumb notebook that's just so great that it's more important than the antidote that has the power to save mankind from literal extinction?"

Ben looked down at the book and chewed thoughtfully at the inside of his cheek. He hadn't shown the pages to anyone. Not even to Sarah, back when she was alive, when he had first started writing, three years ago, when he was still different from what he had become.

"Fuck it," he breathed. He held out the book to his imaginary friend.

Patrick gasped with theatrical astonishment. "Bemme!" He turned on the boulder and reached out, taking the notebook gingerly between his hands. With a great show of reverence, he placed it in his own lap. Then he opened it to a page near the front, chose a random line, and read the words aloud:

"'The blind witch told Patrick his fortune, read from the bones of a fat-fed sow, and in the tapestry of his future, she plucked out the eight threads that would knit together to form his noose in the end: the butcher, the mummer, the light bringer, the siren, the demon's daughter, the running man, the fire drinker, and the hollow man.'"

Patrick looked up from the notebook. Ben's cheeks burned red, and he was intently focused on the dirt between his feet. Patrick closed the book, stood up from the boulder, walked up to the fire. He stared down into the flames for several long moments…then he turned to Ben with a maniac's grin, threw a finger in his friend's face, and cried, "I *knew* you were writing my life story!"

"It's not your life story!" Ben snapped, swiping the notebook back out of Patrick's hands. "It's your…death story," he said, flustered. "It's *our* story. It's the story of…whatever, of…of how things…went." He pulled the notebook in close and turned on the boulder, putting his shoulders between Patrick and the story. "I shouldn't have even shown you."

"My life story," Patrick beamed. "I wonder who'll play me in the movie." He gasped excitedly. "Hugh Jackman!"

"Hugh Jackman is dead," Ben pointed out grumpily.

"You don't know that. He's from Australia. Who knows what sort of weird things you ingest when you grow up in Australia. He might be fine. Oh, and we'll get Rick Moranis to play you!"

"Har, har."

Patrick shook his head in wonder and sat back down on the boulder. "I *knew* you would write my life story. It just feels so good to be right," he decided. He glanced over at Ben, who was still shielding himself from scrutiny. Patrick's tone became softer. "That's why you risked everything? To tell our story?"

Ben sighed. "I didn't risk everything to tell our story," he said. He turned back toward the fire, holding the notebook carefully between his hands. "Our story *is* the everything. Our story is all I have left."

They sat there quietly and watched the fire until it burned low. Ben stood up and put the last three pieces of sun-bleached wood onto the embers. The flames caught, and the fire burned high once more, for the last time.

"How does it end?" Patrick finally asked.

"You know how it ends."

"Can I read it?"

Ben tapped the notebook against his leg. "I haven't finished it yet."

"Oh," Patrick said. He looked down at the notebook. He looked at the pen in Ben's other hand. He looked at the bottle of moonshine within easy reach. "*Oh!*" he repeated as it all finally clicked. "Got it. I'll let you get to work." Patrick clapped his hands together encouragingly and stood up from the boulder. "Make me super-heroic, okay? And maybe bulletproof. I would have liked to have been bulletproof."

"I'll take it into consideration."

"Thanks, Benny Boy." Patrick stuffed his hands into his pockets and took a couple of slow steps backward, toward the night. But he hesitated near the edge of the firelight. "The story isn't *really* everything, you know. You've still got a life. You still have a lot."

"No," Ben said, looking up at his old friend, sadness heavy in his eyes. "I don't."

Patrick opened his mouth to respond...but there were no more words to say. So he nodded goodbye, turned on his heels, and disappeared out into the darkness.

Ben took a deep breath. He drank deeply from the moonshine, coughing some of it back up as it went down the wrong pipe and burned in his lungs.

He wiped his mouth with the hem of his shirt, and when he pulled it away, the cotton was soaked with blood and a bright green strain.

It could be stress, Dr. Bergamot had said about his hallucinations. *It could be dehydration. It could be dementia. It could be the flu.*

Or it could be the final thing, the malady that Ben hadn't let him finish saying.

It could be the Green Fever.

Ben stared dully down at the smear on his shirt. Coughing up the green was an advanced stage.

He didn't have a lot of time left.

He opened the notebook to the back, to where the old and torn foil of a butterscotch Snack Pack lid marked his place. He took a second to gather his thoughts, to remember where he had left off.

Then he clicked open his pen, and he began to write.

Epilogue – Six Months Later.

Kat drummed her fingertips angrily on the table. "Look. I don't see why this is so hard to understand. You want to drink here, you've got to trade something real."

"I am *trying* to give you all of my best things!" the stranger cried, exasperated. "Look at this! *Look* at this!" He spread his arms wide over the surface of the table. "*All* of this can be yours!"

"It's garbage," Kat said, annoyed.

"How dare you!" the stranger replied, clearly affronted. He plucked up an old plastic toothbrush from the pile of goods. "A toothbrush! A *toothbrush!* When's the last time you saw a *toothbrush?!*"

"It's covered in mold! The bristles are black! And fuzzy!"

"A little bit of bleach, it's going to be perfect!" He threw the toothbrush down and picked up a bent, rusty nail. "And this!" he cried. "Tell me you don't need this!"

Kat threw up her hands in frustration. "Why would I need a broken nail?!"

"It is *not* a broken nail, it is a corkscrew!" the stranger hollered.

"Look!" Kat snapped, slamming her hands down on the table. "You want to peddle garbage, go drink at Lou's place."

"But people go *blind* at Lou's place!" the stranger gasped. "His stuff is poison!"

"Then you'd better find some other way to pay, or you can get right the fuck out." Kat nodded at the machete that was propped up against the wall next to the man's chair. "I'd take that," she said.

The stranger gasped. "Killiam Hurt? *No deal!* He is *mine!*" He snatched up the machete and squeezed it close to his chest.

Kat rolled her eyes. "Well, you've got about three minutes to figure it out before I toss you out on your ass." She turned and left the table, muttering to herself under her breath. The cold weather always brought the nut jobs in. She should have opened her distillery somewhere warm, like Florida. Well, maybe not Florida. Florida had its own nightmares. But Texas, maybe. She could handle the people in Texas, now that most of the Texans were dead. Why she'd settled for an abandoned bar high in the Blue Ridge Mountains was a memory that became more and more clouded with each passing season.

She passed behind the bar as the door opened, and she considered telling whoever it was that she was closed so she could throw out the stranger, lock things up, and drink herself to sleep in the cellar, but it was Mabel coming in, with her blue eyes bright, and her dark hair shining, and Kat relaxed some. She liked Mabel. She was a sweet kid.

Kat grimaced at the fact that she was now old enough to consider someone in her twenties a "kid."

"Still serving?" Mabel asked, poking her head inside.

"For now," Kat sighed, waving her in. "Come on, close the door... you're letting all the green in."

Mabel slid inside and latched the door behind her. She climbed into one of the stools at the bar and set a crumpled sheaf of papers down on the seat next to her. "Gin today?" she asked hopefully.

"Just a little left," Kat said, digging around behind the bar. "It's yours, as long as what you've got is better than what this idiot brought." She jerked her thumb at the stranger across the room.

"Foil!" the stranger cried, holding up a sheet of used aluminum foil. There was a tear down the middle that grew longer as he waved the sheet through the air. "Actual, real aluminum foil!"

Kat shook her head. The stranger grumped and went back to digging through his bag.

"I've got something worth a whole *bottle*," Mabel said excitedly. "Maybe even two! But maybe you could give me a little credit time, so I can finish with it?"

Kat snorted. "All right, I'll bite. What is it?" she asked, pouring a measure of gin into a mostly-clean glass.

"Oh, come on!" the stranger whined. "You don't even know what she has yet!"

"*She* is good for it," Kat said, sliding the glass over to Mabel. "*She* comes here. *She* pays. You, I don't know from Adam. And all you brought was trash." The stranger gasped, but Kat ignored him. She poured herself a shot of gin and joined Mabel in a toast. "All right, what do you got?"

"This," Mabel said, her eyes glowing with an impish delight as she picked up the stack of papers and set them on the bar, "is a *book*."

Kat looked doubtfully down at the stack. "It doesn't look like a book," she said. The papers were bound together by three bits of wire that had been threaded through three holes on the left-hand side and twisted shut. Kat flipped through the book; each page was a photocopy of a handwritten notebook page. "It looks awful."

"It's post-M-Day," Mabel said, shrugging off the criticism. "But it's *really* good."

Kat set the half-empty bottle of gin on the counter and topped off Mabel's glass. "What's it about?"

"Are you kidding me?" the stranger said, gesturing wildly from his table. "She gets a whole bottle for a bunch of *paper?* I have paper!" He dug through his bag and pulled out a handful candy bar wrappers. "It's paper that smells like chocolate! Does *her* paper smell like chocolate?!"

"Shut. Up," Kat warned him. She pulled a revolver from beneath the bar and slammed it down on the wood, with the barrel pointing in the stranger's direction. He held up one hand to show there was no harm, then he turned back to his bag and grumbled as he searched.

"It's about this guy and his friend who went on this *wild* journey," Mabel said excitedly, placing her hand on the book as if the details might seep up into her bloodstream through osmosis. "They leave Chicago because they want to go to Disney World. Like, *now* they want to go to Disney World. *Post*-M-Day, not before. And they meet this fortune teller in Memphis, and she gives them these super-ominous warnings. They just left this weird preacher's woods—one of them got a nail through the hand...it's *insane*."

"All right, all right, take a breath," Kat said. "Doesn't exactly sound like it's Dickens."

"It's *really* good," Mabel insisted happily.

"I'll bet. This masterpiece have a title?"

Mabel nodded. "It's called *The Apocalypticon.*"

"That," Kat groaned, "is a terrible title."

"Yeah, it's not great," Mabel agreed. "But the story is really good."

The stranger moved so slowly, so imperceptibly, that Kat didn't notice him approaching until he was just a few feet away. "Hey!" she said, snatching up the gun and aiming it at his chest. "Slow!" Which was a ridiculous thing to say, because the man could not possibly have been moving any slower.

But if the stranger heard her, it didn't show. The warning floated right through him, and he continued to approach the bar, his skin ghostly white, his mouth hanging open, his hands visibly trembling. "Can I—?" he said, reaching out gingerly toward the pages. "Can I—? Do you—?" He seemed to have trouble finding his words, so instead he just moved forward until his hands were on top of the book, and he lifted it from the bar.

Kat moved to jam the butt of the gun against his skull, but Mabel held up a hand to stop her and said, "No, no, it's okay. He can look."

The stranger turned the papers over in his hands, holding the book with the gentleness and care that he might use to hold a baby bird. He slowly turned open the pages, his eyes unfocused, glassing over as they slid across the hand-scrawled words. He closed the book and read the words on the cover: *The Apocalypticon. By Ben Fogelvee.*

"Where did you get this?" he said softly, his voice floating down as if from a distant cloud. Then something in him snapped back into itself, and he jerked his head up, his eyes sharp and bright with excitement. "Where did you get this?!" he said again.

Mabel was taken aback by the sudden change in temperament, and her tongue lost its grip as she stammered her answer. "It's this…uh, there was a…I mean, a train, a guy on the train, he had a bunch of copies."

"Where's that train now?" the stranger demanded. With the book still in hand, he gripped her shoulders and gave her a little shake. "Where's the train now?!"

Kat cocked the gun. "Back off," she warned.

"It's gone," Mabel said. "It left. Three days ago. Headed…I don't know. South?"

"South," the stranger said, letting go of her shoulders and rubbing his chin. "South! I could go south…"

Kat and Mabel exchanged looks. Mabel shrugged.

"Who gave this to you?" the stranger asked. "Who was the man on the train?"

"Oh, that's the really cool part!" Mabel said, beaming. "It was the actual author!"

The stranger screamed then, a caterwauling wail that rose and fell like an ambulance siren. He hopped from one foot to the other, spinning around and kicking his feet out in a confused and clumsy dance. "He's on the train!" the stranger shouted. "He's on the train!" He turned and ran toward the door, forgetting all about his knapsack, his garbage, and his machete.

"Hey!" Kat cried. She leveled the gun at the man's back, but Mabel jumped up and stood between the barrel and the stranger.

"Who *are* you?" Mabel asked, marveling at the stranger across the room.

The man spun around and looked back with wild eyes, his large head bobbing excitedly on his stick-thin body. He raised the manuscript into the air, and they could see a dark purple scar on his right hand, about the size of a quarter. "I'm the Apocalypticon!" he screamed, shaking the papers with excitement. "*I'm* the *Apocalypticon!*"

Then Patrick Deen pulled open the door and blew out of the bar like a hurricane.

By his best guess, he was heading south.

AUTHOR'S NOTE

If you enjoyed this book, please take a moment to leave a review on Amazon. Reviews really do make or break the success of a book for independent authors, and your support would be truly and greatly appreciated.

For more information on the specific ways Amazon reviews help make books more successful, visit:

www.StateOfClayton.com/Why-Review

ACKNOWLEDGEMENTS

First and foremost, I owe a major debt of gratitude to Steven Luna; without him, this sequel--and the upcoming third book in the *Apocalyp- ticon* saga--would not exist. Steven saw something more in the characters and in the world of Apocalypticon than I saw myself, and he wouldn't rest until I at least agreed to explore Ben's story, and find out where it might lead. Well, I did, and in doing so, I started down a path that took my very first novel and developed it into something much, much greater. I am eternally grateful to Steven for his urging to see if my world had more stories to tell.

He also did all of the developmental editing, copy editing, and proofreading for this book, for which I am *extremely* grateful. But also, that means any issues you find in here are his fault, not mine. And I want to be clear about that.

I also want to thank my friends Patrick and Ben (the *real* Patrick and Ben) for continuing to be an inspiration, whether they like it or not. I hope you guys enjoy the continuation of the story! I'm not changing it.

Finally, I want to thank my wife, Erin. I ended up coming down with an extreme case of Life Stuff just after I started writing this book, and I got derailed for a while. Erin picked me up, brushed me off, set me back on the track, and helped pull me along the rest of the way to the end. Thank you, Panda. I love you forever.

ALSO BY CLAYTON SMITH

ANOMALY FLATS

Somewhere just off the interstate, in the heart of the American Midwest, there's a quaint, quirky town where the stars in the sky circle a hypnotic void....where magnetic fields play havoc with time and perception...where metallic rain and plasma rivers and tentacles in the plumbing are simply part of the unsettling charm. Mallory Jenkins is about to experience the unique properties of this place for herself when she accidentally sets off a series of events that could unleash the ultimate evil upon the town and wreak havoc on the world at large.

Life in a small town is like that sometimes.

Welcome to Anomaly Flats. Have some waffles, meet the folks, and enjoy the scenery...and if you happen to be in Walmart, whatever you do, don't go down aisle 8.

Don't EVER go down aisle 8.

APOCALYPTICON

Three years have passed since the Jamaicans caused the apocalypse, and things in post-Armageddon Chicago have settled into a new kind of normal. Unfortunately, that "normal" includes collapsing skyscrapers, bands of bloodthirsty maniacs, and a dwindling cache of survival supplies. After watching his family, friends, and most of the non-sadistic elements of society crumble around him, Patrick decides it's time to cross one last item off his bucket list.

He's going to Disney World.

This hilarious, heartfelt, gut-wrenching odyssey through post-apocalyptic America is a pilgrimage peppered with peril, as fellow survivors Patrick and Ben encounter a slew of odd characters, from zombie politicians and deranged survivalists to a milky-eyed oracle who doesn't have a lot of good news. Plus, it looks like Patrick may be hiding the real reason for their mission to the Magic Kingdom...

IT CAME FROM ANOMALY FLATS

The oddest little town in the Midwest has a thousand demented stories to tell...some of them are horrifying enough to send shivers down the strongest of spines. There's the tale of a man whose utter fear of germs sends him plummeting to the depths of depravity, and the victims he takes with him; the story of a couple escaping Missouri to fulfill their California dreams who take an innocent detour and find themselves trapped in the most unexpected of nightmares instead; the legend of a demonic creature who thrives on human flesh, which may be more reality than fiction.

In this first collected volume of chill-inducing stories from everyone's favorite transdimensional town, you'll find reason enough to question your own sanity, even as you try to reassure yourself that things like this only happen in stories.

Don't they?

Welcome to Anomaly Flats.

How loud can you scream?

MABEL GRAY AND THE WIZARD WHO SWALLOWED THE SUN

All is not well in Brightsbane, the village of eternal night. An evil wizard—the very wizard who swallowed the sun, in fact—has stolen The Boneyard Compendium, a book of powerful spells that could bring about the destruction of the entire town. When an Elder enlists the orphans of St. Crippleback's Home for Waifs and Strays to help track down the wizard, the ever-intrepid Mabel Gray sets out to find the three keys of bone that unlock the Compendium before the wizard gets his diabolical hands on them.

Armed with only her wit and a frightfully small bit of magic in her pocket, Mabel embarks on an adventure that brings her face-to-face with talking scarecrows, high-ranking monsters, babbling witches, ill-tempered daemons, a riddlesome owl who fancies himself a raven, and more. But the wizard isn't a wizard for nothing, and his evil magic may prove to be more powerful than Mabel ever imagined...

NA AKUA

Maui was supposed to be a romantic trip for two. But when Grayson Park's bride leaves him at the altar, a solo trip to paradise seems like just the thing to take him far from his troubles. Then he meets the beautiful and enigmatic Hi'iaka, and his troubles just begin—because when she's abducted by the sinister Kamapua'a, a savage creature bent on draining her life by the light of the full moon, she calls on Grayson to rescue her. With his loyal, new-found Hawaiian friend Polunu as his steadfast guide, Grayson sets out on an incredible adventure that pits him against the very gods of Hawaiian mythology and leads him to the heart of Pele's volcano, into the ocean to find the mythical Hook of Maui, and through the strange and brutal upcountry fleeing from demonic mo'o sent to destroy him. But there are only two nights left before the moon becomes full, and Grayson is running out of time to save Hi'iaka...and himself.

PANTS ON FIRE: A COLLECTION OF LIES

A circus performer leaving behind a trail of ghosts; a castle of bumbling nitwits desperate to prove themselves to King Arthur; a world full of deadly mirrors; a librarian who mistakes Death for a very somber wheat farmer; this pesky little thing called "the Rapture." All these and more pepper the pages of Pants on Fire: A Collection of Lies, a twisted, quirky, macabre world full of hilarious and chilling tales. Equal parts humor and horror, these seventeen surprising stories will leave you thrilled, thrown, and enthralled.

Being lied to has never been so much fun!

ABOUT THE AUTHOR

photo by Emily Rose Studios

Clayton Smith is an award-winning Midwestern writer who once erroneously referred to himself as "a national treasure." He is the author of several novels, short story collections, and plays, and his short fiction has been featured in national literary journals, including Canyon Voices and Write City Magazine.

He is also rather tall.

Find him online at www.StateOfClayton.com and on social media as @Claytonsaurus.

Made in the USA
Middletown, DE
24 June 2025